Terence Strong was brought up in south London after the Second World War. He has worked in advertising, journalism, publishing and many other professions. His bestselling novels (which have sold more than one million copies in the UK alone) include *Cold Monday*, *The Tick Tock Man*, *White Viper* and *Deadwater Deep*. He lives in the south-west of England.

You are welcome to visit the author's website at:
www.twbooks.co.uk/authors/tstrong.html

Wheels of Fire

Terence Strong

POCKET
BOOKS

LONDON • SYDNEY • NEW YORK • TORONTO

First published in Great Britain by Simon & Schuster UK Ltd, 2005
This edition first published by Pocket Books, 2006
An imprint of Simon & Schuster UK Ltd
A Viacom Company

1 3 5 7 9 10 8 6 4 2

Simon & Schuster UK Ltd
Africa House
64–78 Kingsway
London WC2B 6AH

www.simonsays.co.uk

Simon & Schuster Australia
Sydney

A CIP catalogue record for this book
is available from the British Library

ISBN 0 7434 2993 1
EAN 9780743429931

Typeset by M Rules
Printed and bound in Great Britain
Cox & Wyman Ltd, Reading, Berks

AUTHOR'S NOTE

The fictional events described in this book are inspired by the actual work done by the United Nations High Commissioner for Refugees (UNHCR) and other agencies, and by the British Army in particular whilst serving with UNPROFOR under the flag of the United Nations in Bosnia in the early 1990s.

It was often a highly dangerous, daunting and thankless task, not helped by the insanity, hatred and cruel ferocity of the ethnic civil war itself, and further hampered by the indecision and wrangling of the international political community at the time.

This story is set in an unspecified year during the conflict. Because of the nature of the terrain and the precise convoy routes that ran through Bosnia to the capital, Sarajevo, I have swapped two real towns with two of my own invention. The physical layout of these, and more importantly the inhabitants and characters described, are purely my own creation and to my knowledge bear no similarity to those in the real towns I have replaced.

Similarly, it has been confirmed to me by the Ministry of Defence that no such battalion as the Royal Wessex Regiment exists or existed at that time within the British Army and it should not be taken as bearing any resemblance to any other units of a similar name.

Indeed, the 'real life' equivalents of the Royal Wessex in that sector of Bosnia became renowned for their exemplary and courageous conduct in carrying out dangerous and challenging UN peacekeeping duties.

To create this story it has also been necessary to take some small liberties with the geography of the area and the exact chronology of some actual military events that mirror those I have invented.

This is not in any way intended as a factual account of the Bosnian conflict, but a novel that gives the reader an authentic taste of what war and life were like for those who lived or served there.

I am greatly indebted for a wealth of information to my good friend Larry Hollingworth of UNHCR, who was Chief of Operations in Sarajevo at the time and author of one of the best, evocative, factual accounts of the humanitarian operation, *Merry Christmas, Mr Larry*.

It was a chance comment by Larry about British convoy drivers that triggered this whole idea.

More great anecdotal and factual assistance came from both Convoy Leader Ginge Dawes and Mat Whatley, who served as Company Liaison Officer with 1st Battalion, The Cheshire Regiment in Bosnia.

I am so grateful for their interest, time and effort in helping me achieve the background authenticity of this story. Any factual or technical errors remaining are mine alone.

Like everyone else, I initially thought the political, ethnic and demographic dynamics of the Bosnian conflict would be horrendously complex.

In fact, it was all a lot more straight-forward than I had first believed, helped greatly by a few minutes studying the map (see page viii), originally drawn – from memory – for me on a restaurant napkin by Mat Whatley some ten years after the event.

Some things in life, it seems, stay with you for ever.

Terence Strong
London, 2005

For Princess,
with love

And for all those who continue, in both civilian and military capacities, to risk their lives providing humanitarian aid and protection for the innocent in trouble-spots around the globe.

CROATIA

Vukovar

Belgrade

Bihac

Knin

BOSNIA

Banja Luka

Tuzla

Donji Yakuf

Travnik
Zenica

Donji Vrbas

Una
Drina

Srebrenica

SERBIA

Sarajevo

Jablanica

Gorazde

Kamensko

Split

Mostar

Metkovic

MONTE-
NEGRO

Adriatic Sea

Bosnian Government (Muslim) held territory

Approximate territory controlled by Serbs

Croat territory

Croat enclaves

Bihac enclave (Muslim)

Recognised international boundaries

Convoy supply routes

N
W · E
S

0   *miles*   50
0   *kilometres*   80

One

The phone rang at just gone three on that late-October morning.

It drilled into my skull and shattered my dream, unrelenting until I reached for the handset on the bedside table.

They say it's the calls you get in the small hours that are the ones you will never forget. Well, I guess they're hardly likely to be bringing good news.

But I wasn't thinking of that as I cleared my throat.

'Hallo. Hawkins.'

I kept my voice low, not wanting to disturb Marcia in the twin bed next to mine.

The voice at the other end was familiar, the Adjutant of the Parachute Regiment. 'Hi, Jimbo, sorry to disturb your beauty sleep.' He wasn't quite his usual chirpy self; he sounded a little weary round the edges.

'What is it, Bill? World War Three broken out?'

'Nah, that stuff's all over now, Jimbo. You really must keep up with things.'

My first name isn't Jimbo or even Jim. It's Jeff. But with a surname like Hawkins it was inevitable that someone would see the initial J. and make the *Treasure Island* connection. So it had been 'Jimbo' to my army colleagues ever since my induction to the Parachute Regiment as a boy soldier twenty-four years earlier – before I took the 'scenic route' in my career, finally making Warrant Officer First Class before being commissioned.

'Stop pissing about, Bill,' I said, 'and spit it out.'

'How soon can you be ready to leave?'

I glared down at the handset in the dark. 'I'm not on standby . . .'

'I know. How soon? This is an emergency.'

I threw back the duvet and swung my legs off the bed, now fully awake. 'I don't know. Forty-eight hours.'

'Make that twenty-four, will you? There's a lot of hairy shit going down in Bosnia just now. I've had a call from the MOD, asking for you personally. I've got to confirm back immediately. Someone's getting their knickers in a twist.'

I was surprised. 'I'm flattered.'

Suddenly the bedside lamp behind me snapped on, throwing the bedroom into twilight. Marcia was awake and I could smell trouble already.

'Who is it, Jeff?' She sounded anxious. 'Is it my mother; the kids?'

I put my hand over the mouthpiece. 'Everything's fine. It's just Bill. Something's come up.'

'That's ridiculous, you retire next year. Can't they leave you alone?'

I didn't reply, just turned my back on her and returned to my telephone conversation. 'So, what's happened?'

'A liaison officer with the Royal Wessex in Una Drina has gone down with acute appendicitis. Emergency casevac. Bad timing. They want someone with experience to fill his boots. Your name came up.'

Now I knew. The Hereford connection — a while back I'd done a three-year tour with 22 Special Air Service Regiment.

'Liaison' in this context meant negotiating cease-fires with the warring factions, doing some hearts-and-minds and accruing intelligence. Some of the exact qualities that are honed during SAS service.

And, of course, the fact that my step-mother originally came from Belgrade — I'd spent a lot of childhood holidays in the former Yugoslavia — and I spoke the lingo fluently was on their records. Sometimes it's said that Hereford never really lets go of its former members.

Nevertheless, infantry battalion liaison officers – or LOs – were invariably drawn from the same cap badge or brigade. Pulling in an 'outsider', and a Para at that – even if I did have specialist knowledge and experience – was hardly going to make me flavour of the month.

'How long's the deployment?' I asked.

'The Royal Wessex have been there for three months. So you're looking at another three. There's a midday flight out of Lyneham for Split tomorrow. I'll get back with more details.'

I said, 'Can't you count? That's more like nine hours, not twenty-four.'

'Go with the flow, Jimbo. It'll win 1 Para some Brownie points with the MOD.'

It was pointless to resist. I said, 'OK, Bill. Cheers.'

'One more thing.'

'What?'

'Pack your thermals. It can get bloody freezing out there. Ciao.'

I shook my head and smiled to myself as I replaced the hand-set.

'What the hell's happening, Jeff?' Marcia demanded. 'Where are they sending you? Not bloody Bosnia?'

I turned back to look at her. A year younger than me, Marcia hadn't been a bad-looking woman when we'd met and married after I passed out in the Paras. But she'd never been good army-wife material and always resented the way it had become the third partner in our marriage. After our two kids were born, she'd neglected herself and had steadily put on the extra pounds. Long dyed-black hair now framed a still-pretty but pudgy face that seemed to wear a continuously sour expression as if she'd just sucked a mothball.

'At least someone loves me,' I said, standing up and pulling on my dressing-gown. But she missed the sarcasm.

'They said you wouldn't see active service again,' she muttered.

Too bloody true. Due to be pensioned off at the tender age of forty-five, I'd been driving a desk round Aldershot HQ for the past year and it was doing my head in. 'It wasn't a promise,' I pointed out.

'And we've got Ralph and Celeste coming round for supper on Saturday . . .'

Marcia's bridge-club friends. Well, that was one damn good reason to head for Bosnia. I said, 'You'll just have to manage without me. Like you always have.'

I left for the bathroom.

As I ran the shower I stared at my own image in the mirror as the glass began to mist. Forty-four years old, fairish hair that was thinning a little and grey at the temples, a face a little too weathered for my years due to a lifetime in the outdoors, too many cigars and too much booze. But I could still recognize a light of mischievous humour in the blue eyes and the same crooked smile that had been there in the years of my misspent youth. My body had survived better: still muscular, lean and taut from a job that involved relentless physical activity.

I leaned more closely towards the mirror and ran a hand over the bristles on my chin. 'Well, Jimbo, life's full of surprises,' I mumbled under my breath. 'Thought you were on the scrapheap – now suddenly you're getting another slice of the action . . . last-chance saloon . . .'

Of course, there was no way I'd get back to sleep. So after my shower I went downstairs to the living room of our three-bedroom semi on the outskirts of Aldershot, poured a slug of whisky into a mug of black coffee and lit a miniature vanilla cigar. I'd given up cigarettes years before and didn't need to inhale on these strong little fellas to get my nicotine fix.

I started to go through all the tedious domestic paperwork I'd have to clear before I left – bills to pay, a letter from the bank that needed a reply, car tax renewal form – but my mind wasn't really on the job. In those days in the early nineties, television and the newspapers were full of Bosnia: the mayhem, the fighting, the massacres, the ethnic cleansing, the refugees and the humanitarian aid effort by the United Nations.

Of course, being in the army and knowing some of our lads were deployed there wearing the blue berets of the United Nations Protection Force, UNPROFOR, I took a particular interest in the situation. Whereas most of the general public threw up their hands in horror at the complexity of the situation, I made it my business to get a general understanding of what was going on.

At the end of the Cold War, the disparate Balkan states that had been held together under the yoke of Communism to form Yugoslavia fell apart, each seeking independence from the dominant Serbs. Slovenia had managed to slip from Belgrade's grasp early on and Croatia's large and antagonistic population made it impossible for the Yugoslav Army to control for long. Thereafter the real battle was for who controlled the largely Muslim region of Bosnia-Herzegovina in the centre, and its capital, Sarajevo.

The situation wasn't helped by the fact that over the years all the ethnic groups had spread throughout the region, with enclaves or villages or towns full of one group living within an area run by another. In Bosnia there were Bosnian Muslims and Bosnian Serbs, and in some places Bosnian Croats!

It made the Northern Ireland problem look simple.

Germany had been first to officially recognize Bosnia-Herzegovina, soon followed by the rest of the EU countries. Eventually the United Nations followed. At that point the UN was rather obliged to step in with humanitarian aid and try to stop everyone from killing each other. That's when UNPROFOR was formed, to which Britain made a large contribution.

By the time I'd finished my domestic admin, it was seven o'clock and Marcia was up, stomping round the kitchen as she made her morning tea. She had this incredible, almost telepathic way of letting you know she was in a petulant mood and that you were the reason for it. Negative energy seemed to emanate from her very being until her hostility tainted the air like ozone.

I took the opportunity to escape back to the bedroom to pack my bergen. It wouldn't take long, it was permanently half-full with essentials and I had a checklist of stuff I'd need for any type of climate and mission.

The only downside to this sudden deployment was that I'd miss Christmas with the kids. Lucy and Joe, born just a year apart, were both away at university and had gone to Ibiza to work as club reps over the summer, so I hadn't seen much of them that year. Carefully I put a small framed photo of the two of them on the top of my bergen. Then I strapped it up before realizing that the picture of Marcia I always took with me on deployment was still on my bedside table.

I left it there and drove to town to pick up a few crucial provisions I guessed would be in short supply in Bosnia. Whisky and vanilla cigars would be two of them.

When I walked back into the house a couple of hours later the phone was ringing.

It was Bill with the final details. I was a bit surprised when he told me I'd be met off the C130 Hercules transport at Split airport on the Croatian coast by no less than Brigadier Alan Stowell, the Commander of British Forces in the Balkans. It seemed that, in typical British fashion, the MOD had appointed its own commander between our deployed units and the UN general whose orders they were supposed to follow. It was our way of letting 'Johnny Foreigner' at the United Nations know that we didn't fully trust him to play with our soldiers.

I was mystified. My role was to be a fairly humble battalion LO to the Royal Wessex, reporting to its CO on local matters. Brigadier Stowell, on the other hand, as CBF had fielded his own independent network of UKLOs – mostly special forces guys – to report to him direct.

So why was the Brigadier *and* his G2, the intelligence and security chief, going to meet me for the briefing as well as my opposite number, the UKLO in Una Drina?

Marcia came down the stairs just as I hung up. 'Well, I'd better be off,' I said.

Her expression didn't change a fraction. 'I suppose you must. RAF Lyneham, is it?'

I nodded. 'I'll write. And call when and if I can.'

It was my way of saying, don't hold your breath. But I knew she wouldn't anyway.

She gave a bleak little smile and offered her cheek for me to kiss. 'Take care,' she said. She didn't wave me off.

By five o'clock that night I was high over the Adriatic, sharing the noisy, cold RAF C130 with a huge mountain of urgent military supplies that sat under a cargo net in front of me and half-a-dozen other 'replacement' personnel. It seemed that yet again a British government had salami-chopped our armed forces at a time of increasing commitment, so we were topping-up unit strengths in theatre by poaching members from other regiments and increasingly relying on the Territorial Army to plug specialist gaps.

As I felt the distinct cant of the aircraft's wings and its nose dipped for descent over the Croatian coast, my own sense of anticipation soared until the adrenalin rush of old was back the same as ever. I had thought my days in action were over; now it seemed they might return – with a vengeance.

We hit the tarmac with a thud and the old workhorse trundled down the runway towards the terminal building until we gradually came to a standstill and the four propeller-engines wound down. There was a ten-minute delay before the rear ramp went down and I peered out of one of the ports while we waited. It was a dull, pinky-grey twilight, but I could see a frieze of ragged mountains in deep relief on the horizon, beyond the war-damaged perimeter fence of the single-strip airfield. On the grass there were a few old waterlogged artillery-shell

craters and several of the administration buildings were pock-
marked with bullet holes and in bad repair. I could smell the war
and sense the extent of the devastation even from inside the aircraft.

I'd been to Split before. With Marcia in the late seventies on
a package holiday. It had been a lot different then, a much happier place.

I heard the whine of an electric motor and the tail ramp
began to lower, revealing the bizarre and incongruous sight of
Croatian airport officials setting up a wooden picnic table and a
chair, complete with forms and a rubber-stamp for our pass-
ports. Instant immigration control. The message was clear: new
arrivals might know that the Serbs had knocked the shit out of
their airport, but it was still Croatia's airport and the Croatians
were back in control.

Passport quickly dealt with, I shouldered my bergen and
moved towards the gathering of military personnel and vehicles
waiting for the new arrivals. I rubbed my hands together against
the chill air as I scoured their ranks in search of my reception
committee.

At first I didn't recognize the tall, grey-haired man in DPM
camos in the poor light. It was that soft Edinburgh brogue that
gave him away.

'Captain Jeff Hawkins, I believe . . .'

My mouth dropped. 'Bloody hell! Dave McVicar, you old
bastard! What're you doing here?'

McVicar had been a senior sergeant when I'd done my tour in
the SAS; it seemed like he'd been with them since dinosaurs
walked the earth. Nothing had diminished the devilish twinkle
in those grey eyes. 'Staff sergeant now, Jimbo. And G2 to the
CBF.' The smile became more stiff and he turned to introduce
the man standing just a step behind and to one side of him. 'Sir,
this is Captain Jeff Hawkins. Jeff – Brigadier Alan Stowell,
Commander of British Forces . . .'

I saluted and Stowell responded lackadaisically. 'Pleased to meet you, Captain Hawkins.' He was a fairly short and slim man, his body bulked out by extra layers beneath his DPMs. His David Niven voice with its crisp but perfectly enunciated vowels and his black toothbrush moustache were straight out of 1940s Pinewood. 'Jeff, is it?'

'Yes, sir.'

'OK, Jeff. Glad to have you aboard. Impressed you made it at such short notice.' He glanced around the airport and grimaced. 'Welcome to the arsehole of the world! Well, the arsehole of the moment. I expect you've seen others at different times. I know I have.'

I smiled. I was taking a liking to him already. A big man inside a small one.

'Right, it's fucking freezing here. Let's get back to the hotel. At least the electricity came back on today and there's heating.' We started drifting towards a white-painted UNPROFOR Land Rover Defender. 'Have a hot toddy and give you a bit of a briefing. Afraid Cuthbert couldn't make it.'

I frowned. 'Cuthbert, sir?'

'Cuthbert's your oppo in Una Drina. Nigel Cuthbert. He's my UKLO there. Foreign Office wallah – well, you know, MI6's man really, more than mine. In uniform, but actually he's a civvy now. Ex-Guards. He and Captain Wells – not *so* well as it turned out, poor chap – shared the Liaison Office at A Company. Cuthbert was due to be here and drive you back to Una Drina. But the Bosnian Serbs have launched an unexpected offensive from the west and virtually cut the town off. Road in is under artillery, mortar and small-arms fire.'

I didn't understand. A Company had armoured fighting vehicles. 'What about the Warriors, sir? Couldn't one of them get Cuthbert out through the fight zone?'

Brigadier Stowell stopped beside his Land Rover and turned to me. There was a twitch of a smile at one corner of his mouth. 'Apparently the OC, Major Tring, doesn't think so. You're a Para, Jeff, right? And a former Hereford hooligan?'

I nodded.

'Well, you might find that Major Tring isn't quite as robust in his thinking as you are.' He opened the driver's door and slipped behind the wheel. 'And he hates Paras . . . Hop in!'

Dave McVicar threw a knowing glance my way, offered me the front passenger seat, then scrambled into the back.

Apparently Stowell liked to do his own driving and he drove the way he spoke, fast and furious, punctuated by hard braking and jerky little turns of the wheel. He explained that British HQ was at the Divulje Barracks – known, in the typical squaddie way of handling an unpronounceable name, as DJ – next to the airport, but he wanted to speak to me somewhere more private.

'Trouble is, Jeff, HQs are always the worst rumour-mills,' Stowell explained. 'Nature of the beast. Everyone knows too much and they all know too many faces. As a Para filling-in as an LO with the Royal Wessex, you're goin' to stick out like a dog's bollocks. So I want to bypass HQ completely and slip you in quietly. Won't stop the tongues wagging, but hopefully they'll have something else to gossip about by the time you get noticed.'

McVicar added: 'I've found you a room in a small hotel in town. It'll do until Nigel Cuthbert can pick you up.'

I was becoming increasingly puzzled by all this secrecy by the time we got into the town. The thoroughfares of Split were mean and bleak, the street lamps were off and the few people about were fleeting, hunched grey ghosts in the shadows. In the headlight beams I could see the shell damage to the buildings from earlier fighting. Apparently the town was bursting with refugees, filling every hotel and apartment block.

Finally, the brigadier turned into a fairly narrow cobbled side-street. A couple of minibuses and white UNHCR Discoveries were parked half on the pavement outside a hotel that looked as though it had been converted by knocking through three or four old houses. A faded sign above the glass double-doors proudly boasted Hotel Seavu. But my guess was you'd have to be standing on the roof to view anything at all, let alone the sea. Lines of washing hung from many of the upstairs windows, suggesting that this place, too, was now also home to a substantial number of refugees.

Stowell led the way into the lobby and got me signed in at a reception desk that was squeezed under the staircase to the first floor. The red carpet that ran throughout was threadbare, the walls were in dire need of a fresh lick of paint and there was a lingering smell of mildew in the air.

'Drop your kit in your room,' McVicar said, 'and join us for a drink.'

His last words were almost drowned out by a sudden explosion of boisterous laughter from the bar room to the left. It sounded like quite a party.

'British convoy drivers from UNHCR,' Stowell muttered disparagingly. 'Bunch of bloody pirates.'

McVicar just smiled gently and gestured to the 1960s plastic-wood door on the right. 'We'll meet in the lounge. Bit quieter.'

And a bit quieter it was when I joined them ten minutes later. There was no one there apart from the three of us. The lounge was all tired, deflated armchairs in red imitation leather, dusty pot plants and a sense of being trapped in a time warp. A waitress brought us three toddies of coffee and slivovitz as Brigadier Stowell spread out his map of Bosnia-Herzegovina on a tiled coffee table.

'Right, Jeff,' Stowell said, getting down to business. 'BiH – Bosnia – as you know, is geographically a triangle turned point downwards which rests on the Adriatic coast. The whole bloody thing is an invention – there's never been such a place historically, but that's politicians for you.

'After the fall of Communism, Yugoslavia shattered into five pieces. Serbia and Montenegro became the Federal Republic of Yugoslavia, and Macedonia gained independence without bloodshed. But it was different with Slovenia, Croatia and then Bosnia. Trouble was, the various ethnic groups were scattered all over the place. I mean, it was a fully integrated state under Tito. The predominating Serb leadership in Belgrade didn't like this break-up at all – Serbs do like *order*. They wanted things to continue as before.'

I knew all this stuff. 'Belgrade moved against Slovenia.'

McVicar smiled gently. 'Who gave the Serbian Yugoslav Army a bloody nose with a bit of Austrian help. Belgrade also deployed units all over Croatia but in the end they realized it was too big to hold down and they reluctantly had to let go.'

'So then Belgrade turned its attention to Bosnia,' Stowell went on, 'because this was *much* more contentious. The majority of the population in so-called Bosnia is Muslim.'

McVicar added, 'The Bosnian Serbs living there, led by Dr Radovan Karadzic in Pale, were furious at this independence thing. And, of course, they got the backing of the Serbian president Slobodan Milosevic in Belgrade to put up a fight against it.'

'And so this awful mess of a civil war began,' Stowell said with a grimace. 'Of course, most of the warring militias are locals, peasant farmers who used to form the old territorial defence reservists in the Communist era. All their arms were held at the local police stations and there's no young blood in the officer corps. Promotion used to be by dead men's shoes and Buggin's turn. It's rare to find a unit commander under forty, but there are several in their sixties – or older!'

'That's why the battle lines are so static,' McVicar explained. 'Like the trenches of World War One. Old, poorly trained officers, farmers who've got no real stomach for a fight, and no one anywhere who's got a clue about attack. The old territorial reserve only ever studied defence. That's also why there are so many bloody mines about.'

I asked, 'But out of all of them, the Bosnian Serbs are winning?'

Stowell scratched his moustache. 'That's putting it a bit strongly. Predominating, more like. Often depends in a local situation whose side Croat forces are on, Muslim or Serb. But the Bosnian Muslims are between a rock and a hard place. No doubt about that, they're being squeezed.'

The brigadier jabbed at his map. 'Our job, UNPROFOR's job, is to protect innocent civilians and refugees and maintain the flow of aid, negotiating cease-fires and safe passage, escorting the convoys as necessary. Not to get involved in their war. To fire back only if fired upon. Thankless bloody task, but some silly sod at the UN thought it was a workable idea.'

'Where exactly are the Royal Wessex deployed?' I asked.

McVicar pointed a pencil at the top half of a roughly diamond-shaped area in the centre of Bosnia that was nearly all Muslim-controlled territory. 'The main aid-convoy route into this region enters from the south-west near Una Drina, where you'll be based at A Company. As you can see, Sarajevo is almost parallel in the south-*east* – with a near-starving population of three hundred thousand plus, and surrounded by Bosnian Serbs. The route from west to east is a big dog-leg through Donji Vrbas – known as DV – the CO and main body of the Royal Wessex are there. And then on to Zenica, the second biggest city. Then finally through to Sarajevo itself. Some of the convoy drivers call the whole area the "Devil's Triangle".'

Brigadier Stowell pulled a face at that and glanced at his watch. 'Look, I've got to get back to HQ – got a bloody early start for Zagreb tomorrow morning. I'll let Dave fill you in on the detail. Thing is, Jeff, the whole of the Royal Wessex deployment area is key to the failure or success of the entire UN mission in Bosnia. After all, along with UNHCR, it's responsible for feeding and securing the capital and the second largest city. And, frankly, it's losing its grip.'

So this was what it was all about. I raised an eyebrow. 'Sir?'

There was an awkward moment's silence as Stowell tried to find the right words. 'Let's put it this way. The CO of the Royal Wessex is a decent bloke. Colonel Rathbone . . . But he's no

Bob Stewart and the battalion is no Cheshires. Man's got no fire
in his belly, just his eye on retirement. Trouble is, as always in
fighting units, the rot starts at the top. Spreads down to junior
officers and the ranks.'

I asked the obvious question. 'Can't he just be replaced, sir?'

Stowell twitched his nose as though his moustache was irritating it. 'Imagine it, changing the CO when the world's media
attention is on the British Army's work here. Well, sod it, Jeff,
yes, *I* would! But the suggestion has been firmly turned down by
the Defence Minister. And for that you can also read the PM
himself.'

McVicar added, 'Personally, I think the rotten apples have
spread too far. But if we can't even replace the CO, then we certainly can't replace the *entire* battalion.'

I wasn't at all sure I was liking this. 'Look,' I said. 'I'm just one
man and I certainly can't change the attitude of the entire battalion.'

McVicar smiled at that.

Stowell said, 'Won't have to, Jeff. The LOs' work is crucial.
You and the other LOs advise the CO on what action to take,
you try and negotiate the cease-fires, *you* do most of the talking
between the militias. *You* are the CO's eyes and ears on the
ground. *You* can influence decisions more than anyone else in
the battalion. And *you* are my choice.'

I had a feeling I was Dave McVicar's choice. 'But I answer to
the CO of the Royal Wessex, sir, not you. And as a Para I'll be
resented from the off.'

Stowell shrugged. 'Can't be helped. I've had a quiet word
with Colonel Rathbone. Explained your experience, special
qualities and fluency in the lingo. Told him you've come highly
recommended and that I'd appreciate it *personally* if you are
allowed free rein to be a little more *proactive* than your predecessor.'

'The colonel knows you're not happy with the battalion's
performance?' I asked.

'He's not a fool, Jeff. He can read between the lines like anyone else.'

'He'll also be my CO, sir.'

'Yes,' Stowell acknowledged. 'But *I* am asking you to make a difference. And I will back you to the hilt all the way as CBF here. With your experience, I want you to be independent and to push that independence to the wire. Even if it ruffles a few feathers in battalion HQ . . . You retire from the army next year, Jeff, right? Unless you do something bloody stupid, you're not going to get court-martialled or demoted. Falling out with Colonel Rathbone – if that's what it takes to get this job done – can hardly hurt your career prospects now, can it?'

He had a point there.

Stowell stood up, finished his toddy in one swallow and shook my hand. 'Glad to have you with us, Jeff. I know this is an impossible task, but it's our job to make it happen. Right?'

'Right,' I echoed as Stowell turned sharply on his heel and strode from the room.

As we watched him go, McVicar smiled. 'Always reminds me of Montgomery of Alamein. But he's an alright guy.'

When we sat down again at the map, he said, 'Liaison is the key to our mission here, Jimbo. Four officers at DV and the two of you at Una Drina. You guys are the main intelligence-gatherers. On the ground. Local negotiators and collectors of information that British force commanders need to make the best decisions – for their own protection and the success of the UN mission. It's used by your own local unit, of course, A Company, and the Royal Wessex Battalion HQ in Donji Vrbas – DV. Then it all gets collated by me, along with independent special forces and SIS intelligence reports from the UKLOs, for the brigadier.'

'What about UNPROFOR?' I asked. I meant did the British Army share its own intelligence with the overall UN military command?

He shook his head. 'We'll offer advice to UNPROFOR *based*

on our intelligence, but that intelligence itself is strictly for British eyes only. I mean if some Croat commander tells you in confidence – over a bottle of slivovitz – that he's going to launch an assault somewhere, you don't want it leaking out at the UN in New York or Geneva. Trust is everything.'

'Likewise between factions?' I guessed.

'Exactly.' He looked thoughtful. 'Anything we find out from or about the Serbs, Muslims, Croats . . . Nothing is ever said to the opposing sides, no one's ever tipped off. And that can be tough sometimes, believe me.'

I could see that. 'So Cuthbert and I get to know all the local militia commanders, big-wigs, politicians, string-pullers and do the hearts-and-minds stuff.'

'That's it, Jimbo. Though mostly you just want to bang their stupid fucking heads together. Negotiating cease-fires or persuading them to let convoys through is enough to try the patience of a saint. You have to be cool, calm and as firm as a slab of concrete. Otherwise they'll run rings round you.'

I grinned and lit one of my vanilla miniatures. 'So what's the good news?'

'A Company's inherited a good intelligence network but it's not as good as it was. Captain Wells, who you're replacing, let things slip a bit. Reading between the lines, I think his agents – well, informers and contacts, strictly speaking – have felt a bit let down. I expect that's largely down to A Company's OC, Major Tring, who very much has his own ideas about things and spends most of the time with his nose stuck up the colonel's arse.'

That didn't sound too promising, but I shoved it to the back of my mind. 'So how long do I stay here in Split?'

'I'm afraid it could be days, Jimbo. Until the fighting subsides enough for someone from A Company to get down here to pick you up.' He stood up suddenly. 'Well, Alan Stowell might be a party-pooper, but I'm in the mood to let my hair down. C'mon and join the drivers. There's someone I think you'd like to meet.'

McVicar ambled towards the door and I followed him into the lobby.

By the reception desk there was a young and smartly turned-out subaltern engaged in light-hearted and animated conversation with a rather tall and striking blonde. Her hair was pulled back in a ponytail and she wore faded blue Levis and a natural sheepskin body-warmer over a plain rollneck sweater. Two rather expensive-looking cameras, one with a telephoto lens, hung by straps from her neck.

'Johnny Rigg's a PINFO from HQ,' McVicar muttered in my ear. 'Right little wanker.'

Rigg – a Public Information Officer, whose job it was to guide and advise the media in Bosnia – turned at our approach.

'Hi, Dave. How goes it?' The voice was clearly pukka public school and Oxbridge, polished to perfection at Sandhurst.

'So-so, thanks, Johnny,' was McVicar's reply. He didn't believe in wasting words on people he didn't like.

'This is Tali,' Rigg said quickly. 'She's a freelance press photographer.' Rigg's grin nearly split his face in half; he obviously couldn't believe his luck that this good-looking creature, I guess in her mid-twenties, had been put in his charge.

McVicar moved with smooth charm to take the girl's offered hand and press it briefly to his lips. 'An honour, Tali,' he said in his easy Edinburgh brogue. 'I'm Dave.'

I saw the look of mild shock in her powder-blue eyes and the sudden arching of her brows that were so light and fine as to be almost invisible. Her face was a slender almond shape, but a slightly pointed tip to her nose took away conventional beauty and put character and individuality in its place. As McVicar let go of her hand, I couldn't help noticing how very long and elegant her fingers were.

'Tali van Wyk,' she said. Her voice had a soft, melodic lilt to it.

'This is Jeff.' I was glad McVicar remembered how I hated

being introduced as 'Jimbo' to people outside the army, especially females.

'Jeff,' she repeated with a shy smile. McVicar's was a hard act to follow, so I made do with a firm handshake. I was a little surprised when she responded in kind. Our eyes met only fleetingly before she averted her gaze. It was almost as if she thought that to look at me for longer might give out the wrong signals. I decided then that she was fairly new to this and very unsure of herself and I wondered how the hell she'd get on in a hell-hole like Bosnia.

Rigg was saying: 'Tali's Dutch. Just arrived. Working for some of their colour supplements and magazines. Just wangled a room for her. Manager gave up his own bed. Amazing the wonders a pretty face works.'

'What subjects are you interested in?' I asked her.

This time her returning gaze held steady. 'Anything and everything. Anything that might sell. War and peace. Any picture that tells its own story.'

I think Rigg was getting worried McVicar and I would take her off his hands. He intervened quickly, 'You'll find the convoy drivers in there, Tali. But watch out, they eat young ladies alive.'

A smile flickered on her lips. 'And spit out their clothes after?'

With that Tali turned and moved away, her long legs and hips moving with a relaxed and easy grace. As she opened the door the noise from the bar rose several decibels, lots of loud talking, peals of male and female laughter, throbbing background music and a loud voice that sounded like a very bad impression of Elvis Presley doing 'Jailhouse Rock'.

'God,' Rigg muttered as Tali disappeared inside. 'Look at the *arse* on that! And legs all the way up to her armpits. Think I've died and gone to heaven.'

'Lucky to find angels that good-looking,' McVicar agreed.

'Wants to do a photo-story on the convoys,' Rigg explained. 'I was hoping I might keep her at HQ for a bit.'

'There you are then,' McVicar said in fake empathy. 'The

good Lord giveth us His angels and the good Lord taketh them away . . . See you around, Johnny.'

We then followed Tali van Wyk's path into the bar, where the fug of cigarette smoke and the warmth from the crush of per-spiring bodies hit us like a wall. All around faces, male and female, were flushed and shiny with alcohol, voices raised so as to be heard against the background hubbub. The men were of various ages. Some had the tell-tale cropped hair and moustaches that marked them out as ex-military, but as many others had trousers slung around the low tide mark of their beer bellies. Several bright, beautiful eyes flashed in my direction, mostly darkish-featured women whom I guessed were local and just glad to see a good time after all the bad. Tali van Wyk had dis-appeared in the crowd.

I glanced towards the low platform in the corner where a big guy with wild, greying fair hair and a beard to match was cavort-ing with a microphone in his hand. I'd been right. It *was* a very bad impression of Elvis Presley. And, just my luck, it seemed that this was karaoke night at the Seavu.

'Wrap your laughing-gear round that!' McVicar said, fighting his way back from the scrum at the bar with two glasses of beer held aloft.

I took one of them. 'Cheers, Dave. Up yours!'

He inclined his head towards the stage. 'You'll have seen him, then?'

A roar went up from the more appreciative of the audience, including a gaggle of beautiful young Croatian girls getting an eager front-row view, as the huge, mop-headed Elvis did his finale and the background noise thankfully died away.

'Who?' I asked.

'Elvis. The King,' McVicar answered easily. 'King of the Road round here. Rocky Rogers.'

My mouth dropped. Jesus! I couldn't believe it.

The bear of a man, surrounded by his bevy of admirers, was stepping down from the stage as he caught my eye and immediately changed direction to where McVicar and I were standing.

'Jimbo!' the familiar voice boomed. 'What the fuck you doin' here, you ol' son of a gun?'

We embraced like a couple of footballers, his enormous arms and chest crushing the air out of me in a brief but ferocious bear-hug. 'Rocky!' I returned, gasping for breath. 'I'm here with UNPROFOR. Drafted in for liaison. Just arrived . . . But you?'

The ex-Para, whom I'd last seen five years earlier, shook his massive tangle of curls like a lion's mane. 'No, mate, I'm a convoy leader with UNHCR. This bunch of ne'er-do-wells are relief crews. I'm just here to pick 'em up. But the route up to the Triangle's been closed because of fighting. We've got a convoy ready to roll out of Metkovic depot as soon as it stops. Thought I'd join the lads for a shindig. Could do with a day off, to tell the truth!'

'Tough going?' I asked.

I could see as he answered the tiredness in those piercing blue eyes. 'The toughest. But shit, the money's good.' He slapped McVicar on his back with a blow that would have sent a lesser man sprawling. 'Hi, Dave! How ya doin'? You two look after my girlies while I get the drinks set up. This calls for a celebration!'

He left us in the company of his delightful and inquisitive fan club of young-twenties females in their clubbing frocks and Friday-night smiles and, after he returned, we were to spend the rest of the evening with them and Rocky as the drink flowed and flowed like an unstoppable river.

Every now and again I was aware of the distracting pop and dazzle of a photo-flash and guessed it was probably Tali van Wyk. I only properly caught sight of her once, standing in a corner talking to one of the younger convoy drivers.

Later, when things quietened down, Rocky and I got chatting, me sitting next to Jelena, a moon-eyed waif who'd clearly taken a shine to me, and he with a girl called Marina clinging to his arm.

'Take a tip,' Rocky said under his breath. 'If you're waiting for someone from A Company to come and collect you, you'll be here for a month of Sundays. Let's just say Major Tring is the cautious type. Personally, I think he's scared of putting a foot wrong in case it blots his copybook and ruins his career prospects. Got his sights set high, has that one.'

I shook my head. 'Trouble is, blokes like that often get there. But, Rocky, I don't have an option.'

He fixed me with a hard stare. 'Course you do, old son. Ride with my convoy. As soon as there's a window of opportunity, my boys will be down that road to Una Drina like a greasy snake. Be there while old Tring is deciding whether or not it's safe to put his head out from under the bedcovers.'

I grinned. 'I think you're sorta enjoyin' this job, Rocky.'

There was a twinkle in his eyes. 'Tough, like I said, but more fun than in the Paras.' He held up his left hand and counted off on fingers the size of Cumberland sausages. 'Fifteen-ton truck with fifteen-ton load pulling a ten-ton trailer with a ten-ton load. In my convoy, UK Green, we go everywhere flat out up to seventy miles an hour . . . Safest way to avoid being shot up! But coming round a blind mountain bend to unexpectedly find a line of mines across the road' – he paused dramatically – 'concentrates the mind *wonderfully*!' And he roared with laughter.

'When do you leave?' I asked.

'We leave for the depot at sparrow's fart. Be outside the hotel at 0400. Wear civvies.'

'Thanks, mate, it's appreciated.' I rose unsteadily to my feet, aware that the room was starting to swim. 'In that case I'd better crash.'

Rocky stood beside me, unwavering, and nudged my arm. 'Better take Jelena with you, otherwise she'll be upset. She's not a tart, but a few Deutschmarks in the morning will be appreciated. Help her buy a few essentials to survive. You know, oil the wheels.'

By the time he'd stopped talking, Jelena was clutching my arm and helping to steady me as I began to make my way to bed.

I didn't remember much more until I felt her lips brush my cheek and her soft voice in my ear, 'It is time to go, Jeff. You must wake now, or you will miss your lift.'

Cranking open one eye, in the half-light I could see Jelena crouched on her knees beside me on the bed, leaning forward to run her tongue along my arm, her young-girl's breasts swaying slightly as she moved.

'What time is it?'

Her eyes glistened in the darkness. 'Ten minutes to four o'clock.'

'Oh, shit,' I said, forcing myself awake and throwing back the cover.

'I don't want you to go, Jeff. You keep me nice and warm in bed. You are very nice to me, make me feel very good.'

I looked back at her, not knowing whether to feel guilty or chuffed that I could have pleased someone so young. 'You made me feel good too, Jelena,' I lied. The truth was I could hardly remember a thing, just half-remembered dreamlike images.

But she saw through me. 'I didn't make you feel *that* good, Jeff. I think you still have a bad head. I have some aspirin in my handbag.'

I watched her as I started pulling on my clothes, watched her thin, almost childlike body, as she moved purposefully to the bathroom to fill a tumbler of water for me with all the maturity and purpose of a mother caring for her young.

After green thermals, I settled for jeans, my Norwegian army shirt and a blue polar fleece. As I finished strapping up my bergen, Jelena stood naked before me and handed over a tumbler and two aspirins in her upturned palm.

'Thanks,' I said awkwardly, and swallowed the pills. Then I remembered what Rocky had said and pulled out my wallet from my back pocket.

She frowned. 'I don't want your money, Jeff,' she said, but took it anyway. 'You will see me again when you come to Split?'

I hesitated. 'I'm sure . . .'

There was an earnest look in her eyes. 'You can take me to England. That's what I would like. Not your money. There is nothing for me here. This place is shit.'

I didn't answer; couldn't. I just touched her hair and cheek with my hand and kissed her on the forehead. 'Thanks, Jelena.'

'Thank you, Jeff,' I heard her say as I turned quickly and left the room.

Outside in the street, the night air was bitterly cold. The convoy drivers stood around, shoulders hunched and hands in pockets, their breath clouds mingling with the exhaust fumes as the minibuses and four-wheel drives spluttered and coughed into life. In the dim light of the hotel doorway I saw Tali van Wyk, a large rucksack on her back, with the same driver I'd seen her talking to earlier in the bar.

Just then Rocky Rogers, dressed in a tartan lumber jacket with a fleece collar, beckoned for me to join him in his white UNHCR Land Rover Discovery with its emblem of a dove between two cupped hands on the door.

'Christ,' he said as I climbed in beside him. 'Your eyes look like pissholes in the snow.'

I said, 'Haven't been on a binge like that . . .'

He finished the sentence for me. 'For too long, by the look of it.' He started his motor. 'And how was the lovely Jel?'

I managed a smile. 'Nice girl,' I said non-committally.

Rocky nodded. 'Likes a shag, our Jel does. But no young Croatian boys around, all off fighting. Anyway, all she wants is to find some Englishman who'll take her and her mother to the UK. Her mum's got cancer but isn't going to get treatment here. Jelena saves up all the tips she gets from the lads to save for a trip for her mum to go to London to see a specialist. Fat chance.'

If I'd felt bad before, I felt even worse now. I wished I'd

stuffed the whole contents of my wallet into those caring, exploring little hands.

Then we were away, working through the streets of Split for the coast road that would take us the 130 kilometres to Metkovic.

We arrived at the vast UNHCR depot at six, passing through the security gates guarded by Spanish troops wearing blue UN helmets and into the compound that stretched as far as the eye could see. The original brick-built administration buildings had been supplemented with Portakabins to support the influx of UN and UNPROFOR personnel necessary to run this huge distribution machine non-stop, twenty-four hours a day, seven days a week. Under the arc-lights lines and lines of white UNHCR trucks and trailers were backed up into a series of vast hangar-like warehouses where all the provisions and equipment required to keep an entire nation alive were stored. Elderly fork-lift trucks were scuttling about their business, carrying and lifting pallets with that sense of chaotic order and purpose you see in a nest of ants.

Rocky parked up by the admin block and we climbed out. He pointed to a line of twenty gargantuan trucks and their enormous trailers, each gleaming white with a large black 'UN' stamped on its side. 'UK Green,' he said proudly. 'Ready and waitin' to rock and roll!'

It was an impressive sight. Quite as awe-inspiring in its way as any show of military might. It brought a lump to the throat to think that even in this selfish and heartless commercial world of today, someone somewhere cared enough to mount a humanitarian exercise of such dimensions to a people who were hell-bent on their own destruction.

'Magnificent,' I murmured.

'Nah,' Rocky said. 'Just a bunch of trucks.' He waved me to follow him. 'Let's get the latest security report from the Triangle . . .'

On the way he told me the office was run by a brigadier from one of the British regiments of Guards. I gathered this was not considered to be a particularly 'good thing' in Rocky's judgement.

We entered into the welcome warmth of the spartan front office with large-scale route maps on the walls, trestle tables on the floor and a background buzz of radio traffic and the chatter of computer keyboards and Telex machines.

'Hi, Rocky,' the duty officer said, looking up. 'You're fucking optimistic, aren't you?'

'Born that way. I was breast-fed by a mother who drank Guinness.'

The duty officer smiled. 'Even that sort of optimism won't help here. Last A Company sitrep said forward Serb units are still controlling the road into Una Drina. And the Croats still aren't allowing convoys through their sector till the Serbs stop their attack.'

'That's stupid. There's no fighting in the Croat sector – at least we could get up the road.'

'Not stupid,' returned the duty officer with a smile. 'That's the Croats trying to prove to the UN what kind, caring folk they are. Don't want UN convoys getting shelled by accident.'

Rocky said, 'You mean it's the Croats being fucking awkward. Reminding us who's boss in their sector.'

'You said that, not me.'

'When was that last report?'

'At 2300 hours.'

'That was last night. Things might have changed.'

A new voice joined the conversation. 'Don't push it, Rogers.' The Guards brigadier had entered from the adjoining room, an impressively tall, thin man with a nose like a parrot's beak. 'We'll be getting a fresh sitrep at first light. Why don't you go and get some scran down your neck. I'll send someone to you if there's any change.'

'OK, Brigadier, that'll be appreciated.'

As we turned to go, the brigadier said, 'And who's that with you?'

I guessed he'd spotted the bergen slung over my shoulder. I stepped forward. 'Captain Jeff Hawkins, sir, 1 Para. On my way to join the Royal Wessex at Una Drina.'

The nostrils in the parrot's beak flared. 'Not in UK Green, you're not, Hawkins! That's a civilian UNHCR convoy.'

Before I could answer, Rocky stepped in. 'Forgive me, Brigadier, but that isn't your jurisdiction. I decide who rides on my convoys and Captain Hawkins' chain of command is through OC Major Tring and then Colonel of the Royal Wessex. If you care to contact them, I think you'll find they want Hawkins down there pronto, if not sooner!' He grabbed me and spun me round. 'C'mon, Jimbo. Let's get some breakfast.'

The last I saw of the brigadier that day his mouth was opening and closing like a goldfish come up for air. Officers hate it when challenged by civilians who know they're in the right; suddenly rank doesn't count for a hill of the proverbial beans.

And baked beans it was in the canteen. Along with the bacon, tomatoes, chips, sausages, mushrooms and poached eggs floating in a vat of water like gouged yellow eyes. We took our plates and giant mugs of sweet tea along to a long table where I recognized some of the faces from last night's party and those climbing onto the minibuses earlier. I didn't see Tali van Wyk anywhere and idly wondered where she was.

Before tucking into the mountain of food on his plate, Rocky announced loudly, 'Those of you who didn't meet him last night, this is Captain Jeff Hawkins, 1 Para. Jimbo to you lot. An old mucker of mine. He's replacing the unwell Captain Wells down at Una Drina, so hopefully we'll see an improvement in the situation there soon.'

That was one hostage to fortune I could do without, but I could hardly contradict him.

Rocky took a mouthful of sausage and kept on talking, jabbing his fork in the direction of different members of Convoy UK Green: drivers, mechanics, logisticians and storemen. He rattled off the names and I did my best to put them to the faces, but it would take days and even weeks before I got to know them all as individuals.

'Bunch of fucking wankers,' he concluded. 'But they're *my* fucking wankers – and the *best* in the business! No one stops UK Green – we deliver!'

'Piss off, Rocky!' someone shouted back. 'Haven't you sobered up from last night yet?'

'In RADA before he joined the Paras,' another driver quipped. 'Bloody frustrated actor. Wants to play Hamlet.'

'Henry the Fifth!' Rocky came back swiftly. 'You know *nothing*.'

The humour subsided as everyone returned to nursing their hangovers and catching up with the latest sports results from copies of the *Sun* and the *Star* that had accompanied the new draft from the UK.

Rocky lowered his voice confidentially, 'Mostly ex-army. Lot of misfits and hooligans – joined the British Convoy team in preference to the Foreign Legion. Better pay and a better buzz. A few Scandinavians too, and a couple of Ruskies. But I meant what I said, salt of the earth.'

Daylight was just beginning to show in the grey sky outside as everyone moved on to toast and marmalade. It was then that the duty officer from the brigadier's security office came into the canteen and leant over to whisper something in Rocky's ear.

My friend listened carefully, nodded and gave a tight smile. As the duty officer disappeared, Rocky looked along the two lines of faces watching him expectantly. 'Right, lads. A little bird's whispered unofficially the Croats are going to open up the route at any time. Seems like the fighting's subsided around Una Drina – but the Royal Wessex haven't confirmed that bit yet.' He stood up. Convoy security decisions were the leader's alone to make. 'Time to burn some rubber!'

There was a spontaneous scraping of chair legs on the floor as everyone rushed to get up and out to the trucks. It was almost like a Battle of Britain squadron scramble.

I followed out at a trot as the team divided up and ran for their vehicles, climbing high up into their cabs and throwing over the reluctant and mighty engines. The roar was tremendous and absolutely deafening, the air instantly filled with the choking fumes and black smoke of diesel as the monsters came to life.

When Rocky and I reached his Discovery along with his number two – a quiet Irishman called Shaun – the brigadier appeared. '*Mister* Rogers! You are aware that the fighting hasn't yet been confirmed as ceased?' It was a rhetorical question. 'I suggest you wait until it is.'

Rocky smiled sweetly. 'Thank you for your suggestion, Brigadier. But while we wait, children could be dying of malnutrition.'

With that he climbed into the driver's seat and slammed the door. The brigadier caught my eye across the roof as I went to get in. 'I'll be talking to you again, Hawkins. I've marked your card, be sure of that.'

'Sir,' I acknowledged, ducked my head and sat down as Rocky hit the gas, moving down the line of white trucks and trailers to the head of the convoy.

Before us the huge perimeter gates swing open. Behind us twenty twin air-horns let out one mighty co-ordinated scream that filled and shook the air like the wrath of God.

UK Green was go.

Rocky described it as 'bimbling' along. In fact he was as true as his word and led the convoy at a breakneck seventy miles an hour whenever he could.

We hurtled through the autumn mist of the Neretva river valley road towards the city of Mostar, Rocky and Shaun taking it in turns to give a running commentary. As it became light with a sky full of low, bruised cloud, a bleak and soulless landscape was revealed, its natural rugged and mountainous beauty seemingly covered in a grey watercolour wash of misery. Everyone we saw seemed to be dressed in drab clothes that had seen better days, and no one took any notice of the convoy, as though wrapped in their own thoughts and own little world of worry. Frequently we passed ragged little columns of refugees walking one way or another, depending on which ethnic group they were from and where they were heading in search of sanctuary. Scattered throughout the rolling terrain were the wrecked remains of isolated houses and even entire hamlets. Sometimes smoke still spiralled from the ruins. You could smell both fear and death in the air.

Rocky's whispered intelligence had proved correct and we were cheerfully waved through several roadblocks manned by the Bosnian Croat militia.

Beyond Mostar our progress became a slow and steady climb, gaining altitude as we worked our way towards the inner mountainous area of the Devil's Triangle.

I noticed that as we went through built-up areas, the convoy slowed down and tightened up, travelling nose to fender. The tension of high-speed travel on mountainous roads was replaced by the prospect of trouble at every street corner.

'Give some bastards half a chance,' Rocky explained, 'and they'll squeeze some lorry or vehicle in between two of ours and chop off our tail. Some convoys lost a lot in the early days.'

The sense of imminent danger was especially high as UK Green trundled warily through Prozor, which had about it the dangerous air of an old Wild West town. Everything happened here and everything was available in this place awash with warlords, drugs barons and arms dealers. Groups of the feared Croat Black Swan commandos strutted round arrogantly or watched us from street corners with cold, emotionless eyes as we passed.

It was a relief to be out of there and beginning the straining zig-zag climb up to Makljen and the gateways to the Triangle. There was much changing of gears and cursing as we finally made it to the ridge and the last Croat checkpoint before entering Muslim-held territory.

Rocky pulled up at the barrier and threw open his door to get out and stretch his legs.

I noticed that the trucks had stopped in a staggered formation behind us to give each driver a better view of any trouble up ahead.

Two of the militia guards, in mix-and-match bits of army uniform with no insignia, sauntered over, sub-machine guns slung carelessly over their shoulders.

'Morning, gentlemen,' Rocky said, handing over the convoy's inventory to the taller of the two.

'Mr Rogers,' the man acknowledged and studied the list carefully. Rocky shuffled his feet, kicked at the ground. Then the guard found what he was looking for. 'I would offer you some coffee, but we have no sugar.'

Rocky had clearly been waiting for something like this. 'Maybe a box fell off the back of one of the trucks. We'll take a look.'

Shaun climbed out the back of our Discovery and ambled back along the line of trucks.

'Maybe two boxes fell off,' the guard called out. Shaun nodded.

'What's the situation like on the road to Una Drina?' Rocky asked the guard, now that our passage had been successfully 'negotiated'.

'You must ask my commander,' the man replied and nodded towards a rock-strewn area on the ridge a hundred metres from the road. There a Croat officer stood studying the Vrbas river valley below him.

Rocky beckoned me and we walked together across the rough ground to where the officer stood. He was a middle-aged, heavily built man and sported a thick moustache.

'This guy is also the Chief of Security for the town,' Rocky whispered.

Turning on our approach, the Croat officer said, 'Ah, Mr Rogers. How are you today?'

Rocky shook his hand. 'Colonel Markovic, I'll be *happy* if I can get to Una Drina.'

It was a spectacular view down into the mountainous valley, pine-clad slopes diving steeply down to the fast-flowing river which could be seen gleaming like quicksilver between the trees. In the distance, maybe some ten kilometres away, I glimpsed the smudged outline of buildings in a misty depression of land that was to be my home for the next few months. Una Drina.

There was no sign of smoke and no sound of firing. It seemed very tranquil.

'Then maybe you will be happy today,' Markovic said. He had one of those ready smiles that you never quite trusted. 'We have agreed to cease firing while you pass through if the Serbs halt their advance and agree to do the same. We are waiting to hear.'

Then he seemed to notice me for the first time. 'Who is this man? A new face? One of your drivers?'

Rocky turned to me. 'No, this is Captain Hawkins. He's replacing Captain Wells at Una Drina. I'm giving him a lift. No doubt you'll be seeing a lot of each other.'

I offered my hand and the commander accepted it with some reluctance. Despite the unchanging smile, there was no warmth in his eyes. I gathered I'd be expected to earn his respect the hard way.

At last he said, 'The convoy is free to move on, whenever you decide it is safe.'

Rocky and I headed back to the Discovery as Shaun handed over two large boxes of Tate & Lyle. 'Secondary distribution,' Rocky explained. 'That's what the UNHCR lads out here call it. Reckon delivering eighty per cent of something is better that a hundred per cent of fuck all.'

I gave a low whistle. 'Twenty per cent loss of aid? Is that typical?'

He nodded as we climbed into the vehicle. 'Can be. After all, they're all Bosnians and the militias need food and medicine, too.' He picked up the handset of the CODAN radio, a piece of Australian HF kit designed for their flying-doctor service. It was the sort of gear the British Army signals guys would have died for. Rocky punched in his callsign, hit send and waited as we listened to the whirr of the aerial tuning itself. 'Hi, Rocky here. I'm on the ridge. I gather we're waiting for news from the Serbs on a cease-fire to let us through? . . .What? . . . Cuthbert . . . Sure, put him on . . .' He handed the receiver to me. 'Say hallo to your new oppo.'

'Nigel?' I asked.

The voice at the other end was good public school but sounded a little flustered. 'What? Who's this?'

'Captain Hawkins, your new partner in crime.'

'You with the convoy?'

'Yes. We're at Makljen and ready to run.'

'Thank God for that. Will I be pleased to see you.'

That was nice. 'Hear you're trying to negotiate a cease-fire with the Serbs?'

'Not trying, Hawkins. Done it. Just had it confirmed. I should get your arses down here before one side or the other changes their mind.'

'Roger that,' I acknowledged. 'Out.'

Rocky grinned and switched to a close-range inter-truck VHF set on which the drivers were gabbling and joking to each other. 'SHUT THE FUCK UP, YOU LOT!' he bawled. 'Keep the channel clear. We're rolling in five. Anyone got a problem with that?'

No one had. It was time for someone to have a last-minute pee, don Kevlar helmets and flak jackets and finish whatever else they might be doing.

Rocky shoved a CD into his portable player, hit the motor horn three times, long and hard, and started to move. Turning, I could see the first of the trucks rumbling after us, dust clouds billowing in their wake, just as the Discovery was filled with the stirring opening notes of *Ride of the Valkyries*. I guessed it would be picked up by every driver in the convoy.

We gathered speed, the downhill road opening up in front of

us and pine trees flashing by on our right where the mountain-side fell away sharply to the river far below. I was glad we kept a good seven hundred metres ahead of the leading truck, because if we had to stop in a hurry, I wasn't sure the one behind us could.

Ahead and still far below, the buildings of Una Drina were taking shape within the cold mist that wreathed them. The mountain to our left was levelling out now as we raced round its lower slopes, now leaving us exposed on all sides and an open, if fast-moving, hard target.

I glanced anxiously round at the surrounding landscape, but all seemed quiet and I could discern no movement.

I glanced sideways at Rocky and we grinned at each other. It looked like we were going to make it.

Then the road exploded right in front of us as a flash of flame and a geyser of smoke and debris erupted out of the tarmac without warning. A mortar round had narrowly missed us.

In a practised reflex action, Rocky hit the brakes and threw the wheel, then swung it back, just clipping the edge of the smouldering crater. If we'd gone down it, we'd probably have blown two tyres – or been bounced sideways over the precipice into the river valley. More explosions detonated on either side of the road and I heard lumps of dislodged tar and chippings pepper the Discovery's bodywork.

Above all that I suddenly detected the staccato chatter of machine-gun fire. One of the rear side windows shattered as a lucky round found its mark.

'You OK, Shaun?' Rocky bellowed.

After a moment's silence, a slightly anxious Ulster voice replied, 'You know me, Rocks. Shaken but never stirred. I'm fine.'

I turned round in my seat to see what had happened to the truck behind. The driver had coolly straddled the mortar crater, keeping it square between the two huge front wheels.

'The Serbs, I guess . . .' I murmured, half to myself.

'No,' Shaun said. 'That's Markovic's lot, the Croats. They're trying to hit us so they can then say it was those evil Serbs.'

More rounds, this time heavy artillery, exploded up ahead. It now seemed that the Serbs were retaliating. And we were in the middle.

Rocky shook his head in disbelief and gave a wry grin. 'Welcome to fucking Bosnia!'

Two

Fighting was still raging across the valley as UK Green rolled into Una Drina.

We passed a couple of A Company's formidable-looking tracked Warriors parked on the outskirts, no doubt keeping a wary eye out for any attempt by the Serbs to close on the town itself. The commander of one of the armoured vehicles gave us a friendly wave as we passed.

Although it didn't seem as though anyone was actually targeting the town, I saw one or two carelessly aimed howitzer rounds explode on the outskirts. It was enough to send the inhabitants scurrying for cover in case the situation worsened. And, of course, the people never knew when a sniper might take it into his head to indulge in his sick idea of fun.

It was clearly a poor agricultural town. The main street comprised mostly nondescript brick-built buildings with numerous shops, mostly either closed up or with empty windows, and a few more imposing ones with bullet-ridden stucco frontages: a couple of banks, the post office and various municipal office blocks. Off the high street ran side-roads into tight-packed residential housing areas, mostly unimaginative small bungalows of typical Communist uniformity plus a few low-rise flats and a scattering of older Balkan cottages. I also noticed a mosque, set back from the road, and a few small factories.

Towards the middle of the main drag we came to the headquarters of A Company, Royal Wessex Regiment. They had commandeered the biggest industrial premises in town. It was a former brickworks that looked like it had been built soon after the First World War. White UNPROFOR armoured Warriors, Scimitar light reconnaissance tanks, Land Rovers and Bedford trucks were parked up in neat rows behind the high railings of the compound to which additional razor-wire and sandbag emplacements had been added.

As we approached, the two sentries in camo smocks, flak vests and blue UN helmets swung open the huge double gates. Rocky came to a halt and we all climbed out in time to see Major Tring striding across the parking lot with a captain and a decidedly unmilitary looking man in DPM trousers and a red fleece. A fat Staffordshire bull terrier waddled after them.

'That's Tring's dog, Trojan,' Rocky said in an aside to me. 'Fuckin' ugly brute.' Then he was all smiles as the party approached. 'Afternoon, Major! Think we got through in the nick of time.'

'Indeed,' came the rather terse reply. Major Tring was tall and broad-shouldered with a swarthy, unsmiling face and the dark features of a two-shaves-a-day man.

His watchful, almost anthracite eyes flickered in my direction, reminding me vaguely of a motorized camera shutter.

I snapped to attention and threw a sharp salute. Somehow I got the feeling Major Tring was the sort to appreciate strict formality. 'Captain Jeff Hawkins, Major, 1 Para. Your replacement for Captain Wells.'

Those thin lips curled up slightly to one side, which I think was the nearest I ever saw to a smile on his face. But it could have been a sneer, or a grimace of distaste at the word 'Para'. 'Welcome to sunny Una Drina, Captain Hawkins.'

I think that was a joke, which I hadn't been expecting. Maybe things would be better than I was anticipating. But then I noticed Tring had immediately formalized my name and hadn't offered me his own first name. Maintaining barriers. Well, I certainly wasn't going to invite *him* to call me Jimbo.

The major turned to the man in the red fleece. 'This is Nigel Cuthbert, the UKLO here, your colleague in Liaison.'

Cuthbert was quite the antithesis of Major Tring, a fair bit shorter and of slender build. Although probably in his late thirties, his was a boyish, friendly face with well-scrubbed cheeks and slightly crooked rabbity teeth. I was certain the OC didn't approve of his unkempt head of curly blond hair that was in dire need of a trim.

'Hallo again, Captain. Good to speak to you earlier.' Cuthbert had a firm handshake. 'Sorry about the hot state of your arrival. Bloody people – can't trust any of them. Just had Colonel Markovic – that's the Croat commander you met up at Makljen – on the radio complaining about the Serbs breaking the cease-fire and damaging the convoy.'

I said, 'Rocky reckons it was the Croats who opened fire first. Then the Serbs retaliated.'

Tring inclined his head towards Rocky in a gesture that seemed to mean no offence intended. 'With all due respect to Mr Rogers, he is *only* a lorry driver. It doesn't do to jump to conclusions in a confused place like Bosnia. Can get you in a lot of hot water.'

Rocky opened his mouth to retaliate, but I caught his eye and indicated for him to drop it.

Tring didn't seem to notice and continued talking. 'Mr Rogers, would you like to bring your wagons into the compound until the fighting's over. I'm sure we can squeeze you in. How many are you on this convoy?'

'If it's all the same to you, Major, I'll just continue *only driving* my lorries on up to Donji Vrbas.' He turned to Cuthbert. 'The fighting's still confined to the south and west, right?'

Cuthbert nodded. 'Yes, at the moment the road through to DV is clear.'

'Very well, if that's your decision.' Tring sounded weary, a man fed up with talking to brick walls. 'I'll give you a Warrior escort, just to be on the safe side.'

I knew Rocky would prefer to continue 'bimbling', as the heavy, tracked armoured fighting vehicles would just serve to slow him down, but he decided to play along. 'You're too kind, Major.'

'That's why we're here, Mr Rogers. To be helpful.' He turned to me. 'Get yourself settled in, Captain. I'm sure you and Nigel will have a lot to talk about. Colonel Rathbone has been notified of your anticipated arrival here. Would like you to report to him tomorrow in DV, after CO's prayers, at 0900 hours. You can ride up in one of the Warriors.' His bleak eyes scrutinized me briefly. 'I'll see you later on at supper; 1900 hours sharp.'

He turned and strode purposefully back across the compound towards the brick factory. Rocky, Cuthbert and I watched him go, but none of us said anything. Somehow I don't think we needed to.

'I'll just see what damage has been done,' Rocky said, and began walking back down the line of UK Green's trucks and trailers. Cuthbert and I fell in behind him.

'Course, you've heard what the major thinks about Paras?' Cuthbert asked. He spoke in a hurried, nervous sort of way, as if he wasn't sure he should be saying what he was saying. 'Doesn't help that he knows Rocky was one. Or that you are – sorry . . . Bloody stupid, but I made it my business to find out what his gripe is. Pulled in a couple of favours at the MOD and got them to look up Tring's record.'

I raised an eyebrow; Cuthbert really was a crafty little spook. 'Seems his family had a Parachute Regiment tradition. His father actually made colonel and his grandfather died at Arnhem.'

That sounded curious. 'Why on earth should that make him hate them so much? If anything, the opposite, I'd have thought.'

There was a mischievous glint in Cuthbert's eyes. 'Seems he tried to join, but failed Selection. Wasn't the right material.'

'Oh, dear,' I said, suddenly feeling a little empathy with the man.

'Fucking good thing, too,' muttered Rocky, who was a few strides in front of us.

He stopped at the fifth truck, where Shaun and some of the other drivers were inspecting the damage. It looked like a couple of 30mm cannon rounds had gone through the side of the container.

'When did this happen?' Rocky asked the driver, whom I learned was a Liverpudlian known as Lizard.

'Think it was the first rounds fired, weren't they, like?' Lizard replied. He was a thin man in his late twenties, with nervous jerky body movements and darting eyes. 'Same time that mortar shell nearly hit you, boss.'

I looked up. The rounds had clearly been fired from the west, the Croatian lines. Probably an anti-aircraft weapon mounted on a flatbed. So Rocky was right and Colonel Markovic was lying through his teeth.

'What's the load?' Rocky asked.

'Flour,' Lizard said. 'It's like a fuckin' blizzard struck inside. Stuff's everywhere.'

As if to emphasize the point, Tali van Wyk appeared round the back of the truck. She looked decidedly shaken and probably pale, but it was hard to tell because her hair, face, clothes and rucksack were all white with flour.

The truth was they were bloody charmed that the whole lot hadn't gone up in a fireball from the incendiary rounds. Maybe the flour had put the flames out. It was Tali's and Lizard's lucky day.

'Who the fuck's this?' Rocky demanded.

Lizard shifted on his feet. 'Er – Miss van Wyk, boss. She's a photographer.'

'Nearly a fuckin' dead photographer, Lizard, you idiot! She hasn't even got a bone-dome or flak jacket!'

Tali straightened her back. 'I'm sorry, Mr Rogers, it's my fault. I talked him into it. I wanted to take some UN convoy pictures.'

Rocky snorted with derision. 'Got a *good* shot of that tracer coming straight for that *thing* you call a brain, did you?' The barb certainly went home and the girl looked down at her feet in a gesture that acknowledged it hadn't been her brightest idea. It seemed to soften Rocky's attitude a little. 'So, Miss van Wyk, next time you think of smuggling yourself onto one of my convoys, think again and just ask, eh?'

I'm sure she was blushing but it was hard to tell through the flour caked to her skin. 'I was afraid you'd say no.'

He shook his head as if to say that was the most stupid explanation he'd ever heard for anything in his life. 'Get yourself up the front to my Discovery. And shake off that flour before you get in. Don't want the thing looking like Santa's fucking grotto when we get to Sarajevo.'

She managed a quick, 'Thank you, Mr Rogers,' and scampered quickly out of his line of fire.

As our eyes followed her, Rocky muttered, 'Soppy tart.' But I thought I detected just the smallest hint of admiration in his tone.

I said goodbye to Rocky and thanked him for the lift. Then Nigel Cuthbert and I stood and watched as the convoy wound its way out of town under Warrior escort and headed down the valley towards Donji Vrbas. The likelihood was it would shelter there for the night before pushing on to Zenica and Sarajevo the next day.

Thankfully the sound of fighting had finally died away again.

'Let me show you your quarters and then our Den,' Cuthbert said as the sentries closed the gates behind us. 'Get a brew on. Expect you could do with one.'

I shouldered my bergen and walked with him towards the factory. The main works were where most of the company's personnel slept on camp-beds with scrounged material and camouflage netting dividing the huge area into smaller sections for a bit of privacy and to help keep the draught out. By the loading bay doors was an area used by the mechanics to overhaul and repair Warriors and other vehicles. I could hear an industrial blow-heater going, but it was fighting a losing battle.

Cuthbert led me to the two-storey administration block, outside which Royal Engineers had installed Portakabins housing toilets, a washroom and an officers' and Senior NCOs' mess facility.

'I'm afraid it's mostly compo rations here at Una,' Cuthbert explained. 'Just a makeshift field kitchen and zilch in the shops. You'll notice nothing on four legs around the town. All the cats and dogs have been eaten by the locals. Wouldn't surprise me if the buggers ate each other, given half a chance.'

'Sounds grim,' I murmured.

'That's why the lads get rotated every month with a platoon from Battalion at DV. At least they can get some decent scoff there. You and me are a bit luckier, being our own bosses. Well, virtually. I make sure I get up to battalion HQ for a square meal a couple of times a week. Or the local hotel here, the Splendid. The chef normally manages to get something on the menu. Then there's Tring's driver—'

'His driver?'

'Billy Billings. Trained to be a cook before he joined up. Also expert scrounger. Any food in town Billy will sniff it out. Sometimes he'll do a special scoff for Tring and the more senior officers. That'll be you, me and the 2IC, Captain Gordy Cromwell, nice bloke – and, of course, the OC of the Lancers, if he's about.'

The Lancers, about twelve of them, ran the four Scimitar light reconnaissance tanks in support of the Warriors.

Cuthbert pushed open a wooden door into a carpetless corridor, dimly lit by occasional bulb-fittings hanging from a long line of electrical cable. Small offices ran off to the left and right. There was another door facing us at the far end, I noticed, the security of which, judging by the fresh chisel-marks in the woodwork around its shiny and impressive keypad lock, had been recently beefed up.

'That's the Den,' Cuthbert confirmed, before flinging open the last door in the corridor. 'And this is you . . .'

I think it had been a stationery cupboard; in fact, I'm *sure* of it. But at least it was a roomy stationery cupboard. About ten feet by eight. It took a camp-bed, three empty plastic drink crates in different colours, which could serve as either seats or cupboards for personal effects, a galvanized bucket and a length of washing-line suspended between two bent nails from which four wire coat-hangers dangled. Brilliantly dual-purpose for use either as a wardrobe or to dry wet kit. The previous occupant had left behind a pair of cross-country skis. And, bizarrely, there was a real touch of luxury: a tatty but brightly coloured deckchair was folded against the far wall. The trouble was you rather had to decide between the chair or the bed, because there wasn't really enough room for them both to be up at the same time.

There was also a slight problem with the window: there wasn't one. The only light came from a brass Tilley lamp. Still, it wouldn't be draughty.

I said, 'I'm going to feel really at home here, Nigel.'

He gave me a funny look. I was to realize soon that Cuthbert didn't do sarcasm and was anyway never certain when to laugh. Either afraid to offend or show himself up. I thought at the time he seemed nervous and unsure. That was an error of judgement I would live to regret.

'The Serbs knocked out the town's electricity sub-station yonks ago,' he said, indicating the Tilley lamp. 'We don't have enough generators to supply the whole building and fuel's often in short supply. There's water, but no electric to work the pumps, so it has to be collected.'

I dumped my bergen against the wall and turned back as Cuthbert punched in his security number to open the Den. 'This is strictly yours and my territory, Captain . . . ? Er.' He glanced back over his shoulder with that toothy smile.

'Just call me Jimbo.'

He pushed open the door. 'No one else, Jimbo. Except Major

Tring, of course. But even then I don't encourage it. Make sure you keep everything sensitive under lock and key.'

I said, 'He *is* the officer I report to, Nigel.'

'Quite so, quite so. But never any of *my* stuff – that's CBF eyes only – just your own.' He winked. 'And even then, it's nice to keep some things up your sleeve.'

Once a spook, always a spook, I thought. Maybe I should have heard the distant sound of warning bells then. After all, I knew well that the intelligence world and the military don't always march to the beat of the same drum.

I think the Den had once been a manager's office. It was certainly larger than the others I'd glanced into from the corridor outside. The windows had been chipboarded over for protection against flying glass and, I imagined, prying eyes. I clearly wasn't going to see much daylight for the next three months.

The main wall facing us was filled by a large-scale map covered in thin perspex sheeting with lots of locations and the usual military hieroglyphics in coloured chinagraph. Muslim, Croat and Serb lines, unit positions and estimated strengths. Beside the map was pinned a 'rogues gallery' of photographs, just like the units had in Northern Ireland, many clearly taken clandestinely with a long-range lens. Local militia leaders and anyone known to be associated with them. From family and friends to other paramilitary colleagues or those of more suspect association. Others were less controversial: people the Liaison Office considered the movers and shakers of the local community.

And a picture of the glamour model Sam Fox, torn from a magazine and looking decidedly out of place.

I said, 'Nigel, I'm pretty sure *she* doesn't live here.'

'What?' Cuthbert turned his head. 'Oh. Oh no, course not. Except in my dreams.' He looked embarrassed. 'No, actually, in Captain Wells' dreams. He was hoping she might come and entertain the lads here one time . . . I've sort of come to think of her as our lucky mascot.'

I saw there were two desks. Mine with a pile of papers, signals and background files to be read, a couple of telephones and a CODAN radio like the one in Rocky Rogers' UNHCR wagon. I realized I'd be the envy of A Company's signals unit who were still struggling with outdated equipment. Not good in a poor reception area like Una Drina.

By contrast, Cuthbert's desk was devoid of papers. He, too, had his own telephones and a CODAN – and a private satellite telephone. No doubt that was for speaking directly to his masters at Secret Intelligence Service – more popularly known as MI6 – and the Foreign Office in London.

He moved to the far corner where he had a little butane-gas stove on a table with a neat row of jars containing coffee and herbal teas, sugar and a jug of milk. He placed a camping kettle on the stove and lit it.

'Tea or coffee, Jimbo?'

'Either, thanks, as long as it's sweet.'

'First thing you'll want to do is meet the local militia commanders. Normally that would have been the Croats. You saw Colonel Markovic earlier, I gather. The mayor doubles as the town's defence minister. Then there's the nearby Muslim militia commander.'

I nodded. 'But now we've also got the Serbs advancing from the west?'

'Well, they're to the west, certainly, but whether advancing, retreating or digging-in, it's hard to tell. Don't even know who their commander is yet or where he's based himself.'

'So how did you negotiate this so-called cease-fire that isn't happening?'

'Not directly, that's for sure. Had to go the long route, second- or third-hand through the Bosnian Serb HQ at Pale, where their leader the good Dr Karadzic holds court,' Cuthbert said. 'Of course, the current attacks might just be a foray.'

'To test Una Drina's defences?'

'Possibly.'

'I'll make it a priority to find out.'

A smile flickered at the corners of Cuthbert's mouth. 'Yes, Jimbo, I'm sure you will.'

'But this is a predominantly Croat town, right?' I wanted to get all this stuff absolutely clear in my head.

'Yes,' he confirmed, 'the whole of this southern swathe of Bosnia is controlled by Bosnians of Croatian descent. North of here it's nearly all Bosnian Muslim. They are uneasy allies at the moment and the dividing line runs right across the road on the northern outskirts of the town.'

I could see why this was regarded as a potential hotspot with the Muslims and Croats likely to be vying for control of it when they'd both finished fighting off the current Serb offensive.

Cuthbert made himself comfortable on the edge of my desk. 'I tell you what you need to know about this lot, Jimbo.' He held up three fingers on his right hand. 'Croats, Muslims, Serbs. The Croats will talk their way *around* a problem – so it's *still* there when you've finished your negotiations. The Muslims, quite frankly, will just stab you in the back and get it over with . . .'

I smiled gently. 'And the Serbs?'

'They'll simply slit your throat from the front – and say sorry afterwards.'

While we drank very hot and very sweet tea, Cuthbert went through a whole range of problems in our area. He concluded by saying, 'You know, Jimbo, the problem is knowing what these militias are up to. Getting inside their heads. Damn me, it's hard enough speaking to them – and that's without the language barrier! The telephone system is nothing short of diabolical, if it works at all. And their military radios are only marginally worse than ours.'

I put that to the back of my mind as I finished the dregs of my tea. Time was pushing on and I wanted to start work. 'Then let's see just how bad it is, Nigel. What's the best way of getting hold of Colonel Markovic?'

That surprised him. 'Why? It's getting a bit late.'

'We want to know which Serb commander is running this offensive and where he is, right?' Cuthbert nodded blankly. 'If you want to know something about someone – ask his sworn enemies. Because it's their job to know.'

'Er, yes . . . yes, I suppose so.' He shifted his backside off my desk and glanced at a print-out of numbers stuck to the back wall. 'If Markovic's still in the field, radio one of those three call-signs. But unless you're lucky enough to get through to him directly, his aides will just give you the runaround.' He hesitated. 'Otherwise his HQ at the town hall . . . The land line was working this morning. But if he's taking a nap – he likes his drink at lunch – try his house.'

My hunch was that, with the Serb attack subdued but not yet repelled, he'd probably be at Croat HQ discussing tactics. I sat down at the desk, ran my pencil down the print-out and tapped the number into the telephone keypad.

There was a lot of crackle and static and I swear a clanking noise that sounded like metal cogs turning. Suddenly a gruff voice snapped, 'Yah? Markovic.'

In my most polite but firmest Serbo-Croat I said, 'Colonel Markovic, this is Captain Jeff Hawkins, new Liaison UNPRO-FOR, Una Drina. We met this morning when I was travelling with the convoy. If you'd be so kind, it is *imperative* that I speak with you immediately . . .'

I could just imagine him gasping at the handset in surprise. Most liaison officers picked up some of the lingo pretty quickly, but Serbo-Croat is a very tricky language and very few of them would have spoken it anything like fluently.

It was several seconds before he responded. 'Ah, well, Captain Hawkins, nice to hear you made it safely into town.' Smug bastard, I thought. 'And I'd be delighted to oblige you except, as you may have noticed, we are in the middle of fighting off an offensive by those bloody Chetniks. You will understand that I am very busy at present.'

I came back fast. 'Colonel, that is why I must see you.

Information I have that you need to know. Important information.'

'Information? Intelligence?' I sensed he was taking the bait.
Maybe he thought as new boy in town I might say too much.

I cut in. 'I'm on my way, Colonel. Nigel Cuthbert and I will
be with you in . . .' I looked at my SIS colleague who was staring at me open-mouthed. He shrugged and mouthed ten
minutes. 'Five minutes,' I said to Markovic and hung up.

'Christ, Jimbo! You haven't got any information for him.'

'I'll think of something,' I replied, and dived to my room
next door to yank my DPMs from the top of my bergen.

Six minutes later Cuthbert and I piled into his Land Rover
with my allocated interpreter, a Croat called Senic.

Senic was a young man in his late twenties, a former law
graduate who looked as though he'd never quite stopped being
a student. He was a scruffy individual, tall and rather thin with
unruly black hair. He had a rather handsome face with thick
brows and penetrating dark eyes that seemed able to look inside
your head in a way that made you think none of your thoughts
could remain private. His good looks were rather spoiled by a
permanently sullen expression.

Throughout the short dash out of the headquarters gates and
down the main drag, he was staring sideways at me, his expression becoming even more sullen when he learned that I spoke
fluent Serbo-Croat and that his services were therefore somewhat redundant.

I tried to make him feel better. 'Not the best way to get
introduced, Senic, but I'll still need you. My language skills are
a little rusty. And you know all the colloquial jargon.'

He nodded at that, but didn't smile.

Cuthbert had his foot to the floor as we screeched round a
left-hand corner from the main road into a small tree-lined
grassed square. At the far end was one of Una Drina's more
imposing buildings, the town hall. Steps led up to a portico and
tall Georgian-style windows faced out of the cream-coloured

stone that, like everything else in Bosnia, was peppered with bullet holes. The Croatian flag, I noticed, not the new national flag of Bosnia-Herzegovina, hung limply at the ornate crown of the building's façade.

We jolted to a halt in a parking-space reserved for officials and got out. Two slovenly Croat militiamen, one dragging on a cigarette, regarded us suspiciously from the front entrance.

I nudged Senic. 'Go on, introduce us. Tell 'em we've got an urgent meeting with Colonel Markovic.'

Senic ambled forward in no great hurry and began chatting to the guards, being far too polite and almost pleading for us to have an audience. The man who was smoking started to explain how difficult that would be – there was fighting going on with the Serb advance and the colonel was in a council-of-war with the mayor and wasn't to be disturbed. I could have throttled Senic.

Cuthbert whispered, 'I think you'd better save the situation, Jimbo. Senic's afraid to say boo to a goose. Captain Wells used to take my Muslim interpreter when he could.'

'Now you tell me!'

'Sorry.'

The matter was resolved when an upper window in the building opened and Colonel Markovic leaned out. He had a cigar in one hand and seemed in a very good mood. 'What's the matter, Captain Hawkins?' he shouted down in Serbo-Croat, laughter thick in his throat. 'Won't my guards let you in? Well-trained, you see!'

I cupped a hand to my mouth and called back, 'I'm impressed, Colonel!'

More deep mirth from Markovic, then, 'Come on up! They'll escort you!'

And so we were shown into the musty, tiled reception lobby where a few portraits of previous mayors in heavy gilt frames hung on the walls. Despite the sound of voices from various rooms, the clatter of old manual typewriters and a bustle of activity, with Croatian troops walking back and forth with sheets of paper, it had all the depressing feel of a mausoleum about it and felt just about as cold.

We were led up a sweeping staircase with a polished oak banister to a pair of panelled doors over which was mounted the proud town crest of Una Drina. The two other guards here were a lot smarter than our escort and snapped to a salute, which Cuthbert and I returned.

They swung the doors open into the mayor's parlour. It was a large room with a faded red carpet and a scattering of leather club chairs for guests. A military map was pinned to an easel near the window, but the centrepiece of the room was an enormous marble fireplace in front of which was a similarly impressive mahogany desk. Behind this sat the mayor, who rose to his feet as we entered.

Markovic stood at his side, arms folded across his chest. 'You know Captain Cuthbert, sir. And this is Captain Wells' replacement in the British liaison team – Captain Hawkins.'

'Captain Hawkins, this is our mayor, Mr Ivan Jozic.'

Jozic was a short, thick-set man in a threadbare black suit, grubby white shirt and badly-knotted tie. He had a complexion like lumpy porridge and a fixed congenial smile, although it failed to follow through to his eyes which peered from behind pebble lenses in a pair of heavy tortoiseshell frames. He was also a bad advert for Brycreem, which he appeared to have used to stick tramlines of black hair to his balding white crown.

We all shook hands before Jozic resumed his seat and reached for a glass decanter of slivovitz on a silver tray in front of him. 'So, what can we do for you, gentlemen?' he asked in his own language as he poured measures into four tumblers.

I cut in before my interpreter could make another error. 'We won't keep you long, sir. You will be busy with your battle plans.'

Jozic concentrated on pouring and didn't look up. 'Colonel Markovic said you spoke our language well. He was right.'

'My step-mother was from Croatia,' I replied, quickly switching away from the fact that she had actually been a Serb, one of Jozic's avowed enemies. Before I could be cross-examined, I went on quickly, 'We have noticed that the fighting has ceased. What is the situation? Are you holding your own?'

Markovic began distributing the slivovitz. 'You realize that is a sensitive military question, Captain Hawkins?' he admonished, handing me a tumbler.

'Jeff,' I replied. 'Call me Jeff.'

'Yes – er – Jeff. I am rather surprised at you for asking.'

'UNPROFOR have an interest in the safety of the citizens of Una Drina, Colonel,' I replied evenly. 'I'm surprised if you do not recognize the legality of the UN mandate.'

Markovic smiled gently at the parry. 'Well, Jeff, if we are to work together, you may call me Pero. But not in front of my men.' The words were followed by a deep chuckle. 'And whatever else you like behind my back!' He raised his glass.

'To your victory,' I said quickly, and felt the plum brandy scorch my throat.

'. . . Victory,' came the slightly surprised chorus.

Mayor Jozic's eyes blinked like an owl's behind his glasses.

Markovic wiped his lips with the back of his hand. 'Such a toast from an UNPROFOR man who does not take sides?'

I smiled. 'I am not allowed to take sides, Pero. But then Una Drina falling into the hands of the Bosnian Serbs is certainly not going to be in the best interests of its citizens. Tomorrow I may drink to the victory of the Serbs if a Croat force is about to take one of their towns.'

Senic was translating for Cuthbert, who looked horrified and murmured, 'Steady, Jimbo.'

But I thought I had the measure of Markovic. He liked banter and a verbal battle for mastery of position. I felt I was proved right, too, when he chuckled and nodded. 'The status quo, eh?'

I shook my head. 'Not necessarily. Change is fine if it's agreed by all sides. Not by pointless killing. It'll have to stop sometime. Meanwhile, we have civilians to feed and protect.'

Markovic tugged at his moustache thoughtfully. 'Well, I can tell you that Una Drina is safe for the moment. We pushed the Chetnik back two hundred metres and gave him a bloody nose. Our troops hold the road.'

'But it was a tough battle?' I guessed.

'Tough enough.' Markovic refreshed the tumblers with more slivovitz. 'But we are wasting time. You said you had information for me?'

I nodded. 'Who is the Serb commander? Where is he based?'

Markovic's eyes narrowed. 'Who has information for whom, Jeff, I wonder?'

Mayor Jozic interrupted quickly, 'Anyway, that, too, is privileged intelligence, Captain Hawkins.'

This was it, crunch time.

I took a deep breath. 'The commander of those Serb forces that are so tough is not who *you* think he is. They have drafted in' – I plucked a name from the air – 'Marco Tomic.'

'Who?' Markovic asked. 'Never heard of him.'

I replied quickly, 'Marco Tomic is a brilliant young major in General Ratko Mladic's inner coterie. He's been sent from Neversenje to ensure victory here. He's based himself at Dorni Vakuf.'

Mladic was the Bosnian Serbs' top general with a fearsome reputation.

Out of the corner of my eye I could see Cuthbert staring at me in disbelief.

Mayor Jozic didn't believe me either. 'That is not so,' he growled. 'The Serb commander is Zoric and his headquarters is in Stavac! A prisoner confirmed that to our interrogators last night before they—' He stopped himself when he saw Markovic's dagger stare flying his way. But I think Cuthbert and I could have finished the sentence for him. The prisoner-of-war had been executed after torture.

I shrugged. 'Well, that's the information we had which we thought might be useful to you in the defence of Una Drina.' I looked at Cuthbert. 'Isn't that so, Nigel?'

Cuthbert swallowed hard, nodded and buried his nose quickly in his drink.

'Of course,' I said casually, 'it wasn't *confirmed* military information. Otherwise I couldn't have told you.'

Markovic was glaring at me. He clearly realized what I'd done. Then suddenly the anger in his face seemed to melt away like thawing snow. His deep chuckle appeared to come from the heart. 'I like you, Jeff, I like you! We will get on fine. But one thing I tell you . . . your information is shit!' Then he began laughing like a volcano about to erupt.

Mayor Jozic even managed a smile at all the good humour.

'I think we'd better go,' Cuthbert intervened nervously.

'No, no!' Markovic said. 'Another drink – or two – to celebrate Captain Hawkins' arrival here!'

Half an hour later the colonel was well into party mood. Amongst everyone else the conversation was pretty stilted, but he and I seemed to really hit it off. Swapping stories of our military training and experiences, our families and even some dirty jokes. He challenged me to a game of chess, which I decided then and there he'd win hands down. I discovered that if he made the effort he could actually speak and understand English well.

He leaned forward conspiratorially. 'You know what we Croats call that bastard Serb president Slobodan Milosevic? . . . Slobber up and down my cock, you bitch!' And roared with laughter.

I put my arm around his shoulder and steered him gently towards the window, out of earshot of the others. 'Actually, I do have some real information for you, Pero,' I said very quietly.

'Oh, yes?' He bent to catch my words.

I said in a hoarse whisper, 'When I finish this tour, I'm out the army. So I've nothing to lose by saying or doing this.'

He seemed intrigued. 'This? Your information?'

I smiled and spoke with quiet deep menace. 'My information,

Pero, is that *you* shot up my convoy this morning, not the Serbs. If you *ever* pull a stunt like that again and kill or injure any of those UN drivers, I will personally find you, cut off your bollocks and stuff them down your throat. OK?'

Markovic froze. There was uncertainty in his eyes. 'This is your idea of a joke?'

'Do I look like I'm joking?' I faced him down. 'Do we understand each other?'

He nodded, hesitantly.

I grinned widely at him and slapped him gently on the back. 'Then I greatly look forward to our friendship. And to that game of chess!'

As I turned I realized that Cuthbert, spook that he was, had edged closer so that he could hear the gist of what we were saying. His face looked more pale than usual.

Markovic saw him, too, and forced a smile to his face. 'Ah, Mr Cuthbert, you're new LO has a great sense of fun. I think we will all get along fine together here in Una Drina—'

His sentence cut off abruptly as a militia officer burst into the room. 'Colonel, my apologies! Mr Mayor . . .' He skidded on the rug in his haste, then noticed Cuthbert and me. 'I didn't know you had visitors . . .'

Markovic sighed and raised his eyes to the heavens to grant him the gift of patience which he clearly did not possess. 'What is it, Lieutenant? What *is* all the fuss about?'

The lieutenant straightened his back and tried to regain his composure. 'There is a deputation arrived to see you and the mayor, sir!'

'Another deputation?' Markovic said.

'We are in demand this evening,' muttered Mayor Jozic.

'It's Herenda,' the lieutenant added. 'And he's got some of those bastards from the Ramoza Brigade with him.'

Cuthbert picked up on the name and leaned sideways to me. 'Zlatko Herenda,' he whispered. 'Commander of the local Muslims.'

Markovic and Mayor Jozic looked at each other for a moment. Suddenly our little party seemed to be dying on its feet and I got the feeling it was the name Herenda that had burst the balloons.

'We will have to see him,' Markovic said.

Blood was going to Jozic's cheeks, adding a strawberry tinge to the porridge complexion. 'Not if he's got those Arab fuckers with him. I'll not stand for it in my town.'

But Markovic was calm and raised his hand, palm out. 'Steady on, Ivan. I'm not afraid of them. We don't want to be seen as behaving like petulant schoolgirls.'

Mayor Jozic grunted. 'If you say so, Colonel. I shall be guided by you.'

'I think we should go,' Cuthbert urged. 'This may not be the best way to meet Herenda for the first time.'

But I shook my head; this was intriguing.

Markovic turned back to the lieutenant. 'Show them in. And tell our guards to come in as well – just in case.'

Moments later Zlatko Herenda strode into the room.

I don't know exactly what I was expecting – maybe a middle-aged officer of the territorial defence reserve of the former Yugoslavia, because these were the people who ran almost all of the opposing militia forces.

But Herenda was only in his mid-thirties with neatly trimmed black hair, a straight nose, and a determined chin that hadn't seen a razor for a day or two. Immediately his military bearing showed him up as probably an officer who had deserted the rump Yugoslav Army to fight for his new homeland. His camo trousers and shirt were of a slightly strange Third World pattern, but I think his mother or girlfriend had ironed them with loving care that morning. Even his boots gleamed.

The dark raisin eyes were as sharp as the creases in his trousers, alive and darting round the room, quickly clocking Cuthbert and me, and frowning suspiciously.

Behind him stood three other men, all taller than Herenda

and all quite heavily bearded. They moved in with an easy, arrogant swagger and looked round the mayor's parlour as if trying to locate the source of an unpleasant smell.

There was little doubt in my mind that they were Afghans. Their weapons were slung carelessly over their shoulders, but they looked mean without even trying.

'An honour, Major Herenda,' Markovic said, clearly keeping pleasantries to a minimum. The two shook hands so briefly that if you'd blinked you'd have missed it. Then Markovic turned to Cuthbert and me. 'You won't know Captain Hawkins, UNPROFOR's new LO in our town.'

'Arrived this afternoon,' I said. 'Been looking forward to meeting you.'

His grip was like a steel vice and, unlike Markovic, he didn't let go. He held on as he glared fiercely and unsmilingly into my eyes. 'Captain Hawkins. Welcome to the Muslim nation of Bosnia-Herzegovina,' he said tersely. 'Such a shame I had to meet you here first at Croat headquarters and not at my own command post.'

That was telling me. From the corner of my eye I saw Markovic smirk.

'I had to start somewhere,' I said, with the brightest smile I could manage.

'Just a pity it was here.' He let go of my hand and left me to check how many small bones had been broken.

Satisfied that he'd scored a diplomatic point, Markovic addressed the young officer. 'What's the purpose of your visit, Herenda?'

The Muslim soldier commandeered one of the club chairs, perching himself on the edge, his forearms resting on his knees and his hands clenched earnestly together. 'This Serb assault, it is in danger of surrounding our town. Or even cutting it off.'

'It has been repulsed,' Mayor Jozic called out flatly from his desk.

'It has not,' Herenda replied. 'You and I both know that the

Chetniks have only been pushed back off the road. Tonight, tomorrow or the next day they will regain it. They have a free logistics tail back into their own territory. They can bring in men, weapons and ammunition with impunity.'

Markovic was no longer smiling; in fact, he looked like he was suffering a serious bout of indigestion. 'So what do you expect me to do? I do not have the resources. The Chetniks will be pushed back, but it will take a little time.'

Herenda shook his head. 'I've just said. They have an endless source of supply, we do not. Therefore they will win . . . And as for what I expect you to do . . .'

Markovic raised a challenging eyebrow. 'Yes?'

Herenda's smile was as cold as steel. 'Nothing. I *expect* you will achieve nothing. But I will give you forty-eight hours to retake their positions completely and secure our town.'

'Hey now, wait a minute!' Mayor Jozic blustered. 'I am the defence minister of this town! And Colonel Markovic is its appointed commander! You do not come in here making threats!'

'Not threats,' Herenda said, rising to his feet. 'A warning. You repulse the Serbs in the next forty-eight hours – or we will do it for you.'

I saw Mayor Jozic's eyes dart in the direction of the Afghans.

Markovic sneered. 'With the help of your holy Muslim brothers, I suppose? The Ramoza Brigade?'

Herenda ignored the jibe. 'From our positions on the outskirts of town, we will attack behind the Serb lines and cut off their supply tail.'

I couldn't fault his tactics.

'I think you had better go now,' Mayor Jozic growled.

The Muslim commander snapped his heels together, gave a slight nod of acknowledgement to everyone in the room, and turned sharply on his heel. But the tension stayed crackling in the air even after the members of the Ramoza Brigade followed unhurriedly in his wake.

Markovic turned to me, shrugged and smiled. 'See what we have to put up with! Not only the Chetniks, but the fucking Mad Mullah's brigade!'

Mission accomplished, we said our goodbyes and left.

'I suppose they never think to combine their operations?' I asked absently as Cuthbert raced us back to HQ in the Land Rover. He was concerned that we were late for supper with Major Tring.

'Croats and Muslims work together?' Cuthbert thought the concept amusing. 'You must be joking! I think about seventy-five per cent of the town is Croat, the rest Muslim. They've always rubbed along, but the Croats have always held all the key administrative jobs. Like Mayor Jozic. And that's resented. All got worse when Bosnia broke away. Had to become allies to fight the mutual Serb foe, but they ended up hating each other more than ever.'

'And this "Mad Mullah's brigade"?' I asked.

'Recently formed up in the town of Ramoza, over the Croatian border. Sort of Muslim Foreign Legion. Mostly Arabs, and not a few Afghans – like those with Herenda today. Unlike the locals, they get stuck in. Seasoned fighters, some of them. Don't know a lot about them, but my people reckon they're funded by Saudi Arabia, though nothing's been proven.'

I said, 'Not the mayor's favourite people.'

'Sweet Jesus, no! The Croats don't mind the old Muslim community. I mean, most weren't practising and only ever con-verted in the first place during the Ottoman Empire when the Turks ruled here. You know, so they wouldn't get picked on. But this Ramoza lot are *real* fundamentalists. And that's like a red rag to the traditional Catholic Croats.'

I could see now why there had been such animosity back at the meeting in the Town Hall. And I couldn't help wondering just where the hell it was all going to lead.

As our headlamp beams swung off the main road the Royal Wessex sentries recognized us and threw open the high-security gates, which was just as well because Cuthbert seemed in such a hurry I think he'd have been prepared to crash straight through them. We slewed to a halt in the parking lot, narrowly missing a squaddie.

'What's the rush, Nigel?' I asked as Senic scrambled out the back, obviously finding it hard to believe he'd survived the journey in one piece.

'I told you. Major Tring's a stickler for punctuality. Supper was at 1900 hours.'

I glanced at my watch. That was forty minutes ago. 'You're not even in the army now, Nigel,' I pointed out, somewhat bemused.

Cuthbert stared at me blankly. 'I *still* have to live with him.'

I followed my companion through into the admin block and out the other side to a small courtyard formed by three Portakabins placed in a square. One was clearly marked 'Officers' Mess'.

We stepped inside.

The faces of the A Company, Royal Wessex Regiment's leading lights turned towards us as one. They were seated at a trestle table that had been covered in a spotless white linen cloth. The plates in front of the diners had all been scraped clean and their wine glasses were empty.

Major Tring sat at the far end. On the floor at his side, the fat Staffordshire terrier Trojan was slurping his way through some brown meaty stuff in a huge chrome dog's bowl.

On the OC's other side, a thin, weasel-faced squaddie was hovering with a tray of brandy balloons. I guessed that this was Tring's driver, the redoubtable Billy Billings.

'And what time do you call this, Jeffrey?' the major demanded.

Cuthbert jumped in heroically with both feet. 'Got held up at Croat HQ, Major. Bit of a hoo-ha going on.'

'Thank you, Nigel. But I'm sure Captain Hawkins can answer for himself.'

I said quickly, 'It's as Mr Cuthbert said—' My new UKLO chum had told me Tring's first name and how he detested it being used, so creating an unusual 'sir' and 'Major' form of address to him throughout the regiment. In sheer irritation and devilment, I added the form he apparently hated most, 'Reginald.'

The air seemed to freeze instantly. I noticed the glances being exchanged across the table.

Tring glowered up from beneath his angry brows. 'Well, shame about that. Billings here had rustled up something special to mark your arrival. Welcome meal. Thought you weren't coming. Nearly sent out a Warrior to look for you.' He looked pointedly sideways down at the dog, who was now licking his lips. 'Didn't want the food to go to waste, so your loss was Trojan's gain. Still, no harm done, eh?'

Billings wrinkled his nose in my direction. 'Shall I open some compo, gentlemen? Maybe the curried chicken – with some apple flakes?'

Three

'God, Major,' Nigel Cuthbert enthused, 'you should have seen Jimbo at work. He stitched up old Markovic like a kipper!'

I cringed at the words as I began tucking into the compo meal Billy Billings had quickly prepared. And in fairness to him, the herbs and spices and some kind of local sausage he'd added had transformed it into something quite edible.

Major Tring didn't respond, concentrating instead on stroking Trojan's head. I think he'd decided to send me to Coventry or turn me into the Invisible Man for the rest of supper.

But the company's 2IC was interested. 'And how was that, Nigel?' he asked.

Captain Gordon Cromwell ran the unit's day-to-day activities from the Ops Room, which was converted from the former managing director's office on the second floor.

He was in a totally different mould from both Tring and, according to what I'd heard, from the regiment's commanding officer, Colonel Rathbone. Gordon was a tall, broad-shouldered Kentish lad by birth, in his mid-thirties and with an open, happy face and inquisitive grey eyes that didn't appear to miss much. The shaggy, fair-haired moustache emphasized a rather toothsome smile.

'Well, Gordy,' Cuthbert replied, 'as you know I've been trying to find who *exactly*'s commanding this Serb offensive and from where – so I can set up a cease-fire. Serb HQ at Pale isn't being helpful and Markovic wants to keep us out of it. So Jimbo let's on they've got it wrong and we *know* it's some hot-shot sent down here by Ratko Mladic.'

Gordy frowned. 'How did that help?'

'Mayor Jozic got all huffy and blurted out they'd interrogated a prisoner who confirmed the Serb commander was Zoric, and that his forward command post was in the village of Stavac, over the mountain.' Cuthbert laughed and downed a mouthful of wine. 'You should have seen the look on Markovic's face when he realized he'd been had. Talk about thunderous!'

Suddenly Major Tring's interest seemed to return to the conversation. I tried to avoid his gaze, but there wasn't really anywhere to hide around the small table. 'Is this true, Jeffrey?'

I kept the tone of my voice even. 'Something on those lines, Reg.'

He kept staring at me and gave an almost imperceptible shake of his head. 'And do you really think making a fool of the local Croat commander is the way to get off on the right foot?'

Cuthbert sprang immediately to my defence. 'Actually, Major, it seemed to work a treat. Think Markovic respected him for it. Afterwards they seemed the best of mates.'

Tring was clearly irritated by Cuthbert's intervention, and did his best to ignore it by saying, 'Well, Jeffrey?'

I waited a moment as I finished eating. 'With respect, Reg, in my experience bullies only really respect people who stand up to them, and I suspect that Markovic got used to bullying Captain Wells around. That had to change.'

I think that hit home hard. Tring's motorized shutter eyes went into overdrive for a split second. I also noticed a few other eyebrows raised around the table, and Gordy make a face that said I wasn't far wrong.

'You didn't know Captain Wells, Jeffrey,' Tring came back at last. 'He was a good man, very able and an excellent diplomat. He would never have risked putting his relationship with any of the militia commanders in jeopardy by such irresponsible behaviour. You might have got away with it this time, but I suggest you take a far more cautious approach in future.'

'Sure, Reg,' I replied non-committally.

'And I trust a report of your meeting will be with me shortly,' Tring added. 'I'm certain Colonel Rathbone will be interested to see it.'

'First thing tomorrow, Reg,' I replied. Anxious to move things on, I added, 'By the way, now we know Zoric is in Stavac, I'd like to take the earliest opportunity to meet him.'

I had the feeling Tring was trying to think of an excuse not to oblige, but that was difficult for him because we all knew it was his job. He said, 'It'll mean going through Serb lines to get to him.'

That was stating the bloody obvious, of course. 'I know. I was wondering if Nigel and I could have a Warrior escort.'

'When did you have in mind, Jeffrey?'

'Tomorrow, when I return from seeing the colonel in DV. Say 1300 hours?'

Tring added a terse, 'Very well,' as he rose to his feet and made to leave the room with Trojan at his heels.

As Tring left, Gordy Cromwell patted me on the shoulder. 'Well done, Jimbo, excellent. About time someone stood up to Markovic and the Croats here. And all the others for that matter.'

With Major Tring having left the mess the atmosphere lightened immediately and I had a chance to get to know the others around the table: Mervyn Jarvis, commander of the Lancers' Scimitar light-tank troop, and three young subalterns who each commanded one of the Warrior platoons.

One of them, a stocky, ginger-haired lieutenant from Hampshire called Hal Watkins, was decidedly enthusiastic about heading for the front lines. 'My lads are up for it, Jimbo, no worries. We all reckon we've been pussy-footing around too long. 'Bout time we flexed a bit of muscle. If you've got it, flaunt it.' He turned to the Lancers' OC. 'What d'your chaps think, Mervyn?'

Mervyn Jarvis was tall, relaxed and super-cool, it seemed, about everything in his life. He could have been no more than thirty but, despite his youth, he had adopted the rather arch, devil-may-care arrogance of a titled landowner's son who would rather die than bring himself to worry about anything or anyone in life. He seemed to have stepped straight out of the pages of *Brideshead Revisited*. 'My chaps are Lancers, dear boy,' he said, brushing a foppish fringe of hair from his forehead in a somewhat effeminate gesture, 'they don't *think*, they just *do*. Just wind up our spring and point us in the right direction. I like to think we're the Martini girls of the British Army . . . Any time, any place, anywhere!'

'I think that's the artillery, Merv,' Gordy said. '*Ubiquitous*. Everywhere.'

'Ah, yes,' Mervyn said, now waving a long More cigarette around with an elegant gesture. 'But the Lancers get everywhere *first*. Recce, old son, it's our job.'

Gordy Cromwell took me to one side. 'Once this lot get going, they'll be at it all night. I need a break – been on shift since the Serb offensive started. A couple of beers down at the Splendid, then I'm going to crash. You and Nigel want to join me?'

Really I wanted to get my report buttoned up ready for the next morning, but getting out of the atmosphere of Tring's lingering presence was distinctly more appealing.

'Right on,' Cuthbert said. 'Lead on – the fleshpots of Una Drina!'

As I expected, the Hotel Splendid was anything but. It was a concrete block thrown up in the sixties, rendered and pebbledashed and painted white – but it hadn't seen a brushstroke for years. Only the jaunty but wind-ragged striped canvas canopy over the entrance, and an upper outdoor bar area with a wrought-iron balustrade, marked it out as a possible hotel.

It was not easy to pass judgement on the interior because it was lit only by candles and paraffin lamps, but there seemed to be a lot of wood-grained plastic laminate, orange plastic panels in the internal doors and partition windows and another faded red carpet. Refugee children were playing around the main staircase as the three of us made our way to the bar.

No matter what the hardships and deprivations of war zones, how was it, I wondered, that somehow there was always a plentiful supply of alcohol and tobacco? I noticed that the bottled lager came at a high price though, so I guessed that explained some of the economics.

There was quite a crowd around the bar. There were a few DPMs and blue UN berets in evidence together with the mostly ill-matched combat fatigues of Una Drina's militias. It was easy to spot the scruffy-looking local inhabitants who hadn't been able to have a hot bath or launder their clothes for months. They were mostly older men, as the youngsters had all been drafted to fight. Despite the deprivations of living in the place, some of the teenagers and young women had made more of an effort. They looked quite presentable for their night on the town, although I noticed that make-up seemed in short supply.

Cuthbert pointed out the smarter civilians, explaining that both Red Cross and the French charity Médecins Sans Frontières were based at the Splendid, each with a staff of three.

He also spotted an ITN film crew, no doubt up from their usual base in the semi-luxury of DV because they'd heard about the fighting here. Anxious to avoid them, he steered us away to some armchairs in a corner, where we were swallowed up in the gloom and the wafting strains of Phil Collins coming from a battery-operated ghetto-blaster.

'God, it's good to get out of HQ,' Gordy said. 'I can't believe how the company's changed since Tring took over last year. Atmosphere in the Ops Room can be awful, everyone's started developing a bad attitude to everything, very negative. Tring just loves interfering with my decisions and the way I run things. Course, it's been on a slow downhill slide ever since Colonel

Rathbone took command of the Regiment. Nice enough bloke, but . . .'

'Maybe too nice,' Cuthbert suggested. 'I just don't think he's tough enough – and he seems to have taken to Tring like he's his long-lost son. Obviously trusts him implicitly.'

Gordy agreed. 'Runs to him with all the tittle-tattle – so Rathbone thinks he's being kept fully in the picture. Doesn't seem to realize Tring's just toadying up to him.'

'Ever tried putting the colonel in the picture?' I asked.

'Not easy, Jimbo,' Gordy said. 'I mean, you can't just come out and say what you really think. Chances are Rathbone would report it straight back to Tring – and then things would be ten times worse. Both Captain Wells and I have tried dropping big hints, but Rathbone just doesn't pick up on them – or want to.'

It was then that Cuthbert gave me a nudge. On the far side of the smoke-choked room, a group of unmistakably Ramoza Brigade soldiers, tall and mean-eyed with dark Arab features, were being served a tray of orange juice by the barmaid. As she turned she noticed us, gave a wave of recognition and started to approach.

Despite the wave, there was no smile, I noticed. 'The owner's wife?' I guessed aloud.

'No, that's Anita,' Cuthbert said. 'Local schoolmistress. Helps out here some evenings for a bit of pocket money. School's closed because of war damage.'

'The bane of Major Tring's life,' Gordy said with a smile.

'One scary lady,' Cuthbert added.

She wore the obligatory world-wide waitress colour, or lack of it. Black cardigan over a white blouse, a knee-length black skirt that flared nicely on her hips and sensible black pumps. It all seemed to go with her pale white complexion and raven's-wing hair that was scooped severely back off her face in a bun. Dark arched eyebrows above wire-framed spectacles gave her a rather fierce look, which wasn't helped by the fact that her smile came only with considerable reluctance.

'Hi, Anita,' Nigel greeted. 'And how's the prettiest girl in Una Drina?'

She cocked her head to one side. 'How would I know?' she retorted quickly, as though dealing with a wayward pupil. 'I don't know her.'

'Oh, I think you do,' Gordy joined in.

She ignored that. 'What would you gentlemen like to drink?'

Cuthbert ordered three bottles of lager.

Then she noticed me. 'You are a new face in Una Drina?' she said. It sounded like an accusation.

I smiled. 'For my sins.'

This time her smile lasted a fraction longer, and I realized that her face was actually quite attractive. 'And do you sin a lot, stranger in town?'

'Only when I get the opportunity,' I bantered. 'Which is not often.'

Cuthbert said, 'This is—'

I was ready for that. 'Jeff,' I interrupted, and stood to shake her hand.

Her eyes scrutinized my own closely for several seconds as if trying to work something out. Trust, I thought. Could I be trusted? Was I a man of honour? Of course I could have been way out, but it was the feeling I got.

'I am Anita. Anita Furtula,' she said. 'The schoolmistress.'

'And I'm thirsty,' Gordy added.

'You are replacing Captain Wells?' she asked, ignoring the heartfelt pleas for refreshment.

'That's right,' I said.

She indicated the three stars on the epaulette of my DPM smock. 'You are a captain, too. It makes sense, if you are his replacement. How is he?'

'He's better now, Anita,' Gordy answered. 'Recovering in Germany – where I'm going to cure my *dehydration*!'

She gave another brief smile. 'Of course, I will get your order.'

As she went away, Gordy leaned towards me. 'You're in for it now. Think our Anita was sizing you up.'

'For what?'

'Getting the school fixed and the kids behind desks.'

'Why me?'

'Because she's given up on Tring and she realizes that the LOs are the most influential guys in the regiment. She worked hard on Johnny Wells before he went sick – although, to be honest, I think Johnny just made promises to keep her sweet, keep her off Tring's back.'

'Johnny Wells couldn't stand the woman,' Cuthbert confirmed. 'Thought she was just a bloody nuisance.'

Gordy shrugged. 'She's only trying to do the best for the kids. I quite like her.'

It was then that one of the ITN news team, who had been chatting up an attractive female Red Cross administrator, suddenly spotted us. As he began moving our way, past the light of the bar lamps, I immediately recognized his face, although I couldn't put a name to it.

'Gordy Cromwell!' the TV man greeted cordially.

'Gerald,' Gordy responded with feigned enthusiasm and rose to meet him.

I had the name then. Gerald Kemp, a seasoned trouble-spot man who'd been round the block a few times, not to mention the world. I think he was in his late fifties, or maybe older, a consummate professional with a florid complexion and the slightly watery eyes of a heavy drinker. He was wearing a bright yellow puffer jacket and faded corduroy trousers.

After the brief introductions, Kemp said to Gordy, 'Look, we've heard about this Serb offensive. Suppose there's no chance of getting a bit closer to the action? We haven't got any decent footage for a week and London's putting the pressure on.' He shrugged in a way that suggested we would empathize. 'So nothing new there, then, eh?'

'It's been quiet this afternoon,' Gordy pointed out.

Kemp nodded. 'Yeah, but the offensive hasn't been repelled, has it? Just a lull. Bloody good thing, too. I'm after footage, not getting me and the team shot.'

I wondered if there might be some way to turn this to our advantage, but I wasn't yet sure how. I said, 'I'm Jeff Hawkins, the new LO here. I've got to go up and find the Serb commander tomorrow. Maybe you could tag along.'

Kemp looked taken aback; he obviously wasn't used to that sort of co-operation from A Company, or I suspected anyone in the Royal Wessex Regiment. 'Really – er, Jeff, was it? That would be excellent.'

Gordy looked concerned. 'We'll have to clear that with Major Tring, Jimbo. And the Colonel's PINFO at DV . . .'

'Sure,' I said, an idea beginning to form in my mind. 'I'm going to DV tomorrow. I'll square it with the colonel myself.' I looked back Kemp. 'We'll have to rain-check it, Gerald. But have your boys ready to join us around 1300 hours. OK?'

Kemp went away the happiest man in Una Drina.

'Neither the colonel nor Tring likes the media,' Cuthbert warned darkly. 'Not sure that was a good move.'

'Wouldn't want to be in your boots,' Gordy agreed.

I said, 'I was in the Falklands War. In the Paras we looked after the press boys, and most of them were OK. The Royal Marines treated them like shit and wondered why afterwards the public had the impression the Paras won the whole war single-handed.'

Gordy looked a bit uncomfortable as the point went home, and seemed keen to change the subject. 'Ah, our drinks! Thanks, Anita!'

'God, Anita,' Cuthbert said, 'what have you been doing – brewing it yourself?'

Her angry little brows knotted demonically. 'Is busy at the bar, you can see!'

'Thanks,' I said, just grateful to slake my thirst at last.

Anita liked that. 'Ah, at least there is still *one* officer and gentleman left in your British Army.' She touched my sleeve. 'Please, Jeff, I would like to speak with you.'

She started to move away, obliging me to follow. Of course, I could guess what was to follow, but I played along. 'What is it, Anita?'

Those dark, penetrating – and, I had to say, rather beautiful – eyes demanded to be taken seriously. 'For months I have been trying to get the school opened again. First with the last regiment that was here and now with you Royal Wessex people. Captain Wells promises me he will get something done to repair the damage. He promises, promises, promises . . . but nothing ever happens.'

I said, 'As UNPROFOR, that sort of thing is not in our remit, Anita, I'm sure that's been explained to you.'

Now her eyes narrowed like a cat's and seemed to be drilling into mine as her lips formed into a snarl of anger. 'Remits, remits, remits! That is all I bloody ever hear! All of the time it is remits! I am sick to damn bloody death of remits! Remits do not put the roof on the school! Remits do not get our children back to learning! They will be a village of idiots when all this is over!' Now the anger was subsiding in her voice and in her eyes, her tone and expression softening. 'Please, Jeff, understand. There is no one else I can turn to. If your colonel wants something to happen, he can make it happen – remit or no remit. Please persuade him, Jeff. Please!'

For once I had a measure of sympathy for Major Tring and my predecessor. I could imagine what it must be like to be under this verbal barrage week in and week out.

I smiled reassuringly. 'I'll see what I can do.'

She frowned at me quizzically. 'That is a very popular expression in England, no? I seem to hear it all the time here.'

I said, 'I mean it.'

Anita's nostrils flared prettily as she took a deep breath and composed herself. 'Thank you, Jeff. I shall see that you do.'

She inclined her head, gave an oddly beguiling twitch of a

smile and spun on her heel to march purposefully back to the bar.

I awoke in pitch darkness with the floor shaking. Moments before I'd been dreaming that I was with Marcia in our house that wasn't our house and then the earthquake began.

She was still screaming in my head as I realized I was in my windowless cell at company HQ and the shaking and noise I was hearing was that of incoming artillery rounds. The illuminated face of my watch told me it had just turned six in the morning as I struggled out of my sleeping-bag and scrabbled underneath the camp-bed to find my torch.

Then I lit the Tilley lamp and pulled on my DPMs and boots, before heading down the corridor towards the Ops Room.

Gordy Cromwell was already there with sleep-tousled hair, taking over from the duty officer. There was a lot of activity with soldiers rushing backwards and forwards, relaying incoming messages from the radio shack. There was no sign of Major Tring.

'Not doing my hangover any good, Gordy. What's all the fuss about?'

'Hi, Jimbo,' he replied. 'Fucking Croats suddenly started heavy-mortaring the Serb positions – using us for cover. Bloody cheek. Got their fire-position in the timber yard right behind this factory.'

I understood. The Serbs had to return fire by lobbing their shells over the top of us. If the Croats thought it might deter them from trying, they were mistaken. The Ops Room shook again as two more rounds from the Serbs landed somewhere nearby.

'Have we taken any hits in the compound yet?' I asked.

He shook his head. 'No, but close. Got a hole torn in the perimeter fence.'

'What you going to do?'

Gordy looked up at me from the map spread out on the table in front of him. His expression was glum. 'Nothing yet. Major

Tring follows strict rules of engagement. Non-involvement unless we're being directly and deliberately targeted.'

Of course, that was the standing order for Bosnia, but there was always some leeway and a margin of judgement allowed to the commanders on the ground.

I said, 'We should shift those Croat mortar positions before the Serbs end up putting a stray round into the sleeping-quarters or this Ops Room.'

Gordy looked a little irritated. 'That's what you might think, Jimbo. But Tring—'

'Fuck Tring,' I retorted, 'he isn't here . . . Where is he, by the way?'

'In his billet, I should think. I don't expect to see him till around 0700 hours.'

I pushed my luck. 'If you don't want to ask him, make the decision yourself. Tell him later when it's already been done.'

'Is that what *you'd* do, Jimbo?'

Of course, Gordon Cromwell and I were equal rank, despite our age difference, and he was in operational command of the company as its 2IC. I could hardly tell him what to do. I said earnestly, 'If you ordered me to take a couple of Warriors and a Scimitar and persuade the Croats and the Serbs to stop shooting at each other, I'd be more than pleased to oblige.'

More than once when I had been in the SAS, we'd come across Regular Army officers who had not had enough battle-field experience and so had to be 'guided' in the right direction. You can't buy or really even train for that sort of instinctive knowledge. I guess that was why Dave McVicar had chosen me to sup from this poisoned chalice.

He stared at me hard for a moment. 'Sort of LO role, you mean?'

'Exactly, Gordy, and I'll stand shoulder-to-shoulder with you if you get any flak from Major Tring. That's a promise.'

There was a pause for thought, before he reached his decision. He took a deep breath and straightened his shoulders. 'For what it's worth, Jimbo, I think you are right. Let's do it. How do you have in mind to play this?'

I looked down at the map. 'Do we have line-of-sight on any of the Serb firing positions?'

'Only an anti-aircraft gun they're using, probably mounted on a truck. The artillery sites are on the far side of the hill.'

I said, 'That'll do,' and briefly agreed my plan with him before calling over Hal Watkins, the Warrior troop commander, and Mervyn Jarvis of the Lancers. I went over the tactics with them. Suddenly their attitudes transformed and they were brimming with enthusiasm.

Twenty minutes later, with the sounds, flashes and vibrations of exploding artillery, mortars and tracer all round our compound, the sentries threw open the gates. My Land Rover led two Warriors which emerged like two menacing, angry and mud-spattered monsters whose peace had been disturbed.

Mervyn Jarvis's Scimitar brought up the rear, its tracks spinning as it broke away to the right, while I took the Warriors in the opposite direction towards the timber yard, which was situated some five hundred metres farther along the main street.

Darkness was finally giving way to the first vestiges of sunrise and there was now some ambient light. It was enough to make out the outline of the sawmill and warehousing, behind which I could see the sandbagged positions. And there were tell-tale flashes as the rounds were dropped down the mortar tubes, ignited and sent hurtling on their way, over company HQ and into the surrounding hillside.

The timber yard itself was pocked with artillery shell craters and wreathed in acrid smoke from both incoming and outgoing fire. When I was half-way across I switched the Land Rover's lights to full beam and Hal Watkins gave the same order to the two Warrior drivers, who added their spotlamps as well.

In an instant the Croat militia around the mortars and their crews were swamped in dazzling light, turning round and shielding their eyes from the sudden blaze as the rumbling of the

Warrior tracks could suddenly be heard above the noise of their own firing. I swung the Land Rover round tight to their flank and braked hard.

Then I was out. 'Who's in charge here?' I demanded loudly in Serbo-Croat.

The trouble with Croat militia and most of the others is that few carry any insignia or badge of rank. However, I was pretty sure I knew who the leader was, just by his demeanour. I was proved right as a huge bear of a man with a chaotic mass of black hair and ragged beard and moustache stepped forward. He looked both angry and puzzled. Angry because I was talking aggressively and puzzled because of my fluent Serbo-Croat.

'Who wants to know?' he growled back defiantly.

'Captain Hawkins, liaison officer, UNPROFOR.'

There was a sneer on his face. 'So?'

At that moment I heard the dull stutter of the Serb anti-air-craft fire on the hillside and saw the tracer hosing in low over company HQ until it found one of the buildings in the timber yard. Instinctively the Croat commander and I were distracted, watching as the target disintegrated in a fireball.

Dead on cue I heard Mervyn's Scimitar open up, returning a hail of deadly 30mm Rarden cannon rounds back into the Serb fire-position. Immediately the AA gun fell silent.

I looked back at the Croat, who swallowed hard. I gathered it had been some time since he'd seen any assertive UN action in these parts.

I said, 'I suggest you cease fire immediately. You are deliber-ately putting UNPROFOR lives at risk by using this firing position. Under our mandate we are entitled to protect our-selves.'

He glanced back up at the hillside, then shook his head and glared back at me. 'Go and fuck yourself!' he said, and turned his back on me. His mortar crewmen thought that was very funny.

I turned and looked toward Hal Watkins, who was in the commander's turret of the nearest Warrior. He'd been watching and listening intently. I nodded. He grinned and gave me a thumbs-up. Suddenly the engine revved, belching black diesel smoke, and the metal tracks began to clank into motion, edging forward.

It took a second or two for the Croat commander and his crew to realize the armoured vehicle was moving towards them, quite steadily and deliberately. You don't argue with a 24-ton tracked armoured vehicle. You either stay put and get crushed to a bloody pulp or move. They began backing away, not quite believing what was happening.

The front tracks of the Warrior half-mounted and half-demolished the sandbag emplacement, the track teeth ripping the sacks apart as they scrabbled relentlessly for grip to power the beast up and over. It reached a half-way pivot, balanced on the pile of sand and shattered bags, then hovered for a second before belly-flopping heavily down onto the offending mortar launchers. The Warrior moved remorselessly on after the hastily retreating Croats. The sound of metal against metal was clearly heard as the tracks chewed and ground the weapons into a small scrapheap.

Then the Warrior stopped and swung the turret round so that its cannon barrel was pointed at the ragged line of gaping Croats.

I walked forward a few paces so that I was within their earshot. 'I think we now understand each other, gentlemen! Now you have exactly sixty seconds to disperse before I give the order for the Warrior to open fire.'

I just glimpsed the fierce glare on the face of the bear before he turned and disappeared into the early dawn mist with his companions.

Colonel Rathbone scrutinized me closely across his desk. His thoughtful pale blue eyes were set in a fleshy, well-scrubbed face beneath a head of hair that was grey almost to the point of being white.

He lay back in his chair, elbows on the armrests and his fingers interlaced. 'Made quite a mark already I see, Jeffrey. And not been here twenty-four hours.'

I wasn't in a good mood. I'd made the journey from Una Drina in Hal Watkins' noisy cramped Warrior and I hated it. I had felt claustrophobic and sick from the fumes. Worse, I'd felt like a sitting target. Like most Paras I wanted the fresh air and to act on my own initiative, to duck and dive. Yomp or go fast in my own vehicle. I'd even have caught a bus if there'd been one.

'Just doing my job, Colonel,' I replied tersely. I tried to keep my irritation hidden; antagonizing the CO was the last thing I wanted to do.

'Heard about that business this morning.'

Tring on the whinge, I guessed. I said, 'It was Gordy Cromwell's decision, sir. I just carried out the orders. And, for what it's worth, I fully agreed with his take on the situation.'

Rathbone's eyebrows knitted in a frown. 'Major Tring has told me he thought the action unnecessary.'

'With due respect, sir, Major Tring wasn't in the Ops Room at the time. He was still in bed.'

In fact, he'd been out of bed pretty damn fast when Billy Billings told him what was going on. When I got back from our little even-handed, robust peace-keeping, he was waiting and ready to give Gordy Cromwell and me a good dressing-down.

I think Tring was quite taken aback when Gordy stood his ground. And when he realized the mortar fire had stopped, making the Serb counter-barrage unnecessary, he couldn't very well say much. He just went into a sort of silent huff and marched out, trailing Billings and Trojan behind him.

Colonel Rathbone said, 'Well, necessary or not – and whether Major Tring agreed or not in hindsight – the fact is, the fighting stopped.' He smiled a little. 'What do you Paras call that, eh? "Robust negotiations"?'

I was so surprised that my returning grin was involuntary. 'Something like that, sir.'

'Well done anyway, Jeffrey . . . er . . .' He glanced down at my papers. 'Or is it Jimbo?'

'Jimbo's fine, sir.'

'Well, welcome to the Royal Wessex anyway, Jimbo. You come highly recommended by Brigadier Stowell and if the CBF thinks you're the man for the job, then who am I to argue? Of course, I can't pretend that the fact you're not from one of our other Brigade battalions has gone down well in some quarters. But I recognize you have some special qualities of value here. Especially your experience in negotiation.'

'Thank you, Colonel,' I replied quickly before he added any provisos. 'And I'd like to discuss this afternoon's operation with you, if that's OK.'

Rathbone nodded. 'I gather you plan to go to Stavac and speak to the Serb commander. What's his name . . .?'

'Zoric.'

'Of course.' A penny seemed to drop. 'Oh, yes, I've been told by Major Tring about how you obtained that information—'

'And here's my sitrep, sir.' I placed the file on his table. 'I appreciate my method was unconventional, but it worked. Colonel Markovic and I parted on the best of terms.'

He looked relieved. Why did I have the feeling Tring had missed that bit out? 'So, Jimbo, this visit to Stavac . . .'

'I'd like to take an ITN news team with me. Gerald Kemp's lot. If you agree, sir, I'll square it with PINFO.'

'Is that wise, Jimbo?' The look on Rathbone's face said he didn't like that idea at all. 'God, we don't want famous TV journalists getting killed in our care. And I don't know what the Serbs will make of it.'

I said, 'Their presence will make it easier for us to approach. If I can get Zoric to give an interview, it'll massage his ego. Even for him to be asked would be enough. And I think I can use that situation to a negotiating advantage.'

Rathbone frowned, uncertain. 'What does Major Tring think about the idea?'

This was the opening I'd been looking for. 'Well, Colonel, I thought I ought to consult *you* first. All the LOs here are directly responsible to you, I just happen to be stuck out on a limb at Una Drina. But I'd like you to consider me to be your personal eyes and ears on the ground on my patch. I think it especially important that we establish my loyalty to you and the battalion and develop a mutual trust as soon as possible.' I forced a smile. 'Especially as I'm a Para.'

That amused Rathbone somewhat. 'Jolly good, Jimbo. Excellent idea.' I think he was actually beginning to realize that I wasn't the irresponsible maroon-bereted slaphead that Tring had almost certainly described.

'And the ITN team?' I pressed.

The colonel shrugged. 'Well, let's give it a try. I'll be guided by you. But for God's sake don't get any of the little buggers killed or wounded – or I promise I'll have your balls for breakfast. Got that, Jimbo?'

I grinned. 'Sir.'

'Now,' he said, 'any more bright ideas that are going to cause me grief – before I introduce you to a few of our key people?'

Suddenly the dark, accusing eyes of Anita Furtula flashed into my mind. At this very moment she was probably sticking pins into a Plasticine model of me. 'Just the school at Una Drina, sir. If we could have a detachment of Engineers for a couple of days . . . might mean it could reopen.'

Rathbone grimaced. 'Not our remit, Jimbo. I'm sure you know that.'

I nodded. 'Yes, sir. But the townsfolk can't accept that, however often we tell them. I believe it would help restore some confidence in our presence.'

'I really don't think—'

'I think it might take some pressure off Major Tring. The schoolmistress has been giving him quite a hard time over it, and he's got enough on his plate.'

Rathbone regarded me thoughtfully. 'Quite a considerate

chap, really, aren't you, Jimbo? But if you think it would help
Reg . . .'

'And win local hearts and minds,' I added quickly. 'Of course,
we've done a lot of that at Hereford.'

The colonel gave a slow nod of his head. 'Let me see what I
can do.'

Ouch! I swear to God I felt another of Anita's pins go in. But
I decided I'd pushed it enough for the moment.

A promising rapport established, Rathbone took me through
to the PINFO office to square the ITN visit. Then we went on
to meet the four other liaison officers based at Donji Vrbas.
They were four bright, intelligent and enthusiastic men who
were usually stationed at other towns on the Royal Wessex's
patch. It was hard to tell in the few brief minutes we had – especially with the colonel standing right behind me – but I had the
distinct feeling they lacked a sense of direction from above.
Which, of course, was hardly surprising.

I made a couple of anti-Para jokes at my own expense which
went down well and helped to break the ice. And I said I
thought I'd only been drafted in because of my particular and
unusual language skill, not because I was considered superior to
any other officer in their brigade.

They seemed genuinely to appreciate that and I noticed a
new look of respect in their eyes when I made a passing reference to my time in 22 SAS. So we parted on good terms with
the promise I'd stand them a round of drinks next time I was up
at DV. The truth was I hoped that eventually my seniority in
years and experience, if not rank, would allow me to become
the alpha male, so to speak. But I would have to wait and see on
that score.

Then Colonel Rathbone took me on a brief tour of the town
in his personal Land Rover.

Marking the half-way spot on the Devil's Triangle route to
Sarajevo, DV was a good five times the size of Una Drina and
was also a predominantly Croat enclave within Bosnia. Most

important of all it had electricity and its telephone system worked – well, up to a point. The Royal Wessex Regiment's battalion HQ, comprising support and logistics elements as well as two Rifle companies and twenty-four Warriors, was housed in a former technical college.

We drove past a sizeable hospital, apparently straining to cope with the constant influx of war casualties and chronically short of medical supplies, but still operational. And at least here the shops were open, even if the shelves were rather bare. Colonel Rathbone told me that there was a large bakery in the town which used the flour brought in by Rocky's UNHCR convoys to supply the inhabitants and some of the surrounding areas. There should have been a plentiful supply of local fruit and vegetables at this time of year, but even if crops had been planted earlier it was now too dangerous to harvest them in fields and orchards that had become battlegrounds. At least there seemed to be enough food around to keep even a handful of restaurants open on a very restricted menu.

In the centre of town there was a large concrete block of an hotel of typically stark Cold War Communist design, imaginatively called Hotel Donji Vrbas.

'Of course,' Colonel Rathbone announced as he eased himself from the front passenger seat, 'the UNHCR has its HQ here, as does the Head of Office, plus the BBC and other media people. So you can always count on the bar having a full stock of gin and tonics!'

Laughing at his own joke, he ambled through the tiled lobby to the sweeping 1960s bar, lined with leatherette-covered stools and picture windows showing panoramic views of the surrounding river valley. There were little clusters of people standing around on its faded blue carpet, drinking and chatting.

I'd arranged to meet Nigel Cuthbert here, as he said he had some business in town, and we were going to drive back to Una Drina together ready for the afternoon mission into Serb-held country.

I spotted him talking to a large man who was dressed as though he were about to play a round of golf in a bright red sweater and even brighter yellow tartan trousers. He required only a yellow scarf to be Rupert the Bear's stunt double.

Colonel Rathbone leant towards me and spoke in a hoarse whisper. 'Dammit, that's Kirk Grundy, American. Claims to be a stringer for the *New York Times*. But he's fooling nobody—'

But fooling nobody in exactly which way I didn't get to hear, because Rathbone cut himself off in mid-sentence as we came within earshot.

Cuthbert spotted us and made us welcome. While Rathbone made do with a terse nod of acknowledgement to the American, I was introduced and shook the big offered hand.

And Kirk Grundy was big, as big as Nebraska – which I quickly learned was his home state – in size, in voice, in personality. 'So pleased to meet you, Jim-bo! Cuthy here's bin tellin' me 'bout you. Seems like you're a man to watch.'

Oh, shit, that's the last thing I needed with the colonel standing right beside me. 'Only doing my job, Kirk . . . Just like you.'

The large face, rather flat and lacking in contour, suddenly opened up, the mouth like Vesuvius revealing tombstone teeth and emitting a big bubbling chuckle. A few sprays of saliva completed the volcanic effect. 'Yeah, yeah, Jim-bo, right-on! Just doin' our jobs. I gotta keep up with three alimonies, and they're all big-spending gals. My luck, it's always been the sort of gal I go for! Big tits and big spendin' habits! Whadabout you?'

To start with I couldn't work out what was quite so funny. Then I couldn't work out what the hell his question was. 'About me?' I asked.

'Sure. You divorced?'

'Not yet.' Oops! The glib retort tripped out just a little too easily. I pasted a smile on top of the wound. 'Working on it.'

He wagged a big frankfurter finger at me. 'Don't do it. It'll bust your balls. Only she an' her lawyer'll win. Stay put . . . and CHEAT!'

Vesuvius erupted again, but died rather quickly as he suddenly changed tack. 'Heard you're tryin' to stop this Serb offensive down at Una Drina this afternoon?'

I gave a sideways scowl at Cuthbert, who adopted a sudden air of innocence, then I turned back to Kirk Grundy. 'No, I'm trying to negotiate a cease-fire. Subtle difference.'

Out of the corner of my eye I was relieved to see Colonel Rathbone give a tight smile and little nod of agreement, or was it approval?

The big smile on Grundy's face remained and for the first time I got to see his eyes. Not big, but grey and slitted and piggy. And there was not much laughter in them. 'Yeah, Jim-bo. But if the Serbs *don't* cease fire, they might just take Una Drina this week, y'know? So it amounts to the same thing.'

I wasn't following his line of reasoning. 'Not really. If the Croats can't hold them, they'll break through some time soon.'

He wagged another frankfurter at me, then tapped the end of his nose. 'Lot can happen in a week, Jim-bo. A lot.'

I suddenly realized what the end of the colonel's interrupted introduction had been. Grundy claimed to be a newspaper stringer, but he was fooling no one – big, amiable Kirk Grundy was CIA.

Of course, at this time the United States didn't have any involvement in the Bosnian crisis. Well, that was the story at the time.

It was the cue for Colonel Rathbone to make his excuses and return to HQ. Nigel Cuthbert didn't seem to like the way the conversation was going, either, and made a clumsy attempt to change its course. 'Hey, Jimbo, you won't have seen these! Just take a look.'

Distracted, I turned towards the bar where he was spreading out half a dozen black and white photographs. I'm no critic, but I could see that they were brilliant shots. A UNHCR convoy under attack – a huge truck leaping into the frame, the other wagons snaked out behind, explosions to the left and right, live tracer seeming to fly straight at the camera and dust everywhere.

Grundy said, 'Li'l darlin' musta been wettin' herself when she took 'em. Hell, reckon this 'un could make the cover of *Newsweek.*'

I did a double take. This was Rocky's Convoy Green, yesterday. The shots had been taken from the back of Lizard's truck after the container's rear doors had been blasted open. The dust wasn't dust, it was flour. After the shock of being hit, Tali van Wyk must have had the courage and professional presence of mind to crawl to the back of the wagon and grab these shots.

Cuthbert said, 'Kirk says she wants to go with us this afternoon.'

What? Kirk says? I felt suddenly and maybe irrationally irritated. What the hell did Kirk Grundy have to do with Tali van Wyk, or anything else about British operations for that matter?

'Sorta taken her under my wing,' Grundy explained. 'Well, who wouldn't? Reckon I might get to sample the honey-pot if I play my cards right.'

I remembered the shy look in Tali van Wyk's eyes, her nervous gestures and the uncertainty in her stance. In fact I was surprised just how much I did remember about her. 'I don't think so,' I said. 'Think you'd need a collar and lead to get that one into your bed.'

Grundy's eyes narrowed as he looked at me and a long, thin smile spread across his face. 'Yeah! Now, Jim-bo, that's pretty perceptive of you. Maybe that's just what it would take.'

Over his shoulder I suddenly saw her enter the bar. She walked with an easy elegance, her head held high despite the weight of the large rucksack and bedroll on her back. Again her hair was in a ponytail and I noticed the enticing way it flicked as she turned her head from side to side, obviously seeking out Cuthbert and Grundy in the crowd.

Cuthbert said quickly, 'I told her she could have a lift back with us.'

'The hell . . .' I began as my anger flared, but I stamped it out quickly. I didn't want to have a row with him in front of the American. In fact, I didn't want a row with him at all. At the moment Nigel Cuthbert felt like the only friend I had in the world.

'Hi, Tali, this is my fellow liaison officer,' Cuthbert began. 'Not sure you were introduced yesterday at Una Drina, were you?'

She extended her hand towards me. 'No, but we'd already met. At the hotel in Split, wasn't it? Jeff?'

There was that hesitant smile again. I felt flattered that she'd even remembered we'd met, let alone my name. Stupid, really. I scrambled for something, anything, to say. 'Er, sure . . . See you managed to get all that flour off, then.'

Her smile was a mere flicker. 'Well, most places, anyway.'

It took a second to realize what she'd said. I'm never usually tongue-tied, but for some reason I found myself floundering again. 'Er . . . your photographs. They're very good.'

She looked surprised. 'Oh, thank you. I wonder if Mr Rogers will like them.'

Cuthbert interrupted, 'I'm sure he will, Tali. He's not quite the old brute he likes to make out, you know.'

I glanced at my watch. 'Time we made a move, Nigel.'

'Ah, me too, Jim-bo,' Grundy said. 'See my interview subject has just arrived.'

I turned my head to follow the direction of his gaze. Half a dozen tall fighters, unmistakably from the Ramoza Brigade, had entered the room behind the striding, arrogant figure of the young Muslim commander of Una Drina, Major Zlatko Herenda.

Grundy leaned towards Tali and pressed his lips to her cheek. 'You take care yo' self, pretty one. I'll buy you supper back here tonight.' His hand closed around the left buttock of her jeans and gave a little squeeze before he ambled away to meet Herenda. I noticed that she had not flinched.

Tersely I said, 'Let's go.'

Tali gave me a tic of a smile. 'Thank you, Jeff.'

As I led the way out of the hotel I got the inexplicable feeling that I was being set up in some way, but I couldn't put my finger on it. I just knew instinctively that something wasn't quite right.

Only after I'd helped Tali to stash her kit in the back of our Land Rover and climbed into the passenger seat beside Cuthbert did I remember something he'd told me on the way back from the town hall following my first meeting with the town's Muslim and Croat militia leaders.

Major Zlatko Herenda didn't give media interviews.

Four

I waited until we were a good half-way back on the mountain road to Una Drina before I mentioned that matter to Nigel.

'Thought you said Zlatko Herenda didn't give press interviews?'

'Oh, did I?' he said, and glanced sideways at me with an innocent smile. Not a good idea when there's a precipitous drop into a river ravine just feet away. 'Well, I mean, I'd never *heard* of him giving one.' Then he added in a very bad imitation of the American's voice, 'But then dear old Kirk is one persuasive ol' sonofabitch!'

Although Tali was in the back seat, I thought it safe enough to use open code. She didn't seem to be paying much attention to our conversation. 'The colonel reckons he's from Langley, Nigel, is that right?'

Cuthbert made light of it. 'A lot of people think that, Jimbo.'

I said, 'Don't fuck with me, Nigel. Is he or isn't he? *You* had an appointment with him.'

Again he gave a long sideways glance at me, and I suddenly saw a different aspect of him. 'You're a company LO, Jimbo. Just keep to your side of things. I'm the CBF's man *and* I report to the Foreign Office – and that's *my* business. Do we understand each other?'

Keep your nose out, in other words. That put me in my place.

I didn't answer him. I just wondered who might be stepping into whose patch. Me into his – or he into mine? I changed the subject. 'Tell me about this Serb commander we're hoping to see this afternoon. Zoric.'

Thank God Cuthbert's attention was back on his driving. 'Ah, yes, Goran Zoric. I think Pale's given him the rank of Colonel, but he's young. In fact the make-believe story you gave Markovic yesterday wasn't that far off the truth. He's been drafted in from the Yugoslav Army by Belgrade. Bit of a mystery man. No records that we have, not even a picture. Rumoured to be ex-special forces or some secret-police unit, but not confirmed. He's known to get things done.'

I grunted to myself. Well, Goran Zoric was certainly getting things done all right. If Kirk Grundy *was* CIA, then he seemed all too aware of the threat this Serb offensive on Una Drina posed strategically. Trouble was, I was the new boy and I was still trying to get my head round confusing battle-lines and geography. I was just beginning to see that if Una Drina fell, the Serbs could sweep right across the south against crumbling Croat resistance and strangle Bosnia into final submission. The main humanitarian convoy routes up from the south would be completely severed.

At last we reached the town. I could hear the distant grumblings of mortar and light artillery exchanges and see some tell-tale palls of smoke in the hills farther south, but Una Drina itself seemed untroubled at the moment.

An air of expectation hung over company HQ. A troop of Warriors was revving up in the compound, filling it with noise and black diesel fumes. Crews were checking over their vehicles, while the infantry passengers were scattered around cleaning and reassembling their weapons and topping up with ammo. There was a lot of nervous humour and suppressed excitement as they prepared for our expedition.

I spotted the two ITN vehicles, a Cherokee and a G-wagen covered in streamers made from bedsheets emblazoned with 'TV' in large magic-marker letters. I wondered whether it would make any difference to the warring factions – as if cars at home with 'Baby On Board' stickers actually deterred other motorists from crashing into them!

Gerald Kemp stopped talking to his cameraman and sound-man and waved as we passed.

Cuthbert halted our Land Rover at the main building and I went straight into the Ops Room to find Gordy Cromwell.

It was nice to see a big grin on his face for a change. 'Just the man, Jimbo! Heard from Serb HQ at Pale just five minutes ago. They agreed for us to go through their lines to Stavac.'

'That easy?' I asked.

Gordy's grin widened. 'Nothing's ever that fucking simple in Bosnia, Jimbo. You'll learn that. I took a leaf out of your book and said it would be to Goran Zoric's distinct advantage to talk with you and Nigel. I gave the impression you were someone special at UNPROFOR.'

He was learning. I said, 'I am.' And returned the boyish grin.

'Anyway,' he continued, 'they huffed and puffed and really didn't like it, but in the end they agreed.'

'Don't take it for granted, Jeffrey . . .' A new voice joined the conversation. I turned to find Major Tring standing behind me. 'Pale's communications with its front line are piss poor. Just because Pale agrees doesn't mean some sniper in the trenches hasn't heard about it . . .' His eyes narrowed, giving me his total attention. 'That's why I certainly *wouldn't* have recommended taking civilian media with you.'

I made light of it. 'Sorry, Reg, but it all got squared with the CO and PINFO this morning . . . Rather out of my hands.'

I could see the bafflement in his expression. Now he didn't really know whose decision it had been.

Gordy said, 'This couldn't have come at a more crucial time, Jimbo. Rocky's Convoy Green is on its way back from Sarajevo to Split. Be here any minute. And we've got a real mother coming back up the other way from the coast. Ninety fucking trucks and trailers, mostly heating fuels ready for winter.'

If that didn't add to the pressure I was under . . . Over a

hundred and ten trucks waiting for me to stop a war so they could get through.

'Good luck, Jimbo,' Gordy added. Tring nodded in agreement but couldn't actually bring himself to utter the words.

I returned outside to find Tali scampering around between the Warriors, snapping away with her camera at men and machines. Not a few eyes were watching the leggy blonde's antics with more than passing interest.

'Come with me, young lady,' I said as I passed her and made my way to the ITN vehicles.

'Hi, Jeff,' Gerald Kemp greeted. 'Are we still on?'

'Apparently. But don't be surprised if we suddenly find ourselves in the middle of a fire-fight.'

He nodded. 'I know the score. Got the scars to prove it.'

I said, 'When we roll, I want your two vehicles in between these two Warriors.' I pointed to the two that would be in the middle of the small column. 'If either of your vehicles breaks down, leave it and get into the one that's working. Don't stop to unload. Take what you're carrying and leave everything else.'

'And if the shit really hits the fan?' Kemp asked.

I knew what he meant. 'If war breaks out, abandon everything immediately and jump into the Warrior in front of you.'

There was genuine warmth in his grey eyes. 'I really appreciate this, Jeff.'

I said, 'Then perhaps you can do *me* a favour.' I turned to the girl standing behind me. 'This is Tali van Wyk, a freelance photographer. She's a bit new to this game. Would you mind taking her with you, keep an eye on her?'

'My pleasure.'

I realized then he was already keeping an eye on her. I added, 'QM's issued spare flak jackets and helmets. You'll find them over there. Please make sure everyone wears them at all times.'

'Will do,' Kemp promised. As I started to walk away, he

caught up with me. 'Jeff, tell me . . . These rumours that the Ramoza Brigade has moved into this area . . . any truth in it?'

I felt a little irritated. 'You should know better than to ask me that, Gerald.'

'There was a group of them in the hotel bar when we met last night,' he added.

'Well,' I said with a smile, 'that's your answer, then.'

He'd fallen into step alongside me. 'You know they're funded by the Saudis, don't you? All Muslim fundamentalists.'

'Rumours of war,' I answered vaguely.

Kemp chuckled. 'And another of those rumours is the Brigade's being armed by the United States. There have been persistent reports of secret night flights into Tuzla by the CIA. Washington denies it, of course.'

'Of course, Gerald,' I said. 'They would, wouldn't they? Whether it's true or not.'

He turned away then as we were approaching our LO vehicle where Nigel Cuthbert was standing with my interpreter Senic and his own, a Muslim woman whom I hadn't yet met.

'Is Kemp pumping you?' Cuthbert asked. 'Crafty old newshound. Trying to get something out of the new boy before he knows what's what.'

'Just asking about the CIA connection with the Ramoza Brigade,' I replied.

Cuthbert gave an unconvincing look of innocence. '*Is* there one?'

I turned to look back into the compound to see if everyone was ready. 'I wouldn't know, Nigel,' I replied, and topped it with A Company's favourite phrase: 'Not my remit.'

It was then I heard the distant blast of air-horns. UK Green was rolling into town and, sure enough, a few minutes later Rocky Rogers' lead Discovery came into view with the first of the following white UNHCR trucks at his heels.

He pulled up beside me, the big mop of hair and beard appearing at his window. 'How ya doin', Jimbo? Hear you're off to stop a war single-handed.' He laughed throatily. 'Takes a Para to do that!'

'Fuck off, Rocky,' I said.

'Anyway,' he came back, 'you've got a couple of hours to do it while I refuel some of the trucks. That's if UNPROFOR's kind Major Tring will play ball. Doesn't like doing it, y'know. But I refuse to sleep with him – even for a coupla thousand litres of diesel!'

With Rocky's laughter still echoing in my head, I climbed into the driver's seat of the Land Rover beside Cuthbert. I'd persuaded him it would be better to let me drive on this trip.

He gestured to the female interpreter in the back. 'Jimbo, this is Ivana. She's actually a Muslim, but lives in DV. University lecturer in English.'

'Pleased to meet you,' I said as I leaned over the seat and shook hands with the very striking but sad-faced woman.

I revved up and let out the clutch, hitting the horn to let everyone know we were on the move. I checked my door mirror to see the column snaking out through the perimeter gates, a Lancers' Scimitar first, then the two ITN vehicles sandwiched in the middle of 2 Platoon's four Warriors, then an Engineers' recovery variant, and a final Scimitar following up as rearguard.

With few civilians daring to venture outside while fighting could be heard nearby, the streets were virtually empty. But I noticed several faces pressed up against windows, watching our small but impressive show of force as we drove past their homes and headed south on the road to the coast.

On the outskirts there was a Croat roadblock. They had dug machine-gun emplacements on either side of the tarmac and reinforced them with sandbags, corrugated iron and what looked like old railway sleepers. Oil drums filled with concrete were laid out to form a chicane.

As I slowed to a halt, a Croat militiaman wearing a ragged brown beanie hat and smoking a cigarette wandered across to our Land Rover, waving his Kalashnikov at us. 'Hey, you can't go through! Fighting! Not safe, not safe!'

Cuthbert leaned towards me. 'Fucking right it's not safe, Jimbo. Look.'

I followed the line of his pointing finger. Beyond the Croat roadblock they had carefully laid out a pattern of mines. Fairly small anti-vehicle types, but they'd destroy a Land Rover and be powerful enough to blow the track links on a Scimitar or Warrior.

At that point, the voice of Hal Watkins, commander of the lead Warrior behind me, came into my radio head-set. 'Hey, boss, we got company! Twelve o'clock! Looks like a pickup truck!'

From his high vantage point in the Warrior's turret, Watkins had spotted the dust cloud that came into view beyond the mines. I opened the door and climbed out to stand beside the militiaman as he, too, stared towards the small truck as it raced towards us. It was a beaten-up old Toyota variant, slung around with camouflage netting and the open cargo hold filled with Croat militia.

It came to a halt the other side of the mines and I saw some-one climbing down onto the road. Colonel Pero Markovic then picked his way carefully through the deadly circular objects until he was standing right in front of me. 'Captain Hawkins, we meet again.' This time the smile was missing from his lips as well as his eyes.

'Colonel,' I acknowledged. 'We're on our way to Stavac. You were informed this morning.'

He crooked his head slightly to one side. '*Informed*, was I?'

I wasn't taking any bullshit. 'Your HQ was informed person-ally by Captain Gordon Cromwell that we would be passing through Serb lines to get to Stavac.'

Markovic's glare intensified as his face came a fraction closer to mine, into my personal space. 'Well, I have news for Captain Cromwell. To *get to* the Serb lines, you have to pass through our lines . . . because we are in the middle of a FUCKING BATTLE!'

I smiled gently into his raging face and placed my right hand on his left shoulder. 'I understand, Colonel. But look at it this way . . .' I steered him gently away from the Land Rover, out of earshot of anyone. '. . . I'm going there to arrange a cease-fire—'

'Huh!' he interrupted. 'You certainly won't arrange a Serb *withdrawal*!'

'I know that, Colonel. But a cease-fire means firstly that the aid convoys keep rolling and – more importantly for you – you have more time to organize your counter-offensive.' I shrugged. 'But then I shouldn't really have said that.'

He stepped back, so my hand fell from his shoulder. His eyes were still smouldering. 'One day, Captain Hawkins, your cleverness will get you killed. What is that English expression? You are so sharp you will cut yourself . . . Maybe your own throat.'

'Just doing my job,' I replied flatly. 'Now would you mind telling your men to remove the mines so that we can pass?'

He shook his head. 'No, Captain, not without permission from Una Drina's defence minister.'

Bloody hell, I thought, not Mayor Jozic. This was a wind-up. Markovic didn't want to lose face and didn't want to give ground.

I took a deep breath. 'I don't need *anybody's* fucking permission, Colonel. I'm UNPROFOR and the *United Nations* gives me permission to go anywhere I bloody well like in Bosnia-Herzegovina.' He blinked, slightly taken aback. 'So are you going to get those mines moved, or do we do it for you?'

He straightened his shoulders, stared at me hard for a few moments, then turned and yelled at a group of militia hunkered down in one of the emplacements to shift the mines and the oil drums.

Then he walked back up to me, his mood seemingly changed.

'I still look forward to that game of chess, Captain. Let's make it soon.' His smile tried but couldn't quite re-establish itself.

Then he turned and walked back to the pickup; as soon as he boarded, it swung round and headed back down the road to the battle. In the hills on both sides of the valley I could see the large muzzle-flashes and thickening haze of smoke, and hear the deep thud of artillery. With the mines finally cleared, our small column edged forward as the road began its slow and winding climb up the valley to the upper pass. We overtook crocodiles of trudging, ragged Croat militia walking towards the front lines on our right. There were only a few rusted old trucks and pickups to help the fighters on their way.

Cuthbert had a map spread on his knee. 'There's a turn-off on the right, Jimbo. Looks like it's unpaved. If Gordy's intelligence is right, we should be skirting the edge of the battlefield. An SAS team took a look-see last night.'

I nodded my understanding. Last night, last year, last minute. In battle things could change fast, so it really didn't mean a thing. I got through to the Ops Room and told them to relay our position to Serb HQ in Pale and to request they forward confirmation of our approach to Goran Zoric's command post in Stavac.

The track on the right came into view. It ran off steeply up and over a shoulder of hillside; only the first few hundred metres of compacted mud and stone road could be seen before it was swallowed up in the pine forest. I changed down and swung the wheel, feeling the immediate change in the ride, the Land Rover's suspension doing its best to dampen the bouncing effect of the uneven ground. The boys of the Royal Wessex and their Lancers escort were on edge, ready for anything. In my mirror I saw the turrets of the following vehicles jutting the barrels of their cannon and heavy machine-guns alternately to the left and right, covering every angle of fire. And I knew the rearguard Scimitar would have its turret reversed, covering back down the track in case trouble came from behind.

Minutes later the Ops Room came back, saying that a twenty-minute hold-fire had been ordered via Serb HQ in Pale. But a hold-fire isn't a cease-fire. The Serbs would stop shooting unless they were shot at by the Croats. I just hoped Colonel Markovic didn't start his game of chess with me now . . .

The swathe of pines that wrapped the hillside closed in on us, running close to the track on both sides and towering above us. It was claustrophobic, the scent of the pine fronds pungent in the air. In the forest little daylight permeated and it was eerily dark; no birds sang. Just occasionally I glimpsed wraith-like forms moving. Shadows in the shadow, camouflaged militia moving forward or moving back, Croat or Serb, it was impossible to tell. Where the battle-lines were, God only knew.

I continued on, my heart thudding more and more strongly as we drew deeper into the battlefield, not knowing exactly where we were, where the opposing forces were, where instant death might be lurking . . .

And then suddenly we were out of the treeline, in rocky open country as the track rounded the highest point of the hillside shoulder. Now it was easier to spot the slit trenches and gun emplacements, the odd sight of a bobbing head or a scurrying soldier. These were the Serb lines and from here they had a commanding view down into the river valley and the Croat positions.

As I rounded a tight right-hand bend, I was confronted by a group of militiamen spread out across the road. They looked like they were expecting us. They were dirty, unshaven and mud-spattered, and they looked mean. But at least they held their weapons low, even if they regarded us with fierce suspicion.

I hit the brakes and their leader came forward, a tall man in a ragged grey trenchcoat, wild hair and beard and eyes sunken in their sockets after days without sleep. A roll-up cigarette dangled from the corner of his mouth.

I stepped smartly out of the Land Rover before saluting him crisply and offering my hand. 'UNPROFOR,' I said with a tight smile. 'We are going to Stavac,' I added in Serbo–Croat. 'To meet with your commander, Colonel Zoric.'

He spat the remains of cigarette from his mouth and shook my hand. 'We're expecting you. I'll escort you.'

The Serb had no transport. I glanced at Cuthbert. 'Get in the back with the interpreters,' I said.

Cuthbert looked a bit put out, but obliged, and the Serb slumped into the passenger seat. He indicated for me to drive on. I continued to follow the track, round the shoulder of the hillside, then on the slow descent into the next valley. Now we saw Serb militia reinforcements walking towards us along the verge, making their way towards the front line. This was clearly a big operation, and from what I knew of the situation I doubted that Colonel Markovic and his Croats would be able to hold out against it for long. I wanted to talk to Cuthbert about this, but not with our Serb escort sitting next to me.

After ten minutes or so we were back below the treeline, taking the zig-zag trip into the valley and the village of Stavac. As we entered the hamlet it was like slipping back into a medieval time warp. The fifty or so small peasant houses or cottages were of old traditional Slavic design, built using local timber, brick or stone, and with roofs of thatch or corrugated iron. Most of the gardens beyond the rough wood fences had clearly been turned to growing vegetables for each family. There was no evidence of any telephone or electricity connection, no pylons, no overhead cables. In the village centre itself – a square of rough lawn under a cluster of trees – I could see a communal well and a number of wooden benches. No doubt this would be where the villagers gathered to gossip in the shade during the fierce heat of summer.

But where were those people? Apart from small groups of Serb fighters, it was like a ghost town.

On a dirt road beyond the square, our escort indicated for me to pull over beside the most modern building I'd seen so far. It was an artless rectangle of rendered breeze-blocks with some sort of prefabricated roof. All the windows had been blown out. Some pickups and battered Japanese off-roaders were parked outside and two sentries were posted by the door, over which a bullet-holed sign read 'Clinic'. I noticed a number of rickety radio aerials on the roof.

Our escort climbed out and beckoned Cuthbert and me to follow, while the column of Warriors and Scimitars together with the TV wagons parked up on the roadside. I waved to Gerald Kemp to join us, and he hurried across the street to catch us up as we entered Zoric's command post.

There was a lot of activity inside the wrecked clinic, Serb militia officers busy toing and froing, and the sound of radio traffic coming from one of the side rooms. We were led into what I imagined had once been the manager's office.

I don't know what I was expecting Colonel Goran Zoric to look like. Maybe younger, maybe older, but certainly to possess typically dark Slav features.

True, he had dark eyebrows and mid-brown eyes, but the man who looked up from behind the desk also had striking ginger hair, cut in a short military crop. He was thick-set, probably in his early forties and clean shaven with a slightly florid complexion. His uniform was immaculate, marking him out as a professional who had served time in the national Yugoslav Army; perhaps he was indeed here on semi-official secondment to the Bosnian Serb militia.

He pushed back his chair briskly and rose to his feet without a hint of a smile. I leaned forward over the desk and offered my hand. His grip was strong and determined, as though trying to tell me he was not one to mess with.

'Captain Hawkins, UNPROFOR. I've come to talk about a cease-fire,' I said in Serbo-Croat.

Zoric walked around the edge of his desk. 'I know, I have been informed by Pale,' he replied in perfect English, although heavily accented, 'otherwise your military column would have been blown to pieces by my Red Dragons.'

Cuthbert leaned towards me and whispered, 'The colonel's personal commando unit, I believe.'

Well, I wasn't sure Zoric's Red Dragons would have found taking on the Royal Wessex's Warriors and the Lancers that much of a cake-walk, but I let it pass.

Instead I said, 'We have a number of major UN relief convoys trying to enter Una Drina with urgently needed humanitarian supplies for Donji Vrbas, Zenica and Sarajevo over the next few days.'

Zoric's facial expression didn't change from one of total indifference as he gestured to an aide, who scurried off to the adjoining room. 'Frankly, Captain,' he said, 'my concerns are military, not civilian. And certainly not enemy civilians.' The aide returned with a tray bearing a bottle of the inevitable slivovitz and several glasses.

'There are also thousands of Serbs amongst the population at risk,' I came back quickly.

But he remained unmoved. 'Sometimes, however regrettable, civilians have to suffer if they want their freedom. There is always a price to be paid for freedom. After all, my soldiers are laying down *their* lives for them.'

I wasn't at all sure that a Bosnian Serb mother who'd just lost her husband and son in the fighting would agree it was worth it. The thought was interrupted by the pouring of the slivovitz, large tots of which were handed round.

'Skol!' Zoric said, tilting back his head and emptying his glass unceremoniously down his throat. While Cuthbert, Kemp and I followed suit, and gasped to recover our breath, the Serb colonel said, 'Once we have taken Una Drina, your convoys can run again.'

I tried to ignore the fire in my mouth. 'The convoys need to run *now*, Colonel Zoric, not when you – or your enemies – think they should . . . And I should point out that Colonel Markovic has already agreed to this in principle, if you will.'

Yes, I know, but you've got to start somewhere . . .

I added quickly: 'The point is this: Markovic has built very strong defences and has brought in considerable reserves . . .'

Goran Zoric's expression finally changed to one of interest. Cuthbert coughed pointedly.

'So Una Drina will be a tougher nut to crack than you imagine . . . That's only my casual observation, you understand, as a former special forces soldier like yourself.'

His eyes widened. 'Special forces?'

'I'm a Para now, was once with 22 SAS.' I went on quickly, 'It's possible a cease-fire could be in your interest. More time, more preparation, more reinforcements . . . if I were in your position, I'd consider that aspect carefully . . . Besides, your HQ at Pale is *very* keen to see a cease-fire.'

Out of the corner of my eye I saw Nigel Cuthbert roll his eyes heavenward in disbelief as Zoric took the bait. 'Pale have said nothing to me.'

I put my hand on his shoulder in a gesture of friendship; he didn't pull away. 'No, because it's all come through our HQ talking to your HQ – aren't we always the last to know, eh?' I inserted a knowing chuckle. 'But the Croats are making a big thing in the international media about how *you* – the Serbs – are holding up the biggest humanitarian aid convoy this year. The fears of children starving before Christmas . . . Soon the Serbs will not have an ally left in the world, just when they need them.'

Zoric was now clearly thinking hard. 'I will have to speak to Pale.'

I said, 'Before you do, I have a proposition to put to you.' I turned to Gerald Kemp. 'This is a top reporter with ITN – British TV's most popular news programme and syndicated world-wide . . . He very much wants to interview you and let you put *your* side of the story . . . How you agreed the cease-fire first . . .'

Suddenly the face hardened into stone. 'I don't give interviews. Press, TV, radio – anybody . . . Someone should have told you that, Captain Hawkins.'

Gerald Kemp took a step forward and introduced himself. 'I understand your position, Colonel.' He then said, 'but there are ways round that. We can back-light you, distort your voice—'

Zoric was adamant. 'No. You still hold the original video or film.'

But Kemp was just as determined. 'Then we *just* report your words. You write them down and I just report them verbatim – while we show footage of your front-line soldiers effecting a cease-fire and put it together with shots of the convoy rolling.' The old pro Kemp had certainly seen where I was coming from. '*Then* see if the world still believes what the Croats are saying. You'll have been *seen* to have declared the cease-fire first.'

Finally Goran Zoric capitulated. 'Very well. We'll go down to the rear lines, see our artillery and heavy mortars. That will be good pictures for you. I will speak to you off-camera. You will make a note and read them back. No hidden microphones or camera. You will be searched.'

Kemp was all smiles. 'Of course, no problem. I'm most grateful, Colonel.'

'First I will contact Pale. I will see you outside shortly.' With that we were dismissed.

As we wandered out into the grey and sunless afternoon, Cuthbert said, 'Shit, Jimbo, you like sailing close to the wind! What's Pale HQ going to say when Zoric talks to them? You know they don't want a cease-fire.'

I said, 'They will after Zoric talks to them. If he repeats our pitch, they've got to, really. And no one in Pale's going to be bothered who's said what – the game's moved on. It's what's on offer *now* that counts – a big international PR coup for them.'

Kemp was agreeing when I suddenly noticed Tali van Wyk. She was wandering down the street with her camera, casually taking shots of passing Serb militiamen.

'TALI!' I bawled. 'COME HERE!'

She turned, startled, and then grinned as she realized it was me. She loped back towards us, quickly covering the ground with her athletic strides. 'Hi, Jeff,' she said with a disarming smile, 'is something the matter?'

I grabbed her arm roughly and eased her away from Cuthbert and Kemp. 'What the fuck do you think you're playing at?' I demanded.

Her eyes widened with incomprehension and her face crumpled at the reprimand. 'I'm sorry, I don't understand.'

'You're in the middle of a Serb HQ area!' I said hoarsely. 'Highly sensitive! You don't amble around taking happy-snaps, understand? If they suddenly turned against us now, we could be in deep shit. If you were caught and taken off . . . there's not much we could do about it. And you don't even want to know what some of these bastards can do to women . . .'

She swallowed hard. 'I–I'm sorry, Jeff. I didn't think.'

God, she was lovely. That thought just flashed through my brain like a subliminal advert on TV. I shoved it away. 'Well, start thinking. If you want to photograph anything, bloody well ask first. OK? Ask permission. Ask me or Nigel, or ask the Serbs themselves. But bloody well ask.'

She gave a what-a-silly-girl-I-am shrug and a twitch of a smile that asked for forgiveness. 'I won't do it again. Promise.'

I let go of her arm; I think I must have been hurting her. Without another word, she turned and walked back towards the TV wagons.

As I rejoined Cuthbert and Gerald Kemp outside the clinic building, lighting up one of my vanilla cigars, the reporter observed, 'Quite a girl, that one. Created a lot of interest in the DV hotel last night, so I heard. Her presence got the testosterone levels rising somewhat.'

'Media, off-duty soldiers and charity workers away from home,' Cuthbert scorned. 'That lot would get excited over a tin of baked beans if you put it in a skirt.' Then he thought for a moment, watching as she chatted and laughed with the TV cameraman. 'Got that air of innocence, mind . . . Reckon she might even be a virgin.'

'Nigel, this *is* the 1990s!' Kemp laughed. 'Girls aren't even *born* virgins any more.'

Gerald Kemp kept glancing at his watch and then at the clinic, clearly worried about the daylight left for his film-team. Suddenly he said to me, 'Of course, Jeff, you know why Zoric never gives press or TV interviews? He wants to keep anonymous in case they come after him for war crimes. Him and his Red Dragon thugs. Commandos, my arse. Bunch of ethnic-cleansing butchers. Rumours abound all over Bosnia.'

I glanced sideways at Cuthbert and scowled. I could tell he knew why. Spooks and their little piles of dirt. He shrugged. 'Just rumours, Jimbo, nothing proved.'

We did not have much longer to wait before Colonel Zoric emerged from his command post, wearing one of those Yugoslav pill-box officer's caps with a peak. He stood on the top step for a moment, looking at the line of UN Warriors, before putting on some dark glasses and walking towards us.

It was then that I glimpsed Tali, leaning nonchalantly beside one of the TV wagons, lowering a camera with a telephoto lens from her eye. I scowled at her and shook my head; she got the message and instantly retreated inside the vehicle.

'I've cleared it with Pale, Captain Hawkins,' Zoric said as he approached. 'If you follow me, I'll show you to the location that the ITN people can use.'

As he finished the sentence a Russian-built jeep pulled alongside and he climbed in. Our small column coughed and spluttered itself noisily into life and, to the clank and grind of caterpillar tracks, began following my Land Rover as we set off back the way we had come.

Zoric had selected a couple of artillery emplacements and we watched as the two howitzers belched out a couple of shells for the benefit of ITN's before-and-after-the-cease-fire shots. Then the camera crew wandered around with Gerald Kemp, interviewing a few of the fighters. Meanwhile Tali did her own thing and none of the men on the front line seemed to have any objections at all. In fact she was discovered by a young officer who spoke English and was soon sitting down drinking slivovitz with a group of them, laughing and joking.

I turned away.

It always amazes me how much footage TV people take and how little of it ever reaches people's television screens. I wondered how much of the hour they spent shooting would appear on the news item. Probably only three or four minutes.

While I waited, I radioed through to company HQ and told Gordy Cromwell the news. He in turn promised he'd immediately try to contact Markovic and Croat HQ in DV and do his best to persuade them to agree their side of the bargain. We decided to aim for a minimum four-day lull in hostilities, then see if we could negotiate an extension from there.

Finally, Gerald Kemp finished with his piece to camera, in which he quoted Goran Zoric as saying how he had proposed a cease-fire in order to prevent the unnecessary suffering of his people. The hypocrisy was sick-making, but it allowed me to get my job done.

When filming was completed, Colonel Zoric approached me and shook my hand without smiling. 'You have got what you want, Captain Hawkins. Make the most of the time you have. It will not last indefinitely.'

I nodded without comment. But as he turned to go, I said, 'Colonel, just one thing. Where are all the villagers of Stavac?'

His expression didn't change one iota. 'In their houses, Captain, waiting for us to leave. It is a Croat village. Waiting, or they have already left, fearing for their safety. A groundless fear, I might add.'

'No one from here has arrived at Una Drina,' I told him.

A ghost of a smile passed over his lips. 'Then they must have gone elsewhere, Captain . . . Good day.' And he was gone.

Finally the ITN crew packed up and we were able to get

under way, back to Una Drina. We arrived at last light to the news that the Croats, too, had agreed to co-operate. I felt elated, but utterly drained. I wandered off to my windowless cell, fell onto the camp-bed and crashed out immediately.

Over the next few days I was able to get into a routine and find my way round my new surroundings. With the cease-fire holding, the pressure was off, people were out and about on the streets of Una Drina, and I was in high spirits. The sun was even making a regular appearance, doing its best to brighten up the drab little town.

Gerald Kemp had returned to the home comforts of DV with his team, taking Tali van Wyk with him. Rocky's UK Green had headed off for the coast and the awesome hundred-plus UN truck convoy had passed through town very slowly from the opposite direction. It made me appreciate what an important job the drivers did – and what a responsibility I and the other LOs had to ensure that it remained possible.

Other convoys came in thick and fast. I met the guys from UK Red, Rocky's opposite number, and the logistics lads running UNPROFOR's own supply convoys for all the UN troops deployed to the area. Oxfam, Christian Aid, Save the Children . . . all the charities were represented or contributing there in one form or another. And even a little psychedelic minibus carrying a bunch of New Age street-entertainers, jugglers and puppeteers called Wildchild on their way to entertain the kids in Zenica and Sarajevo.

With a little time on my hands, I took the opportunity to put a thick wad of banknotes in a sealed envelope together with a hastily scribbled note. I entrusted it to Rocky to deliver to Jelena back in Split. I hoped it would please her; it certainly made me feel a lot better and helped to ease my conscience.

On the third day, rather to my surprise, a detachment of engineers appeared in the compound and asked for me. They'd been sent on Colonel Rathbone's personal orders to repair the village school. Their boss was an enthusiastic subaltern called Lamb (and known as 'Larry' – what else!) and his men seemed equally motivated to get started and make a difference.

I went round to the school with them to take a look at the extent of the problem. All its windows had been blown out and glass littered the floors, most of the doors had been ripped out to be used as firewood, there were large holes in the roof and no desks or chairs. Apart from that it was in perfect condition. None of this destruction seemed to faze Larry and his number two, a jovial Sikh sergeant from Wolverhampton whom I gathered was one of the British Army's great wheeler-dealers and fixers.

Leaving them to it, I took my Land Rover down to the Hotel Splendid to find Anita Furtula, who was doing the lunchtime shift.

There were only three people in the bar and I was rather surprised to find that one of them was the American, Kirk Grundy. Still wearing his Rupert trousers, this time with a beige sports coat, he was sitting at the bar with two young men I didn't recognize.

Grundy spotted me straight away. 'Hi, Jim-bo, how ya doin'? C'mon over and have a drink.'

One of the worst parts of an LO's job is having to drink with so many people you either just don't like or else downright detest. For me, Kirk Grundy was somewhere in the middle.

As I approached I noticed the photographs placed in a clear plastic folder on the bar in front of him. 'Hallo, Kirk,' I replied without enthusiasm. 'What brings you to Una Drina?'

'Just meetin' my two pals here.' His two companions, who sat hunched with their elbows on the bar, turned round to look at me without smiling.

Both were in olive drab combat jackets, possibly American-issue, and khaki cargo pants, which marked them out as civilians playing at soldiers.

'This is Pieter,' Grundy introduced the taller of the two men, who rose from his stool to tower above me. He had cropped black hair and a neat little moustache and goatee. 'Pieter, this is Jim-bo. British Army.'

'Pleased to meet you, sir,' he said with unexpected politeness.

'South African?' I guessed, but was certain of it. He must have stood six feet six or seven in his socks, and had huge shoulders – a giant like so many Afrikaners brought up for generations on a high-protein diet of beer and barbecued meat.

Pieter just nodded, a man of few words.

'And Lars,' Grundy said.

Lars wasn't as polite as his friend. He made no attempt to stand or shake hands. He just stayed hunched over his beer and gave me a blink of acknowledgement with his brown gimlet eyes and tossed away the fringe of long, dark-blond hair that fell over his forehead.

Grundy chuckled. 'Of course, Jim-bo, Lars has to be Danish with a name like that . . .'

At that moment Anita Furtula appeared behind the bar. She seemed pleased to see me. 'Hallo, Jeff. Sorry – I didn't know anyone was waiting to be served.'

I shook my head. 'That's fine, Anita. Just arrived.'

'What'll it be, Jim-bo?' Grundy asked.

'A beer, thanks.' As Anita reached for a bottle and glass I said, 'Thought you'd like to know, we've got some engineers looking at your school just now.'

She stood upright, placed the bottle and glass on the bar and just stared at me without smiling and without saying anything. I think it might have been shock.

'What?' I asked uneasily.

Her eyes seemed very large, very accusing through the lenses of her spectacles. 'You are playing with me, Jeff. This is your idea for a joke? I don't think this is so funny.'

I had to smile at her seriousness. 'No, Anita, no joke. For real. They are there now. It might be helpful if you could get down there and talk to them.'

Suddenly sunlight burst out on her face as she smiled in disbelief. She was transformed, looking quite radiant. 'This is true? Really true? Oh, Jeff, that is wonderful. I will go straight away now. The owner can serve here, he is just lazy.'

I said, 'But I don't know about desks. There're all missing, looted for firewood, I suppose.'

The mercurial smile melted away. 'Oh, yes, Jeff, looted. But not for firewood. They were looted by Mayor Jozic.'

'I don't understand.'

She crooked an eyebrow. 'You will, I'm sure you will . . . Anyway, now I must go. I will speak to you again soon.' She picked up her coat from behind the bar and came round, passing me on the way to the door. She paused for a moment, hesitated, then gave me a short, sharp kiss on the mouth. 'Thank you.' And then she was gone.

'Gee, Jim–bo,' Grundy observed as she vanished through the doorway. 'Looks like you've tamed the dragon lady.'

I poured the beer into my glass. 'Not sure anyone can tame that one, Kirk. I'm just in her good books. I'm sure it won't last.' I turned my attention to Pieter and Lars. 'You guys with one of the aid agencies?'

Lars smirked. 'Yeah, sure.'

'On contract,' Pieter added.

'You may as well tell Jim–bo,' Grundy said to him. 'He's the LO for UNPROFOR here and he'll know soon enough.' He lowered his voice to a deep, chuckling whisper. 'These LO guys have their spies *everywhere*!'

I'd half–guessed already. 'On contract?' I queried. 'Who with?'

They were still reluctant, so Grundy said, 'With the Muslims. Major Herenda and his lot. Pieter is a former South African recce commando. And Lars is—'

'Lars is Lars,' said Lars quickly. 'That's all anyone needs to know.' He looked up at me with those hateful little brown eyes. 'You are this shit town's fucking policeman?'

The hostile response threw me for a moment. I took a deep

breath to calm my anger and resist the urge to pick the little scrote up by his miserable neck and throw him through the hotel window. Instead I took a sip of beer before just quietly saying, 'No.'

'Then mind your own fucking business,' Lars added, and turned to his fellow mercenary. 'Come, Pieter, we're finished here. Let's get out this shit place.'

He stood up and scooped the folder of photographs from the bar. As he stuffed it in the pocket of his combat jacket, I glimpsed enough to confirm my suspicions.

''Bye, boys!' Grundy called after them, but neither responded.

I said, 'They don't do much to restore your faith in human nature.'

Grundy shrugged. 'Mercenaries – whadya expect?'

'You came down here to meet them?' I asked.

He looked taken aback, thrown for a moment. 'Hell no, Jim-bo. Just needed to get out of DV. Change of air, see what was happening down here. Just got chatting to them, that's all.'

I think I smiled. 'Seemed to bare their souls to you, Kirk. Didn't give me the time of day.'

He looked a bit awkward at that, perhaps realizing that he hadn't been too clever. 'Just a journalist's knack, Jim-bo. You pick up a few tricks along the way.'

I said, 'And what paper is it you write for?'

His smile didn't reach his eyes. 'Any that'll pay. But, yeah, I'm a stringer for the *NYT*.'

'Of course you are,' I replied, draining my beer. 'Thanks for the drink, Kirk. See you around.'

But as I stepped out into the chill sunlight of the street, I felt an inexplicable sensation of anxiety deep in my gut. A feeling that something was going on here that I didn't even begin to understand.

Inexplicable? No, that wasn't quite true. Kirk Grundy was in the backwater of Una Drina to meet two mercenaries away from the prying eyes and wagging tongues of DV.

And he'd just given them a photograph of Colonel Goran Zoric – the enigmatic commander of the Serb assault on the town. That photograph was of the man wearing his topi-style cap and about to put on his dark glasses.

That photograph had been taken a few days earlier when I'd met him in Stavac. It had been taken by Tali van Wyk.

Five

I returned to company HQ anxious to speak to Nigel Cuthbert. He'd hardly been around since our trip to Stavac to arrange the cease-fire, but exactly what he was up to I had no idea.

He'd been due back in Una Drina today, but I was disappointed to find that he still had not returned. I wanted to ask him more about Kirk Grundy and exactly what the American was playing at. He and Cuthbert obviously knew each other quite well, and the CIA and Britain's own Secret Intelligence Service, MI6, had a history of close co-operation. I felt sure he would be able to shed some light on what was going on. Mind you, I was doubtful whether Cuthbert would be willing to share any of his murky secrets with a lowly company liaison officer. He'd certainly been keen to keep me off his patch so far.

Now, with things quiet in the area, I was feeling at a bit of a loose end. I still hadn't had a proper get-to-know-you meeting with the Muslim commander, the arrogant young Major Zlatko Herenda, but that would best first be done with Cuthbert, who already knew him.

So I made my decision and went into the Ops Room. It was unusually quiet and I found Gordy Cromwell actually reading one of the previous week's UK newspapers.

'Don't like this, Jimbo,' he said, looking up from the sports pages. 'This is the quietest it's been since I arrived here. Can't last. Lull before the storm.'

I grinned. 'Were you born a pessimist, or did you have to work at it? . . . Tell me, isn't UK Green due through today?'

He nodded. 'Running late. Called in for a security sitrep from Makljen not an hour ago. Why?'

'I thought I might hitch a ride, get a better idea of the other problems the convoys face in the area.'

'Good idea. Want me to inform Major Tring?'

'Yeah, thanks.' I winked. 'But *after* I've left.'

I returned to my room, grabbed my bergen and went out into the compound. My wait wasn't long before the Warrior at the head of the convoy appeared further down the main street. With the fighting still only on precarious hold, Tring was giving the UNHCR a military escort.

Rocky's Discovery pulled up alongside me, and the window wound down. 'You look like a tart waiting for a punter,' was his opening gambit.

'No, sweetheart,' I returned affably. 'Just lookin' for a lift.'

'Where you going?'

'All the way, big boy.'

He guffawed at that. 'My lucky day! . . . Seriously, Jimbo, you want to come to Sarajevo?'

I nodded. 'About time I took in the whole picture and saw the problems you guys face first hand.'

'Glutton for punishment, are you? OK, jump in.' He reached across and unlocked the passenger door and the rear door so I could stow my bergen and sit beside him. 'We're running late. Nearly lost a trailer on the Diamond Route. Mud track and the thing fishtailed off the road over a ravine.'

'Nasty,' I said.

Rocky nodded. 'Damn near pulled the truck and its driver back over the edge. Lucky a Dutch Army engineer unit was passing, otherwise we'd still be there . . . Can't wait for the ice and snow to arrive.'

'Still quiet on the cease-fire line?' I asked.

'Not a peep out of anyone. Even Markovic's Croats only held us up for twenty minutes . . . Think it'll hold?'

I shrugged. 'Only while it suits both sides. When one of

them thinks they've got an advantage, more reinforcements, more artillery, whatever . . .'

'. . . It'll start again,' Rocky finished the sentence knowingly. Then he called over the radio for UK Green to roll on again and we started off, leaving the Warriors behind as we were now due a safe run up to DV.

The journey was little more than fifty kilometres, along one river valley, then over a high pass and into another, but it was a winding and tortuous road which meant that Rocky couldn't bimble at his favourite speed of flat out. We passed through several hamlets on the way, mostly seeing only women, children and old men as we passed. It was a reminder that somewhere there were still a lot of younger men aiming to kill each other.

We'd covered about fifteen kilometres and were climbing steadily up to the high pass over pine-covered hills when we turned a bend to be confronted by a roadblock. Rocky hit the brakes. It was just as well we were travelling uphill otherwise I doubt he'd have stopped before the front wheels ran over the pattern of mines across the road.

'What the fuck . . .!' Rocky expleted, then bawled into the radio, 'HALT CONVOY!'

There were a couple of fairly modern flatbed pickups in hand-painted green parked across the road; a heavy machine gun was mounted on each. The dozen or so militiamen were wearing the usual ill-matched uniforms of the Muslim Bosnian Army.

'Zlatko Herenda's lot,' Rocky muttered. 'Now what are they up to?'

He threw open his door and eased himself out. I followed, but kept a pace or two behind because this was his show.

'Afternoon, gents,' he said pleasantly. 'What's going on here, then?'

I thought the Muslims looked nervous, edgy. Their leader shook his head. 'You cannot go through. It is not possible.'

Rocky smiled the sort of smile that Paras use just before they hit someone. 'I've got perishable goods here for Sarajevo. You must have some family there. Wives, girlfriends, kids, aunts, grandparents . . . It'll just take a few minutes for us to pass, we're not a large convoy. Just twenty wagons.'

The leader was adamant. 'No one passes.'

'There's no fighting round here,' Rocky said, 'so what's the problem?'

Nervous glances were exchanged between the leader and his number two. 'It is military manoeuvres. You cannot pass.'

'For how long?' Rocky pressed.

A moment's thought. 'Maybe one hour.'

Rocky looked relieved. 'Well, that's not so bad. But only one hour, yes? Time to get a brew on.'

While he radioed the news over to his drivers, who then got out to stretch their legs and light up hexi-stoves for tea, I wandered over to the edge of the road and looked down over the valley below. If had my bearings correct that valley eventually wound its way along to the village of Stavac, which was a little to the south of Una Drina.

I took out my civilian-issue pocket binos and scanned back and forth over the tree tops until I managed to pick up the thread of a road. Of course it was mostly obscured by pine trees, but I found a couple of gaps, probably where there'd been some local logging activity. I was a little surprised to see movement. Vehicles? Men? It was impossible to tell, just that *something* was moving down there.

After a while I got chatting with the Muslim militiamen, but they became very cagey when I tried to bring the conversation round to the military manoeuvres they'd mentioned. My powers of persuasion failed to persuade them to tell me anything.

In fact it was an hour and twenty minutes before UK Green was finally allowed to pass. Rocky did his best to make up time and we finally rolled into Donji Vrbas at four in the afternoon.

He was in a bad mood because he now wouldn't be able to make Sarajevo in daylight and, as that was the most dangerous leg of the journey, the convoy would have to wait in DV overnight. Leaving him to make his wagons secure before sulking in the hotel bar, I made my way to battalion HQ.

I was surprised to find three of my four fellow LOs in an anxious huddle in their allocated Ops Room, not out at their usual locations.

One of them, a chubby little Welsh officer called Williams, looked up and smiled as I entered. 'Good heavens, Jeff, you got here fast. Only just sent a signal to Una Drina to ask you to get up here quick.'

'I just came in on UK Green, Taff,' I explained.

'So not telepathy then, was it?'

I ignored the banter. 'What's up?'

'That's what we want to know,' Williams said. 'As you know, I put myself about round Novi Travnik and Bogojno way. My patch. Well, something's been going on. A lot of Muslim troop movements, but not sure why or where. There's a lot of expectation in the air, a buzz. But the Muslim boyos are keeping very quiet. Even those I almost consider pals, see.'

The other two agreed. They'd picked up the vibes, too, and rumours that the fundamentalist Ramoza Brigade was involved.

Simon Redman, an extremely well-spoken Eton, Cambridge, Sandhurst route officer with a ginger moustache, said, 'The Ramoza Brigade's attracting a lot of recruits amongst the ordinary Muslim fighters. It's all the talk. I mean, dammit, at least they get paid! But there's a big downside. No booze and no women, and you actually have to *fight*.'

I recalled Zlatko Herenda's visit to Mayor Jozic's office with his Ramoza henchmen and his threat to Markovic that if the Croats couldn't stop the Serb offensive then they, the Muslims, would. There was no doubt in my mind that the Muslim–Croat alliance was under threat. And then I remembered Herenda's meeting here in DV with Kirk Grundy.

I said, 'UK Green was stopped fifteen kilometres north of Una Drina by the Muslims. They said because of manoeuvres.'

Williams said, 'Are you thinking what I'm thinking, Jeff?'

I regarded them all. 'I think the Muslims could be about to start their own offensive against the Serbs.'

'Oh, fuck auntie,' Redman groaned, 'that's all we need. The Croats will just love that!'

But Williams wasn't so against the idea. '*Someone*'s got to stop the Serbs. If they take Una Drina, they can sweep clean across the south of Bosnia.'

Redman came back with, 'But if that someone is the Muslims – and the Ramoza Brigade at that – the Croats and the Muslims are going to be at each other's throats! A whole new ball game and a whole new bag of worms for us to worry about.'

I tended to agree with him, but kept quiet. I was still too new to start throwing my opinions around. I just said, 'Look, I think we ought to bring Colonel Rathbone up to speed on all this. I've no real idea how this might affect our operations, but at least the boss should be prepared for the unexpected.'

We all agreed on that and, after securing an overnight billet for myself – a sleeping-bag on the floor of the officers' mess – I strode down the street to the Hotel Donji Vrbas in search of Tali van Wyk.

Reception had her key, so she was out somewhere. I tried the bar.

She wasn't there, but to my surprise Nigel Cuthbert was. And to add to that surprise he was talking to Major Zlatko Herenda, the Muslim leader we'd been discussing at battalion HQ just minutes earlier. This time he just had two of his regular bodyguards with him.

I decided it was time to renew our acquaintance, and hopefully on better terms than at Mayor Jozic's office. Cuthbert must have noticed Herenda eyeballing me as I approached and looked round; he didn't look too pleased to see me.

'Nigel, I've been looking for you everywhere,' I said affably. 'Wanted to get a meeting with Major Herenda arranged and –

blow me! – here you both are.' I turned to the Muslim commander and shook his hand. 'Mind if I join you?'

Herenda's eyes were still as dark, angry and sullen as I remembered. 'That's all right, Captain Hawkins. We have just finished talking our business.'

'Yes?' I asked brightly. 'And what business might that be?'

Cuthbert cut in quickly. 'Nothing that need concern you, Jimbo.'

I said, 'Oh, really? Nothing about the large Muslim offensive that's about to begin?'

Herenda glared at me. 'Who told you that?'

'So it's true?' I asked.

'No, there is no offensive. Who said that there is?'

'Our UNPROFOR office has been picking up intelligence,' I replied. 'A convoy was stopped this afternoon because of Muslim manoeuvres.'

Herenda pounced on that and waved his hand dismissively. 'Just manoeuvres! There is no offensive.'

'Leave it out, Jimbo,' Cuthbert hissed. 'If the major says there's no offensive, there's no offensive.'

I said, 'Then I'm pleased to hear it. We have a huge convoy programme operating over the next week. Vital supplies to get in before the winter starts – predominantly for *your* people. *Your* new nation. I can't tell you what would happen to that if the current cease-fire breaks down.' I offered my hand to Herenda. 'Then I have your word, Major, your word of honour?'

He stared at my palm reluctantly for several seconds before his darkly glowering eyes met mine and he finally shook hands. But it was no signal of friendship, or even a meeting of minds, and I could almost feel the hatred in the power of his grip. I had the feeling I'd just forced him to lie to me, and he didn't like it one little bit.

I wanted to make him feel better, maybe steer him to a different way of handling the situation around Una Drina. 'I appreciate that you and Colonel Markovic and Mayor Jozic don't always see eye-to-eye, Major,' I said, 'but perhaps you'd get on better if you co-operated a bit more.'

'Meaning?' he replied sharply.

I shrugged, indicating I wasn't telling him how to fight his war, just making a useful suggestion. 'Maybe – if and when there is a counter-offensive against the Serbs – you could work together, co-ordinate your military plans.'

His eyes narrowed a fraction, as if considering just what sort of idiot was sitting in front of him. 'That may be a good military concept, Captain Hawkins, *if* we could trust the Croats. Unfortunately they have let us down and stabbed us in the back too many times. Given half a chance they will join up with the Serbs to annihilate us Muslims. Some say they have already signed a secret pact in Belgrade. If the Croats retake ground from the Serbs it may ultimately make no difference. So it must be done by the Muslim troops of the Bosnian government. My troops.'

Of course, Nigel Cuthbert had briefed me on this rumour about a secret deal between the Serbs and the Croats to carve up Bosnia between them. My fellow LOs had also mentioned it. It was a recurring theme, but I never witnessed anything to suggest it might be so. Such paranoia was just another example of the cancer of distrust and irrational ethnic hatred that had burst out again in the Balkans after years of suppression under Marshal Tito.

Herenda continued, 'Remember also that here in Donji Vrbas and in our own Una Drina are predominantly Croat neighbourhoods. And they are strategically placed in the middle of Muslim territory and supply routes to our capital Sarajevo and our second city Zenica. That is why we have to hold firm.'

'I understand,' I said, and it was true. Herenda and his fellow Muslims really were between a rock and a hard place.

Then the major decided it was time for him to go. He stood and his two bodyguards sprang to their feet. Herenda shook hands with Cuthbert and bade him goodbye, but did not offer me his hand again. Things didn't end on an altogether unsatisfactory note, though, because his parting words were: 'You and Mr Cuthbert must come over to my HQ and we must talk some more. Contact me in a few days, Captain Hawkins.'

Cuthbert and I stood, watching Herenda leave, then Nigel said, 'I think it's time we had words, Jimbo.'

I smiled. 'I couldn't agree more, Nigel. We're supposed to be on the same side. Fancy a drink?'

He glanced out of the window; it was growing dark. 'Why not? Sun's over the yardarm.'

We bought a couple of beers and tucked ourselves away on a couple of stools at the far end of the bar. I said, 'I know I'm not a part of your "bigger picture", Nigel, but we've got to start working more closely together. Be more open with each other.'

Cuthbert gave an awkward smile. 'Not always that easy, Jimbo. Decisions are made for me in London – way above everyone's head.'

'You mean London *and* Washington,' I suggested pointedly.

He shrugged evasively. 'Sometimes.'

I said, 'Come on, Nigel – I know as well as you do that America is arming the Muslims and the Ramoza Brigade, and that Kirk Grundy's CIA.'

His head seemed to swivel a full three hundred and sixty degrees in panic to see if anyone had heard, but that was probably an illusion. 'For God's sake, Jimbo!' he hissed.

'You could at least have shared *that* with me,' I replied firmly. 'It's pretty much general knowledge already – and, believe it or not, I can work things out for myself. I've been round the block a few times . . . It would just be nice to think you trusted me with *some* of the stuff that would allow me to do my job effectively.'

That seemed to strike home and he looked a bit sheepish. After all, he must have fully realized that I'd had dealings with MI6 spooks in my SAS days, and that current and former Regiment members are generally regarded as safe pairs of hands on security and intelligence matters.

'Sorry, Jimbo,' Cuthbert said thoughtfully. 'Yeah, maybe I have been a bit anally retentive, so to speak. Maybe I've spent too long around Tring – there's certainly stuff I don't want getting back to him.'

I nodded my understanding. 'Like the fact that the Americans have been encouraging this impending Muslim counter-offensive against the Serbs?'

Cuthbert didn't like that, but realized it would be stupid to deny it. 'Pretty obvious to a blind man, I guess. But strictly off the record. The Yanks aren't officially involved over here.'

'Yet,' I added.

'Who knows? . . . But Washington *is* keen on helping the Muslims. And they'd like them to have a good victory against the Serbs. You know, good media coverage . . . underdog fights back and all that! Also keep the Croats in their place.'

I stuck my neck out. 'Even if that sparks a new round of fighting between Muslims and Croats?'

'I don't think Washington thinks that far ahead.'

'Perhaps *someone*, Nigel, ought to suggest that they do.'

He put both hands up. 'Whoa, there! I'm keeping well out of that. I just find out what I'm asked to find out. No one in the Foreign Office is going to be interested in my humble opinion . . . Besides, we're all guessing. No one knows what the Serbs, the Croats, the Muslims – or the little pixies on the Drina riverside – are going to do next! They're such a petulant, impetuous and unpredictable lot. Half the time they don't know themselves what their own people are up to!'

That reminded me. 'You mean their lack of good military communications?'

'Military, civilian, radio, telephone . . . as you know, half the time it would be quicker to light a fire and send smoke signals. Our own comms aren't much better . . .'

I nodded. 'I remember, you said when you first showed me the Den.'

He frowned. 'So?'

I said, 'I had a thought about that. Not in my remit, but could be in yours. If you could get the funding.'

Now Cuthbert was really intrigued. 'Funding for what?'

'Some good comms equipment for the militias.'

He didn't understand. '*All* of them?'

'Sure, Muslims, Croats and Serbs. Headquarters and other stuff down to battalion level, even.'

'Cost a fortune.'

I said, 'We did something similar when I was in 22. Think about it. The British Army becomes very popular as a result, lots of smiles all round with the gift every soldier wants. It means we can talk to them, they can talk to their own troops and *each other* – hopefully more jaw-jaw, less war-war all round . . . But even more important . . .' I let the words hang.

Nigel Cuthbert wasn't slow, it just took him a few seconds to get there. 'We can listen in to everything via GCHQ!'

I nodded. 'Learn what they're saying to themselves and each other. Give them spanking new comms that are plugged straight into us. GCHQ can patch it straight back through CBF in-theatre.'

Cuthbert drained his drink with enthusiasm. 'Not sure they'll buy it, you know.'

'Can but try, Nigel. Try pitching the idea through CBF himself – can't believe Brigadier Stowell won't support the idea. I'm sure his G2 will – Dave McVicar's an old oppo of mine.'

'Sure, sure, Jimbo.' Suddenly he seemed anxious, on edge. 'Look – er – let's do it. But I have to be off just now.'

'Fine. You at battalion HQ or here tonight?'

He gave an embarrassed, boyish smile. 'Not sure yet. See you around.'

I watched him scurry away. As he disappeared through the swing doors I saw Ivana, his Muslim interpreter, waiting on the other side. They seemed to be looking at each other in a very meaningful way . . . I felt a ridiculous stab of envy.

Then the doors swung shut, and almost immediately opened

again. Tali van Wyk entered, blonde ponytail swinging as she walked.

She didn't appear to notice me and went straight to the bar to order a drink. I crossed the floor, coming up behind her. 'Hallo, Tali, let me get you that.'

'Oh, Jeff!' she said, startled. 'You made me jump.'

The barman brought over a tall glass with ice and a bottle of Coke. 'That all, Tali?' I asked. 'Nothing more adventurous?'

She smiled softly. 'I don't get my adventures out of a bottle.' I thought I noted a mischievous glint in her eye, but wasn't sure. 'And I don't drink much.'

I ordered another beer for myself. 'You can see I'm the last of the big spenders.'

'You can see I'm cheap to run,' she said, pouring the Coke over the ice. 'What brings you to Donji Vrbas, Jeff?'

'I'm on my way to Sarajevo with Rocky's convoy; sort of recce,' I explained. 'And I was hoping I'd get to see you.'

She blinked, a little surprised. I wasn't quite sure if the idea pleased her or worried her. Did she guess what I wanted to see her about? I wondered.

But she just said, 'Oh, yes?'

'When you were with us in the village of Stavac the other day, did you take any pictures of Colonel Goran Zoric?'

Her lower lip pouted a fraction as if she was trying to be defiant. 'Yes.'

At least she hadn't lied to me. 'After I expressly told you not to take any pictures without permission?'

She studied the floor. 'I didn't think it would matter. Nobody noticed me.'

'I saw you.'

There was a sudden look of defiance on her face. 'But you didn't say anything.'

'Of course I didn't, Tali. I was in the middle of negotiating a cease-fire with a bloody dangerous and unpredictable man! Why did you do it?'

She gave one of her beguiling little smiles and a small shrug of her shoulders. 'I don't know . . . It was a little devil in me.'

'And does that devil have a name?'

She looked puzzled. 'What do you mean?'

I said, 'A name like Kirk Grundy? He had copies of your photos down in Una Drina this morning.'

She dropped her shoulders, defeated, and had a couple of gulps of Coke as she decided to come clean. 'I'm sorry, Jeff, I didn't mean to cause trouble. When Kirk heard I was going to Stavac with you, he told me that Goran Zoric would probably be wanted for war crimes one day. Massacres, ethnic cleansing and other horrible stuff. That there's never been a picture of him. Kirk said if I was able to take one, it could be worth a lot of money in the media. He said he had influence and would try and sell it for me. Speak to his picture editor at the *New York Times*.'

I was exasperated by her naivety. 'Hasn't anyone told you Kirk is with the CIA?'

'Is that a news organization?'

Then I laughed, I just couldn't help it. 'No, Tali, for God's sake, it's the Central Intelligence Agency. The CIA, you must have heard of it?'

She looked a little affronted. 'Yes, of course. I didn't know what you meant . . . You mean Kirk's an American spy?'

I shook my head. 'No, he's not a spy, but he probably runs some. And he uses other people to do American dirty work. People like *you*.'

'So he doesn't intend to sell my pictures?'

I shrugged. 'How should I know? But his *main* reason for wanting the pictures is for the CIA, not to help your career.' Then I added unkindly, 'Which is likely to be pretty short-lived, the way you're going.'

Tali looked crestfallen for a moment, but quickly recovered. 'That's me, Jeff. Life in the fast lane and die young and happy.'

I said, 'Believe me, Tali, you won't say that when you get to my age.'

She reached out and touched my arm. 'I don't think I'll get to be your age, Jeff, really I don't.'

That took me aback somewhat, but I wasn't exactly sure what she meant. That she wouldn't or wouldn't want to? God, did that make me feel old.

But anyway, my train of thought was interrupted as the bar doors swung open and my LO colleagues from battalion HQ strode in, clearly looking for me.

Taff Williams reached me first. 'Hey, Jeff, have you heard the news?'

I shook my head. 'I've heard nothing about anything.'

'They've killed the bastard,' Taff gabbled excitedly. 'He was eating in a café with his bodyguards, in Bukovica – a village near Stavac – when two guys burst in with SMGs and blew them all away. Utter carnage, apparently.'

I grabbed Taff's arm. '*Who's* been killed?'

He did a double-take. 'What? Oh, sorry, didn't I say? The Serb commander, Goran Zoric.'

That night my sleep was shallow and fitful, disturbed by dozens of short, vivid dreams like movie clips, one barely starting before another took over. Bizarre, gory and confusing images. It was cold and uncomfortable on the mess floor, despite the sleeping-bag and kip-mat, a bitter draught coming from somewhere in the building.

I dreamt I was in the café in Bukovica, yet it was also the bistro that Marcia and I often used to go to when we were visiting London. Goran Zoric and his bodyguards were writhing on the floor between overturned chairs and tables. Their clothes were ripped to shreds by gunshot and the place was a sea of blood. Tali van Wyk was totally naked, almost dancing between the bodies as she took her photographs. The skin of her feet and calves was smeared with vermilion, as if she'd been treading grapes.

Then two faces loomed before mine, features hideously distorted as though viewed through a fish-eye lens. Pieter, the large Afrikaner mercenary, was grinning at me, his face covered in cam cream. Lars' face pushed in from the other side, lank fair hair over his cold eyes and leering closely at me, his tongue coming out to lap at the thick smear of blood all around his chin. He laughed as he saw me cringe and made a big thing of licking his lips and savouring every drop.

I awoke in a cold sweat and heard the tiny bleep of my wristwatch alarm. Unusually, the image stayed with me like a website cookie while I hurriedly dressed and stuffed my sleeping bag and toilet kit in my bergen. I felt dreadful, sick with tiredness and nauseous at the horrors I'd just witnessed. But I was glad that the night had ended.

There was no proof yet, but I just instinctively *knew* that the mercenaries Pieter and Lars had been responsible for Zoric's execution. I would lose no sleep over his death, but then he'd been murdered by men who were probably no less foul than he was himself. And I'd been used in the process. Me and a rather foolish young woman who had meant no harm.

No one had known what Zoric looked like, he had always made sure of that. So he felt safe to dine out with minimal protection. That was until Kirk Grundy had Tali's photographs in his possession. Then it was a different game altogether. Zoric's end game.

I scurried out into the early-morning dark. Outside it really was freezing, the pavements glistening white and the surfaces of the convoy vehicles covered with a crisp, thick coating of ice. Drivers were busily at work scraping windscreens and the air was filled with the rumble of engines, thick clouds of exhaust fumes mixing with the acrid stench of diesel.

I found Rocky Rogers waiting by his Discovery, its engine ticking over to warm up the interior. He was looking anxious to be under way.

'Mornin', Jimbo,' he greeted, pounding one huge glove into

the palm of the other. His big, florid face was pinched with cold. 'Should be rollin' in five at most, I hope. If we get a good run, I'm thinking we might make the entire way to Sarajevo and back to the depot. It'll be a close call, but I think we can make it.'

'If the cease-fire holds,' I said.

He picked up on my tone. 'You think it won't?'

'Touch and go, is my guess.'

'Zoric's assassination?' There wasn't much that escaped Rocky's bush-telegraph intelligence.

Before I could answer, I became aware of a woman approaching us from the hotel. I didn't recognize her at first in the dark overcoat with upturned astrakhan collar and black headscarf.

'Ivana,' I acknowledged.

She smiled tightly, but was focused on Rocky. 'Mr Rogers, I wonder if you'd be so kind. I need to get to Sarajevo urgently. Could you possibly give me a lift?'

To my surprise, Rocky's face was impassive. 'Sorry, Ivana, can't help you there. This is strictly UNHCR business. Refugees out, not a taxi service in.'

'But my fiancé has called for me to go to him. He is in Sarajevo.'

'Then he'll have to come to you.'

'That's not possible . . .' She turned to me. 'Please, Captain Hawkins, you know me. I'm a Liaison Office interpreter. Couldn't I travel with you? You know, sort of officially?'

Rocky cut in. 'Captain Hawkins isn't official, Ivana, when he's with me. So neither would you be. Now please take no for an answer. It's my decision to make, *not* the captain's.'

She stared daggers at him for a moment, then spared me the merest glance. However low a life-form she thought Rocky, she clearly regarded me as little higher.

When she turned to go, Rocky opened the driver's door. 'Right, Jimbo, we're moving.'

I climbed into the passenger seat and waited while he radio-checked that his drivers were ready, then tooted his horn. To a returning wave of blasts from twenty air horns that must have woken everyone in the town, UK Green began rumbling out of Donji Vrbas on the road to the capital and the city the entire world saw on their television sets every night – the madness that was Sarajevo.

'So what was all that about?' I asked. 'With Ivana?'

He smiled grimly, without taking his eyes off the road. 'You don't know, then?'

'Know what?'

'Her fiancé is the commander of the Ramoza Brigade.'

I did a double-take as I tried to recall his name, technically a brigadier general. 'Almir Aganovic?'

'That's him. One mean and moody sonofabitch.' Rocky leaned forward, straining to see the road through the remaining ice smears on the windscreen. 'Sarajevo's the Bosnian Muslim capital, right? That's why Almir Aganovic is there. But Sarajevo is surrounded by Serb forces. If they found Ivana – the fiancée of Almir Aganovic . . . the man they, and the Croats, consider the fuckin' Antichrist – on a neutral UNHCR convoy . . . Do I have to spell it out? It would give them every chance to play merry hell with us.'

'But she's *our* interpreter,' I pointed out.

'That's her job. For the UNPROFOR military. They know that – and they can't really mess with your Warriors . . . But our convoys are defenceless, vulnerable and at their mercy – and they know it.'

I shook my head in disbelief. 'Another little thing Nigel didn't share with me,' I muttered under my breath.

I was surprised that Rocky heard me; he gave a mirthless chuckle. 'Cuthbert? Oh no, he wouldn't have told you . . . He's shagging her.'

Donji Vrbas was, of course, essentially a Croat enclave within Bosnia, so there was a Croat militia checkpoint as we passed out of the suburbs and into government-controlled Muslim territory, where there was another checkpoint. Then the road passed through another Croat enclave on the route to Sarajevo – so another checkpoint – then out and back into Muslim territory before we approached their capital, which was surrounded and besieged by Bosnian Serbs.

It was quite mind-blowingly complex until you got used to it and I was hastily scribbling chinagraph notes on the perspex window of my map-case. According to Rocky, this part of the route was usually, but by no means always, trouble free as the Muslims and Croats were still uneasy allies.

And today that alliance seemed extremely uneasy. We were held up at all of seven checkpoints on the way. Not for long, but it was easy to see that both the Croat and Muslim militiamen was jittery and on edge. Inventories of UK Green's cargoes were carefully scrutinized and double-checked and every vehicle subjected to a thorough examination in case weapons had been hidden in its chassis. Thankfully, they stopped short of emptying all the wagons for an item-by-item match against the UN's dispatch lists.

We were about half-way to Sarajevo and at a Croat checkpoint as daylight broke, shedding a bleak steely light over the landscape, the mountains emerging out of the night in dark-grey relief all around us. It had been a very hard frost, the road still coated in white film; it wouldn't be long now before the first winter snows.

Rocky climbed out of his Discovery and I joined him. The Croat officer wore a heavy greatcoat and a Russian-style fur cap with the earflaps down; a cigarette dangled from his thin lips beneath a shaggy moustache, damp from his runny nose.

He looked both hostile and weary. Without speaking he accepted the dispatch notes from Rocky, but seemed distracted. He kept looking back over our shoulders from the direction we had come.

It was only then that Rocky and I heard it, above the background noise of the convoy's engines. A succession of deep, low thudding sounds that could almost have been distant thunder. But both Rocky and I had heard that noise too many times before to be mistaken. We both turned. Because of the distance and the mountainous terrain we could see no muzzle-flashes. But there was no mistaking the spasmodic pulses of light that stroboscopically illuminated the dark belly of the low cloud far away.

I said quietly, 'It's started. Heavy artillery.'

Rocky screwed up his eyes as he stared into the distance. 'South of DV,' he said. 'Maybe even down to Una Drina itself. Can't be sure from here.'

The Croat sniffed and cuffed a dewdrop from his nose. 'It's the fucking Mujahedin!' he said in English. He clearly meant the Ramoza Brigade. 'Trying to turn this country into Iran. Just think if they end up running Bosnia. The Mad Mullahs will burn down the churches and put our women into purdah!' He spat out the end of his cigarette from his mouth. 'And it's all your fucking fault if it happens! Fucking UN! Stick your noses in, but know fuck all what is going on here!'

I was surprised to see Rocky put a giant sympathetic paw on the man's shoulders. 'Yeah, mate, what do they know! But we know *your* families have all got to eat and keep warm this winter. Got wood-burning stoves on this load. Hundreds of 'em.'

The Croat blinked for a moment with sad, bloodshot eyes. 'And if you don't get through, maybe we will keep warm this winter standing round the Muslim mosques as they burn, eh? Maybe that's a better way.'

He thought it a very funny joke, but in truth he wasn't unreasonable in the time he took to check the wagons and we were on our way again in half an hour . . . Minus one wood-burning stove for his family.

But it was a different story fifty kilometres down the road on the approaches to the besieged city of Sarajevo. We'd barely begun moving again after the delay at the Croat checkpoint, when Rocky heard over the radio from company HQ in Una

Drina that there was fighting in the area. Not Colonel
Markovic's Croat militia, but an apparent offensive by the
Muslim Ramoza Brigade from the north, cutting into the Serbs'
flank. Security advice from Captain Gordy Cromwell was to
expect hostile retaliatory action anywhere along the supply route
to Sarajevo. In anticipation of any trouble, he'd requested that
Battalion send out a platoon of four Warriors which were in the
capital. They would be escorting the UK Red convoy out
through the Serb siege lines before covering us in UK Green on
our way in.

The reaction of the Croat and Muslim militia manning the
next few checkpoints became increasingly agitated and clearly
they wished we weren't on the road at all to complicate matters.
Both sides seemed to have it in their heads we were somehow
favouring the other or were some part of a Machiavellian plan by
the UN to engineer the outcome of the Bosnian war.

By the time we reached the Serb lines on the approaches to
Sarajevo, we could see their raw anger at the news that their
charismatic and legendary hero Goran Zoric had been murdered – and his now-demoralized troops were under surprise
attack by the Muslims' new Ramoza Brigade.

In retaliation they were pouring artillery and sniper fire into
the Muslim capital relentlessly. Palls of smoke hung in the air
above the rooftops and in the surrounding hills as hidden gun
batteries discharged their deadly loads into the civilian houses.

As we approached the checkpoint, a group of Serb militia
came out to meet us, guns out and aimed at our vehicles. The
officer in charge held up his hand, palm towards us. He didn't
look as though he was having the best day of his life.

'You can't pass!' he shouted in English as Rocky and I
climbed out. 'There is fighting! You'll have to turn round and go
back!'

Rocky was ice-cube cool. 'Hallo again, my friend . . . But it
seems you are doing most of the fighting here. Perhaps you can
stop just while we get the convoy through.'

The officer glared. 'With supplies for our enemies! After what they have just done! Haven't you heard?'

Rocky nodded sympathetically. 'Terrible business . . . but still those things were not done by the citizens of Sarajevo.'

'But they were done in their name!' The officer wasn't in the tenderest of moods. 'Besides, all these convoys supply the Muslims in the city, while the Serb villages outside get nothing.'

I'd heard of this accusation before from Rocky, who explained it was a perception rather than a reality. A city's demands seem so high compared with those of a rural hamlet.

I said, 'D'you think, Rocky, we might be able to help there? In some small way?'

Rocky gave me a steady, knowing look that was well-disguised within the poker-faced expression. 'In return for safe passage,' Rocky said as he handed over his dispatch papers to the Serb, 'I think we might allow a slight diversion of resources to your villagers.'

The officer read the main list items out loud, 'Rice, flour, tinned foods, paraffin, wood-burning stoves, blankets . . .' He looked up at Rocky with a hard smile. 'We will take thirty per cent of all of those items. And the medicines, especially pain-killers. Serb soldiers are having limbs amputated with only slivovitz to dull the pain.'

Rocky shook his head. 'Civilian women and children have priority on pain-killers. *Their* injuries are a result of *your* shelling . . . I will let you have twenty per cent of those and the other items.' He called Shaun from the rear of the Discovery. 'Help the commander here offload these provisions, will you? Twenty per cent. No more, no less.'

Shaun set off in his usual brisk, affable and efficient manner to locate the wanted cargoes. Meanwhile the Serb officer returned to his bunker to radio his superiors for co-operation. In the meantime I used Rocky's radio to patch me through to the battalion's Ops Room in DV to bring them up to speed.

While I was still talking, the Serb officer returned, saying his forces would be instructed not to fire on the convoy, but it was not guaranteed that all soldiers would be aware of that order. The risk, he said firmly, was ours.

I agreed with the Ops Room to wait for thirty minutes to give the Serbs' restraint order time to filter down to all units, then they would send out UK Red under armed escort.

Over the next half hour the artillery exchanges gradually petered out, but it seemed to me that small-arms and sniper fire were continuing pretty much unabated.

It was a relief at last to see the distant white UNHCR trucks of Rocky's opposite number winding out of town behind the grinding metal tracks of two Warriors. Their turrets and 30mm cannon jutted defiantly in opposite directions to cover the mountains on both sides of the road, as if daring the Serbs to take them on.

With much triumphant blasting of air horns the two convoys passed on opposite sides of the road, the Warriors skilfully turning on a sixpence by reversing one track until they were ready to escort us in.

It was an unnerving experience, especially sitting in a vulnerable vehicle like a Discovery, with angry Serb militia peering down at us from the heights on both sides. I'm not personally a great lover of flak jackets and tin hats when fighting, but today I was happy for my blue UN Kevlar helmet and vest.

I will never forget entering Sarajevo. It was like stepping back into history, entering a major European city that had been blitzkrieged during the Second World War. The damage in Una Drina and DV was bad, but in the capital of the fragile, newborn nation of Bosnia-Herzegovina it was dreadful. It was a wreck. No building was untouched, everywhere huge holes were punched through walls and often entire rooftops were punctured and collapsed by incoming artillery, charred rafters pointing upward like accusing fingers at the hills.

We ran the gauntlet of the highway known as Sniper's Alley, where so many innocents had been picked off at random, as though on the whim of a merciless and uncaring God but in truth by a callous part-time soldier down from Belgrade for a weekend's sport. Women shopping in the market with their children, those collecting water from standpipes and even mourners at funerals of war victims were all fair game.

It was a city of scarecrows and ghosts, in a grey and dark and dangerous world. Like living in a harrowing arcade game. Humanity driven to the edge and living in shadows like rats for fear that a stray artillery round or sniper's bead would find them in the open. Today, it could be *you*. A deadly lottery of everyday life.

Suddenly the size of the UN operation necessary to keep this huge city alive and surviving became clear. Truly vast quantities of fuel and water and food and medicines were required, and that was just the beginning.

The situation was made worse by local gangsters and their thugs driving round in luxury limousines, armed to the teeth, vampires feeding on the blood of human misery.

We passed the Holiday Inn where most of the world's media hung out, paying premium rates for rooms at the back which were out of the line of fire. It made me think of the Hotel Splendid in Una Drina and how, by comparison, we had it easy there. But, I wondered, for how much longer would our luck hold out?

If I hadn't realized before, it brought it home to me just how crucial the work of the Royal Wessex was to make sure that it did.

After offloading the convoy's supplies, I didn't feel proud at being so relieved to be leaving Sarajevo and its people, with their world of carnage and barbarity and deprivation, behind me. But surely no sane man would remain in that hell on earth by choice.

UK Green finally dropped me off back at Una Drina at eight o'clock that night. Once they'd refuelled using A Company's diesel bowsers, they would later push relentlessly on, back to

Metkovic depot near the coast. Our town and the immediate surrounds were still thankfully free of fighting. The Serb attackers, who had been wrestling with Markovic's Croats, had now pulled back to protect their own flank and rear from the Ramoza Brigade's surprise offensive.

I left Rocky to organize his refuelling and strode into the floodlit company compound, keen to get the latest update on the military situation. To my surprise I found Major Tring waiting at the door of the brick factory, legs apart, hands behind his back and wearing an expression of disdain. I somehow got the feeling he was waiting for someone in particular – me.

'Well, Jeffrey,' he said, 'I trust you enjoyed your unauthorized escapade to Sarajevo?'

I nodded curtly with a polite smile. 'Very informative, thank you, Reg. We had an LOs' meeting in DV – I think Gordy told you – so thought I'd check the problems on the convoy route at first hand while I was up that way.'

His thin lip twitched a fraction. It really would be difficult for him to argue against the logic of that. He said, 'Got a surprise visitor for you. Young lady. Smuggled herself up on the last convoy through here.'

I frowned in puzzlement as he stepped aside. In the doorway behind him, smiling sheepishly and looking even younger than I remembered her without make-up, stood Jelena, my one-night stand from Split.

Six

'Just what the hell are you playing at, Jelena?'

I led her by the arm, almost frog-marching her away from Major Tring and into a secluded corner of the compound.

She looked up at me imploringly. 'Please, please, Jeff, don't be angry. I didn't mean any harm. It's just that you've been so kind to us – me and my mother . . . Sending that money. I came to see if you could help.'

'Help with what?'

She puckered her lips as she struggled to find the right words. 'You wrote that someone told you about my mother. In the note you sent with the money. I thought that was so nice that you cared. I thought maybe you could do something else for us. For her. Maybe get her to England where they will treat her cancer.'

I shook my head slowly, wishing to God I *could* help in some way. 'I'm so sorry, Jelena, there is no way I can do that. No way the British Army can help. Even the UN doesn't take on such things.'

'But she has been such a good mother to me, and now she is suffering so much.'

I explained as best I could, 'Jelena, there are thousands of sick people in Bosnia. They can't all be shipped out; other countries can't take care of them all. Youngsters take priority. Besides, in England we can't even take care of our own properly.' She sniffed to staunch her tears and I tugged a handkerchief from my pocket. 'Here, use this, it's clean . . . I'm more worried about your safety. I wonder if Rocky will take you back to Split.'

'I don't want to go back. I want to be here, near you. Near your soldiers and the convoy guys. They have always been good to me.'

'What about your mother?'

'I love her, but it makes me cry to see her. There are two aunts who take good care of her.'

I suddenly realized that it couldn't have been that easy for Jelena to have smuggled herself onto the convoy at a guarded and secure depot. 'Who helped you get here?' I asked.

She shook her head. 'No, he will get into trouble.'

I placed my hands firmly on her shoulders. 'Tell me, Jelena. I'll square it with Rocky that he gets no more than a warning this time.'

'Promise me, Jeff?'

'Promise you.'

'It was Lizard. He's such a friendly little guy.'

The same skinny little Liverpudlian snake who'd smuggled Tali van Wyk and who, I got the impression, would do anything to wriggle into a girl's knickers. Rocky would be well pleased to hear this. I had to tell him, of course – he was the man responsible for the convoy's security – but I began to wonder whether I could keep my promise to Jelena and save Lizard's bacon this time.

'Just wait here,' I said, and went off to find Rocky, who was supervising the trucks as they formed a queue to fill up from the fuel bowsers.

I explained the situation to him and the promise I'd made to Jelena. 'I can't have her on the base,' I added, 'and I can't exactly force her to go back to Split.'

Rocky took it all with remarkable calm and even gave a wry grin. 'That Lizard is one randy little fucker. Reckon this is *his* problem, Jimbo. I'll show him the yellow card . . . again. I'll keep him on for Jelena's sake, but he can bloody well sort this mess out himself.' He turned round and spotted the group of drivers who were standing and chatting, having already refuelled their trucks. 'LIZARD!' he bawled. 'GET YOUR ARSE OVER HERE! CHOP, CHOP!'

Lizard came over in a hunch-shouldered little trot, knowing he was in trouble for something, eyes darting furtively left and right for the source of his problem. Then he saw Jelena.

Rocky didn't smile. 'So you know what this is about, Lizard.'

Lizard dragged hard on his thin, wriggly roll-up. 'Yes, boss, sorry. I'm in the shit again, aren't I?'

'Big-time,' Rocky confirmed. 'But we'll talk about that later, and about how I know a doctor in Split who's an expert on castration – Slav-style with two bricks!'

I said, 'It was totally irresponsible to bring her here.'

He nodded. 'I know, but I'm a sucker for a pretty girl. It's in me genes.'

'And that's where you should *keep* it!' Rocky fired back. 'She's got to stay somewhere safe. Take her down to the Hotel Splendid. See if you can get her a room – and pay for it in advance *yourself* – for as long as she's staying here.'

Lizard looked horrified. 'I can't afford that.'

'Either that or you're fired. No such thing as a free leg-over, Lizard,' Rocky said. 'Call it the price of love. Go on, you'd better get down there with Jelena now. I wanna be rollin' in the next thirty minutes.'

For the next three days life in Una Drina remained uneasily quiet and calm. No fighting directly affected the town, but artillery, tank and mortar fire could be heard from further round the western mountains as the battle between the Serbs and the counter-attacking Muslims raged. Each day the sounds of war receded a little more as the Ramoza Brigade pushed home its advantage.

Both Cuthbert and I wanted to get hold of Colonel Markovic and Mayor Jozic to find out what their intentions were, but they were decidedly unavailable whenever we tried to pin them down for a meeting. Similarly, the Muslim commander of northern Una Drina, the arrogant young Major Zlatko Herenda, seemed to be avoiding us.

On the fourth day, a Friday, we had a surprise visit from Commander British Forces' G2. My old pal Dave McVicar, the man with overall responsibility for security and intelligence in-theatre, arrived with a driver in a Land Rover just after lunch.

The three of us disappeared into the Den and locked the doors. Cuthbert got a brew going as we started to chat.

'So bring me up to speed, Nigel,' McVicar said.

'All quiet here,' said Cuthbert. 'The Serbs withdrew from their front lines to reinforce their flank and rear from the Muslim attack. Meanwhile Markovic and his Croats advanced up the side of the valley and took over the abandoned Serb trenches.'

'All movement and no fighting,' I confirmed.

McVicar nodded. 'CBF inserted an SAS observation team overlooking the fighting. Seems like the Serbs have taken a real hammering from the Ramoza Brigade. I don't think they'll be back.'

I said, 'The question is what'll happen when the Croats meet the Muslims on the retaken ground.'

'That's what the CBF and I have always thought,' McVicar said. 'But Washington's paying for this and we're just carrying out their wishes on the ground. We warned the Foreign Office, but frankly I don't think anyone wanted to listen. The government's more interested is cosying up to Bill Clinton and maintaining the special relationship Thatcher had with Reagan and Bush so we can still play with the big boys.' He glanced at Cuthbert. 'One good thing about US involvement, Nigel, is it's prepared to put money where its mouth is. They like your idea of supplying state-of-the-art communications equipment to the militia factions – otherwise you wouldn't have got it.'

Cuthbert smiled awkwardly. 'Actually, it was Jimbo's idea, Dave.'

I somehow wondered if he'd have handed me the credit if I hadn't been sitting in the same room.

'Stuff's being flown into Zagreb,' McVicar added. 'Should be with you in a few days. Of course, as Washington's paying for it, GCHQ has got to share any intelligence gleaned from it. Not ideal, but . . .'

The kettle was boiling, and Cuthbert put teabags into three mugs and poured scalding water over them.

While he was busy, I asked McVicar if Washington had sanctioned the assassination of Goran Zoric.

He gave a wan smile and shook his head. 'God knows, Jimbo. Neither the CBF nor I have been told anything . . . But I'll tell you something, the brigadier wants those two mercenaries' heads on a plate.'

Cuthbert looked round from where he was stirring the teabags round in tiny circles. I thought he seemed a bit sheepish. 'Not sure I can help you there, Dave.'

McVicar raised his eyes skyward. He knew all too well that Nigel Cuthbert was trying to serve two masters, the Commander British Forces as well as the Foreign Office/MI6. 'Trouble is, Nigel, the Serbs are kicking up merry hell. Say they won't stop bombarding Sarajevo until Zoric's killers are brought to justice. One rule for the Muslims, another for us. The usual sort of thing.'

I said quietly, 'I'll see what I can do.'

McVicar nodded his thanks. 'By the way, getting some good reports about A Company just lately, Jimbo. In fact, the Royal Wessex is generally seen to be getting their act together a bit better. The brigadier's delighted.' By 'good reports', McVicar must have meant mostly from Nigel Cuthbert, who answered to him directly. 'And I hear the Engineers have nearly finished repairing the school?'

I nodded and took the steaming mug of tea from Cuthbert. 'They plan to be finished by the end of today.'

'Excellent. The brigadier's asked PINFO to get some media

coverage. Let the masses see we're not just out here for ungrateful Bosnians to take pot-shots at.'

I said, 'I have to go down to the school later to take a look — as it's sort of my baby. Have you got time to join me?'

McVicar sipped at his tea. 'Sure. Thought I might stay over tonight. What's the Friday nightlife like here in Una Drina?'

Cuthbert grinned. 'You just wouldn't believe it!' he enthused.

'Oh dear, that bad?'

'Friday night is Bunker night.'

'Is this a wind-up?'

I said, 'Apparently not, Dave. The Bunker is the hottest disco in town. Mind you, it's also the only one.'

By the time we'd finally finished talking and planning, it was almost dark when we arrived at the school. Larry and his engineers were just packing up and loading their Bedford trucks with left-over materials.

'Bloody incredible,' I said as I stepped inside and the transformation was revealed. The holes in the roof and ceiling had all been sealed, reboarded and painted, the peppering of ricochet bullet-holes had vanished and all the windows had been replaced, this time all neatly covered in crosses of masking-tape to help contain glass splinters in the event of any future explosions nearby.

'Does that mean excellent, Jimbo?' Larry asked.

I smiled. 'Fishing for compliments?'

'Frankly, yes.'

'Then it's excellent,' I said. 'Well done and thanks. If you're staying over tonight, I'll stand you drinks at the Splendid.'

Larry shook his head. 'What d'you think we are, a bunch of tarts? There's a fucking war on and we're needed up DV way. Some buggers have been blowing holes in our road. But we'll have a drink on you next time we're passing.'

'A deal, Larry.'

He paused before leaving. 'By the way, our soft-furnishings department think they might be able to get hold of some fabric for curtains. As long as it's green or brown.'

'Terrific,' I said.

'But none of us useless tossers can sew.'

I grinned. 'I'm sure there are a few women in Una Drina who can.'

'Afraid I can't do anything about the desks. I'll see if I can wangle anything like that through the UNHCR, but school desks are way down their list of priorities.'

'No matter,' I replied. 'In fact, you've just reminded me of something . . .'

And that something was Anita's strange comment that Mayor Jozic had 'looted' the school furniture. Later that night I was able to unravel the mystery.

At around eight that evening Cuthbert, Dave McVicar and I took ourselves down to the Splendid, casually dressed in jeans, sweaters and fleece jackets against the cold. Inside, the body heat from the throng of people in the candlelit bar – mostly military and aid-workers, all keen to relax after a hard week's graft – kept the ambient temperature pleasantly warm.

Anita, actually smiling for once, was working hard behind the bar. To my surprise, so was Jelena, the teacher obviously familiarizing her new charge with the working routines and prices and helping to translate exactly what people wanted in half a dozen different languages.

As soon as she spotted me, Anita totally ignored the next customers in the queue and came over to get my order. 'Jeff, it is so good to see you! The school looks so smart, I really cannot believe it. Please, I will buy these drinks for you and your friends.'

Ignoring my protest, she handed over three cans of beer and refused any money. 'Young Jelena here is going to take over from me, so that I can prepare for lessons.'

'And who is going to pay you to teach?' I asked.

She looked almost indignant. 'Why, I would expect Mayor Jozic. From the town's community funds. He is in here tonight. I shall be talking to him later.'

Jelena gave me a beaming smile; clearly she considered this to be her luckiest day in a long time.

The three of us wandered into the restaurant section to see what gastronomic delights had found their way onto its very restricted menu. It seemed that butterbean soup followed by horse-beef casserole with autumn vegetables was the best of a choice of one. The owner-chef, a jovial and rotund Croat, explained that an old nag had been killed in crossfire in a nearby village.

'Like eating pheasant and partridge, be careful you don't break a tooth on the lead shot.' He added with a wink, 'Be particularly careful tonight, the poor beast was riddled with heavy machine-gun fire!'

In fact the meal was exceptionally good. The horsemeat had been cooked on the bone in a heavy pork stock and carrots, parsnips, plums and potatoes were all served up in a glutinous herby gravy. Having heard about the work on the school, the chef had thrown in three bottles of a local reserve red wine from his personal cellar.

Nigel and I were in the very best of spirits by the time we'd finished mopping up our plates with local crusty bread. That was when Mayor Jozic came into the restaurant with his wife – a dumpy, dark-haired, dour-looking woman who could have been his twin sister.

I waved to catch his eye, but Jozic's usual paste-on smile failed to materialize. Instead he just looked irritated and gave a minimal nod of recognition in my direction as the couple took their seats at a table on the far side of the room.

Anita came in to clear our table, doubling up as barmaid and waitress. 'Ah, I will talk to the mayor now,' she declared, stacking our plates.

I placed a hand on her wrist. 'You were telling me about the school desks being looted,' I reminded her in a low voice. 'What did that mean?'

She glanced hesitantly towards Jozic. Deciding she was far

enough away, she sat down on the spare chair at our table. 'Mayor Jozic is always up to little tricks like that. Apparently always, but especially since the troubles here. He sends a trusted little group of his Croat militia to loot things. Then he gets paid by the UN to "find" them, or buy them back on their behalf. Earlier he did it at the bakery, when it was abandoned during heavy fighting. Took away oven equipment. The same with beds and medicines from the clinic . . . Each time the UN pays money to the town funds to buy replacements. Your British Army even paid for office desks and chairs at the brick factory which he offered to supply.'

'Crafty bastard,' McVicar said.

'Still,' Cuthbert said, 'if it fills the town's coffers . . .'

I spared him a cynical glance. 'Why is it, Nigel, that I somehow doubt that?'

Anita stood up. 'Anyway, I will take your plates, then speak with him about my new job.'

A few minutes later she was back, presenting herself before Mayor Jozic's table and inviting herself to join them for a chat. He looked increasingly annoyed and his wife positively glowered with anger – or was it jealously, or both?

After ten minutes' worth of animated and clearly antagonistic discussion with lots of arm waving, Anita returned to our table with a face like thunder. 'Oh, that bastard! He is *so* mean! He says the town can only afford to pay me a few measly Deutschmarks per pupil! He knows I do not even have one pupil yet! There is no public transport and many parents keep their children at home when there is fighting. I'll be lucky to have ten students! And then I have to prepare for the lessons, find books for them.'

I said, 'I'm sure our quartermaster could find exercise books, pencils and the like for ten kids.'

She turned her head towards me sharply, then, to my surprise, smiled and squeezed my wrist with her hand. 'You are so kind, Jeff.'

I don't know if it was that or the bottle of wine I'd consumed that gave me a sudden surge of courage. 'While we're on the subject, I'll ask the mayor about the school furniture,' I announced, and stood up.

Mayor Jozic must have thought he was never going to have the chance to order his meal that night, let alone eat it. But at least when I approached him properly he had the good grace to stand and shake my hand and introduce me to his wife.

'I'll be brief, Mr Mayor,' I said. 'You are aware that the British Army has repaired the school and that Anita Furtula will be giving up her job here to run it?'

'Quite so,' he said, diplomatic smile at last in place. 'Excellent show.'

'But we have a problem with the desks and chairs,' I went on. 'Is it true that they were looted?'

He averted his gaze to some point in the middle distance. 'Apparently so, Captain. Terrible business . . .' Then for the first time, the smile became genuine and actually showed in his eyes. 'But I do have good contacts. Perhaps I could find some second-hand replacements through a furniture dealer I know. I'm sure the price would be very reasonable.'

I shook my head. 'Thank you, Mr Mayor, but first I'd like to try and find the original furniture. Looting is an illegal act and I hate to think of some crooks getting away with that. As mayor, you would have no objection if I play policeman and try to track them down? For the sake of the poor children . . .?'

He could hardly say no to that, but he hesitated before saying, 'Of course. I wish you luck.'

'Thanks,' I said, then added as I left, 'Strange thing to loot, I'd have thought. Can't be much call for children's desks . . .'

I turned away just as the blood rose up into his cheeks, but not before I caught the look of concern in his eyes.

When I returned to our table, the others were getting ready to leave. Anita said, 'My shift is finished. We are going to the Bunker now, Jeff. Your friend Dave says he has not been. I will teach him to boogie.' Her smiles were coming thick and fast tonight and, as I noticed the dimples in her cheeks for the first time, I thought how amazingly they transformed her features into those of a mischievous elf. 'Do you boogie, Jeff?'

I nearly choked on that one. Laughing, I said, 'Once I get my army boots off, Anita, there's no stopping me.'

By the look on Cuthbert's face he neither boogied nor had any inclination to. The four of us set off into the cold night to find the hottest spot in town. Anita clung to my arm, which brought a knowing smirk to Dave McVicar's face. It was good to be in my old friend's company again.

There was a gnawing cold wind running down the river valley and there was icy rain in the air that stung the skin of my face with spiteful pinpricks. I felt that the first snow would not be long in coming now. Our pace quickened to find shelter in the lee of a residential side road that ran uphill off the main drag. It was a relief to turn the corner and escape the hammering blast of fine rain, and it was in that relative quiet after the windrush that I heard it.

I stopped suddenly, and cocked my head to one side.

'Gunfire,' McVicar said without hesitation.

'If it's on the wind,' I said, 'it's from the south.'

'Oh, shit,' Cuthbert said.

Anita was confused. 'What is it?'

I said, 'Looks like fighting's broken out. And if it has, it'll be between the Croats and the Muslims.'

Cuthbert added, 'Fighting over the ground the Serbs took.'

An expression of horror appeared on Anita's face. 'You mean the Croats and Muslims of Una Drina?'

'And the outsiders,' McVicar added. 'The Ramoza Brigade.'

I nodded. 'Let's hope it doesn't end up with them fighting for the town.'

Cuthbert seemed to be really feeling the cold. 'It'll probably stay restricted to the mountains . . . Anyway, nothing we can do about it now. C'mon, let's get in the bloody warm!'

He led the way eagerly up the street. There were no pavements and no tarmacadam, just compressed mud and clinker running alongside the garden picket fences of the houses. Most were traditional single-storey Slav cottages or prefabricated concrete-slab versions put up by Tito in the fifties and sixties to house the masses. But there were one or two more salubrious and attractive alpine-chalet type buildings, which were most probably owned originally by Communist Party apparatchiks and now by prosperous entrepreneurs. Who were more than likely exactly the same people!

It was into the garden of one of these that we turned, already hearing the blast of heavy metal booming from up ahead in the timber-clad building that resembled an overblown cuckoo-clock.

Anita led the way down some steps at the side of the house, past the firewood logs neatly chopped and stacked against the wall, to the basement door, which was firmly shut. She rang the ornate cowbell hanging by the side and almost immediately a peephole opened, emitting a rod of light out into the darkness.

Once Anita had introduced herself and us, the door was quickly opened. The clamour came as quite a shock after the quiet street, with the pulsing coloured disco lights and heart-thudding heavy bass sound of a rock band gone mad. It seemed that everyone in the town had crammed into the confined brick cavern of somebody's wine-cellar. Several people I'd seen earlier in the evening at the hotel were here, their eyes sparkling and faces lit with an alcoholic glow. Even before we'd squeezed our way through to the bar, which comprised three upturned wine barrels, more familiar figures were arriving at the door. According to Cuthbert, the Bunker had the same reputation as the Windmill Theatre in London, which never closed during the Second World War air-raids. And the underground Bunker in Una Drina had stayed open every Friday night, even under the heaviest bombardment.

Once we'd secured a safe parking-place for our drinks on a

brickwork shelf, it was quite a revelation to see Anita throw her astrakhan-collared topcoat onto the pile of garments by the door, let down her long black hair and throw herself into the scrum of dancers, cavorting like a teenager, tossing her head and gyrating her hips, caught up and utterly lost in the thumping rhythm, head jerking, feet stomping and hair flying in all directions.

McVicar looked at me and grinned. 'Quite a gal when she lets herself go!' he shouted in my ear. 'Guess I'd better go learn how to boogie!'

I watched him join her, slipping effortlessly into a less energetic dance pattern than Anita's that nevertheless seemed to complement it. He was a smooth operator on dance-floors from Hong Kong to Belize and back again.

You didn't have to be a psychiatrist to work out what a release this was for someone as controlled in her daily life as Anita, and how precious were a few moments in which to put aside the ever-constant fear of death that hung over most of war-torn Bosnia . . . In all my years of soldiering, I don't think I was ever in a place that didn't manage to conjure up a nightspot, however bizarre and unlikely in nature, in the midst of the killing, butchery and mayhem of war. It was just another demand of the human condition.

Then the pace changed and, as McVicar wandered back to find his drink, Anita beckoned me to join her. The slow and sexy intro rang a bell in my memory.

'How was Dave's boogie?' I asked.

She took my hands in hers and drew me deeper into the crush of dancers. Peering over the top of her specs and looking very serious, she said, 'That was not a boogie, Jeff.' Then she giggled. 'This is the boogie for me to have with you.'

Then I remembered the song, the sultry duo of Spanish girls called Baccarat who had a smash hit in the seventies with 'Yes, Sir, I Can Boogie' . . . pure, over-the-top acoustic erotica.

Anita smiled, slid her left hand over my shoulder and then,

with the thumb of her right, pushed her specs up off her nose until they were perched on the top of her forehead, holding her hair back like an Alice band. The other dancers crowding onto the floor pushed us closer together, and the whole room seemed to be gently swaying as one to the seductive words and rhythm. I felt myself against her, aware of the surprisingly hard, muscular flesh of her belly beneath the thin material of her dress.

She sensed I was resisting, and slid her hands up over my shoulders. 'You don't have to be on duty tonight, Jeff.' Those angry dark eyes had melted into soft pools of deep hazel light, and her smile hovered on the wicked side. 'Well, not *all* of you.'

It was one of those moments when you think you know what someone means, but daren't risk misinterpretation. I wasn't sure how I felt about Anita; I wasn't even sure I felt anything at all. But mostly I didn't want to compromise the job I had to do.

Nevertheless I'd had enough to drink to let that slip and just relaxed to the next few Baccarat tracks, enjoyed the warmth of her body against mine, and tried to share the mental release I could see she was enjoying so much.

As the song 'Feel Me' ground sensuously and headily on, I found Anita's lips by my ear, felt the quick, teasing dart of her tongue, and her hoarsely whispered words: 'Thank you, Jeff, so much. I cannot tell you what it means to me. What you have done for the school.'

'It was nothing,' I said. 'Just lucky the engineers were around . . .'

'Oh, it was something. After all those empty promises . . .' The music was coming to an end, and she pulled away from me suddenly. 'I am too hot now! It is so stuffy in here.' She grabbed my arm. 'Come, let's get our coats and some fresh air.'

Now she had my hand and was pulling me from the floor. We found our things from the heap by the door and I helped her drape her coat over her shoulders as we stepped out into the garden.

She gave a little shiver and stamped her feet, huddling into her coat.

'Do you smoke?' she asked suddenly. It sounded more like an accusation.

'Yes, do you?'

There was brisk shake of the head. 'No. But I want a cigarette just now.'

That was tough. 'I only smoke cigars.'

She nodded, her expression back to serious schoolmarm. 'Oh, yes, those little ones. Maybe I smoke one of them, please . . .?'

'Sure,' I said, not a little surprised.

As I went to take the packet out she placed her hand over mine. 'No, not here. It is too cold. I need a coffee. If I am to smoke I need a coffee . . .' Again she had me by the arm. 'My place is just across the street. I will make us coffee. I make good coffee.'

Somewhat bemused, I walked with her up the steps and along the garden path to the street. I said, 'I didn't think anyone in Una Drina had coffee any more.'

'Black market,' she confessed with disarming honesty. 'It cost me a week's wages for a small jar when the school was still working. I just make it for special occasions.'

'Then I'm glad you've got some left.'

She paused at the garden gate. In the distance I could still hear the faint crackle of small-arms fire. 'There have not been many special occasions in my life just lately, Jeff.'

Then she linked her arm in mine and we walked a hundred metres to a small block of mustard-coloured flats no more than four storeys high. She led the way along a cracked-paving path between a moth-eaten lawn strewn with litter to the entrance. The concrete stairwell smelled of damp and lingering cooking smells as we trudged up two flights of steps to her floor. A door of peeling green paint swung open into a very neat but dark and slightly oppressive living room. The bare, once-varnished floorboards were covered by a large and faded Persian rug in the centre. The settee and other items of furniture were heavy, dark and uninspired antiques that I guessed she'd inherited from her family. There was a hideous amateur oil painting of a Drina river scene on one wall and a rather kitsch modern icon of the Madonna and Child on the other. But the place was spotless and smelled sweetly of beeswax . . . somewhat offset by the acrid stink of paraffin from the little upright pillar heater in the corner.

'Please sit down.' She patted the sofa, the cracked hide of which had come from a beast that had died long before my father was born. 'I'll put the kettle on.'

She disappeared into a long, very narrow kitchen area and I heard the familiar hiss of an army hexi-stove; I guessed it was maybe the one concession she'd wangled out of my predecessor.

Then she returned to the living room, went to a dresser and produced a decanter of slivovitz and two tumblers. 'To warm us up. We cannot have coffee without a drink. Good health!'

We clinked our glasses and threw our heads back in unison to swallow the contents down in one. As I gasped at the firestorm in my throat I saw that she was standing with her eyes closed, her lips drawn tight, and was trembling slightly.

'Anita?' I asked.

Her eyes opened suddenly as if she were summoning up her courage. 'I am fine, Jeff,' she said, taking a deep breath. 'And tell me, are you married?'

I nodded. 'Yes.'

'A long time?'

'A long time.'

She replaced her glass on the dresser. 'I have never been married. I was engaged. A little late in life, I suppose. But a nice man.' She bit her lower lip and arched her head, looking up at the ceiling. 'He is missing in action nearly nineteen months now.'

I said, 'I'm so sorry.'

She didn't move, just stood clutching the dresser with her left hand and looking away from me. I heard a sharp intake of breath as she fought her tears.

I took a step towards her, took her arm and turned her into me. She fell against my chest, breathing hard, but refusing to cry, determined not to. At last she was able to say what she was thinking, but her words came out in little breathless gulps. 'Before he went missing, I thought . . . one day I might . . . teach *our* child . . . at the school.'

I just hugged her tight and said nothing. There really was nothing I could say.

The moment was broken by a shrill whistle from the old-fashioned kettle as it worked up a head of steam. She detached herself from me, gave a small sniff, glanced at me with an embarrassed quick smile, then went towards the kitchen. 'I won't be a minute. Pour us both another drink.'

I shook my head at the unfairness of it all and at the thought of just how undeserving Anita was of such misery, and walked over to the dresser. I refilled the tumblers and glanced down at an old newspaper beside the decanter. It was dated eighteen months earlier and mentioned a big battle somewhere in Croatia . . .

I'd been reading for several minutes before I realized Anita hadn't returned from the kitchen. I crossed the floor and pushed open the door. Two coffee mugs were filled, steam rising, but she wasn't there.

'Anita?' I called, suddenly worried.

'In here,' her voice replied.

Picking up the mugs, I turned to see that the adjoining door was ajar. It was dark inside and, as I nudged it with my leg, it swung slowly open to allow a slice of yellow light to cut into the gloom. There were heavy drapes at the bedroom windows and an inelegant wardrobe and dressing table in dark and oppressive mahogany.

She was lying outstretched on the bed, propped on one elbow, naked. Her skin seemed almost painfully bleached, contrasting against the dark red of the old-fashioned quilted counterpane.

Against the pale marble skin, her small, dark nipples seemed tightly knotted, angry and defiant, and the thatch of jet black between her legs lashed at my senses.

'Jeff,' she said simply.

I swallowed hard, found my voice. 'I'm not sure . . .'

Her hair hung loose and splashed over her shoulders, her spectacles were missing. 'Jeff,' she repeated. 'Don't say anything. Just come here.'

She wriggled back a few inches and patted the edge of the bed. 'This isn't necessary,' I said as I sat down and twisted round to look down at her.

'Not necessary?' she echoed. 'I know it is not *necessary*. It is what I want to do.' A look of hurt passed behind her eyes. 'You want to go away? You do not find me attractive?'

I shook my head. 'It's not that . . .'

'And it is not because you are married, is it?'

It hardly seemed like a question, because it was as if she already knew the answer. 'No,' I murmured.

She reached over, took the two mugs from my hands, rolled back and placed them on the far bedside cabinet. Then she was on her knees behind me, easing the fleece from my shoulders, her lips by my ear, her voice so soft I could scarcely hear it. 'Relax, Jeff, do nothing. This job is much stress for you, I think. Just lie back, rest and shut your eyes. Say nothing.'

Suddenly I felt immensely tired, the toll of the alcohol and the strain of the week combining to weaken my resolve. It was as if I had no strength or will to resist as her hands eased my shoulders towards her and then down onto the pillow.

What followed passed in a hazy dream of butterfly fingers picking and plucking at buttons and zips, fluttering across my skin, over my face and body, and the delicate moist warmth of her tongue, now here, now there, always unexpected but always knowing where to go next. Then, as my blood began to rush, her mouth found where it had wanted to be and began its exquisite torture until I felt that I would burst. Then she was astride me, slender legs bent and lowering herself, impaling herself slowly and gently, inch by inch. I opened my eyes and saw her smile down at me. She put a finger to her lips.

Crazy, but I felt so pleased that after all the shit in her life, for a short, short while I was making Anita happy. And we rode the storm together until we both came in a series of staggered little explosions that caught one or the other of us almost by surprise. Finally, she let herself down across my chest and laughed.

'Thank you, Jeff,' she said softly and kissed my forehead. 'I have not made love with anyone since a long time before my husband is disappeared.'

'You don't have to thank me,' I said. 'It was good for me too.'

She giggled. 'I am pleased.' Then she was suddenly the schoolmistress again. 'Stay there.'

Seconds later she returned from the little bathroom with a flannel to clean us. Very efficient. 'I think we must get back to the Bunker,' she said suddenly as she began pulling on her underwear. A worn-looking black bra and old-fashioned pants with a touching small hole worn in the material through which her ivory skin showed. 'People will wonder where we are.'

Dave McVicar will *know*, I thought, because he never missed a trick.

As we finally had our coats on and stood by the front door, she turned to me. 'This doesn't have to mean anything, Jeff. It is just a private little thing between you and me.' Those brows fractured with concern. 'Promise me?'

I said, truthfully, 'It never happened.'

She smiled, reassured. 'But you are glad it did?'

'Very,' I said.

The temperature had dropped sharply while we'd been in Anita Furtula's flat, the rain had stopped but now a patina of ice was starting to form on the rooftops. As we passed through the gate and onto the street we immediately became aware of the noise and commotion a few hundred metres away and the blazing lights of two Warriors and other vehicles.

'What . . . ?' Anita began.

I broke into a sprint. The first thing that crossed my mind was that there'd been a bomb planted in the disco – I'm not sure why, maybe too much time spent in Northern Ireland and other places where such things often happened.

But as I neared I could see that it was nothing like that. Apart from the white-painted Warriors and a couple of Land Rovers, the other vehicles appeared to be green-painted pickup trucks and 4x4s of the type used by Markovic's Una Drina battalion. A crowd was gathered by the gate of the chalet garden, a mixture of Royal Wessex troops and militiamen. Even from a short distance I could see that the Croats' mood was menacing and angry. A lot of voices were raised, excitable and threatening.

To one side, by one of the Croat vehicles, I saw Markovic talking to Mayor Jozic. Then I spotted Dave McVicar and Nigel Cuthbert in the gathering; they were in earnest conversation with Major Tring.

McVicar was the first to see me and waved for me to join them.

'Ah, there you are, Jeffrey!' Tring's face was white and pinched against the cold. 'Been lookin' for you everywhere.'

'What's the problem?' I asked.

Tring said stiffly, 'Colonel Markovic claims there's been a massacre at the village of Stavac.'

'Stavac?' I repeated. 'That was Zoric's headquarters before he was assassinated.'

'Yes,' Cuthbert interrupted, 'until the Muslims overran it and sent the Serbs packing. It's a Croat village and it seems that Colonel Markovic's men re-took it from the Muslims earlier tonight.'

McVicar added, 'Markovic claims they've found dozens of bodies in two burnt-out houses. Men, women and children. Says the Muslims did it, blames the Ramoza Brigade.'

I frowned. 'Couldn't it just as well have been the Serbs? Before the Muslims got there?'

Cuthbert said in a low voice, 'In this crazy place it could even have been the fuckin' Croats themselves. To put blame on the Muslims.'

Tring pointed to one of the open-backed pickups at the side of the road. For the first time I saw the small figures wrapped in blankets. Frightened eyes in traumatized little white faces were watching us. 'They say they found those kids hiding in the village and in the surrounding woods. Either orphaned or abandoned – depending whether the parents were massacred, abducted or just fled. Maybe they will throw some light on what happened.'

Anita Furtula, who had been standing just behind me and listening to our conversation, stepped forward. 'What are you thinking of, Major Tring! You cannot leave those children there! Just look at them. They are petrified and shaking with the cold.'

Tring looked irritated, but gave a nod of acknowledgement to the schoolmistress. 'Mrs Furtula, we were just discussing that very point. Where we can put them for safety? It's been suggested the mental hospital—'

'In with the lunatics?' I thought Anita was going to go ballistic. 'Then it is *you* who are mad, Major! I'll hear none of it. We have a school now, there is space and it is dry and it can soon be warm.'

Cuthbert and I looked at each other. 'Not a bad idea,' I said.

'Excellent,' Tring said grudgingly. But I think he realized this would let him off the hook. 'I'll get the QM to rustle up some blankets and get a cook's detail to prepare some hot food straight away. And see if the battalion MO can't give them a once-over tomorrow . . . Then it'll be the UNHCR's remit.'

Anita's eyes narrowed at the use of that familiar word, but she said no more and marched over to the children in the pickup.

Now Markovic had seen me. He left Mayor Jozic and strode across. 'Ah, Captain Hawkins, I hope you are satisfied now! You and your fucking cease-fires! While I oblige you, we leave the Muslims to attack the Serbs – and free to rape and plunder and massacre innocent Croats when they have re-taken territory that is historically *ours!*'

I said, 'Two wrongs don't make a right, Colonel. And *you* did the *right* thing. The world will thank you for it.'

'Bah!' he almost spat out his contempt. 'And those murdered Croats in Stavac will thank me, too, will they? And their orphaned children?'

I know it sounded lame, but I had to hold my ground. 'What this country needs is a little humanity just now, Colonel. Like the humanity you showed with your cease-fire to let the relief convoys through.'

He shook his head. 'And what did you do in return for our cease-fire? You and your swaggering UNPROFOR soldier boys with their smart Warrior toys?' He wagged a pudgy finger in my face. His words were so venomous that droplets of spittle were gathering at the sides of his mouth. 'Fuck all, that's what! You let the Muslims massacre the Croats in Stavac. *You* are supposed to be the UN's *protection* force. Where were you then?'

There is no real way to answer such ludicrous accusations without losing your temper, but I did my best. 'You and the Muslims are fighting and killing each other, Colonel, not us. Remember that when you've calmed down.'

His eyes narrowed. 'Oh yes, Captain, we are certainly fighting and killing Muslims now. The world and the UN can go and stick its humanity up its sanctimonious arse! There will be no more cease-fires. We will not rest until we've driven the Muslims out of the Stavac valley and out of Una Drina!'

He turned on his heel and beckoned his henchmen to follow. In minutes all the Croat vehicles had gone, including the pickup that took Anita and the children down to the school.

Major Tring stared after the last receding truck. 'Looks like we're in for some bad times.' He sighed. 'We'll get a platoon of Warriors over to Stavac at first light tomorrow morning.'

I caught the look in McVicar's eye. I said, 'Just a thought, Reg, but there could be a lot of damage to evidence by then.

The Croats will be keen to bury their dead. We could seal off the site tonight and secure it until UN forensics get there.'

Tring stared at me as though I'd just poked my tongue out at him. 'Are you telling me how to run the company, Jeffrey?'

'Just a thought,' I said.

'I'm very pleased to hear that,' he replied. 'Right, best we get back and put our heads down. It's clearly going to be a long day tomorrow.' He marched off towards the Warrior crews.

I said to McVicar and Cuthbert, 'I think someone ought to get up to Stavac.'

Cuthbert didn't look too keen. 'You mean us?'

'Count me in,' McVicar said, typically. 'Best we go out in uniform and tooled up. Sort of official. Don't worry about Tring, Jimbo. This is on my authorization as G2 to CBF, OK?'

And that was fine by me. We took a lift back to company HQ in one of the Royal Wessex Land Rovers, quickly changed into combat gear, then the three of us left in my own dedicated LO vehicle fifteen minutes later.

Cuthbert drove while McVicar and I rode shotgun with a couple of SA80 Bullpups, me in the front passenger seat and McVicar sitting in the back cargo compartment to cover our rear. We made good headway out of town, scooting through the usual Croat checkpoint which was unmanned. No one had expected anything on the road at this time of night and the guards were shut down in their roadside shed with the light on, no doubt drinking, smoking and playing cards. After we'd passed, the shed door flew open and I could see a small group standing looking after us, but by then we were too far away for them to do anything about it. Thankfully they didn't open fire.

Cuthbert swung off on the incline to Stavac with his foot pretty much going through the floor. I didn't object; the faster we moved, the safer we'd be – well, probably. I couldn't see any reason for this track to be mined.

I told Cuthbert to stop as we rounded the hillside shoulder before descending into the Stavac valley. He cut the engine and we listened and watched. The earlier gunfire of the evening had all but died away. The three of us discussed the matter, and decided that if Stavac was now in Croat hands, then logically the Muslims had been pushed back and the brunt of any fighting must be beyond the village now.

We drove on, the same route we'd taken to organize the cease-fire with the Serb commander Goran Zoric before he'd been murdered by the two mercenaries.

There was a lot of activity in one part of the village. Arc lights had been set up, running off an emergency generator, so that the place looked like a film-set. Croat militia stood around, smoking and looking depressed and sullen. Apart from them were civilians, mostly older women in heavy greatcoats, woollen stockings and headscarves. Some were crying and wailing, others comforting the bereaved. Old men stood separately, just watching, not crying, not talking.

Cuthbert eased up the accelerator and cruised quietly to a halt. None of the gathering spoke to us, but some glared with open hostility. However ridiculous the justification, it was clear they held the UN responsible for whatever dreadful deed had been done here.

We climbed out of our Land Rover in silence, our guns held loosely and in an unobtrusive manner, and edged near to the scene.

It was the stench of the charred bodies that hit us first, both acrid and sickly sweet, causing an immediate gag reaction. Cuthbert quickly backed away, but McVicar and I had been in situations like this before and had learned to breathe through our mouths to avoid the stench.

Only the walls of this house remained. Fire had destroyed the roof and damaged the brickwork with its intensity, and some portions had since collapsed. We stood by the gap and looked at the stinking black sea of bodies. Here and there was a clearly defined hand, charred to the bone, reaching out for help from the quagmire of melted human flesh.

Croat militiamen wearing old Soviet-issue gasmasks, rubber boots and gloves were trying to distinguish individuals from the gooey mess, and putting the pathetic remains onto stretchers. I turned and saw several bodies lined up beside a truck.

I turned to an old woman beside me. She had a kindly, wrinkled face but her eyes lacked all emotion. 'Where are they taking the bodies?' I asked quietly.

Her eyes seemed to notice me for the first time. 'To the Catholic church in Una Drina.' Her eyes narrowed a fraction as she took in that I was a British soldier. 'For a decent Christian burial in consecrated ground.'

I smiled gently, nodded and backed away. McVicar and I rejoined Cuthbert, who'd recovered a little of his composure.

'Don't think we should try to stop them,' I said.

McVicar agreed. 'Not with three of us. Otherwise it'll be three more coffins wanted. See what we can salvage when Major Tring gets up here tomorrow.'

'Let's get back,' Cuthbert said. 'This place is giving me the willies.'

As we moved across to our Land Rover, the old woman I'd been talking to stood defiantly in our path. She said nothing, just gathered saliva in her mouth and spat on the ground at our feet.

Then she turned and walked away.

'Did you notice anything back there?' McVicar asked.

Cuthbert pulled a face. 'What?'

'No heat. No smoke. It all happened quite some time ago.'

Seven

At first light the following morning Una Drina was invaded by the world's media.

I wondered if Dave McVicar had anticipated this, because when I awoke on an early alarm call, he and his driver had already left.

Of course, the Royal Wessex's Public Information Officer had been sweating hard trying to drum up some media enthusiasm to cover the re-opening of the school, but without much success.

In the event, he needn't have bothered. Not only the UK's, but the world's TV, radio and press corps swamped the little town, although the school was irrelevant to them. They wanted pictures of charred and tortured bodies, wailing and bereaved peasants and personal accounts of anyone who had witnessed the horrors of people being locked in a basement and deliberately burned alive.

Major Tring's decision to leave his expedition to the massacre site until the following morning led to a public relations disaster. His sturdy platoon of Warriors were just leaving the company compound at Una Drina as the media vehicles arrived. Naturally they tagged on the end of the column.

Thus the world was to witness the unedifying site of an incompetent British officer, who clearly had no idea how to handle the situation, arriving at Stavac after most of the bodies had been removed, then being jeered, stoned and spat at by angry villagers.

I was to be part of this spectacle. As both the company LO, supposedly skilled in negotiation, and a fluent Serbo-Croat speaker, Tring had insisted I go with him as his right-hand man. I was not in a position to refuse. But in this sad little village, nobody was in any sort of mood to listen to anyone who wore the blue beret of the United Nations.

Finally, Tring left a couple of Warriors and their crews to guard the massacre site against the removal of any remaining body parts or forensic evidence, and set off for the Catholic church back in Una Drina to try to prevent the mass burial of the bodies. In the event he was too late for that, too, because Mayor Jozic had ordered in a JCB to get the job done quickly.

I was thoroughly depressed on the journey back to town. Mostly this was due to a dark and nagging sense of guilt. Dave McVicar had been quite right in his observation the night before. There were no smouldering corpses or timbers, and no heat coming from charred bricks. The massacre could have happened days ago. Even before I had gone there to visit Colonel Zoric.

I remembered the deserted village and glib response when I questioned him. I recalled my sense of unease. But I had let it ride. Now I cursed my own stupidity.

And I could only guess what the media coverage of the Stavac massacre would be like, not helped by the fact that Colonel Rathbone had not seen fit to leave his eyrie in Donji Vrbas and take charge on the ground himself.

At lunchtime I took myself off to the Splendid in anticipation of a conciliatory beer and a cheese, tomato and lettuce sandwich. That doesn't sound much, but it was quite a treat in Una Drina at the time and all home-produced by the hotel's owner, who kept his two prized cows under lock and key in a shed by the back door. To the best of my knowledge, they were the only two domesticated animals in the region to survive the war uneaten.

Of course, I should have realized that the media always commandeered any watering-hole in remote places. The bar was packed with journalists and film crews, and all the cheese and tomato sandwiches had been sold. Jelena served me a can of lager with a smile. 'Thank you for not sending me back to Split, Jeff. I really like it here.'

'I'm pleased,' I said. 'Has Lizard paid up for your room here?'

She pulled a face. 'I wish people wouldn't call him that. He's really very sweet . . . And, yes, he has. For a whole month in advance.'

'That's good, then,' I said. Maybe he really was seriously keen on her, I thought.

'And I'm enjoying working here,' Jelena added. 'I'm getting to save a little money at last.'

'Keep the change,' I said, handing her a note and moving along the bar to where I'd spotted Gerald Kemp in conversation with Tali van Wyk. She was sitting in her usual sheepskin body-warmer with her jeans-clad legs wrapped intricately around those of the barstool.

I'd rather chat to Kemp and Tali than get collared by some of the other redtop tabloid journalists, most of whom I couldn't stand.

Kemp spotted me. 'Hi, Jeff. Bit of a rum show this morning, eh?'

I lit one of my vanilla cigars. 'Didn't exactly cover ourselves in glory, did we?'

The journalist shrugged. 'Shit happens, Jeff. You can't win 'em all.'

Tali put a hand on my forearm and those powder-blue eyes looked at me intensely. 'I thought you were brilliant, honestly. The way you tried to explain to those stupid peasants. It wasn't your fault they wouldn't listen.'

'Thanks, Tali, but I'm not sure that's how it'll look on *News at Ten.*'

Kemp said, 'Tali's right, Jeff. I've seen the rushes and it just looks as though the locals are being thoroughly unreasonable. Blaming the lack of UN protection for the massacre. Besides, viewers won't realize how the Royal Wessex could have handled it differently. They won't know that if you went up to Stavac last night, so could A Company.'

Good news or not, that annoyed me. 'How the hell d'you know I went up there last night, Gerry?'

He tapped his nose. 'I have my sources, Jeff. Nothing sinister, you just can't keep many secrets in a place like this.' He beckoned Jelena to bring more beers. 'If it's any consolation, we've got a new news editor taken over. A woman, bit of a feminist. Not too keen on all the horror stuff. Wants to balance it with a bit of lovey-dovey. She insisted I get the school story she was promised. Does that cheer you up?'

'Somewhat,' I lied.

'I'd like to cover it too, Jeff,' Tali added, 'if that's all right.'

'Fine,' I said. 'Anita Furtula is the schoolmistress. She's there looking after some orphans and lost kids from Stavac. My guess is she'll be very protective. And she can be *very* prickly, so walk on eggshells. Mention I sent you – I seem to be the flavour of the day at the moment. But don't bank on it saving you if she doesn't want the intrusion – which is likely.'

'Where is the school exactly?' Kemp asked.

'North end of town near the Muslim sector. Take the left-hand road at the tyre shop.'

Tali said suddenly, 'Thought I'd stay in Una Drina for a bit.'

I was surprised. 'Donji Vrbas is where it all happens. This place is a ghost town by comparison.'

She gave a coy smile and a shrug. 'Well, Kirk Grundy *also* happens in DV. That's reason enough to be *here*.'

'Oh?' I said.

'Been making a bit of a pest of himself,' Kemp explained helpfully.

But that didn't seem her main concern. 'You were right about the photographs, Jeff, I think. Kirk took me to supper several times and made all these promises, about the picture editors he knew, how he'd sell the Zoric pictures for me.'

'And nothing?'

'Zip,' she replied, looking downcast. 'And Zoric's assassination is stale news now. If they didn't bite then, I don't see them doing it in the future.'

'Are you staying here at the Splendid?' I asked.

She shook her head, her ponytail swinging. 'They've no rooms left. Besides, I can't afford the prices they charge the press. I wondered if you knew of anywhere. Your barracks, maybe?'

'The brick factory?' I smiled at that. The Royal Wessex lads would love to have Tali van Wyk wafting round in her tight jeans, but I knew Major Tring would have none of it. And, of course, he'd be right. 'Sorry. But I'm afraid that's a non-starter. Ask the hotel owner, though; he knows a lot of the locals. Someone might want a paying guest.'

'I'll try that,' she said.

I left them to it then and drove back to company HQ. Almost immediately I noticed a Bedford truck and an unusual but familiar Land Rover variant parked at the entrance to the Ops Room. Both were in standard British Army cam colours, not UNPRO-FOR white. As I walked past the Land Rover I realized my first impression had been right: the Land Rover was the old open-topped long-range variant that had been the workhorse of the SAS Mobility Squadron for years.

I found two of the four-man team in the Den with Nigel Cuthbert. Both looked to be in their mid-thirties, both had moustaches and were unshaven and looked generally in need a bath and a fresh set of DPMs.

'Ah, Jeff,' Cuthbert said, 'these guys are from Hereford Signals. Just brought the radios Dave McVicar promised. Chas and Tiny.'

Chas was medium height with penetrating dark button eyes and Tiny was anything but, built like a rugby player with reddish ginger hair. They shook hands and were friendly, but decidedly reserved. There was no doubt they'd been briefed I was ex-Hereford myself, but it didn't seem to cut much ice. Obviously things had changed since my day.

Chas said, 'This is complicated kit. You'll need us to show your clients how it works.'

'Fine,' I said. 'It'll probably take a few days before we can get to meet all the various militia leaders.'

'We're in no hurry,' Tiny drawled. 'Major Tring's kindly found us somewhere to crash.'

Cuthbert looked slightly embarrassed. 'Up in the roof, in the rafters. Bloody freezing.'

'It's dry,' Chas said flatly.

I said, 'I think we ought to try getting this stuff out to the local Muslim commander, Major Zlatko Herenda, first. I think that's where we need to mend fences most.'

'And the Muslims' Ramoza Brigade,' Tiny added. 'Wherever those bastards go, there's trouble. We've been ordered to make them number-one priority.'

Cuthbert said, 'Trouble is, we're not in contact with the Ramoza Brigade. We've tried through Herenda and through Bosnian Army HQ in Sarajevo, but no one wants us talking directly to them. And, of course, we can't force the Muslims to co-operate.' He shrugged. 'Sorry, there's just no route through to the Ramoza Brigade as yet.'

I looked sideways at him; he certainly looked a picture of innocence.

He wasn't going to like this. I said, 'I think we should have a word with Ivana.'

'What?' Cuthbert glared at me. 'Why?'

'Who's Ivana?' Chas asked.

'Nigel's interpreter,' I replied. 'I believe she's got connections with the Ramoza Brigade.'

'Look, I don't know who's been saying what—' Cuthbert began, but I cut him short.

'Think it's best I handle this, Nigel. You just wait here while I have a word.'

I left the Den and went in search of Ivana. I found her in the rest-room that was the sort of mess for civilian personnel. She was on her own, drinking a coffee and reading an out-of-date *Cosmopolitan* magazine.

She was surprised to see me. 'What is it, Jeff?'

'We need your help on an important matter. But it's a tricky one.'

'Tricky?'

'Tricky for you, perhaps.'

Concern clouded her eyes. 'Yes?'

'I understand you've got connections with the Ramoza Brigade. In particular General Almir Aganovic?'

Her mouth dropped. 'Has Nigel—?'

'No, he's said nothing. I've heard this from a different source. And I promise you, Ivana, it is not a problem. But it means you'll have to trust me – well, us. We need to get a message to Almir Aganovic. We're giving brand-new communications equipment to the leaders of all the main opposing fighting units. So they can communicate more effectively with each other, their own forces and us.'

'Why should you want to do that?'

I said, 'Our thinking is that better communications make for better understanding – and faster. Easier to negotiate cease-fires for the humanitarian work and prevent mistakes and misunderstandings. You know yourself what a nightmare it can be getting all parties to speak to each other, let alone agree on anything.'

She looked less worried now. 'And you just want me to tell Almir Aganovic that?'

'I understands he trusts you on a personal level.'

'I suppose so, yes.'

'Then I'd like you to escort us to him.'

'Just you?'

'Me and Nigel, and four guys from Signals. Technicians who understand the equipment.' I gave her a few moments to think. 'Will you do it?'

Still she wasn't that keen and her agreement, when it came, was reluctant. 'Very well, if there is no other way. I will need to speak to Major Herenda. He has a direct link with Almir Aganovic and the Ramoza Brigade.'

'And where is Almir Aganovic based, Ivana, do you know that?'

She shook her head. 'Almir is never in the same place for long, always moves around. But I think usually near where his troops might be in action.' I think then she thought she may have sounded as though she knew too much. 'At least, that's what I've heard.'

I said, 'Then let's try and make contact with Major Herenda now and get the ball rolling. Wait here and I'll call when I've got some news.'

I walked briskly back to the Den and gave Nigel Cuthbert and the SAS boys an update. Finally, I said, 'See if you can raise Herenda and arrange a meet, Nigel. This afternoon, if possible. If Ivana tells Almir this is legit, then I think there's a good chance Herenda will play ball and put us in touch with the Ramoza Brigade direct.'

Although clearly not overjoyed, Cuthbert seemed to be getting used to the idea. While he got on his personal radio, the SAS guys disappeared up into their loft billet to talk things over with the other two men in their team.

Meanwhile I had something else on my mind. I sat at my desk and opened the file on Mayor Ivan Jozic. Of Croatian descent, he was aged sixty-two and married to his childhood sweetheart. Not surprisingly he was a former Communist Party apparatchik, seemingly having spent most of his working life in the financial administration of the Party, treasurer of this, that and the other. It didn't surprise me that he'd managed to spawn quite a local property and business empire over the years.

I searched down his list of companies. I didn't know exactly what I was looking for . . . Medi-Mental . . . apparently he'd owned the mental hospital in Una Drina for the past six months and received a UN grant to continue the inmates' care and social well-being . . . Mmmm, not very likely, I thought . . . Una Drina Agri-Bank, quite long established, a private bank specializing in loans to peasant farmers . . . BiH Distribution and Logistics, a warehouse facility that was rented by the UN for storing aid . . . then a share in the ownership of the Hotel Splendid . . . My pencil hovered and then went back . . .

BiH Distribution and Logistics . . . I looked at the address. It was on the same road as the mental hospital, down by the river. I swivelled my chair round and went to the radio, calling up Rocky Rogers who was on his way inland from the coast.

After seven tedious minutes of retuning and trying to beat the atmospherics, I finally got through. 'Rocky, where do you warehouse aid material here?'

'Una Drina? Firm run by the mayor. He's got a couple of modern prefab units on the outskirts. We pay a retainer to use them.'

'What about the mental hospital?'

'Eh? Oh, yeah, sort of overspill. There are a couple of old sheds in the hospital grounds. We've only used them a couple of times in emergencies. On the damp side, so no good for perishables, medicines.'

'Thanks, Rocky.'

'By the way, Jimbo, we've had all sorts of bad shit on the road today. Lost a truck and nearly a driver on the ice. Plus mechanical failures. I think we'll have to stop over in Una Drina. Free for a pint?'

'You bet,' I said, and signed off.

Cuthbert had just finished on his own radio. 'Looks like our luck's changed, Jimbo. Just spoke to Herenda's number two and gave him the gist. He sounded interested in the telecomms equipment and said the major should be back in base around four – if we want to be there.'

'Did you mention Ramoza?' I asked.

'No, didn't want to spoil a winning run. We can broach that subject when we're there with Ivana.'

'Good thinking,' I agreed. 'That gives us an hour, say, before we have to leave.'

I left the Den and went to find Gordy Cromwell in the Ops Room.

He looked up as I entered. 'You look like the cat that got the cream, Jimbo. Why're you looking so happy?'

'Haven't got the cream yet,' I replied. 'But I might do if you can lend me a couple of Warriors for a policing mission.'

Gordy was puzzled. 'Policing mission?'

'Locating some looted goods,' I replied. 'Namely, desks from the school.'

'Really?' He looked pleased. 'Well done, Jimbo. Where are they?'

I said, 'Well, if my hunch is right, they're sitting in a warehouse owned by Mayor Jozic – waiting for the UN or some charity to buy them off him.'

'Ouch! That could be a tricky one, Jimbo.' He shook his head, not at all happy. 'I know Jozic's one tricky bastard, but he's an important cog here in Una Drina. Major Tring won't want to be upsetting him unnecessarily.'

'Well, I think it *is* necessary if we're to get the school up and running, don't you?'

A smile finally broke onto Gordy's face. 'You're doing it again, aren't you? One of these days . . .'

I waved his warning aside. 'Yeah, yeah. But listen, Gordy, Jozic can't complain. He *acknowledges* the desks were looted, they're probably sitting in *his* warehouse, and he actually gave me the go-ahead to try and find them.' I tried not to look too smug. 'I reckon that's pretty much game, set and match to us.'

Gordy rose to his feet and picked his blue beret off his desk. 'OK, but I'll come with you. Need a breather, anyway.'

I grinned at him. 'I don't think you trust me.'

He slapped me on the shoulder. 'You *know* I don't trust you, Jimbo,' he said, laughing.

Ten minutes later, I was driving my Land Rover with Gordy in the passenger seat and two Warriors and two Bedford trucks hot on our tail as we headed north up the main drag, then took a right-hand turn into a long unmade road which worked its way gently down the valley side to the riverbank and the location of the mental hospital.

It was a sadly neglected nineteenth-century building with a huge portico and cracked and crumbled rendering, surrounded by ornate wrought-iron railings. I stopped the Land Rover and climbed out. There was no sign of either staff or inmates. I pushed the bell button set in one of the gate pillars. A few moments later a dumpy woman with black hair and wearing a white tunic appeared on the steps of the house, accompanied by a scruffy, gangling individual who wore the typical half-uniform of the Croat militia. He had a sub-machine gun slung carelessly over his shoulder . . . A bit extreme for handling the patients in his care, I thought.

The woman looked fierce and hostile as she approached the gate and saw that we were UNPROFOR troops.

'Yes, what do you want?' she demanded in Serbo-Croat. 'I don't think you are here to visit a relative. This is private property.'

I gave her a winning smile, not always my best point. 'In fact, this is Mayor Jozic's property, is it not? He's asked us to collect some items from the warehouse. Some furniture for the school.'

She looked relieved at that, and almost smiled. Clearly this wasn't hospital business, so if there were any problems, they wouldn't be hers. She jerked her thumb at the man beside her. 'Then you will have to speak to him,' she said.

It was his turn to look suspicious. 'No one said you were coming. Do you have a letter of authority?'

I shook my head. 'No, Ivan said just to turn up. That there wouldn't be a problem. He needs the space.'

'How do I know you're telling the truth?' he asked, trying to play it cool.

I called his bluff. 'How else would I know there are twenty-odd desks in the warehouse here if Mayor Jozic hadn't told me?'

He looked surprised at that. 'So he gave you the key? He has the only key.'

'Yes,' I lied.

'Then I'll open the gates,' he said grudgingly.

They swung open and we drove in, down the gravel track, but where it swung round in front of the entrance portico, we turned off on the track that ran alongside the house. Some fifty metres beyond it we found a large timber shed that looked in imminent danger of collapse.

As we pulled up, a couple of our troopers leapt out of the rear door of the first Warrior and ran to the doors with a pair of heavy-duty bolt cutters. Before the Croat guard could catch up with us and see what we were doing, they'd snapped through the securing chains and began to swing the huge doors open.

Major Jozic had certainly accumulated an Aladdin's cave of goodies here. Indeed, there were the stacks of quaint old-fashioned school desks, each with a flip-up seat attached, pallets of shrink-wrapped tinned foods and other assorted items I knew had come through on UNHCR convoys over the months. Probably all part of the tariff charged at Croat roadblocks and all held here ready for when there was a shortage and the goods would fetch a high price from humanitarian organizations or wealthy individuals.

Gordy gave a low whistle. 'I think we should liberate the fucking lot, Jimbo.'

I grinned at him; this was more like it. 'And Major Tring?'

He knew what I meant. 'If Tring doesn't like it, he can give all the stuff back to Mayor Jozic, can't he? And explain to his UNPROFOR masters why he did it.'

I glanced at my watch. 'Mind if I leave you to it? I think this lot's going to take a few ferry loads and I've got an appointment.'

Gordy Cromwell looked the happiest I'd seen him since I'd been there. 'No problem, Jimbo, leave it to me. You cut along.'

Feeling just a little pleased with myself, I took my Land Rover and headed back to company HQ. There I found Nigel

Cuthbert, Ivana and the four SAS guys ready and waiting. Ivana climbed into the passenger seat next to me and Cuthbert clambered in the back. Two of the SAS soldiers drove their Bedford truck and the other two their long-range vehicle. If we hit trouble, that thing was armed like a battleship with at least three heavy and medium machine guns – and God knows what other lethal goodies they had in the back.

I led our little three-vehicle column back up north, passing Gordy Cromwell's first truck of liberated goods coming the other way. Just a short distance past the turn-off to the school, a new Croat checkpoint had sprung up. There were militiamen all around. Unusually they weren't standing idly by, but actually working hard, digging trenches in roadside gardens and building sandbag emplacements.

'Something's brewing,' Cuthbert said. 'Looks like they're expecting trouble.'

I scratched my chin. 'Or about to start some themselves.'

I didn't know the militiaman who waved us down, but Cuthbert did. Their exchange of greetings was cordial. 'I don't advise you to go through,' the man said through Ivana's interpretation.

'What's happening?' Cuthbert asked. 'You expecting an attack?'

The man gave a sly smile. 'Something like that. Can't say, though – I'm sure you understand.'

'Thanks for the advice,' Cuthbert replied. 'But we're on urgent UNPROFOR business.'

I think the Croat might have argued, but I noticed that behind us one of the SAS guys had left the Bedford to man the second heavy machine gun in their Land Rover. If the two of them opened up, they'd have decimated the Croat militia in seconds.

The militiaman seemed to be watching them and weighing things in his mind. Finally, he waved us through. 'Go on then, but at your own risk.'

Wasn't it always, I thought.

As we passed through I had a better view of the side-streets; they were packed with armed Croat fighters, smoking and looking expectant, nervous, hanging around the half-dozen ancient armoured cars and various heavy weapons mounted in the back of converted civilian pickups.

Barely three hundred metres up the road we were stopped again, this time by the town's Muslim militia, who were in control of most of the open countryside between here and Sarajevo. Of course, they were the official Bosnian Army, but in truth were no smarter, better led or better equipped than any of the other warring factions.

A youth with a Kalashnikov waved us down. He was looking suspiciously back down the road at the Croat checkpoint as he spoke to me. 'Where are you going?' he asked, as though he wasn't really interested in my reply.

'We've an urgent appointment with Major Herenda,' I said. 'Captain Hawkins and Nigel Cuthbert. He's expecting us.'

He took a scrap of paper from his top pocket, looked at the names on his list and then nodded. He didn't smile, but took a step back and pointed to a track to my left that ran up into the hillside before vanishing into the forest.

'Take that road,' he said. 'After about three kilometres there is a farm. That is Major Herenda's headquarters.'

'I know, lad,' Cuthbert replied testily. 'I've been there many times before.'

The young militiaman regarded him sullenly for a moment, then just turned his back and walked away. I shoved the gear lever into first and took off up the unmade road, bouncing over the potholes and ruts, the tyres struggling to grip up the steep incline. After passing through a couple of kilometres of pine forest we burst out of the trees into a shallow mountain pass with undulating meadowland on either side.

The farm as such was not much more than a smallholding. There was a dilapidated chalet-style farmhouse, half a dozen timber corrals and a handful of tumbledown barns and sheds. However, the entire area had been turned into a military camp. There were lines and lines of khaki-coloured army tents – probably old Yugoslav Army issue – and rows of trucks and minibuses used for transport, half a dozen Soviet T34 tanks and a couple of APCs, which had probably been liberated from the Serbs in recent fighting. I noticed two flags flying outside the farmhouse, the new crest of Bosnia-Herzegovina and the plain black flag of the fundamentalist Ramoza Brigade.

When we pulled up in the farmyard, I saw that Major Zlatko Herenda, as smartly turned out as ever, was standing on the verandah of the building talking to a couple of his officers. He left them and trotted down the steps, and threw a quick, snappy salute.

I guess that was an improvement over our previous encounters, but he still didn't smile and those dark eyes still burned with a deep, inner anger.

Quickly I explained why we were there, and what we had to offer. Instead of looking pleased, he looked suspicious. Several times I repeated that the radio equipment wasn't just being given by the altruistic generosity of the British government and the UN, but was necessary to improve communications between us and all opposing militias so that we could get our humanitarian work done.

He didn't seem to be falling for it, until he went to the Bedford truck and saw exactly what the SAS lads had with them. When they explained, interpreting through Ivana what the equipment could do, he began to take a more serious interest. He called over a couple of men who appeared to be his signals officers and let them get on with unpacking and setting up the gear.

'There's one more thing,' I said, and indicated Ivana, who had returned to my Land Rover. 'We want to take some of this equipment to General Almir Aganovic of the Ramoza Brigade. Unfortunately we have no way of speaking to him. And, to be frank, your Ministry of Defence in Sarajevo is being ultra secretive and cautious about anything to do with the Brigade . . .'

For the first time there was a glimmer of a sardonic smile around his lips. 'That, Captain Hawkins, is because they'd rather deny they exist. Our leaders are fools. They don't really want fundamental Muslim foreigners coming here – but they need them. They are the ones who will save our country, because they know how to fight and are not afraid to die.'

At last we seemed to be getting somewhere. I tried to sound sympathetic. 'Spoken like a true military man,' I said, then added, 'I think you know Ivana; she knows all about our objectives with this radio equipment. I believe Almir Aganovic trusts her. If you would be kind enough to arrange for us to speak to him by telephone or radio, I think we might accomplish our mission . . . After all, the bosses in Sarajevo aren't the ones doing the fighting and dying.'

This time the smile broke through like a burst of sunshine, and it transformed the sullen visage into a really handsome, strong and dark-featured face. 'There is no need for that. General Aganovic is actually here in this camp. His troops moved in earlier today.'

I must have looked surprised. He said, 'You are aware that the Croats of Una Drina are accusing us of a massacre in Stavac? It is not true. It was committed by the Serbs before we drove them out.'

'But it suits the Croats to blame you?' Cuthbert interrupted.

Herenda's smile had already vanished. 'I think so. They don't like the fact we're holding the ground we retook from the Serbs. They want an excuse to break their alliance with us. Now they have it. I expect them to try and drive us out of Una Drina completely.'

'So that's why the Ramoza Brigade is here?' I guessed.

He cocked his head to one side in a rather arrogant, sneering sort of way. 'To give them a nasty surprise.' The smile was hovering again. 'And a bloody nose!'

I had no doubt at all it would give Colonel Markovic and Mayor Jozic a nasty surprise to find their Croat militia suddenly face-to-face with the crack Ramoza troops. And the bloody nose was equally likely. But then Markovic had also been reinforcing his lines in recent days and one could only guess at their calibre.

The portents weren't good for Una Drina – the United Nations and UNPROFOR would much prefer an uneasy truce between the two sides than an outbreak of vicious fighting on its streets astride the main convoy route. But the fact that Herenda had revealed his plan to me meant that it had to be so far advanced as to be unstoppable.

As I was turning the significance of all this over in my mind, the major said, 'I will personally take you to General Aganovic, if you'd like to follow me.'

Chas and Tiny left their two SAS oppos talking with Herenda's signals officers and joined us in my Land Rover. The Muslim major hitched a macho ride on the outside, clinging casually and one-handed to my door, with one smartly polished boot in the external footrest, as he directed me along the line of tents.

Suddenly an ostentatious, gleaming silver Cherokee Jeep caught my eye. Its obvious newness and unsuitability for warfare must have attracted my attention, rather than the two men in battle fatigues who were loading luggage into the open rear door – the South African giant and the mean-faced Dane. Our chief suspects for the assassination of Serb commander Goran Zoric.

I said casually to Herenda, 'Those two still working for you?'

He gave a little smirk. 'Not any more.'

'No good?' I asked innocently.

'Too expensive.'

'I met them at the Splendid. Didn't catch their full names . . .'

Herenda wasn't playing ball. 'If you don't know them, don't expect me to tell you, Captain Hawkins.'

Chas leaned over from the back. He didn't miss a trick; he

must have recognized them from the briefing pictures at BFHQ. 'Pieter Visagie is the South African. The Dane's called Thor Larsen.'

The two men noticed our Land Rover's distinctive UNPROFOR insignia and scowled in our direction as we passed by. They didn't look pleased to see us and, judging by the expressions on their faces, they'd decided it was time they were no longer there. When I glanced in the door mirror a few moments later, they and their swanky Cherokee had vanished.

Herenda tapped my shoulder and pointed to a khaki tent to our right which was larger and set apart from the others. A couple of tall and mean-looking Afghans were guarding the entrance flap and held their Kalashnikovs at the ready. The smouldering look in their eyes gave me the impression they couldn't wait for an excuse to fire them.

When I came to a halt outside the tent, Herenda said, 'The rest of you stay here. Ivana, come with me.'

He made no attempt to assist the woman out of the Land Rover, instead he just waited impatiently as she checked that her headscarf was properly covering her hair and drew it across the lower half of her face. She then followed as the guards stepped back to allow Herenda in to Almir Aganovic's tent.

I decided to light one of my miniature cigars as long minutes of waiting started to pass. I had almost finished it when Herenda finally emerged from the tent flaps and approached us. 'Just you, Captain Hawkins,' he ordered. 'And Captain Cuthbert.'

The two SAS guys in the back shrugged in resignation, but my guess was they felt a bit put out. I climbed out, straightened my combat fatigues and blue beret and waited for Cuthbert to join me before following Herenda back into the tent.

After the daylight it was dim under the heavy canvas, the area lit by a single hurricane lamp hanging from the centre of the ridge pole. It illuminated a large trestle table on which an almost equally large sheet of white art card had been placed. The card was covered in a complex pattern of hundreds of tiny balsa-wood pieces that had been glued in position. This odd mosaic was dotted with Arabic characters written in black ink.

Although puzzled over what the hell it was, I was more interested about the man who sat behind the desk. Even this close, General Almir Aganovic remained as enigmatic as ever, the upturned Arab *shamag* he wore in the style of Yasser Arafat casting a shadow across his face.

Ivana stood behind his chair and made the introductions.

At this point Aganovic finally rose to greet us, and just kept on rising. He was a very tall, broad-shouldered man, probably six feet five or more, and immaculately turned out in freshly laundered DPMs emblazoned with the Ramoza Brigade shoulder patch.

His swarthy face sported a wispy moustache and goatee beard. I judged him to be in his late thirties. There was a rather strange, distant look in his dark eyes and I got the distinct feeling he was looking right through me to somewhere far away as he said in a very quiet voice, 'Gentlemen, I have heard a lot about you both.' His English diction was perfect.

He offered his hand, not specifically to me or Nigel Cuthbert, who was standing alongside me, but somewhere in between us. Cuthbert was better placed to grasp it first.

'Pleased to meet you, sir,' Cuthbert said, introducing himself. 'I'm a UKLO, reporting direct to Commander, British Forces. We have also heard much about you. In fact, we have been very eager to make contact with you.'

Aganovic's smile was gentle and seemed genuine, but I noticed that the expression in his eyes didn't really change. 'Our Bosnian government likes to keep us out of the limelight . . . they are a little embarrassed about us because we uphold fundamental Islamic ideals, whereas they do not. Nevertheless, I have no problem with keeping out of the public eye. That helps the Brigade maintain a high level of secrecy about its movements and intentions. It enhances our reputation and helps to put fear in the hearts of our enemies.'

Cuthbert stepped aside, allowing me to shake the man's hand. 'I'm Captain Hawkins, the local liaison officer with the Royal Wessex.'

'Ah, yes,' Aganovic said. 'Here for so short a time, but becoming a legend already.'

I wasn't sure if that was sarcasm; I wanted to think it wasn't. 'I don't know about that, General, but I do know that lack of communication with you can make life very difficult for the UN peacekeepers and aid workers.'

Almir resumed his seat, Ivana still standing demurely behind him, and indicated that Cuthbert and I take the two fold-up canvas chairs in front of his desk. 'I realize that, Captain, but I am here to fight, not to keep ordering cease-fires because you gentlemen want us to. I'd prefer *not* to be on the receiving end of your persuasive charms.'

I said quickly, 'Those cease-fires are to allow your fellow countrymen, women and children to survive this terrible war. Without the food and medical aid you will have no people left in the country you are fighting for.'

Aganovic regarded me fiercely, yet his anger didn't show in those impassive eyes. 'And without the presence of our Brigade, my people will have no *country* in which to live, Captain! The UN sits on the fence and thinks everything can be resolved by drinking coffee around a table in New York – when out there Muslims are being driven from their homes, their towns and villages by Serbs or Croats – and you do nothing to stop them!'

I noticed Ivana place a restraining hand on his left shoulder, as though urging him to stay calm.

I'd been here before with all the opposing warlords. All were keen to blame the United Nations for their troubles, and not one seemed to even consider that they themselves might be in some way responsible for the unholy mess they were in. I decided to save my breath to cool my porridge and went straight to the point. 'Ivana will have told you why we are here, General. Whilst I appreciate you are first and foremost a military man, you are clearly also a good Muslim and follow the teachings of the Koran in your responsibilities to your fellow human beings.'

Almir Aganovic blinked at me. To be honest, I didn't have a bloody clue what the Koran said. But if it didn't preach the qualities of kindness and tolerance and respect for human life somewhere within its pages, then Islam would have the only holy book in the world that didn't.

I pushed on quickly, 'It is vital to save innocent human life – not only Bosnians but UN aid workers and troops – that we are able to have better and direct communications with all sides in this conflict. In fact, Her Majesty's Government in London considers this so important that it is making a rare and charitable gift . . .' I paused and smiled at this point to let Aganovic appreciate my subtle wit, but it seemed to pass over his head. 'They have donated some state-of-the-art communications equipment to all parties. For the British UNPROFOR troops to have improved contact with all sides and for all sides to have better control over all their elements on the ground.'

Cuthbert added, 'So if a cease-fire *is* agreed at any time, everyone in the field is more likely to be aware. There have been some terrible mistakes and accidents.'

Aganovic looked at Cuthbert with thinly veiled contempt. 'And, no doubt, I will have you on the radio every five minutes begging and pleading to stop fighting.'

I said, 'I'm sure you'll find a way of coping with that.' The Ramoza leader allowed himself a discreet Mona Lisa smile. We both knew his minions would just act like good secretaries to any company boss; he'd always be conveniently out of the office whenever it suited him. 'The important thing is that we'll at least know that you've got the messages we send – and vice versa.'

Aganovic lay back in his chair and interlaced his fingers across his chest. 'I have discussed the matter briefly with Major Herenda . . .' He inclined his head in the local Muslim commander's direction. 'And I have decided also to accept your government's generous offer.'

I tried not to look too triumphant. 'They will be pleased to hear that.'

He looked up at some point between Cuthbert and me, his dark eyes again seeming strangely unfocused. 'But I shall warn you now, no persuasion from either of you two gentlemen will distract me from winning this war. And I have it on good authority that the Croats are about to break their alliance with our Bosnian government.'

'That's been rumoured for months,' I replied dismissively. I thought I almost sounded convincing. 'It's never come to anything.'

His voice was a whisper, so I had to strain to catch his words. 'Now they have the excuse they want in the Stavac massacre. Markovic will use that excuse to push the Muslims out of Una Drina once and for all. That is a battle we cannot afford to lose.'

Nigel Cuthbert leaned forward earnestly. 'I suggest that you do not strike pre-emptively, General.' Cuthbert had obviously arrived at the same conclusions as me about what all the troop movements were about, here and with the Croat forces in the north of town. 'It will reflect badly on the Bosnian government and lose you world support.'

Aganovic raised an eyebrow. 'You think I care about world support or otherwise? Politicians blow and bend with the wind whichever way it suits them. If there is to be a battle for Una Drina then we *have* to win it. The Bosnian government has to prevail.'

To be honest, I knew he was completely right. In his position I'd have had the same attitude. 'The UN will ensure that it does anyway,' I said, aware how hollow my words sounded.

Almir Aganovic stared straight ahead. 'Our alliance with the Croats is over, Captain, and they have ended it. That means that our allies are now our enemies. And our new enemies straddle the convoy and supply route to our capital, Sarajevo. Most critically here at Una Drina and at Donji Vrbas. We have no option but to take control of those two Croat enclaves — whatever the cost.' His words chilled me. 'You understand we have to do this. And if you really care for the safety of innocent people, you will keep your UNPROFOR soldiers and your bleeding-heart convoys off the road until Allah's work is done.'

I said quickly, 'I will speak to Colonel Markovic and Mayor Jozic.'

'They will not listen.' Without looking directly at it, he reached out both hands to the strange balsa mosaic in front of him and ran his fingers along some of the pieces at one end. 'This is where Markovic's Croats are amassing ready to assault Major Herenda's Muslim positions.'

It came as a shock to realize suddenly that Almir Aganovic was blind.

The odd mosaic was a sort of map in Braille of Una Drina. Now I examined the pattern more closely, I could identify the main drag, all the side-roads and wood cuttings representing important buildings. And I could hardly deny that the Croats were gathered where Aganovic's finger pointed, because I had seen them myself when we'd left the town earlier.

The general turned his head towards me and his eyes stared straight through me. This time I could see that, although they were dark, the irises lacked the intricate marble patterns and vivid colour you normally expect to find — instead his eyes were slightly opaque and milky. I was distracted so much that I almost missed his words. 'I anticipate that the Croats will attack at dawn.'

I gave a thin smile. 'Then I must see whether we can't persuade them to reconsider.'

That enigmatic smile had returned. 'You must do whatever you must do, Captain.' He rose to his feet. 'Thank you for your equipment and please relay our thanks to the appropriate authorities in England. But you will appreciate that time is short and I have much to do with Major Herenda.'

I explained that we had two signals experts outside who

would stay and brief his own specialists on the new kit, then we shook hands. He gave Ivana a chaste kiss on her cheek and we all started moving towards the tent flap.

'Oh, Captain Hawkins,' Almir Aganovic called after me. 'May I have just a brief word with you in private?'

I hesitated, waiting for Cuthbert and Ivana to leave the tent with Herenda, then turned back to the commander of the Ramoza Brigade.

'What is it?' I asked.

Aganovic shifted awkwardly in his seat. 'You have not known Captain Cuthbert very long?'

'I haven't been here very long and I hadn't met him before.'

'And Ivana, she has worked as an interpreter for the British since the beginning, when the Cheshires were here. Did you know that?'

I wondered where this was going. 'I was told.'

'By Nigel Cuthbert?'

I nodded, then remembered Aganovic couldn't see the gesture. 'Yes,' I said. 'You haven't met Mr Cuthbert before, have you?'

He pursed his lips in a silent no. 'But I know all about him from Ivana. It is my job to know . . . And did he tell you that I am engaged to be married to her, since before all this began?'

Now this was getting tricky. Cuthbert hadn't told me, hadn't even told me Ivana was connected with the leader of the Ramoza Brigade. That had been Rocky. 'Nigel keeps himself to himself,' I hedged. 'He's not one to gossip.'

From outside the tent came a rumble of engines as the blind eyes blazed in an unnerving blank fury. 'I hope you are right, Captain. There are always rumours in times like these. I ignore them because I believe them to be untrue. I am happy for Ivana to keep on working for you. She, too, does not gossip. Even to me about what UNPROFOR is doing. We keep business and pleasure quite separate in our lives.'

I must admit that had concerned me a little. I wondered how

careless Cuthbert might have become during the height of passion. 'That's comforting,' I said.

Aganovic's anger showed plainly in his face. 'But if I find any of these rumours to be true, that I have been betrayed, I will not forgive and there will be a terrible price to be paid.'

I had to act the innocent. 'What rumours are these?'

'Nasty, unpleasant rumours. If you don't know them, then I shall not repeat them.' He hesitated. 'But if you do and you know that there is any truth in them – any at all – well, let us just say you have now had fair warning.'

I agreed politely; what else could I do? Then I reached out my hand to him, once again forgetting his blindness, but before I could withdraw it he had sensed the movement and grasped it unerringly. 'Until we meet again,' I said, somewhat unnerved, and left.

Although it was dull and cloudy outside, the relative brightness of the daylight hurt my eyes. I scanned along the lines of tents in the huge camp, all neat and tidy and empty. Until that moment I don't think I'd realized how quiet and deserted it had suddenly become. I could see that the vehicle park we'd passed earlier with its pickup trucks, minibuses and old T34 tanks was empty. The camp had become a ghost town. So where were all Herenda's Muslim militia and the crack troops of Aganovic's Ramoza Brigade? Suddenly I was sure I knew the answer.

The temperature had dropped markedly since our arrival here and I shivered. But I wasn't sure if that was due to the cold wind, or to something else altogether.

Eight

Cuthbert and Ivana were waiting in my Land Rover and the two SAS signallers were talking to Herenda and a couple of Aganovic's officers. I strode briskly across to their Bedford truck and interrupted Chas, who was giving instructions about one of the new fancy radios. 'We're leaving for town now,' I told him. 'I suggest you do the same just as soon as you can.'

He was in good humour. 'That's OK, Jeff, we're not afraid of the dark.'

But I was in no mood for his well-meant sarcasm. 'Well, you might be tonight.'

Turning on my heel, I returned to my Land Rover and climbed into the driver's seat.

'How long has Aganovic been blind?' I asked, firing up the engine. 'Since birth?'

'No, just two years.' Ivana voice was low. 'Eighteen months after he proposed marriage to me.'

'Blast burn from an exploding artillery shell,' Cuthbert added absently, staring out of the window as we drove back down the line of tents towards the road. 'Not another mark on him. Just singed all his hair and a few superficial burns from where his clothes caught fire. All the shrapnel missed him. His lucky day.'

I wasn't so sure.

Ivana said, 'He was a civilian, a school teacher in Sarajevo. The Serbs opened up with their guns in the surrounding hills. His school was hit, dozens of children killed and maimed.'

'Not a soldier, then?' I asked, rather surprised.

'No, just a teacher. English and art. He was a fine artist and was planning his first exhibition. Mostly landscapes.'

I almost wished I hadn't asked. 'So where did he learn to fight so effectively?'

'I don't know exactly,' Ivana replied. 'He was sent to Saudi Arabia for medical treatment. Then went to Iran and Afghanistan. So there, I suppose. He was always interested in military history, great generals through the ages.'

As we left the camp precincts and headed back down the main track to Una Drina, Cuthbert asked, 'Why did he call you back just then?'

'I'll give you one guess, Nigel,' I replied testily. 'To ask me about the rumours. You and Ivana.'

I saw her silent gasp in my rear-view mirror. She was clearly horrified at what Aganovic might have heard.

Sparing a withering sideways glance at Cuthbert, I said, 'How the hell did you think you'd get away with it, Nigel? Are you really such a fucking idiot? A UK liaison officer and the fiancée of a local warlord – talk about playing with fire.'

'Aganovic wasn't involved when Ivana and I first . . . well . . .' he began defensively '. . . first got close. He was away abroad and she didn't know when – or if – he was ever coming back.'

'Well, he's back now,' I retorted, 'and Ivana is still his fiancée.'

'You're in no fucking position to judge me, Jimbo!' he shouted at me, really riled. 'You don't know the half of it!'

'Well, I can tell you, Nigel, Aganovic *does* seem to know the half of it! And he's just fired a warning shot across your bows. Whatever's going on between you and Ivana, I suggest you stop it *now*! Because if you don't stop it, I think Aganovic very probably will. And it might not be very pleasant!'

But Cuthbert wasn't in the mood to be cowed. 'When I want your advice on how to conduct my life, I'll ask for it! Meanwhile, please keep your nose out.'

Ivana reached over from the back seat and placed a restraining hand on his shoulder. 'Please, Nigel, don't fight over this. Captain

Hawkins has a point. We always knew one day it might come to this. I had no idea Almir knew about us, nothing was ever said.'

We rounded a blind bend in the forest heading down into the Drina valley when I had to hit the brakes. Tanks and armoured cars were lined up under the trees on our right, but still taking up most of the width of the track. I slowed right down and squeezed past. The crew members were sitting outside on the turrets, smoking and playing cards.

Cuthbert turned his head. 'What the hell's going on? That's the stuff that was back at the camp earlier when we arrived.'

I said, 'It's going to be the Muslims' armoured punch against the Croats. You heard Aganovic say he expects an assault at dawn tomorrow.'

'And they'll use that stuff in their counter-attack,' Cuthbert thought aloud. 'Markovic won't like that.'

I shook my head. 'What makes you think it'll be a counter-attack?'

'What d'you mean?'

'What I've seen of Aganovic, I don't think he's one to wait around. He likes to take the initiative.'

'Oh, shit! A pre-emptive attack . . .'

I said, 'I understand that's how the Ramoza Brigade's acted so far in this war. And they've opted for night-fighting on more than one occasion.'

Cuthbert turned back to Ivana. 'Did Aganovic say anything about that to you?'

She shook her head. 'No, but he also knew I wouldn't approve. It's bad enough having to fight in defence, but to actually start the fighting . . .'

We reached the main road and were waved through the Muslim checkpoint on our way back to the town.

The Croats were more cautious at their roadblock and made a thorough inspection of the Land Rover – even though it was clearly a British UNPROFOR vehicle – before allowing us to enter the main street. The side-roads were still packed with militia; it seemed there were a lot of fires and cooking stoves going and the atmosphere was quite relaxed.

My instant reading of the situation was that Almir Aganovic was right. The Croats wouldn't be attacking until the morning. And if they thought they were going to have a quiet night before the storm, they were going to be in for one hell of a surprise.

I swung right at the tyre shop. 'I promised to drop in at the school to see how the TV shoot is going.'

'Fuck media relations, Jimbo,' Cuthbert snarled. 'If the shit's going to hit the fan, we need to be back at HQ pronto.'

'And I need to warn Mrs Furtula that they could be caught in the firing line,' I snapped back. 'Those kids have been through enough.'

I ignored his protests and roared up the unmade side-street for several hundred metres before pulling up outside the school.

Killing the engine and extracting the key, I said, 'I'll only be a few minutes. Why don't you get on the radio to Gordy and tell him what we're expecting to happen? See if he can't set up an urgent meet with Markovic – if we can persuade him to stand his men down, then maybe we can get the Ramoza Brigade to hold off.'

Cuthbert shook his head. 'Flying bushpigs, Jimbo! Markovic is determined to run with this. After the stance he's taken on the Stavac massacre, he'd lose too much face.'

'It's worth a try,' I persisted. Why the hell did everyone give up so bloody easily?

Cuthbert shrugged. 'You're a determined bugger, Jimbo, I'll say that for you.'

I left him to it and strode through the gate in the low railings and across the tarmac playground to the single-storey brick building. It was a utilitarian and unimaginative Tito-era design from the sixties, rectangular with a flat roof. Only a typically Communist embossing of the people's struggle in a concrete panel above the double entrance doors indicated any artistic architectural input whatsoever.

The entrance lobby with its obligatory noticeboards on the

walls was floored with plain linoleum in a faded marble pattern which had been worn away by thousands of little feet over the decades. There was a head's office and a staff room to the left; ahead and to the right were the two classrooms. The door to one was ajar and I peered in.

What I saw brought a lump to my throat. Stupid, really, because what I saw was just normality. But then normality was something that was pretty abnormal in Bosnia. A clean classroom, freshly painted, and windows with glass in them, a ceiling without holes in it . . . and desks. Three neat little rows of desks facing the two large blackboards on the wall.

There were around twenty children, boys and girls, ranging in age from about six to sixteen. They weren't sitting formally but were gathered in two groups, perched on the desktops or seats in any way that allowed them to get close to their two teachers. The older kids seemed to be in hushed conversation with Anita Furtula, the youngsters with . . . then I realized that the second 'teacher' was Tali van Wyk.

She was sitting on a desk with her feet on its flip-down seat, smiling and talking softly, moving her hands around elegantly to illustrate some point or other. Whatever she was saying had her young audience absolutely enthralled: wide headlamp eyes fixed on her, enthralled by every word and gesture, mouths hanging open in anticipation.

Then Anita noticed me standing there and looked up. She stopped what she was saying, excused herself from her young charges and walked over to me. She was smiling as I'd never seen her smile before; an inner light shone in those expressive dark eyes so that they sparkled like gemstones.

'Thank you, Jeff,' she said, clearly choked with emotion. 'Thank you *so* much. Your soldiers delivered the desks a couple of hours ago and even put them all out for us. I can never tell you how grateful I am!'

I smiled at seeing her so happy. 'I'm just pleased we managed to find them.'

'Mayor Jozic doesn't mind?'

'Mayor Jozic probably doesn't know – yet.' I really didn't want to think of what stick I might yet get from Major Tring. 'But what's going to happen to the kids?'

She smiled again. Things had obviously gone well today. 'The UN Head of Office came down from Zenica earlier. A very kind and sweet man with a long white beard like Father Christmas. It was decided to keep the children here under one roof for a while – until we can reunite as many as possible with relatives who might look after them. He is arranging for beds, clothes, food and medicines to be dropped off here later this evening. And some specialist workers and counsellors to help me look after the children.' Her eyes clouded momentarily. 'A lot of mouths to feed and, I think, some bad dreams at night. There will need to be a lot of hugs and kisses.'

'And did the TV people come round earlier?' I asked.

'Yes, that Mr Kemp from your British ITN.'

'I hope you didn't mind? I wasn't sure if I was doing the right thing.'

Anita shook her head. 'He was very nice, very understanding. He treated the children very gently . . . I think the camera helped to take their mind off things a little. And it helped that Tali was with him.'

Tali glanced over at me, grinned and gave a small wave before returning to her story-telling.

'She is a natural with the children,' Anita said. 'They all speak English and they love her fairy tales. She has a big imagination . . . and she is very discreet about the way she took her photographs, I noticed. That is good. She offered to stay and give me a hand until the UN people came . . .'

Even as she spoke I heard the sound of movement and voices in the lobby behind me. Half a dozen men and women in blue UN helmets and flak-vests came in, chatting and laughing and weighed down with rucksacks and holdalls.

'Looks like they've just arrived,' I said.

'That is good, those poor children will be starving.'

I didn't really want to spoil her day with bad news, but I didn't have an option. 'Look, Anita, we've had intelligence reports that suggest fighting might break out tonight between the Croats and the Muslims. If it does, the school could be in the front line.'

Momentarily she closed her eyes as though experiencing a sudden pain, then opened them again. 'Is there no end to it?' she asked herself aloud.

I said, 'It could get worse before it gets better. Is there a cellar in this building?'

She nodded. 'Of sorts. A boiler room for the heating system.'

'Could you get all the kids down there if things get rough?'

'Just about, if we clear out some of the rubbish in there.'

'I suggest you make it a priority right now,' I said. 'Get some of your new UN chums to help. I'd lend a hand, but I've got to get back to HQ.'

I saw the flicker of disappointment in her eyes. 'It would be nice if you could stay, Jeff, see how the children appreciate what you've done. But I understand . . .' She glanced across the room at Tali. 'Perhaps you could drop Tali off at my house. I have said she can stay there until she finds somewhere more permanent.'

Tali looked up. 'It's OK, thanks. I can walk, it's not far.'

I said, 'The streets are full of militia and there could be fighting at any time. Best we give you a lift.'

She shrugged and turned back to the children. 'I'm sorry, we'll have to end the story about the unicorn there for tonight. You all sleep well and I'll come and finish it tomorrow.'

Gathering up her cameras and shouldering her large rucksack, she strode across to us, smiling. 'I think they're very disappointed not to hear the end.' She kissed Anita on the cheek. 'Thanks so much for letting me stay at your place.'

Anita held out a door key. 'You'll need this. And thank *you* for your help today. I really appreciate it.'

I said, 'When the mutual admiration society is quite ready . . .
Time we were moving.'

Tali gave one of those quirky little smiles of hers and then
scurried to catch up with me as I turned and walked out into the
lobby, which was now filled with half a dozen UN workers,
their luggage, supplies and equipment.

The last vestiges of daylight were fading outside and there was
a chill bite to the early evening breeze. A white UN minibus and
a small truck had pulled up behind my Land Rover, but had left
enough room for me to stow Tali's luggage in the rear before the
photographer scrambled in alongside Ivana.

Cuthbert was just signing off on the radio as I got into the
driver's seat. He said, 'Gordy's been trying to speak to Markovic,
but he's apparently not there. So Gordy's angling to at least set up
a meet with you or me later this evening instead.'

I grunted. 'Perhaps we should have given the radio equipment
to Markovic first,' I said, being wise after the event.

'Major Tring wants you to report to him pronto,' he said,
hardly bothering to conceal the smirk on his face. 'He wants to
know where the hell you got this intelligence about an impending attack. Oh, and there was something about Mayor Jozic
having been on the phone complaining about you stealing his
property.'

'So what's the good news?'

'At least Tring believes you. He's ordered all company units to
withdraw to barracks and keep their heads down.'

I shook my *own* head in utter disbelief. Tring should have
ordered the complete opposite – get our boys out in their
armoured vehicles to the north of Una Drina to act as a deterrent to any attacker. If I didn't know better, I'd have said he'd
been trained at West Point.

Cuthbert shrugged his shoulders in sympathy with my frustration. 'And a part-convoy's just rolled in from Sarajevo,' he
added, which explained the arrival of the UN contingent for the
school.

'Part?' I asked, feeling suddenly alarmed.

'A problem at the Muslim roadblock to the north of town.'
The one we had passed through ourselves just an hour earlier.
'They thought they had clearance, then the militia suddenly
refused to let the second half through. They don't know what
the fuck's going on.'

I keyed the Land Rover into life, flung it into a tight U-turn
and accelerated back down towards the main street. It was all but
blocked by a crocodile of gargantuan white Volvo trucks and
trailers that were strung out all the way into the centre of town.
I spotted Rocky Rogers' Discovery parked outside the tyre shop
on the corner and pulled up alongside.

I climbed out to find Rocky standing beside his vehicle, talking on his radio receiver. He waved at me. 'Hi, Jimbo, just the
man!' He told his contact at the other end to wait. 'Can you
explain what's going on? First the Muslims have chopped our
convoy in two . . . And your company HQ is advising us not to
continue south out of town. I've got a hundred-truck convoy this
time – it'll turn Una Drina into one great fuckin' lorry park.'

'I think I know,' I replied. 'There's about to be a Muslim attack
here on the north of town, but the Croats don't know it yet.'

'Muslims?' Rocky echoed. 'Holy fuck, no! So their alliance is
finally over?'

'Apparently. That's why Major Tring will have closed the road
to the coast, in case you get caught in the crossfire.'

Rocky was quick to grasp the situation. 'And that's also why
the Muslims have stopped half the convoy coming in. Shit, it
must be about kick-off time.' He stared at me for a moment and
I could almost hear the cogs of his brain whirring. 'I can't leave
my lads or the trucks stuck out there. Anything could happen.'

I said, 'Whatever you do, make it quick.'

He returned the transceiver to his ear. 'Convoy Leader to
Lizard, are you reading? OK, Lizard, there's about to be a firefight and you might have to run the gauntlet. That's why the
ragheads stopped you. D'you wanna make a break for it? Yeah,

I mean can you crash or skirt the barrier? Yeah, yeah, of course the barrier guards might shoot at you! It's unlikely, but I can't guarantee they won't!' A wicked grin spread across Rocky's face. 'Well, it's a choice between spending the next few days out there in an unheated cab with bullets flying over your head or tucked up with your totty – what's her name, Jelena? – at the Splendid . . . Yeah, thought it might! Hit your air horns to warn the others you're rolling. Good luck!'

Rocky reached into his Discovery and hung up the handset. 'Thanks, Jimbo. Looks like we'll be stuck in town for the night. I'll be owing you a pint if you can get to the Splendid later.'

That seemed fair reward for just doing my job. 'You can bank on it.'

Nigel Cuthbert leaned out of my Land Rover window. 'Can we *please* get on, Jimbo?'

Just then I heard the distant blast of twin air horns coming from the road to the north. I guessed that was Lizard making his move. 'In a minute, Nigel. I want to make sure the rest of the convoy makes it into town.'

Suddenly the ragged answering roar of the rest of the convoy's hundred or so air horns travelled mightily through the twilight like the mating calls of a herd of primeval beasts. It was on the roll. I shifted position to stand alongside Rocky, who'd lifted a pair of binoculars to his eyes.

'Nothing yet,' he murmured. 'I should pick up the leading truck headlights in a couple of minutes . . . Just hope I made the right decision.'

'I'm sure you have,' I reassured, and grinned sideways at him. 'The burden of command, eh?'

At that moment we saw a huge distant flash in the gloom and I didn't need binoculars to tell me what it was. A split-second later the sound of the faraway *crump* of the explosion reached us.

'Oh, fuck,' Rocky breathed. 'Has some bastard opened fire?'

I squinted into the distance, just making out the pinprick glow of the leading headlamps. 'It sounded like a mine.'

'Lizard?' Rocky asked himself.

I said, 'I think the explosion was behind the lead truck, Rocky. Someone must have deviated from Lizard's exact tracks.'

Suddenly there was a repeated defiant blast of air horns, closer and louder now, challenging the unseen enemy in the night. The cacophony of supporting blasts reverberated towards Una Drina, seemingly shaking the very pavement on which we stood.

I watched, dry-mouthed and breathless, as the line of twin yellow eyes, one behind the other, grew ever larger and closer, gathering speed as each anxious second passed. Then the inky outline of the trucks themselves began to take recognizable form in the glimmering remnants of twilight, the tumultuous combined roar of their engines now sounding like an approaching swarm of insects, then seconds later transforming again to a muted roar like an approaching tidal wave of unbridled power. Croat militiamen stopped their preparations for war and joined others who were already gathered at the sides of the main street to watch the convoy approach.

I could see the lead truck clearly now, hurtling into town at full throttle. It was clear Lizard wasn't going to stop for anyone or anything, and I hoped to God the Croat guards had the sense to raise the roadblock pole . . . Well, I think they did, but it was all a bit too late. The front fender of Lizard's truck snapped it like a matchstick as the vehicle rocketed through. Only as he entered the main drag of Una Drina itself did I hear the hiss and squeal of straining air brakes as Lizard reined the big beast in.

Rocky stepped off the pavement and flagged him down. Lizard pulled in and the rest of the convoy rumbled past and down towards the town centre and as close to company HQ as they could get.

Lizard wound down his window. His face looked even paler than usual. 'Best fairground ride I've been on in a long time, boss!'

Rocky ignored that. 'What happened back there? Anyone hurt?'

'Brum Taylor ran over a mine. He's just a bit shaken. Next driver picked him up.'

'And the truck?'

'Fucked, boss, I'm afraid.'

Rocky nodded. 'OK, well done. If it's still quiet come morning, we'll get back there with a recovery crew and see what can be done.'

I'd seen enough and went back to my Land Rover and the increasingly impatient Nigel Cuthbert. I brought him up to date as I started the engine and swung south on the main road, following the last of the trucks towards the town centre.

We were about half-way back to HQ, and I was about to make a short detour to drop off Tali at Anita's house, when it happened.

There was no warning. Something exploded immediately in front of the Land Rover. I barely glimpsed the projectile that struck the kerbside tree. The vehicle seemed to jump and the windscreen shattered and frosted over instantly amid the deafening noise. I hadn't braked but the vehicle had come to an immediate, shuddering standstill. Momentarily I was stunned, paralysed with shock, slowly realizing that the uprooted tree must have landed across the bonnet.

I was suddenly aware of something wet trickling down the side of my face. I put my hand to it and my fingers came away covered in blood.

I glanced sideways at Cuthbert. His face, too, had cuts from shards of the broken windscreen blown in by the explosion of the warhead. 'You OK?'

He gulped and nodded. He said something, but I could barely hear his muffled words. It was then I realized I'd been deafened by the blast of what I assumed had been a rocket-propelled grenade.

I turned to the two women in the back. Tali and Ivana were sheet white and their eyes wide with terror. 'Anyone hurt?' I asked.

They answered me and shook their heads, but their voices

were so muted to me that it was as though I had cotton wool in my ears. I used my elbow to smash a hole in the frosted glass so that I could see.

Through the charred and leafless branches of the tree, I had a view down the darkened main street ahead of us. It was intermittently lit by pulses of light that must have been from explosions that I could not hear.

And something else I could see . . . fireflies! Bloody fireflies? For a second I didn't understand, still not able to think straight.

Christ, as if I hadn't seen enough tracer rounds in my life not to recognize them instantly! I kicked myself for my stupidity until I realized what a difference it made that I couldn't actually *hear* the rounds flying back and forth across the street. I think it had taken vital seconds for all four of us to understand that we were right in the middle of a bloody firefight! That was a profoundly unsettling experience. Indiscriminate death all around you and one of your key senses is down at the critical moment.

At least I could make out the distant tail lights of the last vehicle in the convoy . . . it was some sort of consolation that at least they seemed to be out of the immediate line of fire.

On either side of the street I became aware of shadowy figures, crouched and running, but whether Croat or Muslim I had no idea.

All I knew was we had to get out of here, and fast! I got my head together and threw the ignition switch. If I could pull the Land Rover back from under the weight of the fallen tree, we could make for the cover of the side-streets on the west side of town. But the engine remained stubbornly dead. I tried again, willing it to raise itself back to life. Nothing. The RPG round must have luckily missed us by a whisper before it hit the tree, but the violent shockwave from the blast must have done untold damage to the vehicle's mechanics and electrics.

I realized that Cuthbert was fumbling with the radio, presumably trying to get off a mayday to company HQ. Our eyes met and he shook his head solemnly.

Our faces were close, but I had to shout. 'Get the girls out and under cover!' I jabbed a finger towards a low wall beside the pavement next to the Land Rover.

Then I reached beneath my seat and pulled out the SA80 Bullpup assault rifle with its folding butt. 'I'll give you some covering fire!'

He nodded and beckoned the women to follow him. I forced my door open with difficulty because the frame had warped in the explosion, then scrambled out. Immediately I could see that the damage to the scorched and crumpled bonnet hadn't all been done by the tree. But at least the spray of branches offered some visual cover and the engine block a measure of protection against incoming rounds.

My hearing was starting to distinguish them a bit now, thank God, as I scanned the opposite side of the street. Heavy explosions were becoming more regular, the flagstones trembling underfoot. The sudden jagged light of blasts illuminated the row of buildings. I picked up two cluster sources of muzzle-flashes: from an alleyway at two o'clock and a couple of first-floor windows above a shop almost facing me.

I took loose aim and put a couple of five-round bursts in the direction of each. Immediately their firing ceased as they got their heads down.

Cuthbert had slid across the front seats, his own SA80 out, and exited from the driver's door, opening the rear one for Tali and Ivana.

'GO!!' I yelled.

I saw the three of them sprint across the pavement to the low wall, then returned my attention to the identified targets, putting in a few more single rounds.

Then I turned away and followed the others. A couple of bullets sparked off the flint of the wall as I vaulted blindly over with an agility I thought I no longer had – and crashed into the long, wet grass. I looked up to find Cuthbert and the two girls huddled close in behind the stonework.

It was only then that I realized exactly where we were – in the graveyard of Una Drina's Catholic church. Amidst the macabre setting of ornate tombstones and lichen-encrusted sculptures of angels, dark figures with guns moved slowly and carefully in our general direction and towards the main street. I was pretty certain they were Croats.

I was starting to piece together what must be happening. Almir Aganovic and his Ramoza Brigade of Muslim fighters must have launched their pre-emptive attack. At least some of them seemed to have swept into town in a pincer movement from the east, cutting behind the Croat front line in the north. It occurred to me that they may very well have used the convoy's earlier hold-up at the Muslim checkpoint, and its split run down the main street, to distract the Croats and conceal their advance.

If I was right, it seemed the Muslims were holding the eastern side of the main street, at least in this particular stretch, and were now consolidating.

Meanwhile the Croats, initially caught off guard, were now scrambling to push in from the west to hold their side of the thoroughfare. That put the four of us squarely between the two sides. Not an enviable position to be in.

I looked back towards the church. It seemed from the occasional muzzle-flashes that the Croats were advancing across the northern stretch of the graveyard, darting between the headstones which they were using for cover. I could detect no movement at the southern end.

I said, 'Nigel, we're right in the firing line here. Let's try and pull back to the church, OK?'

Still deafened, he struggled to hear, but finally understood. Then I turned to the women, who were both wide-eyed and clearly apprehensive. 'Watch what I do, then you do the same. But don't start until I stop, because I will then give you covering fire if it's needed.' I saw the look of dismay on Tali's face and tried to make my smile look reassuring.

I quickly cradled the SA80 in the crooks of my arms and

began a rapid leopard crawl through the long grass, keeping my backside as low as possible. It had been a while since I'd done anything like this and my inner thigh muscles began aching as though I'd been riding a horse for hours.

Finally I reached a large stone sarcophagus some fifteen metres away. I regained my breath, put the SA80 to my shoulder and peered around the lower edge of the monument. The Croats were still creeping across the graveyard to the north. Clearly intent on reaching the main street, no one had noticed our party. I looked back and beckoned the others. Tali came first, keeping low and with strong, fluid movements. My guess was she kept herself quite fit and for a split second I found that thought quite distracting.

I chided myself and concentrated of the moving line of Croats.

A couple of minutes later, Tali was by my side, breathless and squeezed up hard against the stone. 'God, Jeff, that was scary.' She grinned, her teeth white in the darkness. 'But pretty exciting too.'

I pressed my finger to my lips and shook my head. 'Sssh.' She gave an apologetic little shrug and watched as I waved for Ivana to come across.

The older woman was slower and more awkward, not helped by the long coat she wore. It seemed to take an agonizingly long time before she reached Tali's side. From the expression on her face, I don't think she found it the least bit exciting.

I didn't have to beckon Cuthbert, the former soldier was already on his way. He had covered half the distance when I saw the muzzle-flashes and sharp crackle of small-arms fire. It came from the Muslim position on the first floor above the shops on the far side of the main street. I heard the whistle of incoming rounds and saw the turf spray up in a dirty fountain around Cuthbert. Ivana gasped.

But our salvation came from the Croats. They interpreted the action as an attack on them. It was their cue to open up on the Muslims with everything they had. A ragged volley of returning fire poured from the Croats' graveyard positions at those who had shot at Cuthbert. It was followed by the swish and crump of rocket-propelled grenades.

All of this provided ideal cover for us to make our escape, not least because the Muslims now lost all interest in poor old Cuthbert and turned their attention to the advancing ranks of Croat militia.

As soon as Cuthbert scrambled to the cover of the sarcophagus, I said, 'Right, let's make a break for the church. I'll bring up the rear.'

I let Cuthbert lead the two women in a crouched run, weaving a course through the ranks of gravestones towards the church. I followed at a slightly slower pace, keeping my eyes and the SA80 sweeping in the direction of the Croats, in case any of them saw our group and got a bit trigger-happy.

I'd nearly reached the large open porch of the church when all hell broke loose across the graveyard. The distant thud of heavy mortars was followed almost immediately by the impact of explosive shells detonating on the ground in dazzling violent flashes that made the earth tremble and sent geysers of debris spewing into the air. I saw the bodies of advancing Croat militia torn apart and tossed aside, while their comrades ran for cover.

I hurried the last few metres to the church and pushed open the heavy metal-studded door. Cuthbert and the two women were standing just inside, looking hot and dishevelled. The cavernous nave was in almost total darkness, just two large candles on the altar painting a glimmer of light on the flagstoned aisle and along the tops of the polished pews.

'What's all that noise?' Tali asked.

'The Muslims have brought up their heavy mortars.'

Ivana looked petrified; I could see she was actually trembling, despite Cuthbert's comforting arm round her shoulder. 'Are we safe in here?'

I glanced up at the dark void overhead and imagined the

effect of a mortar stonk coming through and bringing the roof in with it. 'Not really.'

She realized what I was thinking. 'There is a crypt in here. I heard someone talk about it once.'

I nodded. 'That might be a smart move until things calm down.'

Cuthbert already had his pocket torch out, playing the beam along the walls. For a second he spotlit a single door beside the altar. 'That'll be the presbytery,' he guessed, then swung the beam back along the other wall.

That was where we found a pair of wrought-iron gates guarding a flight of stone steps leading down below floor level. 'Let's take a look,' he said.

The words had barely left his mouth when there was an almighty explosion to the rear of the church. We all looked up instinctively as a brilliant flash outside lit up the huge stained-glass window of the Madonna and Child behind the altar and blew it instantly into a million shimmering coloured pieces. It burst into the building like a vast and spectacular kaleidoscope.

I heard the women scream.

In the instant blackout and silence that followed we heard the faint and bizarre sound of tiny descending glass particles falling like icicles all along the pews.

Aware that a second artillery round could be about to follow the first, Cuthbert moved swiftly to the gates. He pushed them open and shone his torch down the stairwell before beginning his descent into the crypt. We followed him down some twenty feet, where his way was blocked by a heavy timber door. He turned the cumbersome metal ring handle to release the latch. The door creaked open under its own weight and we stepped into a large vaulted chamber.

Cuthbert picked out its rows of family tombs in the beam of his torch. The air smelled dank and earthy, and it was eerily quiet. 'Welcome to Count Dracula's bedchamber,' Cuthbert said with a smile.

Ivana punched him lightly on the arm. 'Don't say things like that, Nigel. It is disrespectful to the dead.'

'And it's spooky enough without all that,' Tali added, suddenly shivering. 'It's so cold down here.'

I took out my own pocket torch and took a look round. On a shelf by the door there were a number of candles and brass holders. I picked them up and put them on the floor. 'It's not much, but it'll provide some heat.'

'We'll sit close together,' Cuthbert added. 'It'll all help.'

I lit the candles while he sat against the wall with Ivana and put his arm round her. Tali sat down next to the interpreter and reached out to warm her palms on the meagre heat from the spluttering flames.

I dug in the cargo pocket of my combat smock and found three emergency ration bars of chocolate and a pack of oatmeal biscuits. 'Not exactly nouvelle cuisine,' I said and handed them out.

I leaned against one of the tombs and munched on one of the bars.

Tali looked up at me. 'You can sit next to me, Jeff.' Her teeth glistened in the candleglow as she smiled impishly. 'I'm all cold on one side.'

There was something about the way she said it. Was she flirting or just being friendly? Some warning bell was ringing deep in my subconscious. But then, if I could hear it, maybe it wasn't so deep after all. Hell, Tali van Wyk was young enough to be my daughter. Well, just.

I went across to the three of them and lowered myself down next to the young photographer. She wriggled and snuggled up again my shoulder. 'That's better, you've blocked off the draught.'

'Glad I have my uses,' I said.

'How long will we have to stay here?' Ivana asked.

I said, 'At least until there's a let-up in the fighting.'

'It's gone quiet,' Tali said, then she giggled. 'But I think I'm still a bit deaf.'

'You must be,' Cuthbert answered. 'I can still hear the thump of mortars. Mind you, it's pretty faint.'

'The noise is deadened down here,' I agreed.

Tali looked at me. 'Aren't you scared, Jeff?'

'Not any more.'

'I am. Feel this.' She took her right hand away from the candle flame and placed the palm against my cheek. 'Still freezing. I think my blood's run cold I'm so scared.'

She took her hand away and I said, 'You'll get used to it. But I *was* scared earlier, when we were hit in the Land Rover.'

She frowned. 'You didn't seem scared. Not the way you took control.'

'I just hide it well, that's all. Training and experience teach you not to panic.' I smiled. 'Or at least to panic in a controlled sort of way.'

'A breed of heroes,' Cuthbert quipped. 'That's us.'

'Knowledge conquers fear,' I added. 'If things get rough, then you should be too busy doing your job properly to let fear get a look in.'

Tali shook her head. 'I couldn't be like that.'

I don't think she realized . . . I said, 'You *are* like that. When you took those photographs as your convoy was attacked – the actual truck you were in.'

'I was petrified.'

'But you still took the pictures, that's what I mean.' I thought for a moment. 'What happened to them, by the way?'

'Kirk Grundy put me in touch with an agent in London. They're with her now.'

At the mention of the American's name I felt my hackles rise, and a distinct feeling of jealousy. I couldn't believe for a moment the rumours that he and Tali could have had any sort of relationship, yet I found the very thought profoundly unsettling. 'So Grundy did actually do something for you?'

She frowned and looked at me as if wondering exactly what I meant. 'Kirk was very friendly and supportive, unlike a lot of people. I know he used me over that business with Goran Zoric, planning the assassination. That was horrible. But if he is in the CIA, I suppose he was just doing *his* job. We're still friends.'

I tried not to dwell on that. 'Has this new agent sold anything for you yet?'

She shrugged. 'I think a couple of London colour supplements are interested, but communications with me here are difficult, of course. I tend to have to beg favours off journalists and TV people. Gerald at ITN's been helpful.'

I said, 'Maybe I could set something up for you to use at company HQ.'

'Don't think Tring would approve of that, Jimbo,' Cuthbert interjected. 'You know how he feels about civilians at HQ, let alone the media. He hates them even more than the Paras.'

I smiled as I imagined the possible scenarios. 'There's got to be more than one way to skin a cat. Massage his ego, see if he can't be persuaded to let Tali do a piece on *him*.' I turned to her. 'Do you just take photographs? Any words?'

She nodded. 'Not really articles, more deep captions. Sort of an introduction, then I let the pictures tell most of the story. Didn't I see Major Tring at Stavac? The officer with the dog.'

'That's him.'

'I get on well with animals.'

'You'll need to with Trojan,' I laughed. 'He'll have your leg off as soon as look at you.'

'How about "The Loneliness of Command" for a title?' Tali suggested brightly.

Cuthbert and I looked at each other and grinned. 'I think that might do the trick,' he said. 'And very true. Tring hasn't a friend in the world.'

'I wish I could take photographs,' Ivana said. 'I do not have an artistic bone in my body.'

'When did you start?' I asked Tali.

She gave a shy smile. 'When I was ten. My first camera, a present from my favourite uncle. We lived on a farm in

Zimbabwe and my parents were very practical. I don't think they approved. They'd have preferred for him to have bought me a bicycle.'

'But you were happy with the camera?'

'Oh, yes. As soon as I got it I was fascinated! I'd always been a bit of a tomboy. I only ever had one doll and I buried it because I hated it so much.'

Ivana looked amazed. 'Why?'

Tali shrugged. 'I don't know. I just hated girlie things. My mum still hasn't forgiven me for that . . . But when I got the camera . . . I photographed everything and everybody on our farm and the nearby town. Landscapes and animals. I couldn't *believe* the results when I got them. I thought some were very good – I sort of surprised myself. After that I spent all my pocket money on film stock and processing.'

I've always been fascinated how people get into out-of-the-ordinary jobs. 'Did you go on to study photography?'

She nodded. 'It was part of my media studies at uni. My family had moved to South Africa by then. I got a job as an assistant to a top photographer in Cape Town. It was murder! He was a real slave driver . . . I made so *many* mistakes! But I learned a lot.'

'Sometimes that's the best way,' I said.

She looked thoughtful. 'Yes, I suppose it is.' Then she smiled. 'But not so much fun at the time.'

It was then that the new barrage struck. The heavy mortar shells fell one after another without warning. We all flinched involuntarily as they detonated just outside the church, closer than any previously. The flagstones on which we were sitting trembled under the shockwave and bits of plaster fell from the vaulted ceiling, crashing to the floor somewhere in the darkness. The candle flames fluttered.

I barely heard Tali gasp, 'Oh, God—' when her words were cut off abruptly by the exploding roar of the second round. It was nearer still and I think it actually hit the outer wall of the church. Chunks of masonry dislodged from the crypt ceiling this time, but the noise of them smashing was drowned out by the next shuddering explosion. But this time it sounded different, coming from somewhere directly above us.

I think we all knew what had happened. The third round had come in straight through the roof of the church and detonated on impact. A terrible noise like an avalanche followed as stone and tiles plummeted onto the floor and burst above our heads. I swear the entire crypt shuddered.

Tali's hand grasped my arm so tightly that it hurt. Her eyes were inches from mine, wide and staring. I knew that look. She thought she was about to die.

More shells exploded nearby, but their focus seemed to have moved away slightly. I took Tali's hand in mine and squeezed it reassuringly, sliding my other arm round her shoulder, holding her close. 'OK, it's OK,' I whispered hoarsely.

'Oh, God, Jeff . . .' She buried her head in my shoulder and I knew she was sobbing, her body trembling against mine.

In the darkness, I kissed the blonde hair of her head. 'Don't worry, Tali. You're safe here, I promise you.'

I felt her free hand on my chest, her palm flat, then felt her fingers curl tightly around the material of my DPM like a child clutching at a security blanket. She was still crying and I think maybe her teeth were chattering with that ice-cold fear you get when you are staring death in the face. Only she wasn't looking to meet it.

I prayed the mortars would stop, but they didn't. They seemed to go on for an eternity, but it was probably only a matter of minutes. Nevertheless, it was quite long enough. I stroked Tali's head absently and muttered a few more words of reassurance.

When the barrage stopped it seemed uncannily quiet. The candles had gone out in the rush of displaced air that had whooshed down the steps from the main body of the church and blown open the door. Somewhere in the darkness water dripped loudly from a fractured pipe.

'Thank God,' Ivana breathed, 'I think it's stopped.'

Cuthbert relit one of the candles. 'Question is, for how long?'

Tali had stopped trembling and drew away from me slightly, the feeble glow of the candle throwing half of her face into deep shadow. The whites of her eyes glistened and she regarded me intently for a moment with an expression I couldn't quite fathom.

Then, taking me by surprise, she reached forward and kissed me quickly on the lips. 'Thank you, Jeff.'

I smiled awkwardly, thinking only how gloriously soft her mouth had been. 'For what?'

'I think I might have died of fright if you hadn't been here. I've never been so scared.'

Cuthbert said, 'D'you think we should see about getting out of here, Jimbo? I can only hear a bit of sporadic small-arms fire.'

'We could take a look,' I agreed.

Tali was very quick to her feet, eager to be gone. Then I noticed the dark patch in the crotch of her jeans and realized why: in her fear, the poor girl had lost control of her bladder. My heart went out to her.

I think that was the moment I realized something was happening to me, something I hadn't felt for a long, long time. Or maybe, even, had never felt before.

Nine

I tried to clear my mind and regain focus as I scrambled up the steps of the crypt and into the church.

The place was a wreck. Through the swirl of dust I could see piles of roof timbers, masonry and tiles obliterating the pews and a gaping hole in the ceiling through which I could see the night sky. I realized just how lucky we'd been. A few more rounds like that and the floor above the crypt would have collapsed on us, and no one would even have known we were buried there.

Cuthbert and I, our SA80s at the ready, moved to the main door, now hanging drunkenly on just one hinge. Crouching low, I peered around the edge of the porch wall and viewed the graveyard. Layers of gunsmoke wafted between the tombstones. Through the murk I could distinguish the vague outlines of moving militiamen.

Things seemed to have calmed down. I guessed the Croats were just holding the line at the church, keeping the Muslims at bay and content to consolidate their positions until daylight. But if we risked a sudden move it was odds-on that some twitchy, trigger-happy local would assume we were the enemy trying to outflank them. But by the same token, I didn't want to stay at the church now that the Muslims had the idea of using it for target practice.

It was time to take a measured gamble. I stood upright and called out loudly in Serbo-Croat. 'Attention please! Hold your fire! I repeat, hold your fire! This is Captain Hawkins of UNPROFOR! I am with a small British Army detachment at the church!' I paused for breath and to listen. I thought I could hear the murmur of anxious voices.

'Christ, Jimbo,' Cuthbert said. 'I hope you know what the fuck you're doing.'

I ignored him and called out again. 'Will one of your officers please make himself known to us! – urgently!'

Then I stepped out of the porch, waving the beam of my torch. I heard the whipcrack of a high-velocity round and the sound of the bullet ricocheting off the stonework somewhere above my head.

'Stop firing!' someone bawled angrily in Serbo-Croat.

I stepped back, keeping most of my body behind the wall. One of the shapes in the mist of gunsmoke was taking more solid form, growing in size as the figure came towards me.

As he approached, I recognized Colonel Markovic. He was flanked by two bodyguards.

'There you are, Captain Hawkins,' he said tersely. 'I wondered what had happened to you. It was reported to me that your vehicle came under fire. I thought perhaps you and Mr Cuthbert here were dead.' He said this in a way that suggested he thought it might be a good idea if we were. 'You are aware that you were not hit by our side?'

I nodded. 'The Muslims.'

A sneer of a smile lingered on his lips but his eyes were blazing. 'Ah, yes, these kind and gentle Muslims you were so anxious for me not to fight. These God-fearing souls who murdered and raped the civilians of Stavac village!'

'That's not true!' The voice was Tali's. She stepped gamely forward. 'That massacre was done by the Serbs before the Muslims drove them out.'

'Shut up, Tali,' I snapped.

Markovic glared at her. 'Yes, keep your nose out of this, girl. You know *nothing*!'

'I spent the afternoon with the survivors,' she retorted, ignoring both of us. 'The children. They told me—'

He gave a dismissive snort. 'The word of traumatized children! What would they know?'

'Clearly more than *you*! You just want an excuse to fight the Muslims!'

I rounded on her. 'Zip it, Tali, let me handle this.'

She pulled a very disgruntled, angry face, but said nothing more.

Markovic thought he had me on the hook, and wasn't about to let me off. 'You try to persuade me not to attack and then this happens! They use the UN convoy for cover to come into town from the east. When will you do-gooders ever learn?'

'They attacked, Colonel, because they knew you were about to,' I retorted. 'You didn't exactly make a secret of your intentions. They pre-empted you and they out-manoeuvred you.'

He smarted at that. I could see in his eyes that the punch had hit home hard. For a moment he hesitated. In the chill air a dewdrop of mucus had formed at his nostrils and he wiped it away brusquely with his sleeve. 'You sound almost pleased, Captain.'

I replied quickly, 'Fighting in Una Drina is the very *last* thing I want, Colonel, and you know it.'

'You knew they were going to attack, didn't you?' he accused. 'You were seen going and returning to Muslim headquarters just before their attack.'

I nodded. 'I guessed that they might attack tonight.'

'And you didn't see fit to warn me?'

I didn't bother to remind him that it was not UNPROFOR's policy to share its own intelligence with the warring militias. Instead I said, 'Our company HQ had been trying to reach you all afternoon, but you were not taking calls.'

He grunted at that. 'Is that why you wanted to talk?'

I hedged. 'I wanted to deliver communications equipment to you so that we *could* talk!'

'But not to *warn* us of this attack, I think,' he replied bitterly.

This was taking us in circles. 'If we could have talked to both you *and* the Muslims, it is possible there would have been no attack, Colonel! No, we are not allowed to share our military intelligence with anyone. But remember, it is our wish to maintain the status quo – unless opposing parties agree peacefully to change it.'

He glowered at me. 'Don't tell me it wouldn't suit you and the UN, London and the Yankees if this town was taken by the Muslims.'

I shook my head. 'No, why should it? This has always been a Croat town. If the Muslims ran it, it would just create more resentment and friction.' Then I pushed the hearts-and-minds bit a little further and touched his arm. 'Pero, in the short time I've known you, I've come to consider you as a friend. Honest and trustworthy. I believe Una Drina's security is safe in your hands. You are a formidable opponent – and I look forward to that game of chess as soon as things quieten down.'

I don't know why the words didn't choke me as I uttered them, but I must have made a fairly convincing job of it, because his posture relaxed a bit and that deceptive smile showed just a hint of returning to his lips. 'I just hope that will be possible, Captain. It won't be if we're overrun by the Mad Mullahs' army.'

'I'm sure they've underestimated both you and your men, Colonel.'

He nodded at that. 'And what *is* this communications equipment?'

I explained briefly and Markovic appeared decidedly interested in the prospect of some fancy comms toys to play with. 'I look forward to seeing your signals people tomorrow,' he said. 'And please pass my thanks up your chain of command to whoever is responsible.'

'I will,' I promised, adding, 'and I wonder if I could ask a small favour in return?'

He looked dubious. 'If it is possible, Captain.'

I smiled. 'A lift back to our HQ in one of your vehicles would be most appreciated.'

'Can't they come and get you?'

'Sadly, Colonel, I have no communications . . . destroyed in our Land Rover.'

I think he understood the irony of that, because the smile returned and actually reached his eyes for once.

Ten minutes later we were in the back of a Croat pickup and hurtling through the maze of side-streets, keeping well clear of the fighting. At my request the driver screeched to a halt outside Anita's apartment block. Tali scrambled out and I handed down her rucksack.

I said, 'Don't leave the house tomorrow if you hear fighting.'

'I promised Anita I'd help her with the children.'

'You can't help her if you're dead, Tali,' I scolded. 'So both of you only go if the shooting's stopped. And use the back way we've just come.'

'Yes, boss.'

'And don't be cheeky.'

Her grin was wide. 'No, boss.' She shouldered the heavy rucksack. 'Maybe I can also talk to Major Tring tomorrow?'

I said, 'We'll see. If things quieten down, I'll come and find you.'

'Thanks, Jeff.' She put her hand to her lips, palm out, and blew a kiss in my direction. 'Ciao.'

I watched as she turned and strode up the path, her blonde ponytail swinging to the rhythmic sway of her hips. The pickup jolted away suddenly and we were swallowed up in the night. My mouth was dry.

Five minutes later we pulled up outside company HQ. White UN trucks were parked up nose-to-tail on both sides of the street outside the compound and a Warrior patrolled menacingly up and down, looking for the first signs of trouble.

Cuthbert and I made our way to the Ops Room. It was absolute pandemonium. A constant babble of military-speak came from the operators in the radio shack as the airwaves were clearly overloaded with calls from observation posts and heavy signals traffic with battalion HQ in DV and the Muslim Bosnian government in Sarajevo and God only knew who else. Major Tring and Gordy Cromwell stood before the main wall map while duty staff updated new militia positions in chinagraph on the perspex cover as intelligence flowed in from various sources.

Tring turned on me. 'Where the hell have you been, Hawkins? You had your radio switched off? Been trying to raise you for hours.'

'Got caught in crossfire when the Muslims attacked,' I replied evenly. 'We had to abandon the Land Rover. Badly damaged and the radio buggered.'

'Any casualties?' Gordy asked quickly.

I shook my head. 'No, we made it back through to Croat lines. Any news on the SAS lads?'

Gordy nodded. 'They radioed in to say they're staying put at Herenda's HQ until tomorrow. They'll get back into town when there's a lull in the fighting.'

But Tring didn't seemed that interested in anybody's personal safety. 'I wasn't informed that you were visiting Muslim HQ until *after* you'd left.'

'It was just a routine meeting.'

'Routine?' Tring's lips twisted into a sneer. 'With those SAS cowboys and a lot of radio equipment? I would have liked to have been consulted *before* you went. Do I make myself plain?'

I counted to ten under my breath. 'For me it was a routine meet with Major Herenda. The SAS guys tagged along on their own mission on orders from CBF.'

Nigel Cuthbert interrupted. 'That's right, Reg. The radio equipment was strictly CBF business.'

But Tring didn't take his eyes off me, aware that he could hardly argue with a UKLO under the Commander of British Forces in-theatre. 'But you, Captain, are *my* company liaison officer. I like to be kept in the picture.'

'With respect, Reg,' I replied, 'you *were* kept in the picture. You were informed where I'd gone. If I have to have a confab with you every time I make a routine daily decision within my remit, I'll never get anything done.'

That seemed to click something in his brain, reminding him of something else. 'Like breaking into a private warehouse and stealing goods from the mayor of this town?'

I glanced at Gordy. 'I'm sure you've been briefed of the full circumstances surrounding that.' My friend nodded in confirmation.

Tring must have realized he wasn't going to get any mileage out of that one. 'We'll discuss that later,' he said loftily. 'In the meantime, we've got more that enough on our plate.' He gestured towards the map. 'The whole situation's gone tits-up! Not only are the Muslims attacking us here in Una Drina, but they've also begun a major offensive against DV. I've just spoken to Colonel Rathbone; it's total chaos there, too. A nightmare!' He looked at me accusingly. 'If you were at the Muslim camp, why didn't you stop them?'

I gave a sarcastic smile. 'Because, believe it or not, they didn't tell me their battle plans.'

Tring seemed not to have heard. 'You should have twisted Major Herenda's arm.'

I said, 'It's not just Herenda you have to persuade. It's Almir Aganovic – and that guy's not for turning.'

'Aganovic?' Tring looked astounded. 'The Ramoza Brigade?'

'They're the ones mounting the assault on this town.'

The blood had drained from Tring's face. 'I don't believe it . . . The last we heard, they were based around DV.'

'Well, they've moved,' I said.

'It's true, Reg,' Cuthbert confirmed. 'We both met General Aganovic. There's a Ramoza camp next to Herenda's HQ now.'

Tring glared at the map. 'This is a disaster. If the Ramoza Brigade get embedded in the town, there could be street fighting for months!'

At that moment a corporal entered the Ops Room, looking as wary as a gazelle entering a lion's den. I got the feeling he knew he was about to deliver unwelcome news. 'Major Tring, sir, there's Mayor Jozic outside to see you.'

Tring turned on him. 'What? That's all I need. Can't you see I'm up to my neck in it?'

'He was very insistent, Major.'

'Oh, for God's sake!' Tring glanced round the room as though looking for some route of escape. 'Oh, very well, show him into my office, will you?'

'Sir.' The corporal turned on his heels.

'Oh, Corporal, don't leave that sneaky little bastard on his own in there.'

'No, sir.' The door swung shut.

Tring said, 'I wonder what the hell Jozic wants.'

'Help, I should think,' Cuthbert replied quickly.

The major grunted. 'He should be so lucky! It's not our remit to get involved in the fighting, Nigel. You know that. Only fire if fired upon.'

I said, 'For all his faults, Reg, Jozic *is* responsible for the town's defences. He's bound to want to discuss the situation with you. It could be a chance to rebuild some bridges.'

Tring scowled at me. 'You mean, after you burned them this afternoon at the man's warehouse.' When I didn't rise to the bait, he added, 'Well, I want you and Nigel to see him with me. He can have a very explosive temperament. You are better at all this sweet-talking stuff than me.'

'It would be our pleasure,' I replied lightly.

Not sure how to take my tone, he gave one of his superior little sneers and strode away towards his office, leaving Cuthbert and me to trail after him.

By the time we arrived, Tring was on the swivel chair and using his large desk as a barrier between him and Mayor Jozic, who sat opposite. For the first time I appreciated just how low the guest chairs were – Tring's armchair-psychological attempt to give his visitors a feeling of inferiority, no doubt. It certainly seemed to work, because Jozic looked decidedly uncomfortable and shorter than ever, like a hunched little dwarf sitting barely clear of the floor. He still had his black overcoat on and was clutching a battered felt hat in his hands. I could see the sweat glistening on his scalp between the tramlines of hair he'd plastered over his bald crown.

'What are you going to do, Major?' he was demanding. 'We will be overrun. Croat men and children massacred, our women raped! It will be like Stavac all over again but on a huge scale!'

I translated, but Tring was unmoved. 'Captain Hawkins and Captain Cuthbert here are working to arrange a cease-fire. That is all our UN remit allows us to do.'

'Cease-fire rubbish!' Jozic blustered. 'Those Muslim bastards will not stop until they've taken the town, you know that! Is that what you want? I think that is what you British have wanted all along.'

'No, no,' Tring protested. 'We want both communities to live in harmony here. With peace talks and the convoys running, we can resolve differences and keep everyone alive and fed.'

'Dream on, Major,' Jozic snarled. 'How can that happen? This has always been a Croat majority town — for centuries! You think people will coexist when it becomes a Muslim town? More ethnic cleansing of my people . . . that is all you will achieve. More of the same!'

Tring started digging his trench. 'I'm sorry, Mayor, but there is nothing I can do. You are the defence minister of this town, it is up to you and Colonel Markovic to defend it in any way you see fit.'

'But *you* are the UN Protection Force,' Jozic returned. 'So *protect* us! You have armoured Warriors; we do not!'

'Our Warrior crews cannot fire at anything or anyone unless fired upon,' the major replied with practised ease.

I could see this was going to go round in circles and could spiral into a huge row that wasn't going to help anyone.

I said, 'Of course, Mr Mayor, we would like to help you stabilize the situation. One thing we could do is send a Warrior patrol down the high street, through the front line so to speak. That may act as a deterrent to the Muslims without us taking sides.'

Tring glared at me. 'That isn't an option. The Muslims will certainly see that as us taking sides.'

Before I could reply, Cuthbert cut in quickly. 'Doesn't matter what they think, Reg. It's our remit to keep the convoy routes open and we have every right to patrol them.'

'And what do you think their reaction will be?' Tring retorted. 'They'll open fire on us if we get in the way. What happens then?'

I said, 'We shoot back.'

'In self-defence,' Cuthbert added, 'as we are entitled to do under our rules of engagement.'

It was good to have Cuthbert as an ally for once. I said, 'Hopefully the Muslims will think twice about firing at us.'

Tring shook his head. 'And if they don't, we get in a firefight with them. That's not why we're deployed. And remember, the Muslims are *de facto* Bosnia government troops.'

I said, 'That doesn't entitle them to shoot at UN troops, does it? And a robust deployment on the convoy route – even with a firefight – will give Colonel Markovic a better chance to make sure they don't get into the town.'

Cuthbert backed me up. 'You said yourself earlier, Reg, street fighting in Una Drina could last for months and make the whole relief operation on this route untenable.'

Tring's face fixed into a grim mask. 'Thank you for your advice, gentlemen. But I don't want to give the good mayor here any false hopes and make promises we can't deliver.'

I'd had enough. I said, 'Forgive me, Reg, but I need to liaise urgently with the other LOs at Battalion . . . it will help you to have a fuller picture.'

It was a white lie, but he fell for it. 'What? Oh, yes, very well. Get back to me as soon as you can.'

Cuthbert gave me a strange look as I left the room; I think he was getting to know me all too well by now.

I strode down the corridor to the Den and sat down at the radio. A couple of minutes later I was patched through to battalion HQ and asking to speak personally to Colonel Rathbone.

He sounded weary when he answered. 'Ah, Jimbo, good to hear from you. Not more bad news, I hope. It's like hell's cauldron here and getting worse by the minute. Muslims and the Croat defenders are going at it hammer and tongs.'

'Sorry, Colonel,' I replied, 'but it's no better here.'

'Bring me up to speed, will you? Not always sure I'm getting the full picture from Reg.' He gave a dry chuckle. 'Sometimes I think he tries to protect me from bad news. Like I'm too senile to handle it!'

I quickly ran through the events at Una Drina. At the end he sighed. 'And I was hoping for the quiet life on my watch. Does sound as bad as it is here.'

I said, 'But there is a hope here, Colonel, if we take immediate action.'

'Oh, yes?'

'But I must tell you that Major Tring is not in favour.'

'You clearly are.'

'I just think it will save the situation here.' I took a deep breath. 'We put an armoured patrol down the high street – virtually between the two sides. That'll virtually enforce a cease-fire, because we'll be in the middle of them. At least give us time to persuade both sides to talk.'

'And we'd be protecting the UN convoy route,' Rathbone said, thinking aloud. 'And if we're fired on . . .?'

'Well, the Croats won't,' I answered. 'And if the Muslims do, we retaliate hard. Really hard, even clearing out their positions. Next time they try to take Una Drina the Croats will be better prepared.'

There was a pause, but it was a short one. 'I like it, Jimbo. Sounds to me it's all we can do – except stay in barracks! I think you should go ahead.'

I smiled to myself. 'I'm only the LO, Colonel. Think it best if it comes from you.'

'Ah, yes, of course. The company will get the orders in the next ten minutes. Thanks for taking the trouble, much appreciated. Alan, er, the CBF said you were an excellent fella. Seems he was right.'

I signed off, left the Den, and headed for the Ops Room. I came across a gloomy looking Mayor Jozic in the corridor, heading for the door.

He saw me and stopped. To my surprise he said, 'Thank you, Captain Hawkins, for your suggestion. I am only sorry that Major Tring is not in agreement with you.'

I'd always thought of Jozic as a rogue and a selfish bastard. But maybe he had some redeeming features, because I saw there were tears in his eyes behind the thick spectacle lenses. 'I fear this is the end of my town. Many will die or be driven away from houses and land that have been in Croat families for generations.'

I placed a reassuring hand on his shoulder. 'Mr Mayor, things are about to change.'

He looked bewildered. 'Major Tring has had a change of heart?'

'Something like that,' I replied. 'We'll be patrolling shortly – but may I ask one special favour?'

'Of course.'

'Make sure your side doesn't fire on us!'

'You have my word.'

He left a happier man and I made my way to the Ops Room. Tring was back there, giving Gordy Cromwell more grief as the major's 2IC was pushing to have an observation post set up behind Una Drina in the hills to watch and report on developments. Nigel Cuthbert watched on in silence.

'What can you possibly have against that, Reg?' Gordy was saying.

'Not my idea' was written all over Tring's worried face. 'We'll find out soon enough in the morning. No one knows exactly where the Muslim units might be. Don't want to put an isolated team at risk.'

Gordy was near despair. 'Reg, they joined the army to take risks!'

'Don't be facetious,' Tring snapped. 'We're line infantry, not SAS.'

'Or Paras,' I said, unable to resist the jibe.

It was probably as well that Rocky Rogers turned up then, ambling into the office. 'OK if I come in? Wondered what the chances are of our convoy moving on to the coast tomorrow?'

Gordy jumped at the chance of breaking off his discussion with Tring. 'Good, so far,' he said. 'The fighting's confined to the north end of town. Trouble is, we don't know how things will develop overnight.'

He shrugged and nodded. 'Got any OPs out in the south?'

I nearly creased up. Was Rocky a mind-reader or what?

'What a brilliant idea,' I said. 'Then we'll have a better idea if it's safe for you to leave tomorrow. What d'you say, Reg?'

That caught him off guard. 'Er, well . . . I suppose—'

'I'll take that as a yes, then,' Gordy said quickly. 'I'll get a four-man team prepared immediately.'

Tring didn't countermand him and let it go.

'By the way, Jimbo,' Rocky said, 'just bumped into those two tossers up at the Splendid.'

'Tossers?' I asked. 'Which ones? This town is full of them.'

'The mercenaries you were asking after. That South African and that scrote of a sidekick of his, the Dane. They've got a room at the Splendid. Tried to buy a ride to the coast.'

I thought quickly. 'Do me a favour and refuse, will you?'

'Already have, mate. Got enough problems without trying to smuggle those two villains.'

Just then, one of the radio operators came in from the shack. 'Major – I've got the CO on, just patching him through to your phone!'

Tring looked irritated as the red telephone on the table rang and he snatched it up. 'Colonel . . .?' A period of silence followed as he listened. His face reddened with suppressed rage, but he remained tight-lipped for several minutes. Finally, he said, 'Er, of course, Colonel, if you think that's wise . . . Yes, yes, of course. I'll implement it immediately.'

Slowly he replaced the receiver and glowered across the room at me. 'You've been talking to Colonel Rathbone, haven't you?' It was more of an accusation than a question.

'Yes, he asked to speak to me. Wanted to know what I thought about the situation here in Una Drina.'

'And you told him.'

'I told him.'

'There's a chain of command in the army, or hadn't you noticed?'

I smiled gently. 'I'm not commanding anyone, Reg. I was ordered to give a view and did. Any decision the CO's made is his alone.'

Tring then cut me dead and turned to Captain Cromwell. 'Gordy, I want two platoons on immediate standby and as many Scimitars as the Lancers can muster. No soft-skinned vehicles. How soon can they be ready?'

'One in five and the second, say, twenty minutes.'

'Right, twenty minutes it is. Then I went everyone in the Briefing Room and everything ready to roll in thirty minutes from now.'

'What do you have in mind, Major?'

'I want an aggressive patrol along the main drag, through the front line between the Croat and Muslim forces,' he said tersely, as if it had all been his idea. 'If those Muslims so much as put a round over your heads, I want full returning fire to be followed up by a house-clearing operation of any building they even *might* be using.'

Gordy took a moment to overcome his surprise. '*Might* be using? They might be using *any* building, Major.'

'Then you'll have to clear them right out of town, won't

you?' He glanced over at me. 'That should satisfy Mayor Jozic, don't you think, Jeff?'

With that he turned on his heel and left the Ops Room.

As a joyous Gordy set about passing on the orders the whole of company HQ became electrified in anticipation of a good scrap.

Cuthbert took me to one side. 'You crafty bastard, Jimbo.'

I feigned innocence. 'Don't know what you mean.'

He grinned. 'Well, here's another idea. Tring won't put out an OP to the north, but you and I could go have a look-see what happens when our patrol goes out. I know just the position. It's been used before. Excellent view over the northern suburbs . . .'

That sounded good to me. 'Let's go before Tring has some other plans for me. Like getting me shot.'

Five minutes later, the two of us slipped out of the gates in Cuthbert's Land Rover and headed into the back-streets to the west where we picked up a dirt trail that wound its way up into the hills overlooking the town and the river valley. It took us half an hour, with Cuthbert getting himself lost twice before he found the spot he was looking for. We pulled up beside an over-grown footpath, climbed out and set off into the pine woods until we reached a rocky outcrop.

It provided a stunning view beneath a vast clear sky, its stars pinhead sharp in the crystalline air. The dim glow of the impro-vised lighting in the houses of Una Drina showed in the darkness beneath us, but to the north there were dozens of tiny fits and fizzes of small-arms muzzle-flashes. These were interspersed by sudden large pulses of light as mortar or artillery rounds deto-nated. The frosty air magnified the sound and the noise of battle seemed surprisingly close.

Cuthbert lugged his daysack of specialist equipment to the edge of the outcrop, zipped it open and handed me a telescopic image-intensifying nightsight. Whoever had kitted him out hadn't stinted on cost. God knows how much the nightsight must have been worth, *and* we had one each.

I settled down, made myself comfortable and adjusted the focus, pulling the grainy green and white viewer image in tighter until it was concentrated on the area of the main street beyond the church.

The battle was still raging pretty much it had been when we'd left the graveyard a couple of hours earlier. Croats amongst the tombstones on one side of the street and the Muslims occupying the building on the other. Fireflies of tracer hosed back and forth across the road.

'Here come our lads,' Cuthbert said suddenly, the anticipation clear in his voice.

I swung the nightsight a little, back along the street towards company HQ. There they were, five magnificent tracked beasts gleaming white in UN livery, turrets and cannons rotating as if seeking out trouble, and two light Scimitar reconnaissance tanks.

Suddenly I felt trepidation. This had been my idea and I was putting the lads of A Company right into the lion's mouth. The Warriors were tough, but they weren't invincible and could still be crippled and left vulnerable by a well-aimed RPG round or portable rocket launcher taking off one of their tracks. And the Ramoza Brigade were undoubtedly the best-trained militia in Bosnia.

To my amazement the Croats stopped firing completely as soon as the UN vehicles appeared. Markovic must have really been asserting his authority, must have already told his soldiers that if we *did* arrive it would be their salvation.

Whether or not the Muslims would have stopped given a few moments more, I don't know. I'd already assumed the Royal Wessex's poor reputation as a toothless tiger would hardly have them shaking in their boots. Big mistake.

Hal Watkins' lead Warrior raced down the road and into a hail of small-arms fire. I imagined I could hear the bullets ricocheting off the armour plates. That was all the Royal Wessex needed this night – their blood was up and they were spoiling for a fight.

In ragged unison all turrets swung to the right and heavy

cannon fire blasted away at the Muslim firing positions in the long-abandoned shops that lined the street. Shells bit into the brickwork with contempt, making it seem as if it were being devoured by an insatiable, monstrous yet invisible insect. Such was the ferocity of the Warriors' returning fire that Muslim guns immediately fell silent as the militiamen dived for cover.

The rear doors of the Warriors swung open and the British troops poured out onto the street. After a brief respite, the cannons opened up again to give covering fire as the soldiers fanned out along the pavement to begin their house-clearance operations.

Even from that distance it was obviously a textbook exercise, perfectly choreographed like a bizarre ballet with four-man 'bricks' working to a practised rhythm of timing and movement. In the narrow streets and lanes behind the advancing Royal Wessex troops I could see blurred figures beating a hasty retreat. Their rearguard barely made a stand, just threw down a feeble attempt at returning fire before following after their comrades.

Nigel Cuthbert drew his head back from the rubber eyepiece of his image-intensifier. The whiteness of his wide grin glistened in the dark. 'Looks like we've won the grand slam, Jimbo.'

I awoke the next morning with a start before my alarm went off.

It was pitch black and very quiet. I read the digits on my watch: a minute or two before six thirty. It's amazing how the army life trains your own personal body-clock. I swung my legs off the cot, switched on my torch and lit the Tilley lamp.

For the life of me I couldn't remember the dream that had slipped from my grasp as I reached out to recall it. But I knew who it had been about. Perhaps it was just as well I couldn't bring the detail to mind because I felt as horny as hell, and that was bad enough. Mental distractions such as those could get you killed in a place like Bosnia.

Using cold water from a galvanized bucket, I splashed my

face, had a quick body wash, towelled off and shaved with a battery razor. Fifteen minutes later I was dressed and on my way to the Ops Room.

Straightaway I could sense the buzz in the air after the success of the previous night's clearance operation. The Muslims had scrambled away down to the safety of the river, from where they could follow it north back to their original lines. Markovic and his Croats had moved in to take over the abandoned houses and reinforce the town's northern defences. The lads of A Company had returned to HQ and broken open a few beers to celebrate. Even Tring seemed to be enjoying himself.

This morning, despite having been up most of the night, Gordy Cromwell was back on station and looking fresh and energetic enough to go ten rounds with a prizefighter.

'Mornin', Jimbo,' he said brightly. 'Seems like we pulled it off. Thanks for pulling that flanker with Rathbone.'

I shrugged. 'It was the CO's decision, Gordy. One problem is he always gets a skewed view of events from Major Tring.'

'Even Tring is on a high today. Maybe he'll have a change of attitude.'

Personally I wouldn't be placing any bets on that one. I said, 'What's the news from DV?'

'Not as good as here. Looks like the Muslims are adopting siege tactics. Reports of mortars and artillery being set up in the hills.'

I lit my first miniature cigar of the day. 'We shouldn't be too smug, Gordy. I reckon that's exactly what the Muslims will do here now they've been pushed back.'

He nodded. 'That's what I've been thinking. Wouldn't be too clever that, would it? Two siege areas across the main convoy route to Sarajevo. You and the other LOs will have your work cut out.'

I said, 'At least things are quiet for the moment. Small mercies and all that.'

Of course, that was the precise moment the radio handset

began squawking on the table. Gordy listened intently for a few moments. 'OK, I'll get a patrol round. Out.'

I frowned. 'What's that?'

'Our sentry tower. Reporting smoke and flame coming from the approximate location of the town's mosque.' He shook his head in disbelief. 'That'll be someone's bright idea of revenge for the damage done to the church earlier.'

On that cheerful note of restraint and reconciliation in Bosnia, I made my way to the mess for some breakfast. By the time I'd finished it and had made my way to the Den, Nigel Cuthbert was able to confirm that a Royal Wessex patrol had found the town's mosque razed to the ground. The commander reported that quite a large crowd of Una Drina's Croat population had gathered and cheered as they watched the building disintegrate into a raging pyre. The happy bystanders had included some members of Mayor Jozic's personal bodyguard unit.

'That man's the biggest obstacle to peace in this town,' Cuthbert said. 'He's always been a big noise in the town. In business as well as local politics. The patrol commander reckons it was his men who set fire to the mosque.'

'When was he elected?' I asked.

Cuthbert gave me a pained look. 'Not elected, Jimbo. Appointed. Self-appointed, more like. Not long after the civil war started. The previous mayor was assassinated.'

'Probably on the orders of the present incumbent,' I said. I wasn't being that smart: the intelligence reports I'd read had hinted at the possibility.

Cuthbert nodded. 'I'd put money on it. Jozic's always had a bunch of thugs close to him. I reckon they put pressure on other local politicians to select him. Jozic runs a bank and a lot of high-ranking people had loans from him. You can see the possibilities.'

It seemed there was always someone willing to make a fortune out of other people's misery, especially in wartime.

After spending some time writing up my report of the

previous day's visit to the Muslim militia camp, I returned to the Ops Room to persuade Gordy to lend me a replacement Land Rover. A REME detachment had recovered the wreck of mine and declared it fit only to be cannibalized for spares.

By eight thirty I was in the compound, inspecting my new vehicle with Gordy's warning that 'You'd better look after this one properly' still ringing in my ears. While I was doing so, the sentries swung open the gates for the SAS signals unit to enter. Their long-range patrol Land Rover and Bedford truck pulled up alongside me. The huge Tiny, with his wild flaming hair, and the diminutive Chas both looked cheerful as they clambered out.

'Hi, Jimbo,' Tiny greeted. 'Gather you had some real fun and games last night.'

'I was afraid you might have got caught up in the thick of it,' I said.

'We're too canny for that,' Chas replied smugly. 'Decided to stay put and get to know as much about the Ramoza Brigade as possible.'

Tiny added, 'Intelligence on them is pretty scant, so I reckon Dave McVicar and the CBF will be pleased to have a bit more info.'

'I'm surprised Almir Aganovic let you hang around,' I said.

Chas laughed. 'He didn't, at first, but we made out we had a few problems setting up the comms equipment. Then we got chatting to his officers and eventually Aganovic actually invited us to join him for a meal.'

'He was pretty chuffed at that point,' Tiny said, 'because his attack on Una Drina was going well. Caught him in a good mood.'

'What was your reading of him?' I asked.

Tiny pulled a small cob pipe and a leather pouch from the cargo pocket of his camouflage smock and began thumbing tobacco into the bowl. 'Almir Aganovic's big trouble, I reckon. Fuckin' Islamic fundamentalist down to his boots.'

'Hates the Croats and the Serbs with a vengeance,' Chas agreed. 'Verging on the psychotic, I'd say. Not the sort to negotiate or give ground. I can see him being a major obstacle to any peace talks.'

I said, 'But Herenda's the local Muslim commander. I know he can be prickly, but he's reasonable enough.'

Tiny put a flame to the tobacco in his pipe. 'Yeah, but Aganovic way outranks Herenda,' he muttered through mouthfuls of smoke that smelled like dried dung. 'And all the Muslim militia seem to be in his thrall. I suspect even Herenda himself. I think Almir Aganovic's going to be influencing events around here.'

'The Bosnian government don't even like him,' I pointed out.

'But they *need* him, Jimbo,' Tiny came back. 'They may not like his fundamentalist views, but they like his fighting prowess. It gives them the military power they need to win this conflict.'

I could see their point. 'Let's just hope that Herenda stands up to him,' I said, but even I could recognize the desperation in my own voice. 'At least the Ramoza Brigade got pushed back out of town last night.'

'Oh, yeah,' Chas said. 'Aganovic wasn't a happy bunny when he got *that* news. Especially when he heard UNPROFOR had a hand in it!'

'A patrol was fired on and retaliated in self-defence,' I said quickly.

Tiny just grinned. 'Whatever, Jimbo. That was when we made ourselves scarce and got back to our vehicles for the night.'

'See the Croats are getting stuck into reinforcing the north defences,' Chas added. 'On our way in just now we passed diggers and cement lorries lined up.'

'That reminds me,' I said. 'Colonel Markovic is anxious to see you guys and get his hands on his communications kit. Promised we'd see him today.'

Tiny nodded. 'OK. Mind if we grab a quick beer at the Splendid first? I'm gagging.'

'At nine in the morning?' I shook my head. 'OK, I'll join you. We can drop in there on the way to the town hall.'

During the short drive in my newly acquired Land Rover I told Tiny and Chas what Rocky Rogers had reported to me the previous evening. That the two mercenaries we thought had murdered the Serb commander, Goran Zoric, were staying at the Splendid and were anxious to slip out of the area unnoticed.

Tiny scratched at the long, fiery stubble on his chin. 'That's interesting, Jimbo. Perhaps we ought to give those two shites a helping hand.'

Chas just grinned wickedly as I parked up outside the hotel.

Rocky and half a dozen of his drivers were at tables in the bar area, tucking into breakfasts of egg, cheese and some sort of local sausage. It didn't look especially appetizing, but at least it was available.

I introduced Tiny and Chas to the convoy leader. 'These two guys are from Hereford,' I said in a low voice. 'They're interested in meeting our mutual friends.'

Rocky raised an eyebrow. 'Pieter and Lars?'

'Are they still here?' Tiny asked.

'As far as I know. Expect they'll be down shortly.'

'I wondered if you'd consider changing your mind. Take them with you on your convoy to the coast.'

Rocky's eyes hardened. 'No way. Don't ask me to compromise the safety of the convoy.'

'You can make it a condition they're unarmed,' Tiny persisted. 'They can be passed off as relief drivers. We can have them picked up and arrested at the other end.'

'Sorry, mate.' Rocky was adamant. 'I've helped you guys before, but I know what those two are wanted for. If they're found on a UN convoy no one – not any of the militias – will believe we're not up to that sort of thing all the time. I don't mind taking some risks, but not that one.'

'Couldn't you just get the Royal Wessex to arrest them?' I asked.

Chas said, 'Problem is, Jimbo, we're on technically difficult ground. The UN doesn't have powers of arrest. It's the Bosnian Serbs laying siege to Sarajevo who are baying for their blood. They're the ones attacking the Bosnian Muslims who are the internationally recognized government here. Only that government could legally arrest them, but that's highly unlikely as — indirectly — it was that government who hired the two assassins in the first place!'

I shook my head. 'What a nightmare.'

'Our instructions,' Tiny continued, 'are to spirit 'em out by fair means or foul and let the lawyers argue the toss after it's done. The only point is to let the Serbs see the international community is not letting the assassination of one of their top commanders go unpunished.'

'Even if the victim was a mass murderer himself,' Chas added. 'Point is to persuade the Serbs to ease up on Sarajevo. They think the world's against them.'

'They are,' Rocky chimed in helpfully.

Suddenly I had an idea. 'I suppose you could call up a helicopter at fairly short notice?'

Tiny looked mildly irritated. 'Yes, of course, but as I've just pointed out, this has *got* to be discreet.'

I said, 'There's a playing field close to the school. It's on the edge of town and some distance from company HQ. An ideal landing zone and a helo could be in and out in seconds.'

Now Tiny looked distinctly pained, as if I'd missed the whole point. 'We'd still have to drag those two screaming and shouting out of a hotel full of the international media and half-way across town.'

My idea was forming rapidly. 'No need. We'll persuade them to go there with us.'

'With the British Army? I don't think so.'

I shook my head. 'They won't know who you two are. You hardly look like regulars . . .'

Tiny's eyes hardened. 'You takin' the piss, Jimbo?'

Chas chuckled. 'When's the last time we shaved or washed? Yeah, I see your point.'

'I'll tell them I want them off my patch. You two are a couple of mercenaries who've been working for the Croats. I make them an offer to join you on a small private convoy.'

'Is there one?'

I nodded. 'Yes, parked up on that playing field. A couple of CARE wagons – the Australian aid agency – a private lorry from some charity in Ipswich and a Dormobile full of a hippy kids' entertainment troupe called Wildchild.'

Tiny stared at me as though I was mad. 'You want us to get them out dressed up as a bunch of fuckin' clowns?'

I had to smile at the thought of that. 'I couldn't put those people at risk any more than Rocky will his crews . . . but Pieter and Lars don't know that. Once they get there, bring the helo in. Grab them, and off you go.'

Tiny studied his pipe for a second. 'Could work,' he said grudgingly.

'His brain's not functioning too well today,' Chas muttered with a chuckle. 'Let's try it – seeing as we don't seem to have a Plan B just now.'

Rocky nudged me under the table. 'Don't look now, lads, but those two creeps have just come in. Looks like they're ordering coffee. D'you want me to make a move?'

Tiny looked at Chas, who gave a slight nod of his head.

Pushing back his chair, Rocky Rogers rose to his feet and ambled over to the bar. The large South African looked around and smiled amiably; the skinny Dane just gave his usual welcoming glower.

'I hope this is a good move,' Tiny said, watching Rocky talking and pointing in the direction of our table. 'We haven't time to think things through or rehearse—'

'Just follow my lead,' I cut in. 'You're English mercenaries just finished a contract with the Croats. You're not exactly wearing regulation kit.'

Chas grinned. 'True enough. Ours is much better.'

There must have been a glimmer of interest, because when Rocky made his way back to us the two mercenaries were in tow.

In order to seize control of the situation, I rose to my feet promptly and stepped forward.

Rocky said, 'I believe you two have met Captain Hawkins?'

I didn't offer my hand, just acknowledged them crisply. 'Mr Visagie and Mr Larsen – please, take a seat.'

Lars clearly didn't like it that I knew his full name. 'I remember you, the village policeman,' he said sarcastically.

'If you like,' I said sharply. 'And I like to keep my beat clean, OK? Now, I don't know exactly what you two have been up to, but I've heard enough rumours to want you off my patch. Mercenaries like you are an embarrassment to the UN.'

'Soldier of fortune,' Chas chimed in with his correction.

Lars glared at him. 'Who the fuck are you?'

Chas's features changed like granite forming. 'Same as you. Soldier of fortune . . . a tidy one, as it happens. Working for the Croats here.'

I snapped back, 'And an equal embarrassment to the UN, I might add. Now Rocky here tells me you wanted to sneak out on his convoy when it leaves later today.'

'He doesn't have the nerve,' Pieter replied with a sneer.

'He doesn't have a mandate,' I came back quickly. 'The UN is squeaky clean and must be seen to be so. Too much is at stake. But there is another small convoy. It's a private one, charities and the like. They'll probably be willing to pass you off as crew . . . if they think you're genuine refugees.'

Lars was looking dubious as he thought about it.

I guessed what he was thinking. 'You'll be as safe as with the UN. The two convoys will travel together and the Royal Wessex will provide an escort out of the valley.'

Pieter seemed taken with idea. 'When will the convoys leave?'

Rocky said, 'If I get security clearance from UNPROFOR,

I'd like to go by midday. If you stick around the bar here, I'll confirm the time as soon as I know.'

I added, 'You'll have to make your own way to the private convoy's set-off point. That's the playing field on the edge of town. Just beyond the school. D'you know it?'

Pieter nodded.

I stood up sharply. 'OK, gentlemen, remember I want the four of you out of this town today. Without fail, do I make myself plain?'

Lars sneered. 'Hey, sure thing, Sheriff.'

Ten

It was ten in the morning and Una Drina remained uncannily quiet. Low cloud had rolled in during the early hours, leaving the morning drab, misty and very cold.

Snow was not the only thing that threatened. At any time everyone – civilians as well as the military – expected the besieging Muslims to begin a bombardment of the defensive Croat positions. It was the only talk at the coffee house-cum-tyre shop on the main drag. That and how the British Warriors of the Royal Wessex had come to the town's rescue the night before.

After our uneasy meeting with the two mercenaries at the Splendid, I took Tiny and Chas on to the town hall. Their two oppos were already there, unloading radio equipment from their Bedford truck.

Colonel Markovic was in an excellent mood, having witnessed the UNPROFOR confrontation with the Ramoza Brigade, and immediately agreed to allow Rocky's convoy to leave the area for the coast at midday in safety and without the hindrance of roadblocks, searches or inventory checks. Even Mayor Jozic seemed pleased to see me and looked genuinely disappointed when I politely declined to join him in a glass of slivovitz.

But I was anxious to return to company HQ, and went straight to the Den to bring Nigel Cuthbert up to speed with the plan to spirit away the two mercenaries.

He listened intently, scribbling down notes on a pad, but

looked a little uncomfortable. Finally, he said, 'You know this is really *my* department, Jimbo. I'm the UKLO.'

'Sorry, Nigel, but you weren't there.' I tried to make him feel better. 'It was only my *suggestion*. Tiny and Chas made the decision. They just want you to arrange for the helo to arrive on station, on time, at the playing field.'

He regarded me a little suspiciously. 'You know, I've never known anyone so good at getting their own way and then blaming it on someone else.'

I said, 'Maybe I should have been a politician.'

'Maybe you should,' he murmured. 'Is that mist still down? It might prevent the helo getting in.'

'It's thinning. The Met Unit forecasts it'll clear by midday.'

'I suggest you tell Tring that. He's twitchy at giving approval for the convoy to run in case the Muslims start their expected barrage.'

I frowned. 'Does that man think the opposite to every other person on the planet? The Muslims will start as soon as that mist lifts. The convoy should go as soon as the refuelling's finished at noon.'

'I know that, Gordy knows that . . .'

I raised my hand. 'OK, OK . . . I'll go to the Ops Room and see what I can do.'

As I went to move, Cuthbert put a hand on my shoulder. 'And about our mercenaries, Jimbo. Not a word to Tring about that, OK?'

I understood. 'Sure.'

Then I went to the Ops Room, where I was absolutely amazed to see Colonel Rathbone and a couple of officers from battalion HQ in discussion with Tring and Gordy Cromwell.

Rathbone spotted me immediately. 'Ah, there you are, Jimbo! Thought I'd better get out of my bunker and see what's going on this end of my patch. DV is merry hell. The Muslims have been bombarding the town all last night and this morning. No let up. Had to make the journey in a Warrior.'

I said, 'It'll start here, Colonel, as soon as the mist lifts. I've just got back from seeing Markovic. That's his intelligence.'

'Reliable?'

I shrugged. 'No way of telling. But Markovic has given me his guarantee of safe passage for the convoy if they go at noon. If that's agreed with us, I'll get on to Herenda and Aganovic and try and get them to stay their hand.'

'Excellent,' Rathbone said. Tring went to open his mouth, but thought better of it. 'We were just debating what to do. Seems you've got it sorted, Jimbo. Nice to see everything's under control here . . . And I was just congratulating the major on his decisive action last night. Probably saved the town.'

Behind Tring's back, I saw Gordy wink his eye in an otherwise straight face.

'Let's hope that smart new comms equipment will start proving its worth,' Rathbone added. 'Hope it makes a difference.'

'All parties seem very pleased with it,' I replied. While I was on a roll, another idea entered my head to catch the CO in a receptive mood. If I'd stopped to think for a moment, I might have decided it really wasn't such a good idea. But all morning I'd been getting flashbacks of the previous night's dream, and the words were out before I could stop myself. 'On another matter, Colonel, I had a request from that Dutch photographer, Tali van Wyk. She wants to do a photo essay on our work here . . . Er, d'you know her?'

Rathbone gave me a curious sort of look that I couldn't quite decipher. 'Course I know her, Jimbo. Well, to look at, anyway. Very pleasing on the eye, too, I might say. And I saw her pictures of the convoy under fire. Impressive. Gather they've just been used in a Sunday colour supplement back home.'

I raised an eyebrow. 'I didn't know that. I don't think she does, either.'

'Really? That's odd.'

'Bad communications out of here,' I explained.

'Of course, yes. Maybe your signals people can do something to help her out. Sensible to keep the press sweet, if possible.'

Tring said, 'Excuse me, Colonel, but, with respect, this isn't a very good time for us here. She'll just get under our feet.'

'Nonsense, Reg. It's a splendid idea. Just get someone to keep an eye on her. Hopefully get some good publicity back home. Taxpayers like to see their money well spent.'

'But, Colonel,' Tring pleaded, 'we're stretched as it is and we don't have a PINFO.'

I said, 'I'm happy to act as minder.'

Tring scowled. 'I think you've got enough on your plate, Jeffrey.'

But the CO seemed not to hear. 'There you are, then. Another problem solved.'

I looked at Tring, and said mischievously, 'Van Wyk wants to include some stuff on you, Reg. You know, "the loneliness of command" and all that.'

Tring didn't respond, but he didn't look impressed. Gordy stifled a snigger behind his back.

Rathbone glanced at his watch. 'Right, I'd best be off back to DV before that expected bombardment. Glad to see everything's in safe hands.'

As soon as the CO left, I started back to the Den. Gordy caught up with me. 'Thanks for back then, Jimbo. Did Markovic really give you that noon deadline?'

I grinned sideways at him. 'In a roundabout sort of way.'

'Tring was coming up with all kinds of excuses to keep the convoy here. I think he's afraid the Muslims will want to shoot it up in retribution for our intervention last night.'

'Well, he could be right. Except they don't hold positions south of the town at the moment.'

'As far as we know,' Gordy agreed. 'Mind you, I've had some unconfirmed reports of Muslim movements south on the other side of the river.'

'Fog of war,' I mused.

'Not sure about that photographer, by the way,' he said suddenly. 'Pretty face, legs to her armpits and all that, but she could be a bit of a liability. A bit young and foolhardy from what I've heard.'

'We were all young and foolhardy once,' I replied, becoming slightly irritated.

'She's been shagging that American creep, Kirk Grundy, y'know?'

I stopped dead in my tracks. 'Tali's told you that, has she?'

'No, of course not. But Grundy has. Been boasting to the whole of Bosnia about it.'

It was all I could do to stop myself from punching Gordy's lights out. 'Is that what we're devoting our intelligence effort to nowadays? Investigating the wet dreams and imagined conquests of an old CIA has-been?'

Gordy was clearly rattled by my angry response. 'Well, perhaps the has-been *has* been, Jimbo! A lot of people seem to believe him.'

'A lot of people believe a lot of things.'

'What's it to you, anyway?'

'She's still a kid,' I fired back. 'Barely twenty-five, inexperienced in this game and vulnerable. I don't like someone like that being character-assassinated behind her back with no chance to defend herself.'

Gordy raised his hands. 'OK, OK. Just don't want her causing any distractions amongst the lads.'

I said, 'A lot of them have met her already and she gets on fine with them. Most of our guys don't even know Grundy, let alone the nonsense he's been spouting. Only irresponsible gossip at officer level will change that.'

He had the decency to look sheepish. 'OK, I get your point, Jimbo. Sorry.'

'I can tell you one thing that *is* true. Grundy was making a pest of himself – that's one reason why she's moved from DV to here.'

Gordy nodded slowly. 'Must say that sounds a bit more plausible.'

I turned off then down the corridor leading to the Den, still angry. But I wasn't sure with whom exactly. It wasn't really Gordy and it wasn't really Kirk Grundy. I think it was more Tali van Wyk – and me for having my own deep doubts about the rumours and then refusing to admit them to myself.

Why the hell should it matter to me, anyway? But, as I tapped the code into the security lock, I think I already knew the answer.

I pushed that disturbing thought from my mind and entered. Nigel Cuthbert looked up from his desk.

'I've spoken to McVicar at CBF,' he said. 'They're sending in a Puma to the playing field at exactly 1200 hours. A crew with special-forces experience. They'll be armed and have the necessary restraints for uncooperative prisoners.'

I smiled at that. 'They may need them.'

'What about the convoy?'

'Well, Tring's reluctantly agreed under pressure from the CO, the Croats have agreed, now it's just a question of contacting the Muslims. We'll need to persuade Almir Aganovic to hold off.'

Cuthbert gave a sheepish smile. 'Best you talk to him, old son. Don't think I'm his flavour of the month.'

'That's what I thought,' I replied, and sat down to raise the Ramoza Brigade on the satellite phone. The comms wizardry did exactly what the instructions promised and I was amazed to find myself through to them in seconds with crystal clear reception.

To my further incredulity, when I asked to be put through to General Almir Aganovic he came on the line at once.

'Captain Hawkins, what can I do for you?'

'Good morning, General, we have a large UN convoy holed up in Una Drina. It's important that it has a clear run out to the coast today. I have spoken to Colonel Markovic and he has agreed to maintain the current cessation of military activities between midday and 1300 hours to allow it safe passage – but only if you, too, will promise not to resume hostilities for that period. Do we have a deal?'

There was a moment's silence at the other end. 'And this is a request from a member of UNPROFOR whose soldiers yesterday compromised the UN's impartiality here . . . Took the Croat side and attacked my holy warriors?'

'Ramoza Brigade troops opened fire on UNPROFOR, General, you know that. Our soldiers fought back in self-defence according to strict rules of engagement. They have to protect themselves.' For good measure, I added: 'They're here to help the weak and innocent, they have wives and children of their own at home who need them to return safely.'

Another pause and the soft voice was back. 'Then it is best they return home now, because if they interfere in my *jihad* to free this country, I cannot guarantee their safety.'

I ignored that veiled threat. 'Do we have a deal to let the convoy run?' I repeated.

'But of course,' he said smoothly. 'I have no intention of obstructing the UN's humanitarian effort.'

Two-faced, hypocritical bastard, I thought.

And, just as bad myself, I replied, 'Thank you very much for your co-operation, General. Then the convoy will run out of town between 1200 and 1300 hours.'

'Well done,' Cuthbert said as I finished.

I passed on the news of the convoy departure to Gordy Cromwell in the Ops Room and by radio to Rocky Rogers. I'd just finished talking to him when Tiny and Chas arrived, knocking discreetly on the door of the Den.

Cuthbert let them in, put a brew on and we went over the plan to get the two mercenaries into custody.

'We want to make sure those two are there on time, not getting lost or having second thoughts at the last minute,' Tiny said.

'So we thought we'd link up with them at the Splendid,' Chas added, 'at around eleven thirty. We'll have bergens, so we look like we're travelling. And we'll stick to them like glue, have a chat, maybe a beer.'

Tiny had the punchline. 'Thought *you* might pick up the four of us together, Jimbo. Drive us to the playing field.'

I shook my head. 'I shouldn't be involved in this. That is, UNPROFOR shouldn't.'

Tiny pulled a face. 'Yeah, Jimbo, but those two bastards know you. And perversely, after your Oscar-worthy performance this morning, they probably trust you.'

Chas nodded. 'They really believe you want them out of here, I'm sure of it.'

I nodded towards Cuthbert. 'Nigel's more your man, guys. He's a UKLO under the CBF. He knows all the sneaky-beaky stuff going on. I'm just a regular chocolate soldier.'

'No disrespect to Nigel,' Tiny said, 'but those two might be a bit tricky and you're rather more handy. More down-to-earth experience.'

'Thanks for the vote of confidence,' I said, 'but what about your two oppos?'

'They'll be tied up at Croat HQ. Anyway, they're only specialist signallers on attachment to Hereford, not the full monty.'

The truth was, I couldn't resist. I wanted to see Pieter and Lars get their comeuppance. I couldn't wait to see the look on their smug faces when the small-town sheriff actually put them in jail, so to speak.

And so 1145 hours saw me pulling up outside the Hotel Splendid in my Land Rover.

Tiny and Chas were standing on the steps, bergens on their shoulders, talking to the two men. The mercenaries' luggage lay at their feet, two bulky 100-litre rucksacks and a very large holdall. I climbed out of the driver's seat and beckoned them. Unceremoniously, I said, 'Stash your kit in the back.'

'I didn't expect such service from the British Army,' Lars muttered sarcastically as he lifted his rucksack over the tailgate.

'Just making sure you don't miss your bus,' I replied flatly.

With all the backpacks loaded, Lars lifted the holdall and made to take it with him into the rear passenger seat. It looked quite weighty and I guessed it was their heavier weaponry.

'Put *everything* in the back,' I ordered sharply.

Lars glared at me. 'Fuck you. This stays with me.'

Tiny was standing behind him and I caught the knowing look in his eyes. We both realized there was more than armoury in the holdall.

I said, 'Do you want to leave this town now, or wait here for a Serb revenge squad to find you?' I paused for effect. 'Because if you're not on that convoy, I'll be on the radio to their Pale HQ pronto.'

Pieter placed a large hand on his friend's shoulder. 'Do what the man says, Lars. It's not worth it. That bag isn't going anywhere.'

The Dane shrugged off the other man's hand with bad grace and slung the holdall over the tailgate with the rest of the luggage.

'C'mon,' Tiny said. 'I wanna get the fuck out of this shit-hole.' He sounded like he really meant it.

The two mercenaries and Chas climbed in the back and Tiny seated himself next to me as I started the Land Rover and swung out into the main road.

We passed the burned-out mosque, the attractive minaret tower and onion dome gone, the building reduced to smouldering rubble. It was a sorry sight, a group of Muslim citizens standing around, looking on in disbelief and gesturing angrily. Further on the huge white UN trucks and trailers were parked nose-to-tail on both sides of the street, as near to company HQ as possible for some semblance of protection. Engines were turning, belching out exhaust to replace the dwindling mist, while drivers conducted last-minute inspections of their vehicles in anticipation of the word to move from their leader.

I swung left at the tyre shop, drove up the side-street and past the school, which thankfully was untouched by the previous night's fighting. Two blocks of residential housing beyond the school buildings gave way to a large fenced sports field. There had once been goalposts and a wooden pavilion, but they had long since been dismantled for firewood, and the grass was over-grown.

The half-dozen assorted trucks of CARE, Save the Children and a private charity had been lined up abreast and the crews were huddled in a circle in front of them, studying a map. The psychedelic van of the Wildchild street theatre was parked some distance away. With their tents still pitched around the vehicle it was clear the members were not planning to leave anytime soon. Tali van Wyk was taking photographs of a long-haired juggler as he rehearsed.

I drove past the convoy vehicles and pulled up fifty metres beyond them.

'Keen to make us walk, are you?' Lars muttered disagreeably, throwing open the door.

'Just a minute,' I said. 'You'll have to leave any weapons behind. You can't take firearms on a civilian convoy.'

'Get stuffed,' Lars snarled.

'Who's rattled your cage?' Tiny demanded angrily. 'You trying to fuck it up for everyone?'

'No one asked you,' the Dane snapped back.

'We want to get out of this piss-hole too, y'know,' Chas rejoined, and pointedly handed over a Browning pistol to me, butt first. 'I've no need for this now. Not with a fuckin' Warrior escort.'

Pieter nudged his friend. 'Let's go along with them. Tonight we'll be in Split.'

As we all climbed out, I said, 'Have you got weapons in that holdall?' I didn't wait for an answer. 'Just take them out and leave them in the back.'

Pieter pushed in front of his reluctant friend, unzipped the bag and extracted four 9mm sub-machine guns of Czech origin. He looked at me. 'Satisfied, Mr Policeman?'

I raised an eyebrow. 'And your sidearms, please . . .' If they were reluctant to leave behind the heavy stuff, they sure as hell hadn't been planning to travel without basic personal protection.

It was Pieter's turn to glower at me. He opened his anorak and removed an automatic from its waist holster; Lars grudgingly followed his example and dropped it over the tailgate.

At that moment I caught the tell-tale *whup-whup-whup* of a helicopter rotor thrashing its way along the valley from the direction of the coast. Lars jerked his head around suspiciously, squinting into the mist that still lingered on the hillside. By the time he looked back, he was staring into the muzzle of my own automatic.

'What's with you?' he snapped. 'We've done what you asked. Let's get out of here.'

I smiled. 'Oh, you're going out of here, Lars, but not in any convoy. Hands behind your backs. Now!'

Simultaneously Tiny and Chas had moved silently behind each man, and as the two mercenaries obeyed my orders Plasticuffs were snapped over their wrists and locked tight.

'You bastard!' Lars spat. He glared at his friend. 'I told you not to trust him.'

The Puma helicopter was now clearly distinguishable as it emerged from the mist, canting as it turned in a wide, descending sweep to approach the playing field.

As the machine hovered unsteadily over the grass before lowering the last few feet, Tiny and Chas shouldered their bergens and frog-marched the two mercenaries between them to the helicopter. I went to the Land Rover tailgate and unzipped the holdall. It hadn't been the weapons that had been so precious to Lars and Pieter; it was the hundreds of twenty-dollar bills, all neatly bundled with elastic bands. Using gloved hands, I dropped all the mercenaries' firearms back into it and zipped it closed. Maybe there'd be some forensic evidence to prove their link with the assassination of Zoric. I ferried the bag and the men's rucksacks across to the hatch of the Puma.

Tiny grinned. 'Thanks, Jimbo!' he yelled above the scream of the engine. 'We'll see you around!'

I stepped back and away from the downdraught as the rotor gathered momentum and the helicopter rose rapidly. It peeled away to the right, beginning a wide ascending circle and setting a flightpath for the coast.

As I climbed back into the Land Rover, I glanced across to the Wildchild encampment and saw Tali van Wyk standing there, legs akimbo, with one of her three cameras to her eye, swinging the telephoto lens after the departing helicopter.

Shit, I thought. I was annoyed with myself rather than her. Somehow I didn't think anything she did would annoy me now.

I started the engine and drove across the field towards her. At least the hippies didn't seem to have given the incident anything more than the slightest attention.

I pulled up and got out. 'Hi, Tali.'

She smiled, her pale-blue eyes wide with curiosity. 'Hi, Jeff, what was all that about?'

'Whatever it was, it never happened,' I said firmly. 'Understand?'

A frown of uncertainty fractured her brow. 'Er, not really.'

'Nice camera. Mind if I take a look?'

'No, of course not.' She unhooked the strap from her neck. 'It's a Leica, top of the range. My pride and joy.'

I accepted it from her, sprang the back fastener, and thumbed out the roll, allowing the cassette to fall into my palm.

'Hey, Jeff, what d'you think you're doing?' She sounded really angry.

I dropped the cassette into the pocket of my smock. 'Sorry, Tali, but as I said, it never happened.'

'You can't do that, Jeff. It's my property . . . What were you doing to those two men?'

'Taking them where they can't do any more harm,' I replied enigmatically. 'Use your imagination . . . but keep your thoughts to yourself.'

She stood her ground. 'That film's my property and I want it back.'

I said, 'It's my property now. I'll make it up to you—'

She wasn't listening. 'I'll report you.'

'Grow up, Tali. Report me to who? Who's going to be interested? Anyway, I'd just deny it.'

Her eyes narrowed. 'I think you're being a complete bastard.'

I forced a smile; the last thing I wanted to do was upset her. 'Tali, please listen to me.'

Her mouth had crumpled into a disconsolate pout. 'Listen to what?'

'I've swung it for you with Major Tring.'

She regarded me with open hostility. 'You think that makes it all right to steal my film?'

'I hope it helps to compensate.'

'Well, it doesn't.'

'You've got the CO's blessing, too. That probably means you've got carte blanche here and at DV, headquarters and probably operational stuff too.'

Finally, I seemed to have her interest and she began to think about it. 'OK, Jeff, thank you . . . But it still doesn't give you the right to—'

'Look, Tali, that's history now. I'm sorry but I *had* to. It's a matter of operational security.'

She stared at me hard. 'I think those two men were mercenaries.'

'I've no idea,' I lied.

'I think I met them once in DV,' she said thoughtfully. 'They were drinking at the hotel bar with Kirk Grundy. Not very nice.'

'No?'

'Kirk suggested we all had a gang-bang.'

Stupid, really, but I said, 'I hope you didn't take them up on it.'

'Of course not. They were just drunk.' She hesitated. 'But I rather fancied the Swedish guy – or was he a Dane?'

'He's pure evil.'

She gave a defiant little smile. 'Maybe that's what appealed to me.' As she said it, I wondered whether she was just trying to shock me. Then she added, 'Anyway, I thought you didn't know who they were?'

'Let's drop the subject, Tali. D'you want a lift to company HQ?'

She frowned deeply as if she'd suddenly realized something. 'Oh, my God, *they* were the two Kirk gave my photos to, weren't they? The ones who assassinated Zoric?' Her eyes widened. 'God, have you just arrested them?'

I turned away, back to the Land Rover. 'C'mon, hop in.'

She seemed to get the message at last and scurried round to the passenger seat and jumped in. I then drove across the field to the line of parked trucks and the group of drivers.

I wound down my window. 'Are you all set? If you'd like to follow me, I'll escort you down to the UN convoy . . . You can tack on the end of it.'

They looked pleased to be on the move at last and dispersed to their various vehicles, ready to form up in a procession behind me. Minutes later I pulled up outside the gates of the company HQ compound. Rocky Rogers was there with his number two, Shaun, standing beside their white Discovery and talking to Gordy Cromwell.

The 2IC leaned in through my window. 'Just the man, Jimbo. With all this speculation about the Ramoza Brigade, I'd feel happier if you went with the convoy in case of any difficulties . . . Just to the top of the valley.'

'No problem,' I replied.

'It's just that you could cut the tension with a knife. The Croats are very jittery . . . Frankly, I wouldn't trust either side at this precise moment.'

'What formation are you using?'

'Just one Warrior in the lead – you drop in behind it with

Rocky's vehicle . . . then one Warrior mid-column, as it's this big, and a final Warrior at the rear.'

I said, 'I've just brought these charity wagons down.'

Rocky nodded. 'That's fine.' He turned to Shaun and Gordy. 'They can follow behind us with the rear Warrior behind them. OK, Gordy?'

'Fine, I'll just brief the rear Warrior commander. Kick-off in five?' He walked off and left Rocky to call up his drivers on the radio.

I turned to Tali. 'D'you want to go in and introduce yourself to Major Tring?'

'How long are you going to be?'

'No more than two hours – if there are no problems.'

'Then can I stay with you? From what I've heard, Major Tring can be a tricky customer. Maybe it's best if you introduce me.'

'You're probably right,' I agreed.

Just then Rocky's Discovery started to move and I fell in behind him, driving between the columns of parked UN trucks until we reached the front Warrior armoured personnel carrier. I received a friendly wave of acknowledgement from Hal Watkins, the cheery troop commander sitting aloft in the open hatch.

I switched over to the convoy's frequency in time to hear Rocky rallying his men: 'OK, lads, let's eat tarmac! But keep it steady, not breaking the world land-speed record today . . . We're too big . . . and we've some charity stragglers at the back! Ride it, cowboys!'

As he finished, he hit the horn of the Discovery and closed up until he was immediately behind the lead Warrior. Hal Watkins took his cue and the giant caterpillar tracks of the Warrior began to turn. I overtook Rocky and fell in behind it. In my mirrors I could see the parked UN trucks feed into the procession alternately from left and right, each blasting its air horns in warning as it pulled away. It was magnificent mechanized choreography.

'It's awesome,' Tali breathed, looking back out of her window.

'Isn't it?' I agreed. 'I always get a buzz when I see a convoy start to roll.'

We picked up speed, then hovered at around fifty kilometres an hour as we passed the Hotel Splendid and the square where the town hall was situated, past rows of boarded-up shops until the centre gave way to the southern residential suburbs and a mixture of hideous concrete low-rise flats and more traditional bungalows and chalet-style housing.

Then suddenly we were in the open countryside with undulating meadows on both sides, running to the foot of the mountains to our right and descending towards the river valley on the left. Only occasional alpine farmhouses and dilapidated outbuildings were scattered across the landscape of dull colours under a sky of low, bruised cloud.

The mist had virtually gone. I glanced around the countryside, feeling decidedly nervous, expecting to hear the Muslim heavy artillery and mortars open fire at any moment. Not – hopefully – at us, because by now the end of the convoy would have cleared the town . . . Yet still there was nothing and the uneasy peace continued.

Then the lead Warrior slowed as it approached the Croat roadblock guarding the southern approach to the town. But the guards just stood back and waved us through, smoking and looking sullen and cold in their tatty greatcoats and scarves wrapped round their necks and heads against the bitter cold.

I breathed a sigh of relief and settled down for the rest of the journey to the high pass at Makljen Ridge that would mark the end of the known danger-zone.

But my sense of rising optimism was badly misplaced.

We'd travelled about a kilometre beyond the roadblock when the Warrior troop commander, sitting in his hatch in front of me, suddenly raised his hand as a signal to halt. I stopped and, yanking the handbrake on, climbed out to see what the problem was.

At this point on the road the terrain was heavily wooded, both up into the mountains to my right and into the river valley on the left.

By now Rocky was out of his Discovery and together we walked forward to the Warrior. Hal Watkins leaned down to us.

'I think the road's mined, Jimbo,' he said.

We looked ahead. The convoy was approaching a tight bend and we couldn't see beyond the outcrop. But I certainly couldn't spot anything immediately ahead. While I was squinting, Watkins had levered himself out of the hatch and sprung down onto the road beside us.

He pointed a finger. 'That pile of stones. A common trick.'

Suddenly I saw what he meant. On the right a few metres in and up the steep hillside was a grouping of rocks that didn't look naturally positioned.

As Rocky and I walked forward with him, Hal said, 'That's the height they like to put them, in direct line with a Warrior commander's hatch.' He gave a boyish grin. 'Don't know what I've done to upset so many folk round here!'

I glanced nervously up into the mountains. If there was an observer up there, no one would be able to spot him. 'Maybe we should pull back,' I said, 'in case that thing's radio-controlled.'

But he continued walking. 'Not this one, Jimbo. There's a trip.'

His vision was sharper than mine. I had to look really hard to see the thin strand of translucent wire stretched across the road. The first vehicle passing would have triggered it. If Hal's eyes hadn't been so good, or his training so thorough, he'd have been a dead man now.

He scrambled up the embankment and peered closely at the stones. 'Yeah, here she is, sir. Nasty little buggers these. Plastic, metal and PE.' Then he looked more closely in the surrounding grass. 'Oh, shit,' he added softly.

'What is it, Hal?'

'It appears to be wired to something else, too. Back down the convoy line.'

'Oh, bollocks,' Rocky said with feeling.

When I glanced back along the edge of the road, where the convoy trucks had come to a halt, I could see several other mounds of stone and clumps of shrubbery – any of which could also be concealing a mine or bomb of some kind. In theory, one trip could have triggered mines all the way down the convoy line.

Suddenly I was becoming paranoid, big-time.

If this mine was linked to others, we couldn't even pass this one by first blasting it with cannon fire. And even if we could, there was no way of telling what lay beyond the next bend. It was very likely we were entering into a very thorough minefield trap.

And on this narrow road, there was no way the huge lorries and trailers could turn round and go back to Una Drina.

Hal said, 'I can request an engineer unit.'

I shook my head. The bomb-disposal boys were well stretched in Bosnia and it could easily be a day or two before they turned up . . . and even then it could be a lengthy operation. 'I imagine this must be a Croat minefield,' I said, 'defending the southern approaches to Una Drina. Easier to ask them to come and remove the bloody things.'

Watkins scratched his head. 'Why should they want to mine the road itself?'

'God knows,' I replied in exasperation. 'No joined-up thinking.'

Rocky said, 'I'll let the drivers know what's going on.'

'Make sure no one wanders off the road for a pee or a crap,' Watkins advised.

The convoy leader nodded his agreement and returned to his vehicle to get on the radio. I went back to my Land Rover.

'What's happening, Jeff?' Tali asked.

I explained the situation then got on the radio to company

HQ to put Gordy Cromwell in the picture. Finally I got him to patch me through to Croat headquarters in the town hall. Hopefully the SAS signallers had the new comms system up and running and it could start paying for itself.

It did. I found myself talking to Markovic. I got straight to the point. 'Colonel, I'm with the convoy right now. We're about one kilometre past your southern roadblock – and have come to a halt. Mines blocking the road.'

'Mines?' A hesitation. 'Not there.'

'I'm looking at them now, Colonel. And this *is* Bosnian Croat-controlled territory.'

Another pause. 'Unless someone is taking a local initiative . . . Or irregulars . . .'

I said, 'Either way, Colonel, I'd be obliged if you find out who planted them and have them removed . . . And quickly.'

'Well, that could be difficult . . .'

'I appreciate that, Colonel, but you owe UNPROFOR a favour for our intervention last night, remember?'

'Of course, of course. I'll tell you what I will do, Captain Hawkins, I will call the local commanders and have them meet me personally at the convoy location to see what this is all about. I will be with you in an hour.'

Three hours later, Markovic finally turned up in his personal Nissan pickup, patriotically flying the red-and-white chequered flag of Croatia. In its open cargo hold were his entourage of scruffy, unshaven and exhausted-looking field commanders. The colonel himself strode up to me, all smiles, and shook my hand.

He turned to a shorter, rotund officer who had comically long hair falling away from a bald head and who reminded me vaguely of the actor Danny de Vito. But from his severe expression, I had the distinct feeling that humour wasn't his speciality. 'This is my new second-in-command, Captain. Arrived this morning. He is Major Josip Zec.'

I had to smile. If I remembered rightly, Zec meant rabbit. And this character was certainly something straight out of Lewis Carroll. He ignored my proffered hand and threw an elaborate salute whilst glaring directly at my eyes.

'He hates the UN,' Markovic added with a ghost of a mischievous smile.

'Pleased to meet you, Major,' I replied politely. 'I do hope we can change your mind about the UN over time – by deeds, not words.'

'Then you will have your work cut out, Captain Hawkins,' Zec replied in a low and ungracious growl.

'OK,' Markovic cut in, 'what's all this about a minefield?'

'This way,' I said, and began walking up the road towards the lead Warrior. I pointed to the pile of stones and the trip-wire, then back down the convoy line. 'A mine here and running to others, probably all wired to go off together.'

Markovic winced. 'Good God, it would tear the whole convoy to ribbons.'

'Quite,' I agreed.

'But it is not our work. Why should we want to do such a thing?'

'I was hoping you'd tell me. To protect the southern approaches?'

'No, no,' Markovic protested. 'From Una Drina to the coast is all friendly Bosnian Croat territory. There is no need. I am afraid I cannot help you. These are *not* our mines.'

'You are certain, Colonel? Not even an independent unit?'

'I have all my local commanders here,' he replied. 'I shall go and check with them now.'

He walked to his pickup and addressed the men in the back. One of them scrambled down and joined Markovic as he made his way back to where I was standing with Rocky and Major Zec. Out of the corner of my eye, I noticed Tali positioning herself discreetly beside the Warrior to take some happy snaps of our meeting.

'This is the commander of this sector,' Markovic explained.

'He assures me this is not the work of any of his units. Nor is he aware of any independent militias operating in the area.'

'Then who would have laid them?' I asked, but even as the words came out I realized there could only be one answer.

Markovic raised an eyebrow in a way that suggested I was the dunce of the class. 'It can *only* be the Bosnian Muslims – led by that Antichrist, Almir Aganovic. Commandos, I expect.' He held out his palm, two fingers extended. He crossed off one with his other hand. 'One, to disrupt our supply lines from the coast.' He crossed off the second finger. 'Two, anticipating we Croats will get the blame for ripping apart a UN convoy. I am sorry, Captain Hawkins, we cannot help you. You will have to get Aganovic to remove them.'

Then it happened so fast, I virtually missed it. I felt a slight rush of displaced air against my cheek and had a fleeting glimpse of a squashed red fly on Colonel Markovic's forehead . . . And, as I blinked, he suddenly wasn't there any more. It all seemed to happen in slow motion. Rocky and Major Zec and the Croat area commander peeled away from me, throwing themselves to the ground. I was aware of their gasps and a scream of horror from Tali.

When I glanced down, I saw that Markovic hadn't gone anywhere. He'd just dropped like a stone in front of me and now lay in a crumpled heap at my feet. His face was turned away and I couldn't see the splattered neat red mark on his brow, but I could see all too clearly the horrific exit wound that had shattered the back of his skull like an eggshell. A mass of blooded grey worms had tumbled out onto the road.

Oh shit, I thought, and found my voice, 'SNIPER! TAKE COVER!'

That was all a bit late, as I seemed to have been the last one to realize what had happened. The shot had to have come from somewhere in the mountains on our right. Wisely, Rocky and the two Croat soldiers had moved for cover behind the left side of the lead Warrior.

Then I saw that Tali, her dangerous inexperience now telling, was crouched on the right of it. I rushed over to her, grabbed her arm, hauled her round to the front of the armoured vehicle and thrust her in an ungainly heap beside the other three.

'Have you got a fix on him, Jimbo?' Hal Watkins yelled down. He already had the turret cannon quartering the most likely firing-position area in the upper mountain slopes.

'You're joking! Didn't see a bloody thing!' I replied. 'Put down some random fire, let them see we mean business!'

That was fine by Watkins. With a clank and whir the turret began to swivel. Then the cannon opened up with short bursts of fire, huffing and puffing angrily amid clouds of cordite, reminding me of the ineffectual indignation of some mechanical dragon. He repeated the process half a dozen times, laying down a field of fire in random sectors of an arc.

Up on the mountain slope nothing moved. And no one fired back.

Watkins glanced down at me and shrugged. We could only hope it would deter the sniper from having another go.

Major Zec took immediate command of the Croats, yelling at the men in the pickup to collect the body of Markovic. We never did have our game of chess; it seemed he'd been checkmated by his Muslim enemies.

With a man grasping each limb, his corpse swung between them as he was carried quickly and unceremoniously back to their pickup.

Zec turned to me. 'This is a set-up, Captain Hawkins! Don't think I can't see through your ploy. The UN and the Muslims have always plotted against us.'

'You know that's not true,' I retorted.

But the man wasn't listening, he just blustered on. 'Well, it won't do you any good. Getting Markovic killed won't do any good. He'll just get replaced by another, and then another . . . we Bosnian Croats will never say die!'

He stormed off in an angry, arrogant little waddle.

'Now what do we do?' Rocky asked.

I'm sure I looked as deflated as I felt. 'Not a lot of options, really, are there?' I glanced up at the mountains. 'There's a Muslim guerrilla unit up there, that's for sure. They'll have laid the mines.'

Rocky looked around the bleak landscape, shades of grey in weakening light. 'It'll be dark before long. You won't get the engineers out here today.'

'Then I'll just have to try Aganovic.'

I returned to my Land Rover and got on the radio.

A few minutes later I was through to the Ramoza Brigade commander, the reception clear and pin-sharp. 'More favours, Captain?' he asked softly, and I could almost see the superior smirk on his face.

I held my anger in check. 'You know exactly why I'm calling, General.'

'I'm afraid you have the advantage over me.' So irritatingly smooth.

'One of your units has mined the south road and put a UN convoy in severe jeopardy. I need the mines removed *now*.'

The slightest pause. 'Not one of my units, Captain. That would be behind enemy lines.'

'Enough bullshit, General, who else would put out a sniper to kill Colonel Markovic?'

'Oh, really?' A gentle chuckle. 'Possibly one of his fellow Croats. He was not exactly loved by his men.'

'Joke over, General. I want these mines removed.'

'Then you will have to go on wanting.' Suddenly the steel edge cut through his soft tone. 'I know nothing about these mines. They are *your* problem. I've no doubt the Croats laid them in order to blame the incident on us.'

I shut my eyes. The old mantra tripped off my lips without me even having to think. 'Our convoys run to keep *your* capital, *your* towns and villages and *your* people alive.'

'We've had that conversation already,' he replied patiently, and the radio cut off.

So that was it. The UN convoy would be stuck on a narrow road overlooking a ravine all night until the engineers could reach it. There was a guerrilla unit in the surrounding forest and a sniper with an itchy trigger finger. Apart from that, everything was great.

Eleven

'God, that was scary,' Tali said as I drove us back towards Una Drina in my Land Rover. 'Thanks for saving me, Jeff. Trust me to hide on the wrong side of that Warrior – I couldn't work out where the shot came from.'

I said, 'That sort of thing only comes with experience.'

'Well, I don't want any more experiences like that. I was actually taking a photograph of Markovic when the sniper fired. Only for a second, but I saw it all in close-up. It was absolutely horrible.'

'I'm sorry you had to see it at all,' I said.

'I wonder if I got the exact moment on film,' she muttered ponderously to herself.

I knew she'd be feeling traumatized. Most of us go through life never seeing the bloody results of warfare or even a serious traffic accident. But when you do, it pulls you up short. It reminds you what frail creatures we really are and you never really become inured to it.

When we arrived at Una Drina it seemed unnaturally quiet, expectant. The Muslims still hadn't begun the bombardment that everyone was expecting and, like everyone else, military and civilian, I wondered why. Whatever the reason, I was thankful for such a big mercy.

I pulled up in the company HQ compound and invited Tali to follow me into the building. 'Be careful what you film,' I warned. 'Be especially careful in the Ops Room. *Always* get permission, and never photograph a map.'

She grinned sideways at me. 'No, Dad.'

On the way in I met Gordy Cromwell in the passageway, taking a mug of hot tea back to his desk. 'What the hell's going on down there, Jeff? You sure the Muslims laid that minefield?'

'As sure as I can be,' I replied. 'Almir Aganovic denies it. Either he's lying, or he's unaware what one of his guerrilla units is up to. And I doubt a fellow Croat sniped Colonel Markovic . . . even in this topsy-turvy place.'

'Whatever the truth,' Gordy said, 'we're well stuffed. An engineer unit won't get here until tomorrow morning.'

'At least the convoy's got Warrior protection overnight,' I said. 'But I'm concerned that Muslim guerrilla unit might still be in the area. They may be tempted to get up to something overnight. You can't necessarily expect rational thinking.'

Gordy raised his eyebrows. 'Too fucking true. And that sniper might still have a taste for blood.' He made his decision. 'I'll deploy a platoon to set up listening-posts around the convoy. Up in the hills and down in the valley.'

It was fairly standard practice in such situations. The British troops would give the convoy warning of militia movement or imminent attack, as well as acting as a deterrent.

As he went to go, I touched his sleeve. 'Where's Major Tring?'

'Back in his office, I think.' He grinned. 'Where he usually hides when the shit hits the fan.'

I turned to Tali. 'Right, let's get this over with. There never seems to be a right time with Tring.'

As I started to lead the way, she said, 'He's not the most popular Smartie in the box, is he?'

I smiled at that. 'Well, let's just say he takes some getting used to. Just be polite and your usual charming self.'

'Perhaps I should show him a well-turned ankle.'

'I'm not sure he's an ankle man. Best not.'

She glanced sideways at me. 'And you?'

'Ankles are fine.'

'I think you're a legs and bum man.'

I felt the blood rush to my face. 'Oh, really? Why should you think that?'

'The way I've seen you looking at me sometimes.'

God, this was embarrassing. 'Sorry, I wasn't aware . . .'

'Don't be sorry. It's nice to be looked at.'

I said, probably too quickly and dismissively, 'I'm old enough to be your father.'

Her eyes glittered with mischief. 'No you're not. He's two years older than you. And you are nothing like him.'

'No?' I wasn't sure I liked the way this was going.

'He seems his age. You don't.'

'Dads always seem their age to their daughters.'

'Maybe. But you're very different. Fun and exciting to be with. Kind, and you make me laugh.'

'Rubbish,' I said. 'It's just a uniform thing with young women. Anyway, I've never told you my age.'

'I made a point of finding out.'

I said, 'Then you probably also found out I'm married.'

Instantly I wondered why the hell I'd said that. Was I really trying to put her off, when in truth my thoughts about her were becoming distractingly frequent and persistent?

The brightness in her eyes clouded momentarily as she replied, 'Yes, Jeff, I know that. Most older men are.'

'A lot of experience with older men, have we?' I goaded, the image of a leering Kirk Grundy flashing unwanted in my mind's eye.

She gave a little laugh. 'I don't have a lot of experience of any-thing. But I do find boys my own age a bit boring, not very mature.'

I liked that and could hardly keep the rather smug little smile from my face.

Thank goodness we'd reached Tring's office. I knocked briskly and entered on his curt command to 'Come!'.

'Major Tring, this is Tali van Wyk.'

He looked up from his paperwork, surprised, his expression of profound irritation immediately melting away as his eyes registered the tall, slender blonde standing in front of him. A smile almost made it to his lips as he quickly stood and stretched out his hand across the desk.

'Ah yes, Miss van Wyk. Pleased to meet you. Seen you around, of course, but we've not been formally introduced.'

She shook his hand a little awkwardly. 'Yes, sir. Pleased to meet you too, sir.'

'I understand you're a photo-feature journalist, whatever that is?'

She nodded. 'I try to tell a story in pictures. Maybe just write an introduction and what we call deep captions.'

He nodded knowingly. 'Sort of thing they use in colour supplements . . . And you want to photograph my company at work?'

She smiled impishly at him. 'Work and play, sir.'

'Not much time for play here, Miss van Wyk,' he chided, taking on the manner of a Victorian father. 'But I think I know what you mean. In the mess, resting up, a bit of recreation like table tennis.'

'Maybe a football game with the local kids.'

Tring frowned. 'I don't like my lads getting too familiar with the locals.'

I said, 'A football match might be a good idea, Reg. Good publicity.'

He spared me an irritated glance. 'Think so, do you, Jeffrey? Well, you know what they say, familiarity breeds contempt.'

Afraid she'd started a row between us, Tali interrupted quickly, 'Oh, it doesn't really matter. But I would like to take some pictures of you, sir. You know, at work, walking around.'

'Look, young lady, this is a busy unit and I don't want you getting under people's feet.'

She shook her head, ponytail flouncing. 'Oh no, sir. I like to be a fly on the wall. You won't even know I'm here.'

'Then see that's the case.' He shot another glance at me. 'Captain Hawkins here has offered to take responsibility for you. He seems to think it's all a good idea, so don't let him down.'

She looked at me and raised an eyebrow, a cheeky smile on her lips. 'I won't.'

I said, 'I thought we could let Tali have pretty much the run of the place as long she's unobtrusive – if you agree, Reg. I've warned her about not photographing maps or anything else sensitive.'

She nodded eagerly. 'I understand that.'

Tring resumed his seat. 'That's fine. Now I suggest you cut along and let me get on.'

'Thank you, sir—' Tali was saying when we heard the first explosion.

The window behind Tring's desk rattled. Before any of us could say anything, the first explosion was followed by a succession of others. They seemed to be some distance away.

'Dammit,' said Tring. 'Artillery. That sounds like the start of it.'

'What?' Tali asked.

'The Muslim assault,' I replied. 'C'mon, the major's got work to do.'

I ushered her out into the corridor. 'Why are they attacking again?'

'Not a proper attack,' I explained. 'They failed at that. So we think they plan to lay siege and start a war of attrition. Artillery and mortar assault.'

'That's dreadful.'

I nodded. 'I'll introduce you to some of the lads.'

Needless to say, Tali's induction tour of the base was an unqualified success. Even the sporadic barrage from guns and mortars in the hills soon went mostly unheeded.

The red-blooded young soldiers, largely confined to camp

and without female company for weeks, had their eyes out on stalks as the svelte, smiling blonde moved amongst them. You could almost smell the testosterone in the air. And Tali seemed to be lapping up all the attention. Time and again, I had to haul her away from animated conversations with small groups of eager and rampant young squaddies and move her on to the next or we'd have been there all night.

She even had the dubious honour of being invited to join Major Tring and his senior officers for supper. The main course was an odd-looking concoction involving pigs' trotters and prunes dreamed up by the inimitable Billy Billings. Dubious or not, it tasted divine and Tali made short work of hers.

She was quieter and shyer with these older men, I noticed, and seemed happier answering questions than asking them. And, of course, the officers were no less enthralled by the unexpected civilian female presence than their soldiers had been. They also had the confidence to flirt obviously and quite outrageously as the innuendos and double-entendres increased with the flow of wine. But she handled it all well enough.

Although she'd somehow already managed to earn the reputation of being a bit scatty, I detected a new respect in the tone of the people around the table as they learned more about her. That she was probably better educated than most of them, had read widely from the classics to travel, was an accomplished horse rider, scuba diver, white-water rafter and skydiver.

'I think life's for living,' she announced boldly. 'You're a long time dead.'

That sort of attitude in a woman always impresses men, especially soldiers. But of course, it didn't stop the innuendos. In fact, they felt on even firmer ground with such a courageous and kindred soul.

The worst was Mervyn Jarvis, the super-cool and laid-back young aristo commander of the Lancers. He may have been plucked straight from the pages of *Brideshead Revisited*, and his chat-up lines may have been somewhat arch, but he managed to capture Tali's attention far too much for my liking. He was sitting on the other side of her and soon the two of them were in a giggling, laughing little huddle which started to exclude the rest of the table.

Gordy must have caught the expression on my face. He smiled and gave a small shrug of his shoulders, as if to say, what do you expect, he's a dashing young buck?

I nodded back, thinking, and I'm old enough to be her old man. But I was annoyed with myself for letting the situation get to me. I tried pushing Tali from my mind and instead exchanged a few jokes with Gordy.

But when the meal was finished and Billings started clearing away, I couldn't resist cutting in on Mervyn when he was in full flow. 'Sorry to interrupt, Tali, but do you want a lift back to Anita's house?'

Fortunately, as it turned out, a heavy mortar round landed somewhere within a hundred metres or so of our compound at that very moment. The table shook, crockery rattled and the empty wine glasses chimed against each other.

Major Tring said, 'It might not be safe to travel just now, Jeffrey. Best if Miss van Wyk stays here overnight while the shelling continues. Nigel's away at the moment; see if our guest can't make use of his billet.'

Tali looked relieved. 'Thank you, sir. I really appreciate that. Anita spends the nights at the school and I find it pretty scary being by myself.'

Tring smiled stiffly, as if embarrassed at being thanked for an act of kindness. I don't think acts of kindness were really his forte. 'Not really something we're supposed to do, Miss van Wyk . . . but as the colonel wants you to work with us, I don't think it'll be a problem.'

I just caught Gordy raising his eyes to the ceiling as I left the table and led Tali into the main building.

'Let me know if you want me to read you a bedtime story!' Mervyn called out after us.

'I don't think so!' she replied over her shoulder. 'You'd give me nightmares!'

I said, 'Sorry about Mervyn. Gets carried away.'

'That's all right. He was very funny.' She glanced sideways at me as we walked. 'Are you jealous?'

I shook my head. 'No,' I lied. 'Why should I be?'

'Shame,' she muttered mischievously, just loud enough for me to catch what she said.

I still couldn't make her out. Was she winding me up or leading me on? Or just having a bit of fun at my expense? She'd obviously picked up that I fancied her, maybe even before I'd realized it myself. But then I wasn't kidding myself there was a chance that she felt anything at all for me. So why did she keep playing this game?

Auxiliary lights were strung up in the corridors, the Ops Room and mess areas and run off generator trucks, but individual offices, billets and the troops' shared dormitory quarters relied on cutting-edge Tilley-lamp technology or candle power. We reached the dead-end passageway to the Den, passing the open door of my room. 'That's where I live,' I said.

She peered in. 'It's a matchbox.'

'Don't worry,' I replied, walking on a few more paces, then opening the door to Nigel's room and shining the torch in. 'Yours is a bit bigger.'

'I see,' she said, taking in the room's unmade camp-bed and its tables and cupboards improvised from packing cases. All work surfaces were covered with clutter: his Walkman and cassettes, old magazines, a pile of very unsoldierly toiletries, and dirty laundry scattered all over the place.

'Sorry it's a tip,' I said, lighting the Tilley lamp.

Tali frowned. 'I thought soldiers had to be tidy.'

'Ah, that's the point. Nigel is actually an *ex*-soldier. Now on sort of secondment from the Foreign Office. Drives the company sergeant mad but he doesn't have any jurisdiction over civilians. I'm sure Nigel plays up to that. Loves putting up two fingers to the army.'

I hunted round, found a large black bin liner and swept the entire contents of his tables into it, then picked up the laundry and stuffed in on top before throwing the plastic bag into the far corner, out of sight.

Tali laughed. 'I don't expect Nigel will like that!'

'As far as he knows it was the company sergeant. OK?'

She giggled. 'That's wicked.'

I said, 'I'm afraid you'll have to use Nigel's sleeping-bag. You shouldn't catch anything nasty if you sleep with your kit on.'

She looked at me steadily. 'I always sleep naked.'

I was aware of my pulse quickening. Impassively I said, 'Up to you.' I glanced at my watch. 'It's 2030 hours. I've got a report to write. I'll be in my room if you want anything. Meanwhile, feel free to wander around the base, just remember the rules.'

'Yes, sir,' she mocked with a smile. 'But I'm a bit tired. I don't suppose you have a book I could read?'

'I'm not sure we share the same taste.'

'It doesn't have to be Jane Austen or the Brontë sisters.'

I grinned. 'Then we may be in with a chance.'

She followed me back to my minuscule billet, where I lit a lamp and dragged out a cardboard box from under the camp-bed. To my embarrassment, I didn't notice the porn magazines on the top of it before Tali did.

She said, 'But I'm not sure *Rustler* is what I had in mind.'

'Not mine,' I replied quickly. 'Most of this stuff was already here.'

'I believe you,' she said, picking up one of the magazines. She sat down on the bed and began flicking through the pages. 'But I wouldn't mind if it was yours. I do understand something about men's needs.'

'Do you now?' I said, aware how patronizing I must have

sounded as I rummaged through the yellowing, dog-eared paperbacks.

'You can be very condescending to me sometimes, Jeff. Did you know that?'

'I'm sorry.'

'I don't think you even realize.'

I said, 'Well, you have done a few pretty daft things. I worry you might put yourself in some dangerous situations.'

She flicked back a loose strand of blonde hair that had fallen over her face. 'I don't mind dying young. I don't want to be old.'

I laughed. 'You won't say that when you get to my age.'

'Anyway, why should you care?' She pouted. 'Care about some silly girl?'

I looked up from the box. 'You're more than some silly girl, Tali, a lot more than that.'

'If that's what you think, you have a funny way of showing it.'

Suddenly that small devil was crouched on my shoulder, screaming in my ear. Screaming for me to tell her, tell her what I felt, regardless of the consequences. It came over me like a brainstorm, but it wasn't frenzied. It was cool and measured, but at the same time I just didn't care.

I opened my mouth to speak, but it was as though my brain had been hijacked by someone else. I was almost startled by the words that tumbled out. 'You know, Tali, Mervyn isn't the only one who fancies the pants off you.'

She blinked and her lips parted in a silent gasp. Then they closed again to form a coy smile. 'I'm not sure I believe you.'

'I didn't want to make it obvious.'

'Well, you didn't . . . Although I did sometimes wonder if you did *really* like me.'

I thought about that. 'Well, for what it's worth, I do. I like you a hell of a lot. But it's a pretty unedifying sight . . . old men leching after young girls.'

Her smiled widened. 'Well, you're not that old and you don't lech. You've always been a perfect gentleman. But women won't respond if they don't know what you think about them.'

'It's a good way to get sniggered at behind your back,' I said defensively. 'Or your face slapped.'

'I wouldn't do that. In fact, I'm rather flattered, I think, that someone like you should think of me like that.'

'Someone like me?'

'I think maturity and intelligence are very sexy in a man. And courage.'

I had to smile at that. 'I was right the first time. You are daft.'

Momentarily there was a hurt look in her eyes as she steadily held my gaze, then she indicated the paperbacks I was holding in my hands. 'Are they any good?'

'Mostly blokes' books,' I said. 'War or adventure. *Peace On Earth* by Gordon Stevens is an excellent thriller. Then there's a Paul Theroux travel book about Patagonia or some such. And a Jilly Cooper, don't know how that got in here.'

'For the sexy bits, I expect,' she suggested brightly.

'Probably,' I laughed. 'Back to men's needs again, are we?'

She reached out for the books and stood up. 'Thanks, Jeff, I'll try them.'

And then she was gone, out of the door and across the passage to Nigel's room. For a moment I felt like a goldfish gulping for air. What the hell had all that been about? It hadn't been a come-on, but then it hadn't been a put-down either. On balance I guess it felt more of a glass-half-full situation than a glass-half-empty one.

But I really didn't want to dwell on it. In a place and situation like this, that way could lead to madness.

I sat on the edge of the bed, drew up a packing case and spread out the fresh report sheet to update my account of the day's events. It took me several long minutes before I could concentrate. As my pen tip scratched its way across the page, I became aware again of the continuing muted sound of guns and mortars firing from the hills.

Half an hour later I'd finished and took the completed report back to the Ops Room.

Gordy was standing by one of the giant wall-maps, stroking his chin and looking concerned. 'Hi, Jimbo, I think something funny's going on here.'

I joined him at the map. 'What's happening?'

'Not sure. As you know, I set up listening-posts with night-vision kit at various points around the convoy. Those in the valley below the road have reported hearing and seeing a considerable number of troop movements.'

'Where exactly?' I asked.

'First indicators were on the far side of the river, militias moving north to south.'

I was being told exactly what I didn't want to hear. It had to be the Muslims, almost certainly elements of the Ramoza Brigade, moving deep into traditional Croat heartland.

Gordy continued, 'Then unconfirmed reports of unidentified units crossing the river to the convoy's side. I'm deeply concerned it could come under attack. It's in a very vulnerable position.' He shook his head. 'Sure, our lads can fire back if trouble starts, but we couldn't stop an immense amount of damage being done. That convoy's a sitting duck.'

I considered the situation for a few moments and lit up a miniature cigar. 'You know what, Gordy, I don't think you have to worry on that particular score.'

'How so?'

I said, 'Look, we're as damned certain as we can be that the mines were laid by Almir Aganovic's Muslims, one of their small commando groups.'

Gordy nodded his agreement.

'So we've got ask ourselves why.'

'To stop Croat reinforcements arriving from the south, presumably.'

I was playing devil's advocate. 'Not to hold up a very large UN convoy?'

'I don't really think so,' Gordy replied thoughtfully. 'Unless you're into the blame-game conspiracy theory, there's not really any point.'

I nodded. 'But just suppose there *was* a point?'

'You mean a tactical, military point . . . ?' he said slowly, and then suddenly slapped his forehead. 'Oh shit, Jeff, of course! So they can use the stalled convoy as cover as they advance behind the Croat lines.'

I added, 'And complete their pincer movement to cut off and isolate Una Drina completely.'

'Oh, shit,' Gordy said, staring at the map as though he could actually see the Ramoza Brigade advancing over it.

'After we prevented them advancing on the town last night,' I said, 'this is their Plan B. Surround it completely instead and begin a siege.'

'Not the best situation we could have hoped for. If they succeed, the Muslims will control the whole surrounding territory and the Croats most of the town itself. They'll both have the ability to shut down the convoy route whenever they choose while they play their little power games.' Gordy sounded very downcast. 'Still, I suppose it's not in the Muslims' interest to stop the humanitarian relief effort.'

I grunted. 'You'd think not, wouldn't you? But I've met Almir Aganovic and I don't think his mind works like ours. I think he'd prefer us and the UN to get out and let them fight to the death. Get it sorted once and for all. I think he'd rather let his own people suffer if it meant the Croats were also suffering.'

Somewhere outside a mortar round landed, the closest so far, and the Ops Room shook slightly in the after-shock of the explosion.

'Bloody Bosnia,' Gordy muttered bleakly. 'Why do we bother?'

Giving him a consoling slap on the back, I said goodnight and wandered off back to my matchbox, as Tali had described it.

I went in, relit the Tilley lamp and closed the door. You have to be ultra-tidy in conditions like that and I'd just begun tidying up my kit when another mortar round exploded close by. The floor trembled and small flakes of plaster fell from the ceiling like snowflakes.

Either the Muslims were getting careless or they were deliberately trying it on. They knew our rules of engagement: if we came under direct attack, we were entitled to fire back in self-defence. The trouble was that over time they'd learned that Major Tring, and to a lesser extent Colonel Rathbone, would engage against hostile fire only as a very last resort. From the sound of it, that round had landed in the main street outside our compound gates.

There was a gentle knock on my door. When I threw it open Tali was standing there, in jeans and a home-knitted sweater, hugging herself as if trying to keep warm. She was smiling sheepishly. 'Sorry, Jeff, that was a bit close.'

Just seeing her lifted my spirits. 'Frightened?'

'Nervous.'

'I thought you wanted to die young?'

She clearly didn't mind being made fun of. 'Not *this* young. And especially not tonight.'

'Oh?'

'My hair needs washing. Can't die with dirty hair, Jeff.'

I said, 'That round was in the street. It's very unlikely the base will be hit. They're just being cocky, getting as close as they can. Just have to hope some idiot doesn't get his trajectory figures wrong.'

She nodded. 'Can I get a drink from somewhere? A coffee maybe?'

'Our mess, such as it is, won't be open now. I can brew you one.' I nodded at the tiny butane stove on one of the upturned plastic milk crates.

'I don't want to be any trouble.'

'You're always trouble, Tali,' I joked. 'Thought trouble was your middle name.' I indicated the door. 'Better close that. Don't want to get tongues wagging.'

She stepped inside. 'You don't think we should give them something to wag about, then?'

I shook my head in mock despair; she was irrepressible. She flirted but in a shy, coquettish sort of way. 'Only in my dreams, young lady.'

'I suppose you could be court-martialled.'

I smiled, filled the aluminium kettle with bottled water and lit the flame. 'You're always breaking some goddamn rule in the army. Once, when I was based in Belfast, my wife and I were put in a house on this grotty army estate. The garden didn't have a fence. And every time our dog escaped, I was fined and given fatigues – even though I wasn't there.'

'That's crazy. Wouldn't they give you a fence?'

'No, it was our fault for having a family pet before I was posted and fences on the estate were against the by-laws.' I hunted in my bergen for a spare mug. 'How d'you take it?'

'Pardon?'

I looked up and saw the cheeky expression in her eyes. 'Your coffee, how do you take it?'

'White, no sugar.' She sat herself on the edge of my camp-bed. 'These aren't very comfortable, are they?'

'Good enough.'

'Yes, but I've strained my back, I think. Well, more my neck and shoulders, really. I always stuff too much in my rucksack. Too many books.'

'How were those books, by the way?'

'I've started the Paul Theroux. Travel books are easiest to pick up and put down.'

I nodded and, without thinking, said, 'I could massage your shoulders for you.'

Her pale eyebrows lifted in an expression of mild surprise. 'Would you? That would be nice.'

Christ, I thought. As soon as the offer had escaped my lips, I'd expected a put–down. Immediately I felt my pulse begin to race. The kettle began to steam and I poured the hot water into the two mugs, hoping the slight trembling of my hands wouldn't be noticed.

I gave her one of the coffees and sat on the bed beside her. 'Would you like some whisky in that?'

'Oh?' Her face brightened. 'Yes, why not? Thank you.' She sipped at her drink.

I extracted my trusty flask from a side-pouch in my bergen and poured in as much whisky as I could until her mug was almost overflowing.

She giggled. 'Are you trying to get me drunk, Jeff?'

'The idea had crossed my mind,' I replied with a fair degree of honesty.

She was clutching her mug to her mouth with both hands and peered at me from over the rim as she took a sip. Then she said, 'You don't need to get me drunk.'

There she was, playing games again.

I said, 'You need to be relaxed for a massage.'

'Relaxed? I'll be comatose.' She took another mouthful. Then she said suddenly, 'I expect you miss your wife?'

The image of Marcia, wearing her usual sour expression, flashed into my mind. It was the last thing I needed at that moment, the very last. I felt more than a little irritated. 'Actually, Tali, no, I don't.'

She shrank back a little. 'I'm sorry. I didn't mean to pry.'

I shook my head. 'No, it's all right. To be honest, just lately I've realized my marriage has just about run out of road.'

'That's sad. Have you been together long?'

I smiled mirthlessly. 'Since the beginning of time.' I took a long, hard swig of the coffee and felt the liquor burn the back of my throat. 'But we grew apart a long time ago. She's not the same person I married, and I guess she'd say something similar about me.'

Tali leaned forward, seeming genuinely interested. 'But you just didn't realize?'

I nodded. 'I don't think I've ever really admitted it to myself. Until now. Just recently.'

'I never want to get married. Or have kids.'

I looked at her pensive expression, as she sat with her elbows on her knees and clutched her coffee with both hands, and I thought that was rather sad. No, I thought that was *very* sad. Because at that precise moment, I couldn't think of anyone else I'd ever met that I'd rather spend the rest of my days with. Mad, impossible dream though it was.

I just said, 'Maybe you'll change your mind when the right man comes along.'

She'd been staring down at her coffee, and now her eyes flashed towards me. 'Maybe,' she said. Then suddenly she sprang to her feet. 'What about that massage, then? Shall I sit on the floor in front of you?'

I looked up at her from the bed. Suddenly I wasn't sure this was a good idea. I said, 'Er, look, Tali, I'm not very good . . . I'm not trained or anything.'

She frowned. 'But you've got a rough idea, I expect?'

'From what's been done to me,' I replied, then couldn't suppress a smile. 'Massage parlours around the world.'

'Oh, I see.' She giggled. 'But we'll keep this clean, eh?'

'Of course.'

She turned round with her back to me and sat cross-legged between my knees. I took a deep breath and placed my hands on her shoulders, squeezed and began to work my thumbs into the tendons below her neck.

Immediately, she said, 'Jeff, you're *not* very good, are you?'

I was puzzled. 'What d'you mean? I haven't started yet.'

'I was about to take off my sweater. You can't massage through wool.' She twisted round to look up at me. 'That is all right, isn't it?'

'Er, of course. I just didn't think . . .'

Then her hands clutched the hem of the sweater and her arms rose to peel the garment up her body and over her head. 'I can't believe you were in many massage parlours with all *your* clothes on.' She shook her ponytail free and flung the sweater on the bed. Again she turned round and looked up. 'Don't worry, I'm not taking anything else off.'

I was just starting to realize that Tali rather liked trying to shock people, to see how they reacted. But she got little reaction from me just then. Her sudden exposure had lashed at my senses for a moment, taking in the slender body I'd only ever seen clothed for weeks and had wondered many times how it would look naked, how it would feel to the touch. Another impossible dream, now unexpectedly a bizarre reality. Her bra wasn't anything fancy, no lace, just sheer and delicate white cotton. From my vantage point above her I glimpsed her small breasts nestling in the cups. Guiltily I pulled back, so that she wouldn't think I was leering.

As I placed my hands back on her shoulders and began to work my fingers into her flesh as professionally as I could, she said, 'I don't suppose you have any oil?'

I chuckled. 'Only gun oil.'

'Oh, course, silly me!'

Then I had a thought. 'Hang on. I think I've got some baby oil.'

She looked at me quizzically, then laughed. 'Now that I *don't* believe!'

I reached into the bergen with one hand and rummaged. 'Keeps leather incredibly supple,' I explained, and located a small plastic bottle that was running low.

'This is looking more promising by the minute,' she said, and closed her eyes.

Well, I certainly wouldn't have disagreed with her there!

For the next twenty minutes I worked slowly and steadily on her neck and shoulders, trying to do a really good job, locating the tension knots in the muscles and kneading them with my thumbs. I thought I wasn't doing too badly, and about half-way through Tali confirmed what I'd thought. After a purring little moan she murmured, 'Oooh, God, that's good, Jeff. You'll be sending me to sleep.'

I started moving my hands further up into her hair at the nape of her neck.

'You don't know how to Indian head massage as well, do you?' she asked.

'I've seen it done,' I said. 'But it would be a bit hit-and-miss.'

'Well, if it's half as good as what you've just done,' she said enthusiastically, 'this is my lucky day.'

No, Tali, I thought, this is *my* lucky day. But I just said, 'I can give it a try if you want.'

'I want,' she said. Immediately she reached for the band that retained her ponytail and deftly unravelled it to let her hair fall free to her shoulders.

It was like an explosion of wavy molten gold and I scooped it up in my cupped hands, raking my fingers hard back against her scalp. I heard the barely audible gasp of pleasure and surprise escape her lips, and sensed then I knew what she liked. And, so far, I'd got it right.

For the next ten minutes I concentrated hard, massaging my fingertips deeply from the front of her head and back across the crown, then starting from her temples and back along both sides, then down to the nape of her neck, working my thumbs into her skin.

I didn't really know what the hell I was doing, but Tali just closed her eyes and leaned back into me a little, increasing the pressure against my fingertips.

Eventually I stopped and she sighed languidly. 'I'm half-way to paradise.'

'Only half-way?' I countered as I manoeuvred my right leg behind her back, picked up my mug and dropped down to sit beside her on the floor.

She finished her coffee. 'I'm not complaining at half-way.'

'Another drink?'

'I'm fine.'

'Just the Scotch?'

She turned to face me, a slightly devilish look in her eyes. 'Are you trying to lead me astray?'

I held her gaze. 'Yes.'

'Oh, all right, then,' she replied, and offered me her empty mug.

Without moving position, I reached for my flask and poured in a seriously over-generous measure of whisky. 'Thanks,' she said and swallowed hard. 'I feel so much more relaxed now. Mellow. I'm feeling mellow.'

'That's a good word.'

'It's a good feeling.'

And, feeling a bit like a kid on a first date, I slipped my arm behind her shoulders, her hair now brushing my cheek. My mouth was dry and suddenly my head was empty of anything sensible to say. So I said the first thing that came into it: 'You've got lovely hair. Very soft.'

'Thank you,' said Tali.

Her eyes closed and we sat in silence. Every now and again she'd take a sip of her whisky. I waited for some physical response from her, a signal, but there was nothing. I caught some strands of her hair and idly curled them in my fingers. It had to be obvious to her that I was making a play but still there was no reaction.

I had just decided that I was making an idiot of myself and had got it all wrong when suddenly I felt her bare foot rubbing teasingly against my leg. I did a double-take. Had I imagined it? I looked down and saw the deliberate movement as her toes curled themselves along my calf in a stroking motion. Now there was no mistake.

'Tali,' I breathed as I ran my right hand over her hair, caressing the side of her head. She sighed softly and snuggled up against me. I knew then we'd done it – at last we'd made the connection. I leaned sideways and kissed her ear.

I will never forget the tiny tremor of her whole body and her sudden breathlessness as I trailed my fingertips down across her throat. I swear it was one of the most erotic experiences of my life as she turned her head to me and opened her velvet mouth.

Our first gentle kiss grew rapidly into a madness, then a frenzy. Her hands were around my neck, in my hair, her mouth and tongue exploring mine with a feverish intensity. It was almost as if we were devouring each other, and I suppose in a sense we were.

I ran my fingertips down along her throat again, eliciting that same tremor and gasp that told me it was a very sensitive zone for her. And she groaned as I momentarily tightened both my hands around her neck before releasing her and moving my palms down over her breasts, aware of her hardening nipples on my skin through the thin stuff of her bra. My right hand glided down across her stomach and moved hard in between her legs. She hadn't been expecting that quite so soon or quite so roughly, and gave a sharp intake of breath. It flashed through my mind that I was staking a claim, the territory was her body and I had no intention that she should suddenly change her mind and demand it back. I'd waited too long for this moment, desired her too long until it had become almost a physical agony inside me.

And at that moment I could have believed she felt the same.

Already I was becoming aware of a sort of rhythm about the way we were doing things. Whatever I did to her, every pleasure I gave her, she immediately returned, with not a little interest. As I moved to unhook her bra and free her breasts, her fingers were already working nimbly at the buttons of my shirt. After I kissed and bit her nipples lightly, she did the same to me.

It seemed only moments before we were naked and entwined on the floor, my head reeling with fleeting glimpses of her naked body.

Our natural rhythm continued for many long minutes, by turns gentle and exquisitely cruel, ebbing and flowing as we both seemed to know what the other liked and then, as my hand was between her thighs and she clutched at me, I found I was looking close into her face again. She was making a soft, almost whimpering sound, as though she was struggling to breathe, and her eyes were half closed as she neared orgasm.

Then she shook her head, biting at her lip. 'Oh, Jeff. I can't quite get there.'

I kissed her damp forehead. 'Don't try so hard, sweetheart. Relax.'

I felt her shoulders drop as she obeyed the direction. I ran my left hand down along her spine, my fingers trailing feather-like into the cleft of her buttocks.

Mere seconds later she muffled her scream into my shoulder, biting hard into my skin with her teeth as her whole body was racked with the explosion of her release.

Her trembling in the after-shock seemed to linger for several minutes as I held her close, feeling her hair soft against my chest. 'Jeff,' she said, still sounding breathless, and looked up, her eyes wide and her pupils dilated. 'Fuck me now, Jeff. I want you to fuck me.'

Momentarily I was stunned. Not at her language, her choice of base words, but the softly spoken, slightly breathless delivery of them.

I looked down into those appealing powder-blue eyes and felt a renewed surge of blood to my loins. 'I'll just get—' I began.

But she cut me short. 'No, no, don't use anything. There's no need. Unless you want to?'

The rumours about her and Kirk Grundy flashed through my head, but suddenly I didn't care. Didn't care about her age – Jelena had been younger still, even though I'd been drunk – and at that moment I didn't care about any other risk either. Like a male praying mantis, I'd have been willing to die immediately afterwards. I just wanted to fuck Tali then and there, regardless of the consequences to my morality, my body, my career.

She placed a hand on each of my shoulders and pushed my back down onto the threadbare carpet, spread her legs wide, feet firmly on the floor. Then reached down to me and began very, very slowly to impale herself on me.

'I want you to fuck me to my core.'

I said, 'We call that a spy's fuck.'

She frowned. 'Why?'

'Don't stop, I'll tell you later . . .'

She smiled, and her eyes closed as she sank down on me. She wasn't listening any more, lost in her own world.

And I was lost in mine.

Twelve

I awoke to the pneumatic drilling of my alarm clock and felt like death.

Too much whisky and lack of sleep had left me disorientated for a couple of seconds, until I remembered where I was. I reached towards the luminous dial of the clock and hit the off switch.

Then the memories came tumbling back. Where the hell was Tali? When I'd fallen asleep she'd been up tight against me on the narrow camp-bed, her buttocks mashed warmly against my groin.

I swung my legs off the bed, found my torch and turned it on. Of course, she'd gone. There was no place to hide in my matchbox.

Although it would have been lovely to wake up with her still in my arms, I was in a way glad she'd made good her escape before HQ came to life. Besides, I felt I needed time to think, and I certainly couldn't think straight with her lying naked next to me.

Next I noticed how quiet it was. The sound of background shelling that had gone on into the early hours had fallen silent. I lit the Tilley lamp and put the kettle on the small stove, pulling on my fatigue trousers, Norwegian Army shirt and regulation-issue khaki sweater while I waited for it to boil. Later in the day I'd grab a shower in the improvised ablutions block when there'd be a better chance of some hot water.

In the meantime I poured a cup of strong, sweet tea and lit up one of my miniature cigars. I was starting to feel better already, even more so as I slowly began to recall the tenacious love-making of the previous night. We'd talked a lot too, in whispers so that no one passing in the corridor would hear. It had been the first time I'd really had fully joined-up conversations with her, and I'd been surprised at just how bright and intelligent she was – and how we'd simply got on so well. Looking back, it really did seem that the age gap between us had melted away. Of course, given her relative youth, she was a bit innocent and naive, and I tended to find myself cast more in the role of mentor than I'd have liked. But she seemed not to mind, and was apparently eager to garner the benefits of my experience. And she wasn't beyond some wit and humour at my expense, either. There were definitely hidden depths beyond that shy and innocent façade of hers.

And as for the sex, that had blown me away. I couldn't remember a time when I'd ever felt such physical harmony with a woman. It had almost been like dancing, moving and counter-moving, giving and taking, always seeming to know exactly what the other wanted. One minute rough, almost violent, the next gentle and soothing, playing to an unheard rhythm. It had been animal, instinctive.

I tried to push the thoughts from my mind. If my head was full of Tali van Wyk all day, I'd be worse than useless to anyone.

Just as I drained my coffee, I heard it. The barrage had started again. Distant thuds of artillery and heavy mortars from the hills, followed moments later by the resounding crash of the rounds exploding nearby. Not too close, but close enough. But this time, the firing was immediately answered by returning fire from the Croat lines on the edge of town.

Time, I decided, to find out what developments there had been overnight.

Stubbing out my cigar, I killed the lamp and went out into the passage. As I did so another shell landed a short distance away and the walls shook, flaking off some loose plaster. The string of overhead bulbs that were powered by our generator truck flickered uncertainly.

I glanced at the door to Nigel Cuthbert's billet and hesitated. Immediately my resolve weakened and I stepped across to the door, and tapped lightly. There was no reply. Gently I twisted the handle and allowed the shaft of light from the passage to open up over the floor towards the camp-bed in the corner.

Tali was curled up on the bed, the blanket she had found tossed aside to reveal the short silk jade nightdress she wore. She was fast asleep and looked so peaceful, so angelic with her blonde hair splashing over the pillow like a halo.

Quietly I shut the door again, thankful that she couldn't hear the surrounding sounds of death.

The base was coming to life as I strode through the corridors to the Ops Room. Gordy Cromwell was just taking over from the night duty officer and finishing off a thick bacon wedge he'd grabbed from the canteen.

Licking his fingers, he looked up. 'Mornin', Jimbo.' He frowned. 'You had a rough night?'

I smiled. 'Does it show? Couldn't sleep.'

He nodded. 'I know. Worrying, isn't it?'

I let it pass. 'So, what's happened?'

'Well, you were right. Most importantly, the convoy's OK and the mine-clearance boys should be here soon after first light. And so far, according to our OPs, the Muslim barrage has been directed at Croat lines. But our listening-posts have been reporting more Muslim movements all night. Seems like they've taken up new positions to the south. Una Drina's completely surrounded.'

'And the Croats?' I asked.

'Woke up to what was going on quite late, but they've started reinforcing their southern defences.' He stared at the wall-map. 'But I don't think they're going to be in a position to counter-attack. My guess is it'll be more of a stand-off, more like trench warfare.'

Of course, that had been the thing about the Bosnian war.

Most of the Yugoslav-trained officers were only really trained in defensive warfare and the largely rural peasant population had no real stomach for heroics. It was easier to stay put in their trenches and lob stuff half-heartedly at the other side. Sometimes it really felt that you'd entered a military time-warp and were back on the Somme.

I said, 'Still, better that than for either side to believe it can actually achieve an objective.'

Gordy nodded. 'More likely to talk, you mean?'

'If they don't think they can really get anywhere by fighting,' I replied with more hope than conviction.

I left Gordy to it and visited the canteen for some eggs, beans and a sweet, strong black coffee to kick-start the day.

After that I opened up the Den and played with the satellite phone, once again getting through to General Almir Aganovic far more easily than I'd anticipated.

He was in high spirits. 'Good morning, Captain Hawkins. I trust you slept well.'

'I would have done had it not been for your infernal barrage,' I replied.

'War is never easy.'

'And civil war is barbaric. I'm for jaw-jaw, not war-war. You'll all have to talk in the end.'

'Have you called to give me a lecture on the thoughts of Winston Churchill, Captain?'

I was reluctantly impressed that he had recognized the reference. 'No, General, but as I understand you now have Una Drina surrounded, I am calling to ask you if your men will *now* come and remove the mines that are blocking the convoy.'

But he was still playing games, refusing to admit responsibility. 'No, because they are not our mines – as I have explained already.'

'Then you will not hinder UNPROFOR clearance teams or the convoy?'

'Of course not.'

Well, at least we were getting somewhere. 'Good. Our men will begin that task shortly. I was also calling to suggest a meeting between your good self and the Croat administration in Una Drina.'

I was aware of a gentle laugh at the other end. 'A meeting? What for, in the name of Allah?'

'To see if you cannot resolve some of your differences, General.'

'Captain Hawkins, I represent the forces of the *de facto* government of Bosnia-Herzegovina. As such I demand the surrender of the hostile Croat forces in Una Drina, because we cannot continue to allow the enemy to choke our supply line to Sarajevo either here or in Donji Vrbas. Do you think the Croats will want to discuss that? I think not.' Then he gave a menacing little chuckle. 'Not *yet*, anyway.'

'You and the Croats were allies until a few weeks ago,' I pointed out.

'A week is a long time in politics, Captain, as another of your leaders once said.'

Touché! 'Better to talk early than to let old animosities become set in stone,' I persisted.

'It is too late for that. Already the town's Croat authorities have allowed the mosque to be burned down. We all know what will happen next.'

That made me angry. 'Ethnic cleansing will not be tolerated in this town by *anyone*. Not while the British represents UNPROFOR here. But the longer both sides refuse to talk, any mutual dislike will simply fester. You know that, General.'

'Regrettably, there is nothing I can do about it.'

It was like squeezing blood from a stone, but I thought I might just have him on the back foot. 'So *you* would come to a meeting if the Croats agreed?'

I was wrong. Aganovic said, 'Only if the Croats agree beforehand to disarm and disband their militia. *Then* I would be prepared to meet to discuss the fine details.'

Dammit, I was back to square one. Aganovic knew as well as I did that the Croats would never do that, even if it were logical and in their best interests. It would entail too much loss of face.

I gave up on him then, finished the call and returned to the Ops Room.

At ten o'clock a detachment of Dutch Army engineers arrived to sort out the mines that were holding up the convoy and Gordy gave them a Warrior escort to the south of town. Meanwhile the rest of the company's armoured vehicles began patrolling the town or deploying themselves to protect key civilian locations such as the clinic, the hotel and the school where Anita Furtula was still trying to look after and teach a dozen or so children. By stationing themselves as closely as possible to these buildings, the Warrior commanders could adjudge any attack on that target to be an attack on themselves and justifiably return fire under the rules of engagement. But so far the sporadic Muslim barrage had been confined to known Croat positions.

However, there was lot of toing and froing of Croat forces, mostly militiamen in battered pickup trucks being ferried south to reinforce the defences following the advance of the Muslim pincer movement. They would always be a temptation for the Ramoza Brigade's artillery observers in the hills.

It had just gone eleven when Major Tring appeared with Tali, loaded down with cameras, by his side. I noticed that, even by his exacting standards, he was exceptionally well turned-out. Even if the full dress uniform did look ridiculously out of place. Of course, everyone else was in the usual combat trousers and khaki woolly-pullies.

'Blimey, Reg,' Gordy said. 'Didn't know we had a regimental dinner planned.'

'Don't be facetious,' Tring replied tartly. 'Miss van Wyk's taking photographs. Have to create a good impression for the press.'

Gordy chuckled. 'Yeah, right! Don't want your mum to think you're letting your standards slip.'

While the other duty staff suppressed their laughter, Tring decided that selective deafness was the best way to handle the situation and instead turned to Tali. 'Where would you like me to be? At a desk; in front of the wall map . . . ?'

The young photographer looked awkward. 'I'm not actually doing a portrait, Major. I'll just take pictures as you go about your usual business.'

He hesitated. 'Oh, er, I see.'

At that point she caught my eye and held my gaze for a moment, her lips parting a fraction in a shy smile. 'Hallo, Jeff. Did you sleep well?'

'Best in years,' I said with a knowing smile.

Tring frowned. 'With that barrage going on half the night?'

'Well, there was certainly a lot of banging going on.'

Tali's faced reddened. Before I could dig a deeper hole for myself, the line of conversation changed abruptly with the arrival of Tring's aide, Billy Billings. 'Major, sorry to interrupt. You've got a deputation.'

Tring looked irritated. 'Oh, yes?'

'Mayor Jozic and 'is new commander. That Major Zec bloke.'

The fat rabbit, I muttered under my breath, the Danny de Vito lookalike with the sense-of-humour bypass.

Tring raised his eyes skyward. Then looked straight at me. 'Look, Jeff, you and Gordy handle this, eh? I'm tied up with this press nonsense, and as you know the CO's keen on it . . .'

I was feeling in a flippant mood. 'OK, Reg, I'll tell them how important it is.'

'No, for God's sake, Jeffrey!' Tring looked seriously worried. 'Of course, don't tell them that. They wouldn't understand. Say I'm not available, in conference. Just play the bloody secretary and PA card.'

'They'll probably want something,' I pointed out.

'Yes, undoubtedly,' Tring retorted. 'And undoubtedly something I don't want to give them. All the more reason for me not to be around. Any problems, just say you'll have to ask me.'

'When I can find you?' I added for the hell of it.

He gave me a stare as sharp as two ice-picks, then turned to Tali. 'Come on, Miss van Wyk, I can make an inspection of the men's quarters. That should give you some good material.'

And with that he swanned off with Tali, out of the Ops Room and down the corridor.

Gordy glanced sideways at me and shook his head gently. 'Unbelievable, isn't he?'

'C'mon,' I said, 'let's see what the deputation wants.'

We'd decided to see them in Tring's office. Gordy had barely taken his place behind the desk in the boss's chair when Billy Billings showed in our two visitors.

Mayor Jozic, wearing an expression like a smacked arse, was huddled in a black winter coat and clutched his felt trilby hat with both hands. Josip Zec was even shorter and rounder, and his camo fatigues had obviously defied his quartermaster's best efforts. No one would envisage making a uniform for his odd shape; as a result the arms and legs were too long, so he ended up looking a bit like a crumpled parcel that had been lost in the post for a couple of years.

'Gentlemen,' Jozic began gruffly as I took up position, standing beside Gordy, 'may I introduce Colonel Zec?'

'Colonel?' I echoed, before I could think better of it.

Zec's black gimlet eyes pierced me across the desk. 'We met yesterday, of course, Captain Hawkins, where the convoy was halted. I was promoted in the field after Colonel Markovic was murdered.'

Mayor Jozic looked genuinely saddened and fleetingly I felt sorry for him. 'A great loss, Captain,' he agreed, 'he was a good friend and an excellent soldier. Major Zec was to have been his new second-in-command. But in the event I have had no option but to appoint him as the new commander of our forces here in Una Drina.'

I was not at all sure this was good news, but I replied,

'Markovic's death was indeed very unfortunate.' Then I turned my attention to Zec. 'Nevertheless, Colonel, I must congratulate you on your promotion, despite the regrettable circumstances.' And I said it with as much sincerity as I could muster.

'Of course, you *know* what has happened?' was Zec's somewhat aggressive opening gambit.

'The Muslims have encircled the town,' Gordy replied evenly.

'Oh, yes, they've done that all right!' Zec exclaimed, and jabbed his pudgy forefinger in Gordy's direction. 'Those bloody turban-heads of the Ramoza Brigade used *your* UN convoy as cover! That's why they planted those mines – as if you didn't know! They used the vehicles as a screen so we didn't know they were there until it was too late. Then we couldn't engage them for fear of hitting the convoy! And if we had, no doubt your Warriors would have retaliated!'

'Yes,' Gordy confirmed. 'They would have.'

Zec placed both fists on the edge of the desk and leaned across, scowling, his chin jutting and greasy black hair hanging like a rope curtain. 'But they *didn't* see fit to engage the bloody turban-heads trying to destroy this town, did they?'

Gordy said, 'Because the Muslims didn't open fire on the convoy or on any UNPROFOR vehicles. You know the rules, Colonel.'

Zec wound in his neck a little and grunted. 'Or is it because it is all a conspiracy? The UN is the puppet of the Americans! And the Americans have demanded that the Muslims win this conflict! We Croats are an inconvenience! Never mind that this has been traditional Croat territory for hundreds of years! And you British are just America's lap-dog to dance to their tune.'

The metaphors were getting a bit mixed, but I got the gist. I interrupted with, 'Colonel, you are well aware that things have changed. The Muslims were your allies, but the alliance has broken down. Now they see your hold on this town and Donji Vrbas as a threat to the convoy route to Sarajevo.'

Zec gave another snort of disgust. 'Well, we were no threat, but we are *now*! They are exactly right about that. From now on, no convoy will pass through any Croat-held territory from here to the coast! Do I make myself plain!'

'Your own people will suffer from any action so rash as that,' I pointed out.

But, as usual, the military commanders were unswayed by the humanitarian argument. It usually took diplomatic and political pressure from their peers to make them change their tune. 'We Croats are a resilient people,' Zec continued. 'And, in this town at least, we will survive.' He glanced at Mayor Jozic, who gave a little nod of agreement.

I realized this was probably an oblique reference to the UN supplies Jozic had pilfered and stockpiled over the years. One thing was certain, he wouldn't be giving them away. He'd stand to make another tidy sum on the black market.

Zec added, 'There will be no more convoys through this town until the Muslims call off their siege and return to their old front-line positions in the north.'

I said, 'Do you realize the Muslims are demanding the same, just different conditions? No let-up of the siege and no convoys until you stand down and disarm the town's forces.'

The two round, outraged faces in front of me reminded me distinctly of a couple of red balloons. But before they could retort, Gordy said quickly, 'So you can see it's all a bit of a farce really, isn't it? Both sides are saying no convoys unless their conditions are met. And those two conditions are diametrically opposed.' For effect, he turned and glanced up at me. 'I guess we're not going see many convoys for a while, eh, Jeff?'

I nodded. 'It could be a bleak Christmas for a lot of innocent people.'

Zec didn't like that. 'Then the UN will have that on its own conscience! You should have thought about that before you conspired with the Muslims. You have only yourselves to blame!'

I went to reply and decided I'd be wasting oxygen. Besides, I was feeling utterly exhausted and really couldn't be bothered with such nonsense. Gordy Cromwell, too, kept quiet.

Mayor Jozic seemed to realize he wasn't going to get any further. 'Come on, Colonel,' he said to Zec, 'we are wasting our time here. We have said what had to be said.'

The two of them started towards the door, then Zec hesitated and turned. His brow furrowed over his black olive eyes and he almost spat his parting words of defiance. 'We Croats will *not* be the first to break. Be assured of that!'

The two of them had barely left the office when the Muslim barrage of Una Drina began again.

Later that day, the Dutch engineers managed to clear the mines and the trapped convoy departed for the coast, but now that the siege had begun in earnest I did not expect to see another for a long time. Understandably, Rocky Rogers was not in the best of moods when he left. The main humanitarian aid route into the Bosnian capital Sarajevo had been effectively severed. It was a gloomy and depressing time.

For the rest of that week the Muslims tightened their stranglehold on the town. The artillery and mortar barrages onto Croat defensive positions fell into a pattern. They started early each morning for an hour or so, just to let the Croats know that the Muslims were still there, and again towards twilight so that the enemy would sleep uneasily in their beds. Then there would be the odd and totally unexpected round that could be fired at any time, day or night, just to keep everyone on their toes.

There were inevitably some civilian casualties, but it was impossible to know if these were deliberate or accidental. It could have been worse. Then it *was* worse, when Nigel returned and Tali moved back to Anita's.

As the days passed, the barrages lost their earlier intensity. According to our intelligence sources, this was due to ammunition resupply problems.

Thankfully for the townsfolk, those problems worsened for the Muslims when, a week later, the first winter snow arrived.

The icy winds that had buffeted Una Drina for several days had dropped suddenly late in the afternoon. And, as the temperature rose a few degrees to just above freezing, thick white petals began falling from the low pinky-grey cloud. By the time twilight had faded into night, it was settling quickly on the cold ground. By daybreak the following morning everywhere was cocooned in three feet of soft snow, muting sounds and for once making the ugly agricultural town almost as picturesque as a ski-resort postcard.

As a bonus that day, under a clear sky and wintry sun, the breathless hush of the place remained unshattered by the Muslim bombardment; I guessed they were fully occupied digging out their weapons. It meant that the kids of the town were tempted out to play, build snowmen and toboggan down the steeper side-streets on tin trays, plastic sheeting or any other ingeniously improvised sled.

And, of course, when I say kids I also mean the men of A Company. Like soldiers everywhere, they were certainly not slow to take any opportunity to break the boredom and monotony of routine duties. As soon as patrols and chores were done, full-scale snowball wars broke out between rival platoons.

I took the cross-country skis from my billet that I'd inherited from my predecessor, and gave Tali her first skiing lesson on a secluded slope on the outskirts of town. She was her usual cheerful and daring self and would launch herself down the steepest slopes with total abandon – usually only to crash heavily at the bottom. That was mostly because she wanted to miss out the boring bits of instruction I gave her, such as learning to turn or slow down. We laughed a lot, enjoying the thin sunshine and innocent fun, and kissed frequently. Suddenly I couldn't remember a time I'd enjoyed more, or had ever wanted a woman as much I wanted Tali then.

Her final crash was into a deep drift in a sunlit depression surrounded by pine trees. I caught up with her to find her in a tangled mess with her legs crossed and unable to move because the skis were still attached and deeply embedded in the snow. There was no one around.

'Help me, Jeff,' she pleaded. 'Don't just stand there laughing.'

I looked down at her. 'I've got you at my mercy.'

She reached for my hand. 'My lucky day, then.'

I unsnapped the fastenings of her skis to free her legs, and helped her up. Then I kissed her snow-wet mouth and felt the madness within me. 'God, I want to fuck you now,' I said.

She glanced around, saw that we were out of public view. 'I want you to fuck me now, too. Right here.' She began unbuckling her damp jeans.

I hadn't exactly been expecting that response. I should have known better. I said, 'You'll have to take those boots off.' I wasn't sure how practical this was going to be.

But then Tali was rarely practical. 'I don't care.' Her jeans fell to her ankles. 'No, wait. I can keep the boots on. Fuck me from behind. I prefer that, anyway.'

Yes, I'd already learned she preferred that. Typical of Tali, it was more abandoned, more animal. That was the way she liked her loving. So I rolled her over as she drew up her knees, and roughly pushed her face into the snow when I took her. For once it was fast and furious rather than slow and lingering. I heard her muffled cries but didn't stop. I knew she wouldn't want me to, that she would rather suffocate or choke than have me stop before she came.

And when she did, her whole body shook as if in spasm. When I pulled back and lifted her face from the snow it was icy wet and flushed and she was gasping.

When she finally got her breath, she was smiling. 'You nearly bloody killed me.'

I kissed her on the mouth. 'I'd never do that.'

'That's how I'd like to die.'

'You're crazy.'

'Fucked to death in the snow.' She laughed. 'That was something else.'

I lit a miniature cigar and watched her as she pulled up her snow-sodden pants and jeans. 'No, Tali, *you* are something else.'

We'd grown very close since the siege had begun. Major Tring had clearly taken a shine to her, especially when he was the focus of her professional attention, and she was free to come and go from HQ whenever she wanted. For the first few nights that Nigel Cuthbert remained away on some mysterious errand, she used his billet but my bed. We talked a lot and made love even more. I got little sleep, but I really didn't care. During the day I just kept going on autopilot.

After that first snowfall, the lull in battle lasted for twenty-four hours before the barrages began again. But they lacked their earlier intensity, as the Muslims eked out their dwindling munition supplies.

Far worse was the arrival in the heights above the town of an elite Ramoza Brigade sniper squad, apparently trained in Afghanistan. The news came from Nigel and although, in his usual enigmatic way, he refused to confirm or deny it, I think it was the result of an intercept via GCHQ Cheltenham of a conversation on one of the militia's new satellite phones.

At least it meant we were able to warn Mayor Jozic, who put up notices telling the townsfolk to beware. As usual in these situations, the war-weary paid little attention until something actually happened.

Two days later the first victims were an elderly man and a young teenage girl who were in the water queue at one of the high-street standpipes. The rest of the people scurried for cover, screaming, leaving only the two corpses and discarded buckets and plastic containers scattered all around. A Warrior raced to the scene, but there was nothing much it could do except retrieve the bodies. No one knew where the shots had come from.

I was in contact with Almir Aganovic almost immediately to protest. But in his increasingly smug and smarmy tone, he assured me that the source of any sniper fire was not from his lines. He understood it was the Croats shooting their own kind in order to blame it on the Muslims.

'General, that pretty fourteen-year-old girl,' I pointed out, 'who died with a fist-sized exit-wound in her chest, was a Muslim.'

He did not reply. But after a short hesitation, he simply hung up. It left me seething and with a terrible sense of my inability to do anything about the situation. That has to be the very worst thing about peace-keeping work. The sadness and utter frustration of it.

After the incident, civilians rarely walked the streets. Where possible they would resort to using the town's sewer passages and manholes to get about, or creep around using the walls of buildings for cover where they could, and then run for their lives across any open spaces. A Warrior was stationed almost permanently at the standpipe after that, but the snipers continued their disgusting work, and the death toll of innocent civilians and Croat front-line fighters rose steadily and inexorably.

On one occasion the mental hospital was targeted, probably because it was owned by Mayor Jozic. A platoon of Royal Wessex had to spend a day rounding up the escaped lunatics wandering around the nearby woods in their pyjamas. It was reminiscent of a zombie horror movie.

For their part, the Croats under the new leadership of Colonel Josip Zec had improvised a new heavy mortar weapon with which to retaliate. Always short of ammunition themselves, but with plenty of gunpowder at their disposal, the defence force of Una Drina resorted to firing car engine-blocks at the Muslim positions. Apparently they had been stockpiled in one of Mayor Jozic's warehouses prior to the siege, in readiness for just such an event. Although very unaerodynamic, when the mortar crews got lucky this new weapon could strike with devastating effect.

Thankfully, two weeks later in mid-December, I woke up one morning to find the valley and town shrouded in heavy white fog. It wafted thickly over the snow-covered pavements and the grey slush of the main drag. No targets could be seen by either side and the guns and mortars had fallen silent. That included those of the accursed snipers.

At once the place was touched by the magical hand of peace and tranquillity; all sound, even the clanking tracks of the Warriors, was oddly muted by the combination of fog and snow.

I stepped out into the compound, my boots crunching on ice, to light my first cigar of the day and to take in the welcome atmosphere of serenity. Nigel had been away again for a couple of nights and Tali had joined me again for some nocturnal activity even more adventurous and experimental than before.

But he was due back today and she'd been packed and gone when I woke up, so I was not surprised to see her taking photographs out on the main street, making the most of the unusual weather conditions to snap wraith-like grey figures of haggard townsfolk emerging from the drifting fog on the dank streets.

I wandered over to her. She looked up. 'Hi, lover.'

'I wondered where'd you gone.'

She smiled. 'Nowhere far. I love this light. I wanted to make the most of it.'

I indicated her rucksack leaning against the compound fence. 'You weren't going to say goodbye before you left?'

A frown creased her brow. 'Of course I was, Jeff. I knew you'd be out here before I went. Don't be so possessive. I can't stand that.'

I felt awkward. 'Sorry. Didn't mean to be.'

'Anita wanted me to help her with the kids today. She'll probably want to take them up to the playing field if there's no shelling. They've been stuck in that school for days.'

'I'll give you a lift.'

'I don't want to put you to any trouble.'

'It's me you're talking to, Tali. It's no trouble. When do you need to go?'

'Soon, I suppose.'

'Let's get the Land Rover.'

We headed back to the compound gates, where she shouldered her rucksack. 'Do you know how long Nigel will be here this time?'

I shook my head. 'He's a law to himself.'

'I'll miss you. Unless we meet at Anita's place while she's at the school some time.'

That made me feel uncomfortable. Since Anita and I had made love, I'd rather avoided her. Not because I didn't like her – I did. In fact, I liked her a lot. But I felt that she was treating me like some sort of hero, and had expectations of me that were much too high to be realistic. And at the moment I was finding my relationship with Tali quite distracting enough. I didn't need any more complications in my life.

Bedding Tali in Anita's flat just wouldn't feel right, it would seem like a betrayal. And God forbid that she would ever come back home unexpectedly . . . it didn't bear thinking about.

I'd just said, 'We'll see,' when to my relief Gordy Cromwell emerged from the office entrance, waving a sheet of signal paper.

'Jimbo! Great news! The Serbs have stopped their bombardment of Sarajevo! They've just publicly announced the cessation!'

I halted beside my Land Rover. 'That's bloody incredible! What on earth persuaded them to do that?'

Gordy was slightly breathless as he reached us. 'They say those two mercenaries who killed Goran Zoric have been arrested by British authorities, pending a war-crimes hearing in The Hague.'

I could feel the rush of blood to my face, but I did my best to bluff it out. 'Really?' I said with all the innocence I could muster.

'Must say it's the first I've heard of it,' Gordy agreed. 'Anyway, sodding good news.'

Tali said, 'But that won't mean the aid convoys will be able to get through.'

'Not by this route,' I confirmed. 'But at least the poor bastards aren't being shelled and shot at.'

'She's got a point,' Gordy said. 'You can be shot dead or die of starvation. Starvation takes longer and affects virtually everyone. Not only Sarajevo. At least they should now get some supplies via other routes. It's worse here and in DV. Malnutrition is on the increase and deaths from hypothermia are mounting – especially amongst the old timers.'

I knew that. I had heard the forlorn ringing of church bells at funeral ceremonies all too often in the past few days. I said, 'I wish to hell I could make General Aganovic see sense. I speak to the bastard every day, but he's stubborn as a bloody mule.'

'Yeah, well,' said Gordy, 'but *he*'s not starving, is he? Anyway, there's mounting concern at the UN and big conflabs going on between UNHCR and the other NGO charities. Everyone thinks something has to be done soon.'

I thought aloud. 'Maybe I should have another go at Major Herenda.'

Gordy shrugged. 'But Herenda's yesterday's man, Jimbo. Aganovic is the big banana these days with his Ramoza Brigade. Herenda hasn't got the sway or effective manpower to compete. The Bosnian government might not like Aganovic, but they need him as the only effective fighting force they've got.'

The conversation left me in a depressed mood as I drove Tali to the school, creeping through the dense freezing fog and even then almost overshooting the turn-off by the tyre shop.

I carried Tali's rucksack into the building for her. The first thing I noticed was how cold it was. The children were gathered round Anita in the first classroom, all huddled in scarves and winter coats, while they listened intently to her as she talked and scribbled sums onto the blackboard.

As we entered she stopped what she was doing and smiled. It was good to see her looking so happy. 'Jeff! Tali! How lovely to see you.' She told the children to work out the answer to a new sum and walked over to us. 'Jeff, you have been avoiding me, I think? I have not seen you in weeks.'

'Sorry, I've been very busy.'

She peered over the top of her specs at me, very sexy-school-marmish. 'I think you are afraid I will be asking more favours of you.'

'Anything you want, Anita, you know that. If it's at all in my—'

'Remit!' she said in a flash, with a mischievous smile on her lips.

'I was going to say power.'

'Ah, now that is a distinct improvement.'

'How are the kids getting on?'

'Better this morning with no shelling. Come, let me show you.' She led Tali and me to the second classroom. This had been turned into a makeshift dormitory with a dozen or so beds, a dining table and chairs and lengths of string running across the room from which clothing hung on wire coat-hangers. There were lots of kiddies' crayon drawings on the wall.

'Ingenious,' I said. 'Quite homely.'

Anita frowned at me. 'Not really, but we've done our best. It doesn't help they spend last thing at night and first thing in the morning in the cellar. When the Muslims do their shelling.'

'But no near misses?'

'Not yet, but I think there might be if your Warrior wasn't usually parked outside.'

'You're down to around a dozen?'

'Yes, these are the orphans with no close relatives to look after them – or none the UN has been able to find. The others used to return for day classes, but not since the siege began. The relatives tend to keep them at home.'

'How are you for food?'

'It is getting bad. We have UN workers come to cook one meal a day, but their supplies are nearly gone. Often now it is just thin soup and bread. It is like that for the whole of Una Drina. Some of the children with their relatives are even worse off now. Some are resorting to digging up their gardens to eat tulip and daffodil bulbs.'

I winced. 'I knew it was getting bad.'

She raised an eyebrow. 'There was nothing much in the first place, Jeff. Of course, that fat pig Mayor Jozic has done well supplying black-market food he has stolen from the UN. People have been handing over their life savings for a bag of sugar or coffee.' That ferocious pout was back on her lips. 'But even that pig's warehouses are bare now.'

I indicated the dark overcoat she wore. 'Do I gather the school's out of fuel?'

She nodded. 'For a week now. And since the siege began we cannot hunt for wood on the outskirts of the town.'

I said, 'You should have let me know.'

'And what could you do about it, Jeff? I know your own conditions are not that good.'

'I'm sure we could find a kerosene heater and fuel. The lads would be pleased to give one up for the kids.'

She looked at me. 'Is your room heated?'

'Just a candle. We have to huddle to keep warm.'

Tali giggled, and that rather irritated me. Anita said, 'A heater would be wonderful, Jeff, really. We would all be so grateful.'

'At least UNPROFOR's own convoys still run,' I pointed out. 'Trouble is, we can't be seen to supply the civilian population.'

She nodded, well aware of the finer points of how we were obliged to operate under various agreements with the warring militias. 'Well, I will keep the secret. Anyway, you may not have to help for too much longer. The UNHCR wants to evacuate these orphans now the town is under siege. And any other children in Una Drina whose parents or relatives are prepared to let them go. To somewhere safe on the coast. I think they are preparing an old tourist hotel.'

I could see the hurt in those expressive doleful eyes of hers and my heart went out to her. 'Your school will have no pupils.'

She forced the smile back onto her face. 'It was here when it was most needed, thanks to you, Jeff. And this crazy war cannot last for ever, can it?'

I reached out and touched her arm. 'All wars end eventually.'

She bit her lip, I'm sure to hold back her tears. 'I just wish the UN convoys could run again, before any of my children are killed or injured.'

'We're working at it,' I reassured her, but I felt like a liar as I spoke the words. Working at it, sure, but failing miserably.

She looked at me. 'I *do* know what you British would *like* to do, Jeff.'

I nodded. 'Use armed force to drive the convoys through and shoot the hell out of any bastard who stands in our way,' I confirmed. 'It's the only language these militia warlords understand.'

'Maybe the UN will realize that? They must do soon, surely?'

I said, 'Don't hold your breath.'

She looked away and smiled at Tali. 'Thank you for coming. You will help me with the children?'

'Of course, Anita, that's why I'm here.'

The schoolteacher glanced at me. 'You think it will be safe to go to the playing field? There will be no bombardment today?'

I said, 'I can't guarantee it, but it's unlikely while this fog is down. Besides, an empty playing field is not an obvious target.'

Anita smiled thinly. 'I am not sure logic like that still applies in this country. But the children need some fresh air and exercise.'

'And some fun!' Tali added cheerfully.

'Don't we all!' Anita replied with feeling. 'I just hope it will be safe. I don't even trust our own side. The Croat soldiers are very nervous at the moment, scared of the Muslims. Too many nervous fingers on the triggers.'

I said, 'I'll come with you, if you like.'

Anita's eyes lit up. 'Would you? That would make me a feel a lot happier.'

I added, 'And I've a flask of hot coffee in the wagon.'

She laughed. 'Then I am even happier still.'

A short while later I was crawling up the hill in the Land Rover beside the crocodile of school children, all laughing and chatting, skipping, slipping and sliding on the snow-covered pavement. Anita led the way and Tali brought up the rear, to prevent any stragglers getting lost in the fog. It lifted my spirits to see so many smiles on faces I had not seen smile before. I had no doubt their lives would be forever blighted by what they had witnessed at the massacre in Stavac, but seeing them now I could see a glimmer of hope for their future. It made me realize what a difference just a few people who care can make.

There was an ancient tractor and empty trailer parked by the entrance to the playing field, a Croatian flag hanging limply from a broomstick lashed to the tailgate. No militia were to be seen.

I drove past it and through the entrance and stopped some fifty metres beyond. By the time I climbed out, the crocodile had broken formation and the kids rushed into the deep snow, shrieking with laughter and excitement. I think I counted thirty seconds before the first snowballs were exchanged.

Anita and Tali reached my Land Rover, the schoolteacher calling out, 'Come on, children, who wants to have a snowman competition?'

'Me! Me!' came the chorus of shouts.

'All right, so you must form yourselves into teams. Let's have four teams of three. That doesn't divide equally, so one team will have four with our youngest pupil.'

'Can I join a team?' Tali pleaded, a wide grin on her face.

Anita laughed. 'No, Tali, I want you to be the judge. I know you will be impartial.'

Tali feigned a look of deep disappointment, which had the children laughing and mocking. 'You can't play-y! You can't play-y!'

A little boy put his hand up. 'Please, miss, there are trees at the top end of the field. Can we go and get some twigs and cones and things?'

Anita glanced at me. 'D'you think that's all right?'

I shrugged. 'I guess so. There's a perimeter fence, so they won't get lost or wander off.'

'I'll go with them,' Tali offered. 'There might be some nice pictures to take.'

'Thank you,' Anita said, 'they so like to be with you.'

We watched Tali disappear into the swirl of fog with half the children skipping in her wake like she was the Pied Piper of Una Drina. The others started work on the snowman foundations while Anita and I looked on.

I took the flask from the Land Rover and poured Anita and myself two coffees in old-fashioned tin army mugs. 'She is a wonderful girl, that Tali,' Anita said as we leaned with our backs against the vehicle's side. 'Always such fun, full of mischief and always looking for adventure. The children love her. I wish I could be like her.'

'You're fine the way you are.' I lit a small cigar. 'Besides, Tali hasn't had the sorrow and grief you've had in your life.'

Anita clutched her coffee in both her wool-mittened hands. 'I wonder if that would make a difference to someone like her? She seems so happy . . . sort of from the inside out, if you know what I mean. She will always have friends.'

I savoured the aroma of the coffee; it was a Billy Billings special requisition. 'I must admit she's very popular.'

'With the men especially, I've noticed.'

I could hardly deny that. 'I guess so,' I murmured.

She glanced sideways at me. 'Including you. I see the way you look at her.'

'Oh no, I don't think so.' Why the hell did I feel the need to go into immediate denial. But it was out before I could stop myself. 'She's just—'

'A girl?' Her voice had adopted a slightly mocking tone. 'Young enough to be your daughter?'

'Only just – and anyway, no daughter of mine would be that scatty.'

Anita laughed. 'Don't be so defensive, Jeff. *All* the men look at her, desire her, not just you. I don't mind competition . . . even if it is from a younger model.'

'She is not competition,' I said flatly.

She slipped her arm through mine. 'I have made love with you once, Jeff. It was very nice, you were very kind to me and I am very content to have shared that with you. Of course, God willing, I hope one day we will do it again. You know, in happier times. But if not, so be it.'

I turned my face to her and kissed her on the forehead. 'Anita, you are one of the most remarkable women I have ever met.'

She smiled. 'But I scare you?' she challenged.

'You scare every soldier in the British Army, Anita. That's why we like you on our side.'

Now we could hear the children calling from far away in the fog and Tali calling back, warning them not to get lost and to keep together. Meanwhile, just in front of us the torsos of three snowmen were growing rapidly.

Anita stared out into the mesmerizing swathes of fog eddying aimlessly in the still air. 'I just hope Tali will be wise in the choice of men in her life. If not, maybe she will not always be so happy.'

I frowned. 'Meaning?'

'To be so pretty, so popular. To have the choice of any man you want. It is easy to make bad choices.' She turned her head to me again. 'You know she was seeing that awful American? I forget his name, ya, that Kirk Grundy.'

I felt the blood pulse in my temples. 'It was just a rumour; they were only friends.'

'They were more than that, I assure you. A friend of mine works at the hotel in DV. He saw her leaving his room in just her nightdress, getting back before the day staff arrived.'

I gritted my teeth. 'She's over twenty-one. It's her life.' I threw away my cigar butt. 'Besides, she's fallen out with him now.'

I stared ahead, aware that Anita was still watching me intently. 'She says . . . But then, Jeff, you are right. It is no business of ours. I just would hate to see her hurt.'

There was a brittle silence between us, lasting several seconds. Then we both became aware of male voices drifting through the fog from the direction of the entrance.

I turned. There was a group of shadowy figures gathering around the tractor and trailer. 'Ah,' I said, 'the Croat militia. I wondered where they'd got to.'

Anita was watching too. 'No mystery. Two orphaned sisters in their twenties live in a cottage over there. They prostitute themselves to make ends meet. Very sad.'

One of the militiamen suddenly spotted us, waved his submachine gun and shouted something.

'What did he say?' I asked.

'I couldn't hear. God, this is what I was afraid of! Does he think we are Muslims?'

The man shouted again. And again his voice was distorted by his apparent anger. He began running towards us, the other Croats following.

Suddenly, I was seriously alarmed. I yelled back in Serbo-Croat. *'British Army – UN here! Children here! Do not fire!'*

The man slowed, out of breath from running in the snow. He cupped his hands to his mouth and shouted. 'I can see who you are! Come away! Mines!'

But the words had barely left his mouth when I heard the dull thud of a detonation. I spun round, staring up towards the end of the playing field. I was just in time to see the sudden flux of yellow light somewhere deep in the swirling drifts of fog and to hear the second mine explode. And the unmistakable sound of Tali screaming.

Thirteen

'Oh, my God!' Anita gasped.

I just couldn't believe it. Minutes seemed to pass as I stood rooted to the spot in abject horror, though in truth it was probably only for a split second. I hurled aside my mug of coffee and began racing across the playing field, plunging into the blinding white fog, towards the top end where I'd seen the mine explode. I slipped and skidded in the snow that seemed to have developed a malign physical presence, sucking at my boots to try to slow me down when I had never wanted to run faster in all my life.

I was vaguely aware of Anita shouting at the children by the Land Rover to stay where they were, then her laboured breathing close behind me.

'Help! Help, someone!' It was Tali's plaintive voice some-where up ahead, hidden within the swirling white vapour that created and dissolved strange images before my eyes. 'Help, Jeff! Please help!'

Her cries spurred me on. My muscles, not used much since my deployment here, screamed at the punishment as I powered them on through the pain barrier, my lungs raw and stinging from the effort and the cold damp air.

Ahead the shapes of trees drifted in and out of focus through the writhing fog like a mirage.

Then I heard Tali's voice again in a low, desperate whisper. 'Don't move. Don't anyone move. Stay where you are.'

I altered course, veering to the right in the direction of her voice. At last the trees came into sharper focus, a thin copse of silver birch, and beneath them dark and indistinguishable shapes lying on the snow, nothing moving.

'Jeff, is that you?' Tali shouted.

One of the shapes moved and I knew then they were bodies. One of them was waving.

'I'm here!' I shouted back. 'Are you hurt?'

'I'm OK, but some of the children are injured.' I could see now that Tali was sitting on the ground. 'Jeff, be careful! Don't come any closer! There are mines here.'

I shuffled to a halt, breathing heavily. Then I could hear the children, some crying, some whimpering softly. Cursing the cocooning layers of fog, I stared into the stuff so hard that my eyes hurt, but still I had difficulty seeing exactly what had happened. Tali was lying almost directly in front of me, maybe thirty metres ahead. There were three children near to her, pathetic little bundles in overcoats and woolly hats, sitting rigidly in the snow, scared even to breathe.

Tali pointed to her right. 'Over there, Jeff.'

I peered hard, then as a swathe of thicker fog wafted away, I finally had a clearer view. Some fifteen metres from Tali were two darkened patches in the snow where the exploding mines had thrown up the underlying turf and soil. The two small craters were themselves some ten metres apart. A child lay beside one and two others were sprawled close to the next. I knew they were all injured; at least one of the poor mites was wailing in pain.

'Jeff!' Anita was suddenly beside me, panting hard, glancing around in shocked disbelief. 'Oh, my poor babies! Jeff, look, they are hurt!'

She began to run forward, but I grabbed her arm and hauled her back. 'Don't go any closer, Anita! The mines could be any-where.'

'I must go.'

'We don't need any more casualties,' I said sharply. 'Tell those on this side of the trees to make their way carefully towards you, then wait here. I'll go and get the injured.'

Just then the Croat militiaman who'd been shouting at us near the entrance appeared through the fog, coughing. I turned round. Despite his run, he still had a thin, hand-rolled cigarette hanging from his lips.

'Why the hell you bring kids in here?' he demanded in Serbo-Croat. He was an unkempt individual, with a beard and scruffy long hair beneath a woollen hat.

I turned on him. 'Because it's a fucking playing field. When did you lay these mines?'

'Two days ago.'

'Why, for fuck's sake?'

'Because the Muslims could break through here. We haven't enough soldiers to cover everywhere.'

'Why the hell didn't you cordon off the area and tell us you'd laid the bloody things?'

He was incensed at that. 'The fucking UN isn't running this war, we are.'

'And making a good job of it, blowing up your own children,' I replied testily. 'Aren't you supposed to be guarding this approach?'

'We are, that's why we're here,' he said, jutting his chin in defiance.

It was all I could do not to hit him. 'Yes, guarding it, not shagging the local women.' He looked a bit sheepish at that, but I had no time to pursue the point. 'Where exactly are the mines laid?'

He shrugged. 'Around the trees, right the way across from left to right.'

'Are we safe here and back down behind this line?'

He gave a sarcastic smile, showing bad teeth. 'You haven't been blown up, have you?'

I took that as a yes, and turned back to the minefield. 'Tali! I want you to stand up very carefully and retrace your footsteps through the snow. I want the three kids with you to do the same. Very slowly, very carefully. They needn't be afraid. If they stick to their own footprints, they'll be safe.'

Most of the children had a good grasp of English, but Anita repeated the instructions in their own language to make sure they fully understood.

I turned to the Croat. 'Right, you can give me a hand with the injured. I'll go first and you follow in my footsteps. OK?'

In fairness, the man nodded in agreement without a second's hesitation.

As Tali climbed gingerly to her feet and gave words of encouragement to her young charges, I tentatively studied the ground in front of me to work out which were the most likely footprints of the injured children.

I made a quick decision, took a deep breath and my first step. Of course my size-ten boots were twice the size of the kids', so my safety wasn't exactly guaranteed. But there was nothing I could do about that. If I got unlucky, I might as well get unlucky quickly as slowly. The Croat waited until I was some seven metres ahead of him, then set off himself.

It was a horrible experience, moving into that fog as the scene of the carnage was slowly revealed like a picture coming into focus. The soft moaning became a little louder as I approached the first crater; it sounded like a girl's voice. I found it difficult to distinguish her at first and couldn't quite work out why, because I could clearly see a little boy just a few metres further away from the crater.

But as the last few gossamer wafts of fog cleared I could see why. The force of the blast had blown away her clothes so the girl, maybe nine or ten, sat in just her baggy knickers, her skinny undernourished body the same colour as the snow. She was shivering with cold and shock. The mine had taken off her right leg at the knee and she was now nursing the bloody stump with a scrap of what had once been her skirt.

She was startled at my approach and looked up. I have never

seen such an endearing, terrified little face, wide dark eyes like saucers framed in a cute bobcut of black hair, tears running down her cheeks.

'It's OK, sweetheart,' I said softly. 'You'll be fine. Just be a brave girl for a few minutes more.' Swiftly I removed my belt-order and camouflage smock which I draped over her shoulders. I waved at the little boy, who was a similar age to the girl, a few feet away. He had a hand to his left eye and I could see the blood on his cheek. 'I'll be with you in a minute.'

'Don't worry, mister. Mara's worse than me. I've just got something in my eye.'

Mara tried to smile but didn't quite make it. 'I feel dizzy. My leg's gone. I like to play hockey. I shan't be able to now . . . Oh, Mama, it hurts . . . !'

I reached for the morphine syrette that hung round my neck as part of my battledress and snapped it off. I reckoned on a half dose for a child of her size. 'I'm going to give you an injection to take away the pain.' I found a vein, pushed gently, and fired in a half load. 'They'll make you a new leg, poppet. You'll play hockey again.'

'Ouch!' She looked at me, unsure. 'Really?'

'Really,' I replied, opened a belt-order pouch, extracted a field-dressing pack and ripped it open.

The Croat arrived at my side. As I worked on binding the girl's wound, I nodded in the direction of the second crater and a third child. 'Can you check out that boy over there for me? See what his injuries are?'

There was no immediate response as I saw the militiaman look at the intervening stretch of snow. He said, 'There are no footprints to step in.'

I said, 'Then you'd better pray it's your lucky day. Maybe next time you'll be a bit more careful when you lay mines.'

He looked down at me with contempt. 'Fuck you, English.' Then he set off, steadily and softly, placing one foot after the other, clearly expecting each step to be his last.

It was his lucky day.

I patched up little Mara as best I could, then moved around to the boy. He had something in his eye all right; a fragment of plastic mine casing. Although he hadn't been aware of it, another piece of shrapnel had severed a tendon in his leg and he couldn't walk.

As I worked quickly just to bandage his wounds, I saw that Tali and the other children were safely out of the minefield. Anita now followed my footsteps and joined me.

'This is all so wicked,' she said, looking around her. 'Would you like me to take Dario?'

The boy smiled at up at her. 'Please, miss.'

As she scooped him into her arms, the Croat returned, cradling the second boy.

The militiaman had the body completely covered in his own anorak. Blood dripped copiously into the snow. He said, 'This child is dead. I am sorry.' There was a cold-weather dewdrop hanging from his nostrils, and tears in his eyes.

Gently I collected Mara in my arms. She was nearly asleep and nuzzled against my chest, groaning softly, as I led the slow procession back across the minefield to safety.

I looked up to the click and whir of a camera motor drive. 'Tali, for God's sake, what the hell d'you think you're doing?' I snapped angrily.

She was standing with the other three children gathered round her. They were watching us, silently and with curiously emotionless expressions, as we carried their friends towards them.

Tali took the camera from her eye. 'My job, Jeff, that's what I'm doing.'

Of course she was right. I was seething with anger and lashing out at the wrong person. In truth, I blamed myself for what had happened. Anita had asked me if I thought it would be safe to bring the kids here. I'd said yes with barely a second's thought. Of all people, I should have known that *nowhere* is safe in a war zone.

But that didn't stop part of me thinking that taking photographs of things like this was cashing in on other people's misery.

Thankfully, I took my first step onto safe ground, but there was no time to relax. I said, 'Just put your camera away and follow us with those kids, will you?'

She nodded as I turned away and headed for the Land Rover as fast as I could, Mara still in my arms, with Anita and Dario and the Croat following. As soon as I reached my vehicle I put the little girl in the back on some soft sacking and stood back as Anita laid the boy beside her.

The Croat stood back with his tiny corpse. 'Not with them,' he said.

I nodded. 'Put him in the front passenger well.'

Anita pressed her teeth into her fist, but she couldn't stop the tears welling in her eyes. I put my hand on her shoulder and gently kissed her cheek. 'I know,' I said softly.

Tali arrived with the other children. Anita sniffed heavily and straightened her back. 'I'll take the others back to the school,' she told her. 'I'm so sorry you were caught up in all this. It is not your war.'

The young photographer smiled uneasily. 'Somehow I feel it is now.'

I said, 'Will you get in the back with the kids? They all like you a lot. Try and keep them calm.'

As Tali scrambled into the rear, I got on the radio to company HQ and explained the situation. As always, Gordy Cromwell was immediately on the ball. He told me to take the wounded directly to the public clinic and he would immediately dispatch our MO to meet us there with additional medical supplies and equipment.

I resisted the urge to do my usual Formula One racing-driver impersonation and drove steadily back through the fog to the clinic. To my great surprise Rocky Rogers' white UN Discovery was parked outside.

Before I'd opened the door, the company MO, a man called

Figgis, came out to meet me together with the head of the clinic, a Croat with a white coat so smeared with dried blood that he looked like a butcher. Another doctor, a woman working for Médecins Sans Frontières, came out to help. Between them they lifted out Mara, Dario and our pathetic little corpse.

Tali and I followed them in. It was a dreadfully depressing place. The outside walls were peppered with bullet holes, broken windows had been covered over with cardboard and inside the paint was peeling off the damp walls. A row of grubby, unshaven and dishevelled Croat fighters, most nursing minor wounds, sat on the floor against the walls of the central passage while they waited to be examined. A distinctly fetid smell of death hung in the air.

The original small office now served as living-quarters for the exhausted duty staff, who had been working round the clock since the siege had started, as well as providing a desk and antiquated typewriter for what little administration got done. One of the two treatment rooms had become a makeshift operating theatre and the second was an examination room.

It was into here that the doctors took the two little survivors. Mara had come round now and looked frightened. Tali and I both did our best to reassure them they were in good hands before leaving.

The French doctor said, 'Since the siege began we have commandeered two large empty houses nearby. We try and keep all the children together there in a separate room once they are in a stable condition.'

'How many children are there?' Tali asked.

'Too many,' the doctor replied. 'But we do our best to keep them happy. They are very resilient. Unfortunately fluffy toys are not the UN's priority.' She gave a weary smile. 'But they aren't ours either just now. We are running out of everything, including fuel for the generator. Today we had to do two operations by torchlight. That is not easy when you are removing shrapnel from a man's intestines.'

'Can't we give you some fuel?' I asked.

She gave me a curious look. 'According to your Major Tring, you are running low yourselves.'

Well, that was probably true. Our own military convoys were getting through, but far less regularly, and they were being harangued and delayed for hours at every Croat checkpoint from here to the coast. Then they had to endure the same treatment at the Muslim ring around Una Drina. Nevertheless, my guess was that Tring just didn't want to be accused by the Muslims of breaking neutrality by assisting in the recovery of wounded Croat fighters.

I expressed my sympathy, then headed back up the passage with Tali.

The door to the original waiting room was open as we passed. It was now the nearest thing the clinic had to an intensive-care ward. Just inside, Rocky Rogers stood talking to another of the doctors, a man I'd once met at the bar in the Splendid. Before the war he had been the town's vet, but in his new role he had successfully completed some very complex surgery on several human patients. And by the look of it, he still had his work cut out. The room was crammed with sick fighters and civilians, including four children, lying side by side on the floor. Grubby, dirty bandages were much in evidence along with various drips either on stands or held by the patients themselves.

The vet spotted me first. 'Hallo, Captain Hawkins, good to see you again. I was just telling Mr Rogers here . . .' He lowered his voice, and took a step out into the passage, ' . . . we are going to lose a lot of these patients over the next few days if they cannot be properly treated.'

Rocky nodded at me. 'Hi, Jimbo, I'm just doing an assessment.'

'Of what?' I asked.

'Just about anything and everything, including the sick and injured. We need to get this lot to the hospital in DV or evacuated out completely.'

The vet said, 'Unfortunately, DV is running out of medical supplies, too.'

Rocky shook the man's hand. 'Thanks for your time, pal.'

He turned away and grinned at Tali. 'Hi, gorgeous. You still causing trouble?'

She frowned. 'What do you mean?'

'Aw, nothing. Forget it. You two fancy a drink? I bloody need one . . . the journey here was total shite. Took me all yesterday and I had to spend last night in the car. Fucking freezing it was, too. My balls were like dried peas this morning.' He glanced at Tali and winked. 'Pardon my French.'

'How'd you break through the blockade?' I asked.

Rocky scratched at his beard. 'Five hundred ciggies and a crate of slivovitz.'

'Nothing new there, then.' I shook my head in wonder at how bizarre life was out here. 'A drink sounds good, though. We've had our work cut out today; I'll tell you about it at the Splendid.'

Rocky slapped me jovially on the back and nearly knocked my fillings out. 'See you in five, pal.'

And five saw Tali and me arrive at the bar in the Splendid. Rocky, anxious to get a beer down his neck, had beaten us to it. As we walked in, he was setting up the first round and talking to the last person I wanted to see right now, the American Kirk Grundy.

I deliberately took a stool at the opposite end of the bar so, when Jelena served the three bottles of Belgrade-brewed lager, Rocky was obliged to bring them over to the two of us.

Even if it was a rather obvious snub, it didn't stop the rhino-skinned Grundy from waving at us. 'Hi, Tali! . . . Jim-bo! How you doin'? I just got in from DV. Cost me two hundred green-backs to get through the roadblocks. Bloody Muslims are getting as greedy as the Croats. At least you've still got beer here. DV's just about run dry.'

'Guess we will soon,' I replied flatly, hoping that would be the end of the conversation.

'Hey, Tali,' he called, 'you gonna come and chat to your Uncle Kirk? I been missin' the brightest smile in Bosnia – and the prettiest ass.'

I whispered in her ear. 'Just ignore him.'

She looked at me. 'It's OK, I don't want to be rude.'

That riled me. As she slipped off her barstool, I said quietly, 'I thought you came to Una Drina to get away from him?'

'I did, but I think he's got the message by now. We're still friends.'

I watched her walk across the room and Grundy greet her with an arm round her waist and a kiss on her mouth. He patted her backside and said something to her, then they both laughed. I noticed he'd left his hand on her rump, and she didn't attempt to move it away.

Rocky shifted position and leaned against the bar, blocking my view. 'You won't hold on to that one, Jimbo.'

I felt irritated. 'What d'you mean?'

'I know you've been shagging her, everyone does.'

'Who the hell says?' I snapped.

'That doesn't sound like a denial, Jimbo. You should know what this place is like. I heard about it at army HQ in Divulje.'

'Bloody gossip mill,' I snarled.

He gave a knowing smile. 'So it *isn't* true?'

'I didn't say that.'

He took a swig from his bottle and placed it on the bar. 'Pal to pal, I'm just saying, don't set yourself up for a fall. Don't expect to keep her. She's one wild spirit.'

I said, 'If I want a fucking agony aunt, I'll write to a professional, OK?'

He raised both hands in a gesture of surrender. 'Sure, none of my business.'

I quickly tried to steer him onto another subject. 'So what's happening out there in the big wide world?'

Rocky grimaced. 'Well, as you might imagine, the UN's getting very anxious about the situation. Food and fuel are down to critical levels in Sarajevo, DV and Zenica – and here, of course. Plus all the villages in between.'

'I know,' I replied, 'but what are they going to *do* about it?'

Rocky took three hard gulps from his bottle of lager, then wiped his mouth with the back of his hand. 'Well, the UN's been putting pressure on the Bosnian government to call off the sieges that are blocking the convoy routes. Seems the lights are on, but no one's at home. More accurately, it seems the Ramoza Brigade is running the sieges and not listening to their political masters in Sarajevo.'

I nodded. 'General Aganovic's got his own agenda.'

'Now the UN's talking about pushing a convoy through anyway. And it'll have to be a real mother of one to make a difference. That's why I'm here. To see if it's going to be feasible in the next day or two.'

'And what do you think?'

'I think we don't have an option. You saw the wounded and dying at the clinic. It's on a much bigger scale in DV and Sarajevo itself. And that's just the medical evacuees, before we look at refugees, food, medicines and general essential aid.' He shook that curly mane of hair. 'No, we don't have an option, we've *got* to go in.'

'I agree,' I said. 'Both sides will huff and puff, but if they're confronted with an actual convoy, determined to get through, then it's more likely to concentrate their minds. Especially if there's a good media presence and the eyes of the world are on them.'

Rocky winked. 'Well, we couldn't have a better man in place to negotiate it all.'

I didn't even want to think about that. I said, 'At least the Serbs have lifted the Sarajevo siege – for the time being, at least.'

'Yeah, and you know why, of course?'

I shook my head. 'No, I only heard about it this morning and I haven't been back to HQ.'

He dug in the back pocket of his baggy jeans and yanked out

a folded, crumpled copy of the *Sun* newspaper. 'This was flown in just before I left yesterday.' He spread it out on the bar.

The front page was filled with one headline and one picture. The words read: 'SAS SNATCH BOSNIAN ASSASSINS'. The picture showed a couple of men being bundled into a helicopter by three British soldiers. And one of them was me.

'Oh, fuck,' I breathed.

He jabbed his forefinger at the photo credit. 'Taken by our very own Miss Tali van Wyk.'

I could not believe my eyes. I looked across the bar in a rage. 'Tali! Come here!' I shouted.

In her surprise she almost fell off her barstool. She turned round, alarmed. 'What is it, Jeff?' she asked as she rushed over to me.

I indicated the newspaper in front of me. 'What the hell's the meaning of this?'

'What?' She looked down. 'Oh, oh goodness, I hadn't seen this. Fantastic, the front page! Bit grainy, should have used a faster film.'

I grabbed her by the shoulders and twisted her round to face me. 'The hell you should! I thought I'd destroyed the film.'

She smiled in a sort of impish defiance. 'Well, you'd destroyed the *faster* film – probably my best pictures. I've got more than one camera. I'd decided I wanted a faster film and had just switched when you snatched it off me.'

I couldn't believe her. 'You *know* I didn't want you photographing what happened!'

Suddenly her eyes blazed into mine. 'Why should I care what *you* want? I've got a job to do – and if I don't do it, I don't see *you* paying my wages.'

'Do you realize how bloody embarrassing this can be to the British government?' I snapped back.

But Tali stood her ground. 'If you don't want to be photographed doing something, then don't do it in the first place.' She glanced at the picture again. 'Anyway, you can't see your face, or the two other English guys'.'

'Stupid girl, you just don't understand, do you?' I let go of her shoulders. 'How the hell did you get the film to London?'

'I asked Hal Watkins to drop it in to Kirk when his patrol went to DV. Kirk arranged everything.'

I saw red at that. 'I might have known *he'd* be involved in this.'

A new voice joined the conversation. 'Hey, go easy on the kid!' Kirk Grundy had decided to join us and make my day. 'You Brits come out of this smelling of roses! Your famous SAS heroes in action and as a result the Serbs stop bombing the crap outta Sarajevo!'

I said, 'We hardly needed that in every newspaper on the planet.'

Grundy smiled a patronizing fat smile. 'Let me tell you something, Jim-bo. The Bosnian Serb leadership in Pale got it in their heads that the UN and the Brits had their commander Zoric killed.' He nodded towards the newspaper. 'When, to reassure them, your guys abducted the killers, Karadzic and his cronies chose not to believe what your diplomats told them. It took that picture and the world's press to do that.' He grinned at Tali. 'So shells stop falling on the capital. I call that a result.'

I said, 'That's conveniently forgetting that you Americans set up Zoric's assassination in the first place.'

'We weren't alone. Zoric had to be stopped before our strategy for this conflict went tits-up.'

'I didn't think the US was supposed to have a strategy for Bosnia,' I reminded him.

Grundy's eyes narrowed. 'We have a strategy for everywhere, Jimbo.'

I nodded. 'You know, Kirk, I do believe I'm sadly all too aware of that.'

Rocky said, 'Hey, cool it, you two! What's done is done. Let's all kiss and make up. I'll get another round in.'

I shook my head. 'Sorry, I've got to get back. I'll catch you later.' I turned to Tali. 'Would you like a lift?'

'No thanks, Jeff, I owe Kirk a drink.'

'Of course you do,' I said quietly and walked out.

I can't say I was thinking rationally as I drove back to company HQ through the fog. My head was reeling. It felt like there was an electric storm going on inside my skull, raw emotions of anger, guilt, helplessness and jealousy were exploding together like colliding atoms.

Swinging in through the compound gates, I caught sight of Nigel Cuthbert unloading his Land Rover, which looked as though it had been driven to hell and back, covered in snow-grime, dented and pock-marked with half a dozen bullet holes.

Then I noticed Ivana standing by the passenger door, wearing a long overcoat and black headscarf.

Something told me that, despite my warnings, they hadn't just been away on business.

I drove on to the main entrance and had barely stepped inside when I heard Major Tring's voice behind me.

'Captain Hawkins! My office! Now!'

Even as I turned he was stalking off down the corridor. I followed and entered to find Tring standing beside his desk. 'Newspapers have just arrived from the UK. And just what is the meaning of this, Captain?' A copy of the *Daily Mail* was pointedly opened at the centre-spread. The same picture or similar to the one I'd seen earlier in the *Sun*.

'Not a good likeness, I'm afraid,' I replied coolly.

He glowered at me. 'That is you, isn't it? Body-shape, posture . . . with those two hooligans from Hereford . . .?'

'I can't deny it, Reg. They needed my help, it was an awkward situation.'

'I bet it was!' He took a deep breath. 'Now, am I or am I not the officer commanding this company?'

'Of course.'

'So why didn't you seek my permission to get involved? Why deliberately keep me out of the loop?'

I said, 'It was a sensitive operation. Need to know. I was told not to say anything.'

'It took place on my patch,' Tring retorted. 'And you are one of my junior officers. God, what the hell's happened to the army nowadays! Hasn't anyone ever heard of the chain of command?'

There was suddenly a quick, loud rap on the office door before it suddenly opened and Nigel Cuthbert peered in. 'Ah, Reg, sorry to interrupt, but I need to talk—'

'Not now, Nigel, I'm busy,' Tring answered snappily.

All the same Cuthbert stepped inside. 'Sorry, Reg, but it really can't wait . . .' He saw the open newspaper on the table. 'Ah, you've seen that, have you?'

Tring nodded. 'No doubt there'll be hell to pay over this. And it happened on my watch, so I suppose *I'll* be the one to get it in the neck!'

'No way,' Cuthbert replied, shaking his head. 'It was supposed to be a secret operation. It didn't have UN approval or anything. Only the Serbs were told in confidence . . . to persuade them to stop shelling Sarajevo. Trouble is, they didn't believe us, thought it was a trick.' He inclined his head towards the newspaper. 'Until this story broke. Now we're seen as heroes.'

Tring frowned. 'Not at the United Nations, I'll wager. Our politicians are going to have to do a lot of explaining.'

'It's what they're paid to do,' Cuthbert replied with a shrug. 'Anyway, that's part of the reason it's been decided to push through with a big convoy in the next few days. At least now there's a lull in Sarajevo.'

Tring walked round his desk and sat down. 'But not here, Nigel, or DV. I'm not sure that's a smart idea.'

'Out of our hands, Reg,' Cuthbert said. 'It's a UN decision. Reports from our UKLOs and OPs suggest that the snow cover is hampering troop movements and ammunition resupplies to both the Croats and the Muslims. It might be the best opportunity we get.'

I said, 'I just met Rocky. He's checking out the viability.'

'That's right,' Cuthbert confirmed. He looked at Tring. 'We might have to be quite robust in our handling of the situation. That's the word from the brigadier. Would you be kind enough to brief Colonel Rathbone on my behalf? I need to get back to Divulje Barracks soonest . . . ah, and by the way, the brigadier wondered if he could steal Jimbo here to ride with the convoy? They'll want a top negotiator with them.'

Although Tring pulled one of his po-faces, I think he'd have liked nothing more than to get rid of me as soon as possible. 'I suppose we can spare him for a day or two.'

I said, 'Anything else, Reg?'

He shook his head. 'No more of this irresponsible behaviour, Jeff, do I make myself plain?'

I stood up. 'Of course, Reg, understood.'

'Before you go, Jeff, one more thing. These pictures were taken by Miss van Wyk. I've decided she's a real liability. I don't want her back in company HQ. Tell her when you see her.'

I was caught off guard and devastated by his words, but I was in no position to argue the toss. Part of me was even starting to agree with him. I left and walked with Cuthbert back towards the Den.

As he punched in the security code he said, 'Things are coming to a crunch, Jimbo, and a lot of it is down to you.'

'Me?'

'Your idea about the satellite phones.' He locked the door behind us. 'It's paying off. GCHQ has been monitoring all the traffic from Almir Aganovic and the Ramoza Brigade. SIS and BFHQ here have decided the general is the biggest obstacle to lifting these sieges and getting the convoys running again.'

I nodded. 'He's a stubborn bastard, I know that. Won't listen to reason.'

'He won't listen to anything – or anyone,' Cuthbert agreed. 'Not even his own high command in Sarajevo. He's become too powerful. So, it's been decided he's got to be taken out.'

'Taken out?' I echoed. 'Not another assassination like Zoric?'

'No, the Yanks have learned their lesson over that. Just get him removed from the scene.'

I frowned. 'Don't tell me the Americans are behind this again?'

Cuthbert's smile was cagey. 'Well, they do seem to be taking an increasing interest in the situation here. And the Foreign Office likes to keep them sweet.'

I shook my head in exasperation. 'The Americans were behind setting up Aganovic and the Ramoza Brigade in the first place. American arms and Saudi money.'

'You don't know that, Jimbo,' Cuthbert chided.

I said, 'But you do.'

'It was necessary at the time, as you know. The Muslims needed an effective fighting force to hold their own.' He shrugged. 'It's just grown into a bit of a monster.'

'Like Ho Chi Minh and Saddam Hussein,' I pointed out. 'America and the CIA are good at spawning monsters. I wonder who'll be next?'

He ignored that. 'We'll want Zlatko Herenda to fill the vacuum. I can't see he'll object to that. We'll make him an offer he can't refuse.'

'Well, I wish you luck,' I responded icily.

'I'll need your help.'

'For what?'

'Getting close to General Aganovic, working out how to get to him. I can't do that.'

That got me rattled. 'Because you're still shagging his fiancée?'

Cuthbert didn't like that. 'At least she's out of puberty . . . and I don't do it in *your* billet when you're away!'

So even Cuthbert knew about Tali and me. But then I suppose information and gossip was his stock-in-trade. '*Touché*,' I acknowledged. 'But I might have to make use of Ivana.'

'No bloody way, Jimbo. Not again. She's finished with him.'

'Is that your idea or hers?'

'Ours.'

'Has she told Aganovic yet?'

'Of course not. It would be too dangerous until she can get out of here.'

I hesitated. 'I'll give it some thought.'

'Thanks. Right, now I've got to be off. Got a meeting with Kirk Grundy at the Splendid.'

I said, 'Now why doesn't that surprise me? You'll probably find Tali with him. Do me a favour and tell her Tring's banned her from HQ, will you?'

He raised an eyebrow at my tone of voice, and just nodded.

I spent the rest of the day discussing and drawing up contingency convoy protection plans with Gordy Cromwell for the big one that was so desperately needed. I also spoke by satellite phone to both Croat and Muslim militia HQs as well as the Ramoza Brigade. Neither Colonel Zec nor Almir Aganovic was available, or they just didn't want me bending their ears yet again.

I left a message saying simply that under the UN mandate a very large emergency convoy would be passing through their siege lines within the next few days. Both warring parties' cooperation would be expected and appreciated. There was likely to be a very strong media interest in the operation – the eyes of the world would be on them. Subtle, I thought, but not too subtle.

In addition, I managed actually to speak to the young local Muslim commander, Major Zlatko Herenda, direct, delivering the same uncompromising message.

He sounded despondent. 'You will have no problems with *my* militia, Captain Hawkins. But you must understand that the Ramoza Brigade is running the sieges.'

'I know that,' I replied. 'But if you can bring your influence to bear on your colleague, General Aganovic, and emphasize the importance of this work to him, it will be greatly appreciated.'

'If only I had such influence, Captain Hawkins,' Herenda replied gloomily, 'I would gladly bring it to bear. But General Aganovic does not listen to the likes of me. However, I shall do my best.'

It didn't sound too promising, but was no worse than I'd expected. That afternoon I heard that Rocky had carried on through to Donji Vrbas to assess the siege situation there and discuss it with Colonel Rathbone and the UNHCR's head of office, their top man in-theatre. He'd left word for me to meet up with him again that night at the Splendid. The following morning I would travel with him back to the coast.

With my essential work for the day complete, I decided to drive back to the school and see how Anita Furtula was coping after the shock of the minefield incident that morning.

As I entered the classroom, I was immediately struck by the sombre mood. The children were unusually silent, some drawing at their desks, others writing carefully and thoughtfully in their exercise books. Their little faces looked drawn and haunted and there were, I noticed immediately, a lot of tear-stained cheeks. A female UNHCR worker was talking quietly to a small girl who looked very distressed.

Anita herself, still in her overcoat, was hugging her body as she paced slowly back and forth in front of the blackboard. She looked up when I entered, but didn't smile.

She walked across to me. Quietly she said, 'Did you know that Dario has lost his eye?'

'No, I haven't been back to the clinic. I'm sorry. What about Mara?'

'She's stable. But the clinic needs morphine and antibiotics urgently.'

'How are the rest of the kids?'

Anita looked across at her young charges. 'I have asked those who want to, to write or draw about their experience this morning. Or their private thoughts, maybe put them in a poem. Apparently such a process can be very therapeutic.'

I said, 'I imagine Tali might be good at that sort of thing. The kids seemed to like her.'

Anita regarded me closely, her eyes dark and bleak. 'Tali isn't here.'

I was surprised. 'I thought she was coming back here this afternoon.'

'She came back, Jeff, but I told her to go.'

'I don't understand. Why?'

'Earlier this afternoon I went to the clinic to see how Dario and Mara were. I was so upset I called in at the Splendid for a stiff drink. I met that American journalist there, Kirk Grundy, his name is.' Anita didn't take her eyes off mine. 'He told me something that made me even more upset than I could believe possible.'

I frowned. 'What?'

Anita took my arm and steered me out of the class and into the hall. Her voice was low and hoarse. 'He told me you've been sleeping with her, with Tali.'

I felt my jaw drop.

'Don't bother to deny it, Jeff. Don't tell me again that she's no competition,' Anita said. 'Apparently everyone knows about it. Anyway, Tali was here when I got back, so I asked her. At least she is honest. She's told me it is true. So I told her to go. Also that she was no longer welcome to stay at my house.'

I shifted awkwardly. 'I see.'

'You did not make love to her on my bed, did you? Tell me that, at least.'

Of course, I now realized where she was coming from. 'I only ever went to your flat that time with you.'

Her eyes seemed to bore into my skull. 'Thank goodness for that. I hate to think that you are trying to make a fool of me. It is bad enough to think that I am just another notch on your bedpost.'

I said, 'I haven't done anything to spite you, Anita. That time we spent together was good, but it wasn't any kind of commitment.'

'So I see. Better for you to be able to boast the conquest of a mere girl who is half your age.'

'It's not about conquest.'

'You are telling me you are in love with her?' She didn't bother to hide the raw cynicism in her voice.

That drew me up short. 'I don't think you would believe me if I said yes.'

'If I believed you, then I'd be thinking I was talking to a fool.'

I said, 'Maybe you are.'

Her lips curled back in a bitter smile. 'Better that, I suppose, than to think you just used me like a whore.'

I didn't remind her that it was she who had led me to her bed, not the other way round. But Anita had been through enough in this dirty war, and she didn't need to be belittled as well. I said, 'You know I like you very much.'

The bitter smile twitched again. 'A sort of *fucking friend*, isn't that what they call it?'

I said, 'I'm sorry, Anita, but I don't know exactly what I feel. I admire you and like you a hell of a lot; let's leave it at that. The last thing I wanted was to upset you.'

She seemed a little more composed now, and took a small step back while she continued to watch my face closely. 'Perhaps I am expecting too much. I think that night meant more to me than to you. I think I am jealous, but also disappointed in you.'

I said, 'You can't always choose who you fall in love with, Anita. Sometimes it just happens.'

That seemed to touch a nerve and this time the hint of a smile was sweeter. 'Like I have fallen for you . . . ? Yes, of course, you are right. I am being silly, behaving like a petulant schoolgirl. I am sorry.'

'It's all right, don't worry.' A thought suddenly occurred to me. 'How well do you know Kirk Grundy?'

'Kirk?' She shrugged. 'Since nine months, a year. I met him at the Splendid when he first arrived here. I did some translating for him, showed him the area, explained all the local personalities and politics. We still chat from time to time. Mostly, I suspect, when he wants some local gossip or information.'

'Did you ever tell him anything about us?' I asked.

Anita shook her head. 'No, nothing personal. But maybe he has an idea by the tone of my voice, or some rumours about when we left the Bunker nightclub together and disappeared for an hour or so that time.'

'Always the rumours,' I murmured.

She reached out and touched my arm. 'Can we still be friends, Jeff? Just friends?'

'Of course.' I leaned forward and kissed her cheek, reminded again of the fragrance of her.

She said, 'But I am sorry, I cannot have Tali back. Here or at my home, I just *can't*.'

'I understand,' I replied.

'I don't think she is good for you, Jeff. She will break your heart . . . and not even realize she is doing it.'

I edged away towards the door. 'We'll see.'

It was a relief to step out into the moist chill of early evening and I gulped down a lungful of air. Deep in thought, I retraced my footsteps to the Land Rover. The fog, having thinned a little during the day, was thickening up again. I had to take it really steady driving back to the Splendid and was in a way thankful that the concentration needed to avoid hitting a pavement, let alone anything else, took my mind off things.

The bar was filling up with UN and other aid workers, winding down with an early-evening drink. I spotted Nigel Cuthbert huddled in an alcove with Kirk Grundy, deep in earnest and whispered conversation. Tali sat alone at a table by the window, nursing an empty glass and staring out at the eddying fog.

'A drink?' I asked, startling her.

'Oh, Jeff!' She put her hand to her chest. 'You made me jump. I was miles away.'

I bought two bottles at the bar and rejoined her.

'Have you forgiven me?' she asked, an uncertain look in her eyes. 'About the photographs?'

'Looks like it,' I said, placing a bottle in front of her and sitting down. 'I think you know I'd probably forgive you anything.'

'Silly,' she said, her smile deepening as she reached out and put her hand on mine. 'I seem to be in everyone's bad books.'

'I know.'

'I don't see Major Tring being so forgiving.'

'He's not in love with you. Doesn't know what an angel you are.'

She looked awkward. 'I'm no angel.'

'I saw the way you helped Anita with the kids and how you were with them in that minefield this morning.' I put my other hand on top of hers and squeezed it. 'You're an angel to me.'

'No.' She shook her head and laughed lightly. 'I'm just your little devil on the side.'

I caught her mood. 'That sounds good enough to me.'

'And please don't fall in love with me, Jeff. I couldn't handle that.'

I watched her carefully, saw that little glint of fear behind her eyes. I said slowly, 'I don't mean anything heavy, Tali. I can't say you haven't bewitched me somewhat . . . but I realize there's probably no future in it.'

She raised her eyebrows and drew her lips into a little pout. 'Sorry, but I suppose we each regard our relationship slightly differently . . . Hey, I still enjoy being your little devil . . . despite what Anita said to me.'

'Oh yes,' I said, 'I've just seen her. She's disapproving of me, too, you know.' That reminded me. 'Have you anywhere to stay now? I could speak to my local contacts, I'm sure one of the villagers would be pleased take in a paying guest.'

'That's OK. Kirk arranged something with the owner here. I've got a little attic room at a reasonable price.'

I felt the blood pulse in my temples. 'Kirk? Why should he do that?'

'Because he's a friend, like you.'

'So you haven't fallen out?'

'We had, but we've patched it up.' She giggled. 'He's promised to behave himself while he's staying here.'

I said, 'You know it was Kirk who told Anita about us?' Tali shook her head. I added, 'He's bloody crafty. I think he knew what her reaction would be and guessed the result . . . you'd be homeless and he'd get you under the same roof here.'

She shrugged. 'It doesn't really matter.'

'It does to me.' I hesitated, and lowered my voice. 'There have been a lot of rumours about you and Kirk.'

The smile melted from her face. 'I can imagine.'

'Are they true?'

She hesitated and I tried to read what was in her eyes. 'If you mean did he fuck me, yes he did. Quite a lot, actually.'

It felt like I'd been hit in the solar plexus by an invisible steel fist. My silence can only have been for a second or two, but it seemed to stretch for eternity while I took in confirmation of the one thing in the world I didn't want to hear. 'For God's sake, Tali, why?'

She shrugged and I could tell she was trying to make light of it. 'I suppose because he took an interest in me. No one else did. Sure, there were a lot of leers and jokes. A lot of offers I could easily refuse. But no one took me seriously, or my work. I was solo on my first job in a war zone, inexperienced . . . I know people were laughing behind my back. But not Kirk.'

'Because he saw he could use you,' I said quickly. Too quickly.

'I know that now,' she replied evenly. 'But I think he genuinely liked me.'

'I'll bet.'

She ignored that. 'He treated me like an adult, we had a lot of laughs. And he really has helped get my work seen . . . pulled strings. I was a bit in awe of him.'

'You didn't have to sleep with him.'

Her powder-blue eyes met mine, and held them in a defiant gaze. 'I haven't got the prettiest face, but he said nice things, very complimentary. A man like Kirk has never said things like that before. Then one night . . .' She hesitated.

Perversely, I wanted to know. 'Go on.'

Tali sighed. 'One night in his room we had a lot to drink, talked a lot. He had a portable radio playing romantic music. I was feeling mellow. Then he kissed me and I kissed him back. He didn't ask if it was all right, he just started fondling me and undoing my buttons.

'I resisted, sort of, but he wasn't having any of it. He was very masterful, very overpowering. Then he forced his hand into my jeans. He knew exactly where to hit the spot. I'd come for the first time before I even realized, suddenly I was so hot, so frustrated . . . I just thought, what the hell, what does it matter?'

I shook my head slightly, disapproving. 'I don't need to hear any more.'

There was a sadness in her eyes as she watched the expression on my face. 'You need to know that it's finished. I enjoy sex, Jeff, you know that. I like to explore, be adventurous . . . I think maybe I was too adventurous. Kirk started talking about threesomes, watching me with other men . . . I realized it was time to end it. That was all before I came down here to Una Drina.'

'Before we happened?'

'Before we happened,' she confirmed, and squeezed her palm over my fist. 'I'm not a slut, Jeff . . . well, not that way . . . I only had sex with one man before Kirk, that was with my fiancé at the time. And that was three years ago.'

I was calming down a little. 'Twenty-two. You were a late starter for this day and age.'

'It was the way we were brought up in Africa. Strict Calvinist and church every Sunday. Family and friends were all the same. I had boyfriends, but they were governed by the same rules. Holding hands and a kiss on the cheek. One grope was one too many.' She laughed suddenly, that sweet musical sound she made. 'Me and my friends were the original little girls who always said no.'

I couldn't resist a smile. 'You've made up for lost time.'

She nodded slowly. 'Are you going to be here long, in the bar?'

'I'm waiting for Rocky. He could be some time yet.'

Her voice was soft. 'Telling you all that has made me horny. Come and see my new little attic room.' She raised the beer to her lips and drank, watching me over the bottle with a teasing look in her eyes, waiting for my reaction, knowing exactly what it would be.

I did too. 'That's the best offer I've had all day.'

She lowered the bottle. 'I'd like you to do something for me.'

'What's that?'

She leaned forward and whispered in my ear, so low I could barely make out the words. 'I want you to fuck my soul.'

Fourteen

While I was enjoying my own private heaven with Tali that evening, I was blissfully unaware that all hell was breaking out on the streets of Una Drina.

Our lovemaking seemed to take on a new reckless dynamic. Her confessions about having been with Kirk had perversely aroused me and I think I somehow wanted to punish her, use her like some kind of whore. I was rough and demanding, pushing her to her limits. But as she perspired and moaned and once or twice even yelped with pain, it became clear that this was what she wanted, and it spurred her on to respond in kind.

We seemed to go on for ever before I finally fell back on the crumpled sheets of the bed in her small attic room, and she lay her head against my chest.

She murmured sleepily, 'That was the best ever, Jeff. I thought I was going to die then for a moment.'

My anger had emptied, was gone. She had turned it back on itself, and I thought how sex would never be like this with any other woman, how I'd never find such a match again. I looked sideways at her and smiled. 'Then I must have found your soul.'

'You did.'

I raised my left arm and pressed the light button on my wristwatch. The digits 2145 shone back at me. 'Christ, is that the time?'

'What is it?'

'Quarter to ten.'

Her mouth dropped in surprise. 'I can't believe we've been here two hours.' She moved her legs and sat on the edge of the bed. 'I hope Rocky hasn't been waiting.'

I got up and started pulling on my clothes. 'If he is, it'll be my round all evening.'

'What's that noise?' she said suddenly. 'I can hear voices.'

She stood and moved towards the dormer window with an easy grace. I watched the arch of her spine and thought how comfortable she was with her own nakedness. She pushed the window open and peered down, her hair fluttering in the chill air. 'Something's happening, Jeff. I can't see very well but there seem to be a lot of people out there.'

I could hear it now, the faint but distinct tones of excited, gabbling voices. Pulling on my boots, I headed for the door. 'I'll catch you later.'

I didn't quite hear her reply as I left the room and ran down the four flights of stairs to the bar. It was deserted apart from Jelena who was collecting dirty glasses.

'What's going on?' I asked. 'Where is everyone?'

'Outside,' Jelena replied, looking concerned. 'There is trouble, fires are being started. They say the Black Swans are in town.'

I did a double-take. The Black Swans were a vicious group of Croat militia elite normally based at Prozor. 'When did they get here?'

She shrugged unhappily. 'Some time this afternoon, they say. I am Croat, Jeff, but I do not like those people. They are evil.'

I moved swiftly towards the door. Jelena was not wrong in her assessment. They called themselves elite commandos, but their chosen enemy were usually defenceless old people, women and children. My best guess was that, if the rumour was true, the Black Swans had used the fog to slip through the Muslim siege lines to reinforce the town's Croat defence forces.

In fact, they'd made it just in time, because there was a chill breeze now and the fog was definitely thinning. Outside the Splendid's entrance, groups of regular drinkers were standing in the slushy snow, talking and arguing among themselves and exchanging heated conversation with a growing crowd of angry townsfolk. Beyond them I could see the dark figures of people, heads bent, moving hurriedly along the main street. Most seemed to be heading north.

As I looked in that direction I could see a couple of blazing buildings, other small crowds there gathered to jeer and watch the flames from the wrecked shops lick at the night sky.

A big paw of a hand landed on my shoulder. 'Where you been, pal? Not shagging that girl of yours again?'

I turned round. 'Something like that, Rocky. Sorry if I kept you waiting.'

He shook his head. 'No, only arrived ten minutes ago. The road from DV was hell. Refugees everywhere, all going in different directions.'

'What's been happening?'

'My best guess is an orchestrated attempt by the Croats to drive the Muslims out of DV. Started at dusk there, but I don't think anyone quite realized how widespread it was until it was too late. I reckon there are hundreds or even thousands homeless. Then some Muslims started retaliating by torching Croat properties. Bloody mayhem.'

I glanced at the angry crowd around me. 'Looks like it's started here now.'

Suddenly an elderly man in a tattered old coat and flat cap realized he was standing next to a uniformed British soldier. He prodded me in the chest with the tip of his walking-stick. 'You fucking UN! You here to protect us! What you do? You do nothing!'

I edged away from the crowd with Rocky. The presence of members of the UNHCR or UNPROFOR would only antagonize them.

It was then that we heard the familiar clank and rumbling sound of approaching Warriors from our HQ in the middle of the town. We turned and saw the glowing orbs of their lights and waited for the first huge bulk to take form through the dissipating fog.

The young commander, a man called Foster, saw me wave him down and told his driver to stop.

'What's the situation, Foster?' I shouted.

He leaned out of the top hatch. 'Ethnic cleansing, sir. Bigtime. Happened in DV earlier, so we were half expecting it. Torching Muslim houses all over, but it's worse in the Muslim quarter down south. We've been told to patrol the southern districts as a deterrent.'

I indicated the burning shops further up the main drag. 'Looks like you might be too late already.' I watched as the column of four Warriors clattered past us, then turned to Rocky. 'I'm going down to the Muslim quarter. Want to take a look?'

'Sure, never mind that I'm gagging for a beer.'

Although the fog was lifting, I couldn't drive the Land Rover at any speed because the main street was filled with desperate looking people, mostly the old and mothers with babies or small children. Some looked as though they'd fled with just the clothes they were wearing. Others had rapidly packed a few bags or suitcases and thrown them into wheelbarrows, prams, handcarts or toboggans, deciding that to stay any longer in their homes was too dangerous.

More sinister were our occasional glimpses of heavily armed men in camo fatigues and balaclavas. The notorious Black Swan commandos. They stood in the shadows, perfectly still, and just watched the growing flow of humanity, admiring the result of their handiwork. Hundreds of vulnerable, innocent people with nowhere to go.

If they went out of town they'd be walking into the front line of the battlefield, if they stayed where they were they'd be burned in their houses or even shot. So they went to the only place they could think of, the company HQ of our UNPRO-FOR force.

As I drove past there was a growing mass of people pleading

with the guards to be let in. The gates remained firmly shut.

'Sad, that,' Rocky said, shaking his head.

I agreed. 'But we can't take them in. There's just not the space, let alone facilities.'

'And more snow forecast.'

I said, 'It's going to be a fun Christmas.'

The Muslim quarter was lit with burning buildings and the streets filled with terrified and suddenly homeless people. Four Warriors had been deployed and their troops were out on aggressive foot patrol of the area to prevent any more torching of property. But I guess the men responsible, the Black Swans, had melted away before they'd even arrived.

I pulled up beside the familiar figure of Captain Gordy Cromwell, out on the ground to make a first-hand assessment of the situation.

'Welcome to Beelzebub,' he greeted as Rocky and I approached.

'Under control?' I asked.

He nodded. 'After a fashion, but we can't be everywhere at once. It was well co-ordinated. Virtually all the fires were started at once. So by the time we responded the damage was done.'

'I hear the Black Swans are in town.'

'Yeah, and that little scrote Colonel Zec is well connected. Major Tring's just gone to the town hall to complain to Mayor Jozic. This is clearly pre-planned and deliberate, not people acting on impulse.'

I said, 'Jozic will just deny it.'

Gordy shrugged. 'What else can we do? At least Tring's mad and talking tough for once.' He gave a faint smile. 'Your bad influence, I suppose.'

'Any civilian casualties?' I asked.

'One nasty situation. Three under-tens being looked after by a deaf grandmother. Didn't stand a chance, all burned alive.'

'Christ.'

'Apart from that a dozen or so with burns or gunshot wounds.

Nothing too bad, as far as I'm aware. Our medics are looking after them or taking them to the clinic.' He stared at the haunted, tear-streaked faces of the helpless women, children and pensioners around us. 'But it's cranked up the pressure here. Like a balloon that's about to burst.'

Rocky asked, 'Where the hell are all these people going to go?'

'We're trying to identify any commercial properties not already used for refugees,' Gordy explained. 'But if they're not being used already, they'll be in a pretty dreadful state.'

I said, 'A lot of people won't feel safe here any more. There's going to be a lot of refugees.'

Rocky scratched at his beard. 'If that big mother of a convoy wasn't a priority before, it sure as hell is now.'

Next morning at around nine, as I was hastily packing my bergen and satellite telephone prior to joining Rocky Rogers on his journey to the coast, Gordy Cromwell knocked on the door of my billet.

'Looks like we've got our own personal siege, Jimbo,' he announced. 'Nothing more scary than a crowd of angry women. Major Tring wants you to lend a hand.'

'What?'

'Outside the gates. They're complaining about no convoys for weeks.'

I slung the bergen strap over my shoulder and picked up the satellite phone case. 'I'm due to go with Rocky.'

'I know. But, believe me, Jimbo, you ain't going nowhere unless we can appease this lot.'

I strode down the passage and out into the compound, where I found Major Tring pacing back and forth, head down and hands clasped behind his back. A group of armed troops stood nearby, fingering their rifles nervously.

Behind the mesh fence with its razor wire was a large crowd of women in shabby winter coats and headscarves. It looked as though they came from both sides of the community. They were shouting out, trying to get attention, and only stopped when Rocky Rogers' white Land Rover Discovery edged slowly through them from the main street, forcing them to part. As they realized it was an UNHCR vehicle, they began pounding its roof and windows with their fists.

The gates parted to allow the Discovery to enter and half a dozen Royal Wessex soldiers had their work cut out to prevent some of the women from squeezing through with it.

'We need to address these people, Jeff,' Tring said. 'Reassure them, send them home. If they stay here in this mood they'll hamper all our operations.'

'I'll see what I can do, Reg,' I replied wearily and walked with him across the compound to join Rocky by the gates as he climbed out of his Discovery.

'What do they want?' Tring demanded irritably.

I'd already picked up a lot of what different people were shouting. 'What *don't* they want?' I said. 'They're asking where the convoys are. Humanitarian supplies are needed urgently. Their children are starving. Many people are now refugees and need shelter. There are no medicines in the town, no food or fuel. They're demanding action—'

'Yes, yes,' Tring said testily. 'I get the picture . . . Well, Jeff, tell 'em something. Reassurance, whatever it needs. Just get them off my back.'

Rocky intervened. 'I'll talk to them, Jeff, if you translate.'

'Fine by me.'

Scrambling onto the bonnet of his Discovery, Rocky used it as a stage and held up his hands to get the attention of the crowd. All eyes turned in his direction and the voices died for a moment.

'I am from the UNHCR!' he shouted. I climbed up alongside him, and repeated his words. 'We fully understand your plight! . . .'

Clearly the audience thought that the UN did not. Individual women began calling out their requests in plaintive, pleading voices.

'My children have nothing to eat! I need powdered milk for my baby!'

'I am breaking up my house bit by bit to burn on the fire!'

'She is lucky!' Contempt in the voice. 'Since last night I have no house!'

'We are boiling weeds to make broth!'

'My child is dying in hospital because they have no drugs!'

'Last night my grandmother died of the cold! We bury her today!'

'I want to leave this accursed place with my family, but we are trapped!'

Rocky tried again and raised his hands. 'We are going to try and bring in a very large convoy in the next few days. Its arrival will solve many of your problems.'

As my translation percolated through the crowd, the shouting faded as the individuals thought about what they had been told. It was something – if they really believed it – but still not nearly enough. And everyone knew it.

I added a point of my own. 'Please remember, the only reason the convoys can't get through is because of the fighting or the sieges operated by your *own* people. Croat and Muslim. Please make it clear to your leaders and your fighting menfolk that you *must* have the convoys running. They must listen to *you* – the ordinary people. You are who *matter*! Make your voices *heard* like you have to us here today!'

In the silence that followed, I heard one person slowly start to clap with approval. I turned and saw the huddled figure of Anita Furtula, half-hidden in the crowd. Around her others began to clap, too, the sound beginning to spread through the throng like ripples on a pond.

Rocky leaned towards me. 'Looks like we've won some of them over,' he said quietly.

I nodded. 'For today.'

As we climbed down, the crowd began to disperse and drift away. I had hoped Anita might stay and say something to me. For some reason it was important to me to know that we were still on good terms . . . But she had melted away with the others.

When Rocky and I drove out of the company compound in the Discovery, the legacy of the previous night's ethnic cleansing was plain to see. A squatter camp had materialized in the icy slush along the pavements of the main street, people seeking the relative safety of the town centre. Here they were less likely to be preyed on by the loitering gangs of Black Swans. Every few metres there was a small fire of burning wood scraps or anything combustible, and a huddle of people under a makeshift shelter of plastic, polythene or old packing cases. Old people shivered in blankets and mothers tried to console their children or suckle babes in arms. It was a pitiful sight.

It was a relief to get to the outskirts of town and put the awful sights behind us. The fog had finally cleared, leaving behind a dank day with low, pinkish-grey cloud that held the threat of more snow to come. At least the Muslim guns had not yet opened up again, which was probably why we were waved through the Croat checkpoint with barely a second glance.

Beyond it we could see the Croat trenches on either side of the road, in snow-covered meadows and in open woodland, newly dug and manned to defend the southern approaches of the town from the surrounding Muslims.

A couple of kilometres further on we were flagged down at a checkpoint mounted by the Ramoza Brigade. Their spokesman was unkempt, bearded and bellicose.

He demanded to know why the UN had allowed the previous night's ethnic cleansing of his 'brothers and sisters' in the town. Patiently I explained to him that the Royal Wessex had been quick to put a stop to it and that the UN regarded the matter very seriously. The Muslim militiaman seemed unimpressed, so I pointed out we were bringing in convoys again with medicines for injured and sick Muslims and to take out any Muslim refugees who wanted to go to the safety of the camps on the coast.

He smirked at that. 'So again the UN assists with the ethnic cleansing of our people, like they do when the Serbs do the same thing!'

In the Balkans it often seemed that you could never win an argument with simple logic. You had to turn it on its head to get anywhere. Losing my case cost us a carton of cigarettes and a jar of Maxwell House, but at least we were out of Una Drina and speeding up the valley towards Makljen Ridge.

It was then I heard the first distant explosion from back in the valley. The bombardment of Una Drina had resumed.

I was suddenly overcome by a sense of freedom, almost euphoria, at being away from that place. It made me realize just how trapped and claustrophobic the citizens must feel, just like the peacekeepers who had come to protect them.

Then, after clearing the ridge, we began our slow descent towards the coast. Of course there were the usual Croat road-blocks along the way, where our identity papers were checked, but a single UNHCR vehicle and two accredited passengers raised little interest. There was just a cursory inspection of our personal luggage in the back, a routine request for cigarettes, and we were on our way again.

Finally we arrived at the huge UNHCR depot at Metkovic. This time it was Egyptian troops in blue UN helmets who opened the security gates for us. The first thing that struck me were the number of trucks parked here this time. With all convoy operations on this route suspended, dozens and dozens of the monstrous white vehicles and their trailers were grounded here. Line after line after line of them. It was all such a shame and a waste, resulting in people near to starving, the old battling against hypothermia and the sick and injured dying for lack of essential medicines.

Following a quick snack lunch in the canteen, we went to the

UNHCR meeting in one of the administrative Portakabir
extensions to the base.

Inside it was bare apart from an army-style conference table
with collapsible legs and a scattering of metal stacking chairs. A
forlorn-looking plastic Christmas tree stood on top of the only
other item of furniture, a filing cabinet.

I listened in as an UNPROFOR observer while the team or
half a dozen aid and refugee experts heard Rocky's latest update
of the situation in Una Drina and Donji Vrbas. The debate that
followed was fast, furious and decisive. Arguments were quickly
settled with a lot of well-balanced give and take which I thought
was quite impressive for a bunch of civilian bureaucrats.

The chairman of the meeting, a tall Swede in his late thirties
with an impressive blond beard, hunched over the sheet of paper
before him on the table. 'Right, the decision is made, the
convoy runs. It's been cleared by the UN high commissioner
through her special envoy in Sarajevo and our chief of operations
in Zagreb. The detail is down to us.' He turned to Rocky.
'What's your latest reading of the situation, Mr Rogers?'

'Of course, some convoys are now reaching Sarajevo by other
routes,' Rocky replied thoughtfully. 'And the suspension of the
Serb bombardment of the capital is very helpful. But its demand
on supplies remains huge and, of course, will remain so. But the
plight of Una Drina, Zenica and Donji Vrbas, on the main
convoy route from the coast, has become absolutely desperate,
almost critical.'

The Swede nodded his understanding. 'These are all Croat
towns, of course. Will we have problems with the Croat militias?'

Rocky nodded in my direction. 'I've been talking to Jeff
Hawkins on the way here. He's LO with the Royal Wessex, as
you know. It's our joint opinion that there'll be no major problem if the right pressure is applied. Maybe just a little
prevaricating at local level by some individual commanders.'

The Swede stroked his beard. 'Now, what about the Ramoza
Brigade? These are the Muslim fundamentalists besieging Una

Drina and DV who, I understand, are still not responding to requests from the Bosnian government in Sarajevo to let any convoys through. Even if they don't open fire on us, how do we pass through their lines?' He then reminded us of what we all knew all too well. 'We don't have a mandate to shoot our way through their roadblocks – and no UNPROFOR escort could effectively protect a convoy of this size.'

The faces of the other UNHCR workers round the table look glum.

Rocky cleared his throat as if preparing to swallow something that might choke him. 'There is a possible way.'

Everyone looked up.

'But I hesitate to actually recommend it.' He glanced again at me, looking for moral back-up for what we'd discussed on the long journey from Una Drina. Suddenly it seemed a totally hare-brained idea. 'Makljen Ridge marks the start of the "Devil's Triangle", as some of us call it. Anywhere beyond that we can now expect to run into Ramoza units hostile to the UN. Una Drina is the first town of any size beyond Makljen, but there are now major Muslim deployments in that area.' Rocky glanced pointedly at me, I guessed wanting me to share some of the flak for this crazy proposal. 'Maybe Jeff would be kind enough to explain.'

I stood and walked across to a large-scale map on the wall. 'Just before Makljen there is an unmade track that veers off to the right. It runs up into the hills of the valley, running broadly parallel to the main road to Una Drina. The locals call it "the snake", which gives you some idea of what it's like. Narrow and very twisting as it winds through the hills and with precipitous drops in some places. Only sensibly usable by a mule cart or a four-wheel drive. Or skis and sleds in winter.'

The Swede looked concerned. 'What about our lorries?'

'Jeff said *sensibly* used by,' Rocky pointed out. 'No one would normally use it for trucks when there's an alternative road, but there's no reason why the convoy *couldn't* negotiate that route.

It'll be long and not without dangers – including two rather iffy bridges – but I reckon we could do it.'

I picked up the baton. 'The beauty of it is that it eventually meanders down through the hills to Una Drina from the west.'

'Through Muslim positions,' the Swede pointed out.

I nodded. 'But we should have the element of surprise. It's a very short distance from the scattered Ramoza Brigade positions to the town. Our observers haven't placed any hostile units near that track.'

'By the time they wake up to our presence,' Rocky added, 'we should be safely through – before they can do anything about it.'

The Swede was massaging his beard again. 'That's a very high risk strategy . . . and couldn't such a huge convoy be spotted by hostile forces at any time while on this so-called "snake"?'

'It's always a risk,' I agreed. 'But actually it's a very sheltered and secluded route with a lot of tree cover. The only villages it comes close to are Stavac and Bukovica, which are both Croat-inhabited.'

Rocky added, 'And we're looking at a couple of other things we can do to improve our chances.' He glanced at the faces around the table. 'At the same time we run a smaller convoy down the *main* road to Una Drina as a sort of diversion to catch the Ramoza Brigade's attention. If it's held up or has to turn back, it won't matter.'

Everyone seemed to see the sense in that and the mood round the table lightened noticeably. I said, 'I'm also looking at the possibility of jamming all Ramoza Brigade signals traffic during the operation. If the convoy is spotted, it'll be more difficult for the Muslims to organize any sort of effective response.'

'In theory,' the Swede said shrewdly.

'In theory,' I agreed.

'That gets us into Una Drina. We still have to reach Donji Vrbas beyond that, and then Sarajevo itself.'

I said, 'I'm hoping our arrival will take the wind of the

Ramoza Brigade's sails, so to speak. This huge convoy will be in-theatre and with a big international media contingent reporting on events. Even if the bombardment continues and the siege is later renewed, I'm hoping they'll see the sense in not interfering with it. We'll also then have full armoured back-up from the main Royal Wessex force at DV.'

'It's not perfect,' Rocky admitted. 'But I reckon this'll be as good as it gets.'

The expressions on the faces, watching us in such earnest, suggested that they agreed. I stayed on for the rest of the meeting while they refined decisions on exactly which essential supplies would be carried and how they would be distributed. Fundamentally, of the hundred-odd trucks and trailers, some fifteen would supply Una Drina, thirty-five would supply Donji Vrbas and Zenica, and the remaining fifty would roll on all the way to Sarajevo. Each would return with the most urgent medical evacuees and as many refugees as they could carry. This would be prioritized in situ by the staff of the UNHCR's head of office in Zenica.

The meeting moved towards its conclusion with the decision that the diversionary 'Convoy Silver' would set out in around forty-eight hours' time. The mighty 'Convoy Gold', as it became known, would follow an hour or two later. It was planned to reach the area of Makljen Ridge just after dark when it would divert off down the treacherous 'snake', the back route into Una Drina.

The Swede dealt with 'matters arising' and 'any other business' before giving a droll Nordic smile. 'Thank you, everyone. Of course, if Mr Rogers succeeds with this, it will be one of our biggest successes in the Balkans and one of our biggest ever convoys of humanitarian aid. Even so, remember that even this will not begin to do the job needed here . . . but it may make Christmas for the citizens of this wasted land just a little happier.'

Or just a little more endurable, I thought to myself as the meeting broke up.

Rocky left to meet up with his drivers and check over the loading procedures. I went to the lorry-park to await the arrival of transport from British HQ at Divulje Barracks by the airport.

I wasn't exactly expecting VIP treatment, so was surprised when a gleaming Land Rover Defender staff-car pulled up. Nor was I expecting my old friend Staff Sergeant Dave McVicar to be my chauffeur.

'You're coming down in the world.' I grinned, throwing my kit in the back and getting in beside him.

'I know, I know,' he said, shaking his head. 'Here's me, supposed to be G2, head of operational intelligence and all that . . . and I end up being a driver for oiks like you.' He headed out of the compound on the road to Split. 'Change of plan. We're not going to DJ. The brigadier's in town and wants us to meet at your old stamping ground.'

I groaned. The Seavu Hotel.

We chatted on the two-hour drive to Split but I noticed that McVicar wasn't up for talking business. When we arrived, the hotel was just as grim and dowdy as I remembered, but this time there were refugee children playing on the stairs and in the lounge where I'd received my initial briefing from McVicar and the CBF. Suddenly it all seemed like a lifetime ago.

It came as a mild jolt as I suddenly recalled it was in this very reception area that I'd first noticed and been introduced to a rather tall and striking young blonde with her hair in a ponytail by the name of Tali van Wyk.

I shooed the kids out of the lounge while McVicar ordered a pot of coffee, and we'd just settled down as the diminutive Brigadier Stowell breezed in. He had a newspaper tucked under one arm and was rubbing his hands vigorously. 'Christ, I'd forgotten how cold this place is! Bloody heating seems to be off again. Ah, coffee, Dave, just the ticket!' His raisin eyes focused on me and the lips beneath the toothbrush moustache fired a quick smile. 'Jeff! Good to see you.'

He plucked the newspaper from under his arm and held it up

for me to see the front page. It was the *Washington Post* and showed a large photograph by Tali of me carrying a wounded child from the minefield near the school. 'Well done, Jeff. That's the sort of publicity our work needs. Might help to get the Americans more involved. Excellent job you're doing. Keep it up.'

I felt a bit ashamed when I remembered how angry I'd been at Tali for taking the picture at the time. Now I felt pleased that she had.

Brigadier Stowell sat down on one of the red leather chairs grouped round the coffee table. He plucked some foam stuffing from a split in the upholstery with consummate distaste. 'Now, Jeff, bring me up to speed on the plans for Convoy Gold, will you? Gather you've just come from the final meeting.'

I began while McVicar distributed the coffee and Stowell produced a hipflask of brandy and offered it round. The brigadier didn't interrupt, but just nodded from time to time if he especially approved of something. He clearly liked the plan that involved sneaking through the back route to Una Drina, the diversionary Convoy Silver and jamming the Ramoza Brigade's communications. 'I'll get that checked out immediately, Jeff. I'm sure our signals boys will be up for that one.'

McVicar added, 'And I'll get an SAS team to inspect your route along the snake. Make sure you don't have any nasty surprises waiting for you.'

'Good idea,' I agreed.

Stowell said, 'I've had talks with the Croatian military and they are putting pressure on their country cousins in Bosnia to co-operate. Of course, Una Drina and DV are Croat towns and are both desperate for aid. Doesn't mean you won't find some local commanders playing silly buggers, of course, but shouldn't be anything you can't overcome by persuasion – or bribery! As far as they – and us, for that matter – are concerned, the only fly in the ointment is the Muslim Ramoza Brigade. The Croats don't want their towns to be strangled. We've assured them we're working on the problem . . .' He let his words hang in the air as he looked pointedly at me.

I said, 'Is this about General Almir Aganovic? Nigel Cuthbert mentioned you wanted him . . .' I hedged to find the right word, '. . . neutralized.'

Stowell pulled a thin smile. 'Disappeared. Any ideas?'

I'd been racking my brains over this one. 'We need to get him on our territory, and I don't think that will be easy. He's not going to show himself personally unless it's a powerful lure.'

From the corner of my eye I saw Dave McVicar nodding his agreement.

'The best I can come up with,' I said, 'is to suggest that the Croats are ready to agree to his terms of surrender to end the siege. Invite Aganovic to negotiate the detail of how the Croat militia will either stand down or withdraw from Una Drina.'

Stowell pursed his lips thoughtfully and nodded his head. 'Neat, Jeff, I like it. But will he believe it? He'll no doubt want to verify that position with the Croats. Mayor Jozic and Colonel Zec might play along if they knew what we were up to . . .'

McVicar got there first. 'But we can hardly make that public.'

'I realize that,' I replied. 'So we need to be a bit cunning. Use a go-between that Aganovic trusts. Tell him the Croats secretly *want* to negotiate, but can't afford to lose face.'

'Who would he trust that much?' Stowell asked.

I took the plunge. 'Ivana.'

Stowell grimaced. 'Ouch. Mmm, you know the problem there, Jeff?'

'Yes, sir. I know Nigel won't like it.'

'And I suspect neither will she.'

I said, 'Maybe she would if the reward was good enough.'

'Such as?' McVicar asked.

I shrugged. 'British citizenship, new identity . . . something along those lines.'

McVicar and the brigadier glanced at each other and I knew they could see the possibilities. I added, 'And maybe we can also put some pressure on Mayor Jozic to play along with the ruse.'

Stowell looked bemused. 'How?'

I said, 'Look, the man's an out-and-out villain. We know enough about him and his operations to ... how can I put this?'

McVicar saw it coming. 'Blackmail him?' he suggested helpfully.

'Something like that,' I replied. 'I'll work on it.'

Stowell looked pleased. 'Excellent. I think I can see a way forward here.' He stood up sharply. 'Now, there are also a couple of technicalities to work out. I've got to get back to HQ, so I'll leave McVicar here to go over those with you. Well done, Jeff. I'm well pleased with your efforts.'

McVicar watched the brigadier cross the lounge and disappear through the door. 'Nice one, Alan,' he murmured. 'Leave me to sort out the *technicalities* . . .'

I frowned. 'What's the problem?'

'You're not going to like it.'

'Why?'

'Because it means going behind Rocky's back. Naturally his loyalty is to his job and the UNHCR, so I can't risk putting him in the loop.'

I was starting to guess what he was on about. 'You want to use the convoy in some way?'

McVicar nodded. 'We've got to get a snatch team into Una Drina and we've got to get General Aganovic out. The convoy's a perfect solution. Four from Hereford as truck crew and a false compartment in one of the vehicles to smuggle Aganovic back through the Muslim lines. Some engineers are already working on one of the container trailers.'

'What about the paperwork?' I asked.

'Not a problem. We can get that fixed by contacts in the UN.'

McVicar had been right in guessing that I didn't like this one bit. 'And you're sure you can't let Rocky in on this?'

'Sorry, Jimbo. You know it's more than likely he'd turn us down. Understandable, of course, because it breaks all the UN rules. But we've got to think of the bigger picture.'

As a soldier you get used to that sort of excuse for many things; it was just odd hearing it coming from a good friend like Dave McVicar.

I forced a smile. 'Then the bigger picture it has to be.'

An evening of heavy drinking lay ahead in the hotel bar with Dave, Rocky and a number of the UNHCR drivers. Although there were plenty of pretty young women clearly available, I steered well clear of them. All I wished was that the bar door would open and Tali would magically appear. She didn't.

The next day I spent nursing a hangover at British Army HQ in Divulje Barracks. After liaising with the staff there and also by radio with Gordy Cromwell and Colonel Rathbone's staff at battalion HQ in DV on the fine detail of the plans, it was decided that a large UNPROFOR army replenishment convoy would also travel the same route as the smaller diversionary Convoy Silver of the UNHCR, following close on its heels. Apart from carrying supplies desperately needed by the Royal Wessex, it was felt this would put added pressure on the renegade Muslims to let both convoys through. If it worked, it might mean that Convoy Gold could also go by the main road and not need to take up my hare-brained scheme of travelling along the snake.

Later I tried making contact with General Aganovic on the satellite phone, but the leader of the Ramoza Brigade proved elusive and I had to make do with an aide the first time I called. I referred only to the Silver and UNPROFOR convoys and asked for a guarantee of their free and safe passage through the siege rings around Una Drina and Donji Vrbas. The aide said he was not able to make such a decision but would pass on my request. Before hanging up, I reminded him how much the supplies were needed by the Muslim inhabitants of the area as well as the Croats. He seemed unmoved.

It was another two hours before General Aganovic came back

to me, and his opening words were spoken with quiet, restrained anger. 'Captain Hawkins, are you aware of the military *purpose* of a siege?'

I lit a cigar and exhaled. 'Of course.'

Obviously he wasn't convinced. 'It is to deny access and provisions until the enemy is forced to capitulate.'

'Your "enemy", General,' I said, 'comprises women, children, old people and the sick. Muslim and Croat.'

'My enemy is the Croat militia,' he growled back venomously, 'and the town authorities who want to drive my people from their ancestral homes.'

I said, 'Your government in Sarajevo want you to allow the convoys through.'

There was a low menacing laugh in my earpiece. 'That's what they tell you. They want my sieges to succeed as much as I do.'

'Then you've both got what you want.'

'Meaning, Captain?'

'Una Drina at least is at breaking point,' I said, beginning to plant the seed of belief in his mind. 'There is talk that the Croats may concede what you ask.'

But Aganovic was dismissive. 'Talk! Yes, *talk* until they get their precious aid. Then they change their minds. Don't treat me as a fool, Captain.'

'Believe what you want, General. Your blindness is sadly irreversible, but there is no point in also being deaf to the truth.'

I heard the hiss of outrage. 'May Allah be merciful when your turn comes to die . . .'

I pushed on. 'UNHCR and UNPROFOR convoys are coming into the territory you hold tomorrow. Do not defy the mandate of the United Nations, General. The media eyes of the world will be on you and there will be a heavy price to pay if you do not allow them free passage. For you *and* your cause.'

I left it at that. Aganovic wasn't the sort to back down in a direct conversation with me, but left to think about it overnight and then being confronted with the reality of the situation, there was just the slimmest chance he'd come up with some sort of face-saving solution.

Obviously the UN and British government publicity machine had swung into action, for all flights arriving that afternoon at Split were bursting with television news crews from around the world.

That night when I returned to the Seavu, the bar was heaving with media types, newcomers being briefed by veteran reporters and news crews of the Balkans campaign who where already stationed in the country.

I had no desire to get mixed up with them and no doubt pressured for information I had no intention of giving. As I turned away from the door, I saw Gerald Kemp of ITN trudging wearily up the hotel steps with his suitcase. Behind him, with a huge rucksack weighing on her back, was Tali.

'Hi, Jeff!' Kemp called. 'Can I have a word?'

'You may indeed,' I replied. He was the one media man I felt I could trust implicitly on a personal level. 'Come into the lounge for a coffee and a shot of something. Looks like you need it.'

'I do!' he said, shuffling past me as I held open the door. 'What a sod of a journey. Held up at every bloody checkpoint from Una Drina to here, then the fucking car expires. We were stuck in the snow for three hours before some Russian Army engineers came across us and fixed the engine, bless 'em.'

As Kemp dumped his suitcase on the carpet and began unravelling the bright yellow scarf from around his neck, Tali followed him in. Her face looked pinched and white, her eyes watery from the chill air outside.

I kissed her on the cheek, her skin cold on my lips. 'Hi, Tali,' I said.

She stopped and looked at me for a moment with something like disappointment. 'Not good enough, Jeff.' To my embarrassment she threw her arms around my neck and kissed me long and hard on the mouth, her tongue teasing open my teeth until she got the response she wanted.

Kemp coughed politely.

Tali relaxed her grip and drew back. 'I've missed you,' she said quietly.

'I've missed you, too,' I said quickly, then changed the subject. 'Presumably you came with Gerald?'

Kemp said, 'And a bad decision she made too. Freezing in that car with no heating. Still, huddling together to keep warm made up for it.'

Anger flashed in my brain like a bolt of lightning. Bloody jealousy! What the hell was happening to me?

At that moment, the waitress came in and took our order and the diversion gave me the chance to calm down. If this was the thing called love, then I don't think I'd ever really experienced it in my life before. And, to be honest, I wasn't sure I cared for it much.

As we settled down on the red leather suite and poured out mugs of hot coffee from a huge pot, then laced them with the contents of a bottle of slivovitz, Kemp said, 'I've heard rumours, Jeff.'

I groaned inwardly. 'Oh, yes?'

He must have read the expression in my face. 'Don't worry, I don't think anyone seriously believes them . . . That if the convoy isn't allowed through, it's going to try and get down some dangerous and little-known goat track.'

So much for security, I thought. At least the rumour was only half right and didn't appear to have much credence.

I said, 'For your ears only, Gerald. Part of the convoy may well try something similar to that. If it does, I want the press horde to stay with the main body of the convoy. But I'd be happy for your crew, and your crew only, to come with us on the alternative route. The condition is, this is strictly between you and me.'

Kemp's smile widened. He knew a scoop when he saw one. 'You have my absolute word on it, Jeff. I won't even tell the rest of the crew.'

'It could be hairy,' I warned.

He raised his coffee mug in a toast. 'Hairy's what I do, Jeff. Made my living out of it for thirty years.'

Later that evening, Tali left her hotel room and came to mine as we'd arranged after Gerald Kemp had set off to round up his crew and buy them some drinks.

I was lying on the bed when she opened the door to my room, her slender body a silhouette in the light from the gas-lamp in the corridor. She didn't say a word, just entered and began undressing in the faint glow from the window. Her clothes were left where they fell and my eyes adjusted quickly to discern the shadowy contours of her breasts and belly. Her hair glistened like pale platinum as she released it and allowed it to tumble down over her shoulders.

'Are you watching me?' she asked in a hoarse voice.

'Of course.'

She laughed shyly. 'Well, I'm up for it, if you are.'

I smiled. 'Can't you see? I've never been more up for it.'

She glided elegantly to the side of the bed, lowered herself and ran her hand up my naked thigh. A soft laugh. 'I see what you mean. I think he likes me, even when you don't.'

'I love you. He adores you.'

'Don't love me too much.'

'I'll try not to.'

'Jeff?'

'Yes?'

'Let's go soul searching. Find my soul again.' I felt her mouth close on me.

It must have been an hour or more later when I drifted into a contented sleep, with Tali snuggled against my chest. I was the happiest man in the world.

Then suddenly I was aware that she was no longer beside me. I raised myself onto one elbow and looked across the room. She was standing at the foot of the bed, looking down at me, my DPM fatigue top keeping her warm and barely decent.

The whites of her eyes glistened in the ambient light. I

thought she was frowning. 'I've been thinking, Jeff,' she said suddenly, realizing I was awake. 'Does this include me?'

I cleared my throat. 'Does what include you?'

'Going with Gerald's crew on this breakaway convoy?'

I really didn't want to handle this now. I shook my head. 'Sorry, Tali. I can't put you at risk.'

'That's not fair,' she countered. 'What about all the convoy drivers and crews? Doesn't it matter if they're put at risk?'

'They're not female,' I replied, grasping at a chauvinist straw. 'And, as you know, Major Tring has you marked down as a security risk.'

But she saw through that one. 'Major Tring doesn't run the convoys.'

'But he is responsible for military security and protection of the convoys,' I came back. 'I'm sorry, but that's the way it is. You can travel with the primary convoy on the main road, though.'

She didn't reply immediately, but I could sense her anger as she dropped my fatigue top from her naked shoulders and turned her back on me, quickly pulling on her pants and the rest of her clothes.

Moving towards the door, she paused with her fingers on the handle. Suddenly she said, 'You're being a real bastard, Jeff. You don't own me, you know.'

Then she was gone and the door slammed shut behind her.

Fifteen

I slept badly for the rest of that night, worrying that I'd handled it all wrong with Tali and anxious about the prospects for the convoy the following day. Sleep must have caught up with me eventually, but it seemed like only minutes before I was disturbed again by the bleep of my wristwatch alarm.

Although I was drenched in sweat, I could remember nothing about the bad dream I must have just had. My mouth was parched and my eyes felt like glue. There was no hot water in the mildewed shower cubicle, but at least the icy lancing needles cleared my head and woke me up.

Feeling better then, I quickly shaved, dressed and ran a comb through my hair. I double checked my watch; it was just 0700 hours and the sky was lightening outside to reveal low bruised cloud. There were flurries of snow in the air.

Downstairs, the hotel was absolute bedlam. There were UN workers, convoy drivers, journalists and TV crews with their mountains of equipment everywhere, scoffing huge breakfast fry-ups in the dining room, milling round in the lounge or having coffee and a smoke in the bar while they waited for the locally hired minibuses and taxis to arrive to take them the 130 kilometres to the convoy depot.

Although I looked everywhere, I could see no sign of Tali. I pushed my way to the front of the queue of people trying to check out at the reception desk. The girl working there was the friend of Jelena I'd met on my first night; she recognized me and smiled brightly. 'Can I help you, Jeff?'

'Miss van Wyk . . . which room is she in?'

The girl smiled. 'The tall blonde lady?'

'Yes.'

'She checked out about an hour ago.'

'Where did she go?'

A shake of the head. 'I don't know. She was picked up by that big American guy, the journalist. I can't remember his name.'

'She left with him?'

'In his car. He picked her up.'

The man behind me in the queue nudged me. 'Do you mind, mate? Some of us are in a hurry.'

I mumbled an apology and turned back into the foyer.

Rocky Rogers was standing there in his tartan lumberjacket with the fleece collar and clutching the small holdall that contained all his possessions in Bosnia. 'Hi, Jimbo, you had your scoff yet?'

I shook my head. 'Not hungry.'

'Then let's make a head start and get up to the depot,' he suggested, 'while the road is clear. And before we get any fresh snow.'

I said, 'Fine. Let's go.'

It was as busy outside the hotel as it was inside. Drivers and UN staff standing around, hunched against the cold and the swirl of snowflakes, minibuses and taxis backed up nose-to-tail down the street. I walked with Rocky the hundred metres or so to his Discovery.

We set off at a steady pace out of the depressing city and took the road to Metkovic. Several times we overtook white UNHCR trucks and trailers making their way towards the assembly point at the depot.

About half-way there we passed four more large trucks pulled over in a lay-by with an ostentatious Cherokee four-wheel-drive cruiser parked behind them. As we flashed past, I just caught a glimpse of its driver as he was about to get back in, his face almost hidden by the fur hood of his slate-coloured parka. Kirk Grundy.

I nudged Rocky. 'Hey, pull over for a second, will you? Just seen someone I need to talk to.'

As my friend slid the Discovery neatly into the remaining length of the lay-by, I had the door open and began slipping and sliding on the ice-crusted snow on my way back past the huge white UNHCR trucks to where the Cherokee had stopped.

Grundy watched me approach with an apprehensive sort of look. 'Hi, Jim-bo, what you doing here?'

I smiled without feeling. 'I could ask you the same thing.'

'Just stopped to stretch my legs. On my way to Metkovic to join the other press guys.'

As he answered I peered into the Cherokee. There was no one in the passenger seat. 'Isn't Tali with you? You picked her up from the hotel this morning.'

His eyes glittered mockingly from within the fur hood. 'Hey, cut the girl some slack, buddy. You're not her father, are you?'

I felt my anger start to boil, but slammed the lid on tight. 'Just need to talk to her, Grundy, that's all.'

'Have the lovers had a tiff, then?'

My eyes narrowed. 'Where is she? That's all I want to know.'

'No idea, buddy. All I know is she called me to pick her up and take her to another hotel. I dropped her at the Medina around seven this morning. Maybe she's still there, maybe not.'

Suddenly I wondered if I'd been a bit unfair on Grundy. I forced a polite smile. 'OK, Kirk, thanks. See you around.'

He nodded. 'Sure thing.' And I felt his eyes watching my back as I retraced my steps to the Discovery.

I fell into a sullen silence for the rest of the journey to Metkovic, and Rocky knew me better than to ask any probing questions. But by the time we reached the compound itself he'd managed to break down the ice wall I'd built with a couple of cracking jokes. When I got out of the vehicle my spirits had lifted considerably.

Inside the gates I was absolutely staggered by the number of trucks being loaded; there barely seemed a spare centimetre in

the place and other vehicles and their trailers had been parked on
the side of the approach road. Some of these were non-government wagons belonging to the big charities like Save the
Children and Oxfam. They would be tagging on to one or
other of the official two UNHCR convoys.

I had to smile when I saw the Wildchild hippy van again; two
of its members were dressed as clowns and were giving an
impromptu performance in front of a group of bemused drivers
and mechanics. I guessed their mission was to bring a bit of
Christmas cheer to the kids in the besieged towns. I just hoped
I wouldn't let them all down.

The ten vehicles and trailers that would make up the official
Convoy Silver were lined up just inside the compound gates as
they would be leaving first. Then there was row after row after
row of trucks that would follow in Convoy Gold. Drivers and
crews who had already arrived were checking over the engines
and suspension with the mechanics and fitting snow chains to
the giant wheels.

Over the past forty-eight hours those mechanics had had a
particularly frantic time implementing the master-plan that
Rocky and I had concocted. That was, if we were forced to take
Convoy Gold down the snake, we would do so in stealth,
unseen by any potential hostile forces. And that meant using
convoy lights, a white reflective disc fitted on the rear axle under
the body of each truck. These were illuminated by a small bulb
and visible only to the driver of the following truck. Around
forty per cent of the vehicles we were using were ex-British
Army, and needed no modification. But each civilian variant
needed an hour's work on it to fit a disc and lamp-fitting and
splice it into the electrics.

Of course, in snowy conditions there was often enough ambient light for a driver to see the truck in front, but not always. As
this was a civilian UN operation, not a military one, we had to
play it as safe as possible.

Meanwhile I set up my stall of radio and satellite telephone communications equipment in Rocky's cramped office while he went off to check loading-bills, inventory lists and all the reams of bureaucratic paperwork that these UN operations demanded. That was one aspect I didn't envy him at all.

There was good news from company HQ. Gordy Cromwell had received a report from one of CBF's SAS teams who had driven down the snake during the night. Although they opined that they couldn't recommend the route for a convoy – as if I didn't know that! – rarely was the snow much deeper than twenty centimetres. There was some drifting in places, but not enough to give any headaches. This was pretty much as I anticipated because in the mountains the wind tended to prevent build-ups of deep snow. Unfortunately it could also have a polishing effect, turning the top layer into glistening hard ice.

The SAS survey team also warned that the two bridges on the route were suspect and thought that they might not withstand the pressure of a hundred trucks and trailers of over fifteen tons each. One was ancient stone that looked solid, but it was impossible to gauge its real state. The other was a fairly new timber affair. Before the outbreak of the civil war, the local authorities had imposed upon it a maximum weight recommendation of seven tons.

On a brighter note, the team reported that the track showed no signs of having been used in recent days; they themselves encountered no one. There appeared to be no mines on the route – which, of course, didn't really mean a lot – just that their vehicle hadn't happened to have gone over one. It might be a different story with the convoy's giant wagons. They also identified and pinpointed what they thought were a couple of Ramoza Brigade artillery positions overlooking the proposed convoy route. If the Muslims were awake and looking behind them rather than forward to the targets they were aiming at in Una Drina, it was possible that the convoy would be spotted.

Gordy then informed me two of our company's three Warrior platoons, a total of eight cannon-toting APCs, would be at

Makljen Ridge to meet us and act as escort to Convoy Silver. In his wisdom, Major Tring had decided that the whole idea of sneaking into Una Drina by the back door, so to speak, would be seen as an act of provocation by the Ramoza Brigade. He had proclaimed that UNPROFOR should play no part in that aspect. And it seemed that Colonel Rathbone had been persuaded to agree.

Although I was saddened by this return to former attitudes, I wasn't that concerned. Stealth would be everything and Warriors were damn noisy bits of kit and their military presence alone in Convoy Gold might be seen by some fundamentalist Muslims as a legitimate excuse to open fire.

My next call by satellite phone was to Colonel Zec. 'The Rabbit' immediately let me know that he was one very unhappy bunny. 'You will know, Captain Hawkins, that I am not in agreement with the decision made by our Croatian brothers. They sit smugly in the mother country and make decisions over our heads – while it is *we* who have to live with the situation here in Bosnia. Croatia has no jurisdiction over us Bosnian Croats.'

I gave an inaudible sigh. 'Does that mean you are going to halt Convoy Silver?'

'What about the Muslims?' he countered quickly. 'Are they going to allow the convoy through?'

'We're negotiating.'

He pounced on that. 'Ah, so they have not agreed. Again you expect us to capitulate first.'

I said, 'It's hardly capitulation to let a relief convoy through to feed your own townspeople . . .' I let the words hover for a moment, then went for the one crack I had noticed in his armour, ' . . . but then I was forgetting; you are not from Una Drina, are you, Colonel? It will not be *your* dear old mother dying of hypothermia, *your* wife and children forced to boil up weeds for a stew to survive.'

His voice deepened an octave as he tried to restrain his anger.

'Get that Antichrist Aganovic to agree and we will consider it, too.'

'The international media will know of your decision,' I replied evenly. 'Mayor Jozic should be aware of that. Therefore, as defence minister of the town, I need to speak to him.'

Zec didn't like that. 'You will get the same response.'

'I'm sure I will,' I lied.

There was a few minutes' wait while someone went to fetch the mayor from his chambers in the town hall. When he came on the line he sounded polite, but wary. 'What can I do for you, Captain?'

I repeated what I had told Zec, but added, 'There are some special consignments of coffee and sugar on the convoy for the town, Mr Mayor, but it is difficult to know who to entrust their distribution to. So many rogues and villains around.' I couldn't keep the smile from my face, knowing full well that Jozic's black-market warehouses were bare. 'As a public servant beyond reproach, I wondered whether you'd be kind enough to help the UN out?'

There was a pause and I could almost hear his mind ringing like a till as he relished the prospect. 'Ah, well, of course I shall do everything I can. How big are these consignments, Captain?'

'Sorry, I don't know the details, I'm not UNHCR, but my friend Mr Rogers will explain when the convoy arrives . . .' I hesitated. ' . . . But sadly I've just been informed by Colonel Zec that you will be refusing to let it pass.'

'No, no,' he said quickly. 'A misunderstanding. The subject is under review, not quite the same thing. As defence minister of Una Drina, I have the final word.'

'Which is?' I pressed.

'The convoy may pass.'

That was a welcome little triumph. After thanking the mayor politely I then had to go through the hoop of speaking to General Almir Aganovic again.

He didn't seemed pleased to hear from me, but at least listened while I told him, 'Our convoy is leaving at noon, the Croats have guaranteed it free passage, the Bosnian government wishes you to do the same and the international media will be there to witness events.'

There was a brittle silence. 'Captain Hawkins, how many words for *no* do you have in your language?'

I said, 'Croat resolve is weakening, General. Now would be a good time to co-operate and negotiate with them.'

'I seem to remember having this conversation before.' He hesitated. 'Send your convoy by all means, but they will be wasting their time. I advise you to make sure they have supplies and warm clothes for a long wait. Now, if you'll excuse me . . .' The line went dead.

I'd expected nothing more, but it was my job to keep trying. I still hoped that when Convoy Silver actually turned up the Muslims of the Ramoza Brigade would have a change of heart.

As the designated departure time approached, the activity in the compound reached a frenetic level. Now all the crews of over a hundred and ten trucks and trailers were swarming all over their vehicles, making last-minute mechanical checks, securing loads and supervising the loading of supplies delivered by an army of little fork-lift trucks scurrying back and forth from the warehouses with all the chaotic order of an ants' nest.

Incredibly, everything on the ten truck-and-trailer combos of Convoy Silver was ready on time as noon approached. With it were half a dozen four-wheel-drive vehicles and people carriers belonging to the media, most flying makeshift 'TV' or 'Press' banners – with their understood sub-text 'so please don't shoot us'. I wandered over to them and had a good look for Tali, hoping that she had decided to travel with them. There was no sign of her and I could only suppose she was sulking in her hotel room back in Split.

I made a special point of checking with Gerald Kemp, whose ITN news team would hang back and later latch on to Convoy Gold. 'No, Jeff, I haven't seen her. And I wouldn't be surprised if you don't again, either.'

That took me aback. 'What do you mean by that?'

He shrugged. 'Look, I don't know what's going on between you two, none of my business. But she's done you and the Royal Wessex proud with some of her picture coverage, even if you haven't always approved. I think you should have let her come with my team.'

'Out of my hands,' I lied, feeling increasingly guilty. 'She's unpredictable . . . besides, she'd be at risk.'

Gerald shook his head. 'Risk is part of our game, like yours. I'm a journalist, so is she.'

'Maybe it was a harsh decision,' I admitted.

'Then better do what you're so good at,' he suggested.

'What's that?'

'Mending bridges.'

But as I walked away from him, I wondered if it might be too late for that.

One by one the trucks' engines spluttered into life and the quiet of the afternoon was desecrated by the deep background rumble of diesel power. I watched as Jock, the 'wagon-master', strode through the flurrying snow to his Discovery; he was Rocky's opposite number and arch-rival, who usually ran Convoy Red. He climbed into his vehicle and went on his intercom to the drivers. Almost immediately the cacophony of twin air horns burst out with near-volcanic force in answer to their leader. The Discovery edged forward and behind him the wheels of the first huge truck began to turn.

There was no mistaking the adrenalin rush I felt, watching the ten monsters and their trailers roll out of the compound gate and swing onto the road that would take them to the 'Devil's Triangle'. Behind them followed the little trail of media cars like small animals tailing a herd of prehistoric beasts.

Their absence, however, made hardly any difference to the appearance of the overflowing compound. It would be twenty more minutes before the gigantic Convoy Gold followed, after which the lorry park would finally be empty.

I went to the canteen and grabbed a mug of hot tea before joining Rocky at a table where he was just winding up the briefing to his key drivers. Each of them would have special responsibility for a ten-vehicle sub-section of the convoy. These were Rocky's most experienced men and I'd got to know a number of them quite well.

Despite his chequered history, Lizard was among them, puffing nervously on a straggly roll-up. Others I knew were Rocky's number two, Shaun, the cool, quiet Ulsterman; Rick Ashton, a Mancunian with a wild beard, thick glasses and a beer gut, whose party-piece was farting to music; Brum Taylor, born on a Birmingham sink-estate but able to quote passages of Shakespeare and Oscar Wilde *ad nauseam*; 'Chalky' White, a cheerful black guy who'd formerly been a Royal Marine and police officer until he'd got bored; and a big Russian nicknamed 'Sputnik'.

'A final word, lads,' Rocky said, winding up. 'If we decide to go down the snake there is to be a complete blackout – convoy lights only – and total radio silence, except in an emergency. Breaking any of those rules will be a hanging offence. Also, keep your hands off the air horns. If those Muslims get wind of us, there's no knowing what might happen. That's it. Good luck!'

As everyone shuffled towards the door, tossing plastic tea mugs into the wastebin as they left, Rick Ashton on rectal trumpet, gave an impressive rendition of 'Rule Britannia' to an appreciative audience. Spirits were high.

I joined Rocky and we were striding across the compound towards his Discovery when the bearded Swede I'd met two days earlier emerged from one of the admin buildings, calling and waving some papers.

We paused and waited while he caught up with us. 'Ah, good news, Rocky! We have four more trucks and trailers just arriving! Their repairs are finished ahead of schedule.'

'Good news for you, Oscar,' Rocky growled. 'But not for me, we've got no time to load them.'

The Swede shook his head. 'No problem. My colleague in Split got them loaded straight off the dock facility. Here is the inventory.' He thrust the papers at a disgruntled Rocky who glanced at them quickly before stuffing them in his pocket. 'See, we at UNHCR can think and act fast when necessary.'

Humour glistened in his eyes, but Rocky had no intention of smiling. 'Just when I've finished the convoy plan and the briefing. Brilliant!'

Oscar shrugged. 'Sorry to mess you around.'

Rocky grunted. 'Get them into Ten Section under Rick, he can handle the extra vehicles. I'll brief him how you've buggered it up.'

The Swede offered a rare smile. 'You know you love me really.'

As we reached the Discovery, the four errant UN trucks and trailers arrived and rolled into the compound. Rocky called up Rick Ashton and gave him the good news. Rick, being Rick, cursed and blustered and no doubt farted, but in truth nothing much ever fazed him.

Meanwhile, all around us the sound of engines turning over was rising to an almighty, earth-shaking rumble and wafts of diesel smoke belched skyward, providing a contrasting background for the swirl of light snowflakes.

'Right, you shower,' Ricky spoke into the intercom, 'on your marks, Convoy Gold, it's Christmas Eve tomorrow and Santa's on his way! Let's rock and roll!' He reached forward and flipped on the CD track he'd decided on. Suddenly the deafening overture of the 'Dam Busters' March' shook the interior of the Discovery and was carried into the cab of every truck.

But even that was drowned out by the blast of over two hundred air horns as headlamps and hazard-lights were switched on and the first of the trucks jolted forward and out through the gates.

We sat and waited as Rocky watched them pass and checked that everything was to his satisfaction. First to go were the fifty trucks and trailers of One to Five Sections. These were followed by a recovery truck with spares and a crew of mechanics.

Sputnik, the lead driver in Six Section, waited while the private charity vehicles that had been parked up outside the compound moved forward and tagged on behind the recovery truck. I watched as the Oxfam, Save the Children, CARE and several smaller charity lorries moved off. The Wildchild entertainers had followed Rocky's advice, left their van behind, and hitched a lift for themselves and their equipment in a truck hired by the Women's Institute in Watford. Maybe it was because Christmas was just a couple of days away, but I found it quite touching. Ordinary people with their collections, raffles and bring-and-buy stalls actually caring enough to make a difference.

As these moved away, Sputnik hit his air horns again and moved off to sandwich the non-government element safely in the middle of the convoy. Seven, Eight and Nine Sections followed, then Ricky followed with Ten Section, the four newly repaired trucks feeding onto the end, and finally the second recovery truck which brought up the rear.

Satisfied that all was well, Rocky threw the Discovery into gear and followed onto the main road, slowly overtaking the crawling procession that was now spread out over an incredible two and a half kilometres.

On reaching the first truck of the convoy, he slipped deftly into the lead position and eased his foot down on the accelerator. Behind us, Brum Taylor in the lead truck acknowledged us with a blast of air horns.

Big convoys were always notoriously slow, held up by the speed of the least powerful vehicle or least experienced driver; and with so many more trucks, there were so many more things to go wrong mechanically. Nevertheless, soon Rocky was coaxing the tortoise of a convoy nearer to his favoured 'bimbling' speed, cruising through the slushy roads that carried us steadily up into the mountains of the interior.

Two incidents held us up. The first was when a cat ran out

across a village street and a driver braked hard on instinct. The truck behind him was driving too close and shunted the rear of the trailer in front of him. The result was one burst radiator and one vital load out of commission. Rocky radioed for help to get it towed back to the depot.

All the official Croat roadblocks were opened up for us grudgingly; although we were also going to the Croat-dominated towns of Una Drina and DV, many Croat militia took the view the UNHCR was essentially supporting the Muslims and their capital Sarajevo.

That was certainly the attitude of the only 'unofficial' checkpoint we came across, manned by a mean-looking group of renegade Black Swan commandos. Their battered four-wheel-drive Land Cruiser was parked across the middle of the road where it passed through a steep-sided cutting. I knew this was a maverick group because when Convoy Silver had passed through half an hour earlier, there were no reports of it having been there.

Rocky and I got out to negotiate our passage. The wagonmaster began with a smile and offered his hand, which was pointedly ignored by the obvious leader of the four men.

He looked back down the long line of the convoy, clearly surprised at the sight of so many vehicles. 'That is one hell of a lot of supplies,' he murmured in Serbo-Croat and scratched at the stubble on his chin. 'More than enough for you to have some to spare.'

What really hacked me off was that it would have been so easy to take these guys out with the SA80 I had with my kit in the Discovery. Yet we had to pussyfoot around, sticking to polite United Nations guidelines, smile sweetly and play patsy with every thug and villain in Bosnia.

So with a level voice I explained the importance and the need for the convoy to go through unmolested and that the Black Swans' ultimate superior authority had so ordered.

But the scruffy individual in front of me just kept eyeing the long line of trucks, almost drooling. 'In that case we must check your loads against your permitted inventory. What is in the first truck?'

I noticed Rocky flinch as I translated. 'Medical supplies,' he answered.

And I knew why he was flinching. The bastards loved checking medical supplies, whether they were Serbs, Croats or Muslims, because it took for ever! Hundreds of boxes containing thousands of packs of pills, or syringes, or bandages . . .

Rocky turned to me. 'I've an idea, Jimbo. Tell him about the truck we had to abandon, just a few kilometres back down the road. Those supplies aren't going anywhere, they can have them if they let us past now.'

Smart move, I thought, and translated the offer to the Black Swans leader. He clearly liked that and smiled slowly. 'What is in that load?'

Rocky consulted his sheaf of consignment notes. 'Toiletries. Women's stuff.'

'Toiletries,' I repeated in translation. 'Soaps, shampoos, smelly stuff for women.'

The Croat turned that over in his mind. I could tell he thought he could make money out of that and maybe make a lot of new female friends. 'Maybe we have a deal.'

Quickly I shook his hand before he changed his mind. Rocky leaned into the Discovery and spoke to the driver of the abandoned truck. 'Got some Croat friends of ours – Black Swans – coming to take the load off your hands. Suggest you make yourselves scarce until the recovery people turn up. Oh, take the tarpaulins off, will you? They won't need them.' He smiled. 'I know, but just do it, OK? Out.'

'All done,' he said, and also shook the Croat's hand, before we both climbed back into the Discovery. Waves were exchanged and the convoy rolled on.

I felt reasonably pleased that we'd got off so lightly. Rocky was grinning to himself, so I guessed he was also reasonably satisfied with the outcome too. 'What made you think it was soap and shampoo?' he asked suddenly.

I frowned. 'You said toiletries.'

'Ah, that covers many things,' he replied. 'In fact I was just wondering what our heroic Black Swan friends are going to do with a whole wagon and trailer full of tampons.'

Our laughter exploded in the confines of the car and kept us chuckling nearly all the way to Makljen Ridge, where Rocky drew the convoy to a halt before getting on the radio to the wagon-master of Convoy Silver.

'How goes it, Jock? Over.'

'Just been stopped at a Ramoza checkpoint, Rocky. About five kilometres out of Una Drina. They're saying no, no, no. I tried to get the press and television boys out but they were made to get back in their vehicles at gunpoint. I'll keep trying. Over.'

'Keep me posted. Thanks, Jock. Out.' He hung up the handset and turned to me. 'We'll give it an hour. Give the boys time for a rest and get a brew on. If the Muslims haven't relented by then we'll just have to see exactly how crackers our plan is.'

I climbed out of the Discovery and lit up two hexi-burners, one for a brew and the other for a mess tin of curried beef for Rocky and me to share. It promised to be a long, cold night. The sky had cleared and we had a grand panoramic view of a spectacular Canaletto sunset in orange and crimson as the temperature began to plummet.

We'd just finished the meal when I noticed a British Army Land Rover racing towards us past the long line of parked trucks. It slewed to a halt alongside us and Nigel Cuthbert scrambled out, hunched in a bright red puffer jacket and rubbing his hands against the marrow-numbing cold.

'Hi, Jimbo,' he greeted, 'how's tricks?'

'Convoy Silver's been stuck at the Muslim checkpoint for around forty-five minutes,' I said. 'No sign of them giving way. Want some char?'

He shook his head. 'No, I'm fine. Thought I'd keep you company. Didn't want to miss the fun.'

'One man's fun . . .' Rocky muttered darkly.

'By the way,' Cuthbert added casually. 'Those four repaired trucks that joined you at the last minute . . . They are here, aren't they? Not with Convoy Silver?'

From the corner of my eye, I saw Rocky frown. I said, 'Yes, why?'

'Oh, nothing. I was chatting to the drivers earlier, that's all. Met them at a lay-by.'

It was all so casual, too damn casual. And mention of the word lay-by suddenly rang a bell somewhere at the back of my mind. It came back to me in a flash. I recalled my drive from Split to the UNHCR depot at Metkovic when I'd spotted Kirk Grundy pulled over beside four trucks. At the time my head was full of Tali and where she might be. Now I recalled the anxious look in the American's eyes when he'd realized it was me. Anxious, worried I'd land a fist in his face over the girl? Or was it guilt, I suddenly wondered? But not about her, about the four trucks with him.

But I played it cool. I didn't want to alarm Rocky or ignite some sort of ruck between him and Cuthbert just before we set off to break the siege. So I said, 'Oh, right', and pulled out my hipflask of Scotch in order to take everyone's mind off the subject. It worked a treat. If Rocky's suspicions had been aroused, they were immediately forgotten.

However, I couldn't stop thinking about it. My best guess was that one of the trucks had the hidden, sealed compartment to carry General Almir Aganovic if we were lucky enough to get him. Cuthbert probably didn't know that Dave McVicar had taken me into his confidence as an old and trusted friend. And, of course, Kirk Grundy suggested some sort of CIA interest, but then that should hardly surprise me.

I was turning this over in my head as the darkness crept over the mountains. The twilight was melting rapidly into an intensely black sky, the stars sharp like glittering pinpricks of light in the crystalline air.

Rocky again spoke to Jock on Convoy Silver. The Ramoza Brigade Muslims were standing firm, adamant that the convoy would not proceed into Una Drina.

'Looks like we have no option,' he said grimly, replacing the handset.

I said, 'Then let's get on with it.'

He got on the net and called up the drivers. 'Right, lads, we're leaving in five, taking the scenic route. Remember, radio silence except for real emergencies, and convoy lights only. Good luck.'

That done, he returned to the rear of his Discovery, snapped two little chemical light tubes that would give off a feeble green light for four hours, and fixed them to the rear bumper so that the first lorry in the convoy could see us.

Rocky resumed the driver's seat and cranked up the heating. I'd purloined a couple of pairs of night-vision goggles from British Army HQ. But Rocky, like most of the former British Army drivers who made up the team, was trained to drive without them and would use them only as a last resort. He checked his watch and I checked mine. The illuminated digits flashed up, reading 1800 hours. He engaged first, and edged forward, checking in his rear-view mirror that the first truck was following.

He grunted with satisfaction and I lit a cigar to help my concentration as I navigated from the map on my lap.

It was very eerie and not something I'd done in a long time, travelling in almost total darkness, yet knowing that there were over a hundred trucks and trailers crawling after us with none of the usual blast of air horns and the dazzling array of blazing headlamps.

'Ahead on the left,' I said. 'About a hundred metres.'

My eyes were quickly becoming accustomed to the dark, greatly helped by the ambient light of snow and stars. There appeared to be a steep drop over the left-hand side of the road, and the exact location of the track was not immediately obvious.

'Slow up a bit,' I said, and Rocky dropped from around thirty kph to a crawl.

The reason I couldn't see the start of the track was because there wasn't one. As I peered out of the side window I could see down to a break in the treeline about a hundred metres away; that, I guessed, was the start of the track and the embankment slope to reach it was pretty steep.

'That's it, I reckon,' I said.

Rocky came to a halt and leaned forward. 'Fuck me, Jimbo, I thought we might at least start with some easy stuff. It'll have to be straight over the top.'

I knew what he meant. You can't even take a Land Rover down a gradient like that on a slant without rolling it, let alone a truck and trailer.

So Rocky swung out to the right first, before spinning the wheel left so that our front tyres were at right-angles to the embankment and we could go down straight, more or less aiming for the gap in the distant treeline.

'Here we go!' he announced with a grin, cigarette clamped in the corner of his mouth.

Over the edge we went, feeling our wheels crunching through the ice-crust and biting into the softer snow beneath. In low gear the snow chains held us back, but I could still feel the gravity of the steep slope trying to pull us free. Any later in the evening, when the top ice layer would thicken, some of the trucks would have been in trouble.

Eventually we slewed to a halt beside the pine trees at the start of the track and looked back up the embankment as the first truck began feeling its tentative way over the top. To the driver in the cab it must have felt like he was staring into an abyss. But Brum Taylor was an absolute pro with vast experience. He picked the right gear and speed to keep rolling steadily without the vehicle sliding away out of control, or causing the trailer to jackknife.

The next followed, then another, each following the example of the truck in front.

Rocky was just about to start moving again and pick up the lead when the fourth truck driver lost it. Somehow he got his positioning wrong, the front wheels finding a deep rut or hollow which caused the truck to cant. Then he braked too hard, or a tyre burst, or both. As the truck shuddered to a halt, the trailer developed a mind of its own and determined to continue down the gradient and overtake. As it did, it dragged the truck over onto its side and both vehicle and trailer began an agonizingly slow and unstoppable slide over the ice crust. Finally it came to rest beneath the pine trees.

'Bloody hell,' Rocky muttered. 'And we haven't even started yet.'

There was nothing that could be done, apart from picking up the driver and his number two, who were more angry with themselves than even shaken. At least the sight of the gargantuan pile-up seemed to concentrate minds and unbelievably the rest of the convoy made it down without further mishap.

Meanwhile Rocky had picked up the lead and was feeling his way down the track that meandered on a slow downward route along the contours of the pine-covered hills. Adjusting the door mirror on my side, I was fascinated to view just the slow-moving bulky black shapes that gave no clue there were over a hundred vehicles crawling through the darkness behind us.

We hadn't been going long when we heard the first rumble of that night's artillery barrage on Una Drina by the Muslims and the night sky pulsed with light from somewhere beyond the mountain tops. It was a timely reminder of the dangerous situation we were in. If the Muslims realized there was something on the track, whether they thought it was us or their Croat enemy, our fate would be in the lap of the gods.

But my mind was soon distracted elsewhere as the track began to climb and the pine forest on our left began falling away to be replaced by a precipitous drop into a river valley far below. And the higher we climbed, so the drop deepened into a seemingly bottomless inky void. My mouth was dry and my eyes smarted from the effort of trying to peer ahead and determine each turn of the track.

'Ice,' Rocky murmured and changed down a gear.

This part of the route was exposed from the wind across the valley and I could see that the surface of the track had been polished to a dull gleam. Behind us I knew the drivers would have increased the gap between each vehicle to allow room to slow down gently through the gears. To touch the brake pedal on this stretch could be a death sentence. Even with our four-wheel drive and snow chains I could feel the Discovery jinking, trying to take a direction of its own, on ice that was like greased glass.

Only when we turned another bend, leaving the valley wall to cross a high pass between the summits of two hills, did I realize I'd been holding my breath for most of the time.

I'd barely begun to relax when the track began to drop quite rapidly towards the next valley, and we were back to more steep drops as we turned into a zig-zag that eventually led to the river below.

This was really tough on the drivers. Negotiating each tight hairpin on the narrow track in a huge lorry and towing a large trailer was a nightmare and demanded almost superhuman skills. On most of the bends it could be done in one precisely gauged movement, but every inch of track had to be used with none to spare. Most of the drivers were professional enough to get it spot-on, but one or two made a small error. To avoid going into an abyss, it meant carefully halting on sheet ice, backing up in total darkness, repositioning the front wheels and starting forward again.

Everything was held up when this happened. And two of the bends were so tight that every truck had to go through this manoeuvre. It all took hours and one driver got it wrong, ending up with his front wheels spinning out over the drop. It took another half an hour before the recovery truck managed to squeeze past the rest of the convoy to get to him and pull the thing back onto the road.

By the time we reached the river it was one o'clock in the morning, and we were faced with the first of our two unsafe bridges.

Rocky and I climbed out to inspect it. After the heat of the Discovery, the raw intensity of the cold was like a slap in the face. The low rumble of idling truck engines was drowned out by the excited rush of mountain water, black and frothing, beneath the old stone bridge.

'How many centuries old, d'you reckon?' Rocky muttered.

'Nineteenth century,' I said glibly.

'Oh, yeah, smart arse?'

I pointed to the inset stone inscription. 'Builder's mark – 1876.'

'Well, it looks well built and it's lasted all this time.'

I pushed quite hard at the stone coping on top of the parapet. It toppled over and landed in the water with a loud splash.

'Till you arrived,' Rocky added quickly.

I said, 'Well built, but not so well maintained.'

I moved onto the crown of the bridge and examined the parapet. There was a quarter-inch crack running in a line through the mortar. I pulled an old cigar tin from my pocket, leaned over the parapet and wedged the tin into the crack on the outer wall of the bridge. It was a tight fit.

'We're not turning back, Jimbo,' Rocky said as I returned. 'Let's get the first wagon across.'

He waved to Brum Taylor, who geared up and edged forward. He inched his wheels onto the bridge and crawled over the low hump. There was about a foot clearance on each side of the truck. And the bridge didn't collapse. But when the second truck crossed, the cigar tin fell out of the gap where I'd jammed it and disappeared into the raging torrent below.

Rocky looked at me, but said nothing. He didn't have to. If the gap on the bridge widened after the passing of one truck, how would it be after a hundred of the monsters had passed over it? I saw him take a deep breath before he beckoned the second wagon.

One by one they crawled tentatively over the slowly weakening bridge and parked up on the road on the other side. I couldn't believe we'd done it when the final lorry crossed. Before I rejoined Rocky in the Discovery I made a final check on the bridge. The gap had widened to a good two inches. I chipped at the ice on the hump with the heel of my boot. A hairline fracture showed in the tarmac. I was no engineer, but you didn't have to be a genius to know that the bridge could have given way at any moment.

As soon as our Discovery reached the head of the convoy, it moved off again like some huge, dark caterpillar. This time the track was ambling along the level beside a black and fast-flowing river, the stars reflected in its ruffled mirror surface.

Much more like it, I thought. At last we could relax a little and make up some lost time. Rocky eased the Discovery forward so that we were back to the standard five hundred metres beyond the first truck.

And just as I decided things were getting better, we saw the militiamen standing in the middle of the track. As we were travelling without lights, I don't know who was the more surprised, them or us.

Sixteen

Rocky snatched up the convoy intercom. 'All vehicles halt!' he hissed. 'Repeat, all vehicles halt. No noise and no lights. Suspected hostile force ahead!'

I glanced over my shoulder. I could barely distinguish the outline shape of the first truck, driven by Brum Taylor, which was half concealed by a bend in the riverside track. Being very dirty and slush-smeared white, the vehicle was well camouflaged against the mixed surroundings of the snow-covered terrain with its black water and inky treelines.

As Rocky slowed down, he said, 'I think the bastards are laying mines.'

But they weren't laying mines any more. They'd recovered from their surprise and were approaching us, waving Kalashnikov rifles. They were Muslims, but looked more like local men than foreigners.

When Rocky stopped, I threw open my door and stood up to greet them in Serbo-Croat. 'Hallo there, don't be alarmed! I'm a British Army officer and we are doing a UNHCR survey.'

'The fuck you are,' said the man I assumed to be their leader. 'In the middle of the night?'

'An urgent convoy recce,' I explained, and proffered my tin of small cigars. 'Fancy one of these?'

He peered down at them. 'Serbian?'

'German-made, Cuban leaf.'

'Smell good,' he said, sniffing and pocketing half the pack. 'So they were right?'

'Pardon?' I said, not following. 'Who was right?'

'The rumours that the UN runs a convoy through here.'

I shook my head. 'Not after what we've just seen. That's why we're inspecting the route. Two unsafe bridges, a very rough road and that zig-zig they call "the snake". No convoy's coming *this* way, I can tell you that for nothing.' I gestured towards the neat formation of mines. 'If I were you, I wouldn't waste those things here. No point.'

It was bitterly cold and a dewdrop was forming at the man's nostrils. He sniffed heavily. 'The mines stay.'

I shrugged. 'Up to you, of course. But will you let us pass? I'm exhausted, just want to get back to Una Drina and crash out.'

There was a hint of a smile on the man's face. 'Ah, no such thing as a free cigar, eh?'

'A fair exchange, I think.'

The smile actually reached his eyes. 'Well, it is Christmas.'

I grinned. 'And you a Muslim . . . that's kind of you.'

'Listen, I'm in the Ramoza Brigade, but me and my friends are not fucking rag-heads,' he said with sudden venom. He produced a hipflask from his tatty combat smock. 'See, alcohol!' He unscrewed the cap, took and swig and handed the flask to me. 'Fuck the rag-heads.'

I accepted his offer and took a mouthful of some fairly obnoxious neat spirit. 'Fuck the rag-heads,' I rejoined.

'Stopping the convoys is stupid,' he added, and his two friends nodded in agreement. 'But orders are orders. Look, I've got family in Una Drina and they're having a bad time. They need the convoys to run.

'We always got on OK with the Croats,' he continued. 'Get rid of that fucking racist crook of a mayor of theirs, and the ordinary people will still get on . . . But General Aganovic is *another* politico – and turned into a fucking rag-head himself now.'

'Politicians,' I agreed with his condemnation, as he took his flask back.

He took another swig and wiped the back of his hand across his mouth. 'Yeah, fuck the politicos!'

One of his friends said, 'Keep to the far right of the track.' He pointed his finger. 'There is a gap of about a truck's width. When the snow covers these mines, our own people will have to know the way through.'

The third man thumped a small wooden signpost into the snow. It was painted white with a black skull-and-crossbones and the words in red: WARNING! MINES! 'There, job done, boss. Can we get back now, before my balls freeze and drop off?'

Their leader nodded as the other two sauntered off to an open agricultural tractor and trailer which I only now saw was parked up under some trees on the other side of the mines. 'Goodbye, English. Thanks for the cigars. I will smoke them on Christmas Day.' He laughed throatily and turned away.

I returned to the Discovery and explained the situation to Rocky as we watched the leader and his two men hanging on precariously as the tractor and its trailer chugged away into the dark.

'Tonight,' Rocky decided, 'the gods are smiling on us.'

And he was pretty much right. It took a while for the convoy to jink its way very tentatively around the small minefield before we gathered speed along the riverside track for several kilometres until we reached the second bridge.

This one was wooden, but looked stout and very well constructed within recent times, I'd guess not long before the Balkan wars had exploded. That was just as well because the bridge had to carry our trucks over a deep gorge where the vortex of water could be heard raging angrily over a cataract far below.

It had clearly been designed to carry the weight of most agricultural vehicles, cars or light trucks, not our sort of monsters, yet although it creaked in mild complaint and the thick wooden planking bowed visibly, it held up well to the punishment.

Once clear, we began an upward zig-zag climb that was nothing like as tight as the previous descent had been. Eventually we would reach a high pass between two hills from where we should be able to see Una Drina stretched out below us. We'd be on the final run home.

I was dog-tired, and could only imagine how Rocky and the truck drivers must have been feeling. Having been certain we'd make the town under cover of darkness, now I wasn't so sure. I didn't have to look at my watch. The sky was already lightening perceptibly and the stars fading behind a thin veil of broken light cloud. That meant it was around six thirty in the morning.

Leaning forward in my seat, I tried to peer up the slopes on either side of the track for any sign of Muslim positions. None was obvious, but I could now make out individual trees and boulders in the pre-dawn light. If a militiaman had been standing in the open, I'd have had little trouble spotting him. And if I could see him, he'd sure as hell be able to see us.

This was the time of day when men would be crawling, shivering, out of their sleeping-bags, getting brews on and taking their first pee of the day; it was only a matter of time before we were spotted.

I willed us on, desperate to see the crest of the pass. Three times it appeared that we were there – but each proved to be a false summit. Then, suddenly, I realized we'd finally made it.

As I took in the grey vista of the winding river valley and the dreary urban sprawl of Una Drina, a hail of small-arms fire rained down on us from somewhere on the left. A couple of rounds punctured the bonnet metal right before my eyes and I flinched instinctively.

Rocky veered off course, but quickly regained control. 'Right, that's it, Jimbo. Time to pull out all the stops.' He reached forward and flipped on the convoy intercom. 'Leader calling Convoy Gold. We're taking hostile fire. It's time to rock and roll. Lights on, hit your horns and let's go!'

I was pushed back in my seat as Rocky's right foot went down.

I wasn't at all sure that I agreed with the last of his orders, but I knew Rocky well enough to know where he was coming from. It was sheer morale-boosting bravado.

He and all the UNHCR drivers had been frustrated for weeks by the Ramoza Brigade and indecisive action from the UN. Now the boys were back in town, and telling Almir Aganovic's Muslims that they could go and fuck themselves because one of the biggest aid convoys ever run had stolen through their lines, right under their noses, to get the job done.

I wondered what would be passing through the minds of the militiamen as they peered down from their mountainside eyries to be suddenly confronted with a never-ending crocodile of blazing lights and the primeval call of air horns reverberating around the hills.

I hoped they'd be sufficiently stunned to think twice before opening fire. At this early hour they would still be half asleep and slow to react. Local recruits, like those we'd met on the road earlier that night, might hesitate to open up. Though I doubted most of the Afghan fighters would stay their hand.

It would take vital minutes to redirect artillery or mortar weapons presently aimed at Croat lines in Una Drina. But rocket-propelled rifle grenades were another matter, and if one of those hit a truck it would be curtains.

The thought had barely come to mind when a firestreak rocketed across the track in front of us. It exploded in the opposite embankment.

'Holy shit,' murmured Rocky, crouching low over the steering wheel and cranking up the revs. We were shifting at a full seventy, hazardous enough in dry summer conditions, let alone through ice-crusted snow.

I glanced in my door mirror. The convoy was keeping up, each of the drivers allowing an extra gap to lengthen between his vehicle and the one in front. And, hell, would they need it.

Quickly I got on the radio to company HQ. 'Captain Hawkins here with Convoy Gold.'

'Jimbo, how's it going?' It was good to hear Gordy Cromwell's familiar voice. 'Expected you a couple of hours ago.'

'We're about eight kilometres out of town and the shooting's started. Can you get us an escort?'

'You got it! Two trigger-happy Warriors primed up and waiting. They're on their way.'

'You're a star,' I said.

'Bet you tell that to all the girls.'

I signed off and stared ahead, mesmerized by the speed at which the landscape was rushing at us, yet Una Drina itself remained tantalizingly distant.

Suddenly I heard an explosion; we both did. I looked over my shoulder. 'Oh, fuck,' I said.

Rocky glanced in his rear-view. 'Brum Taylor's bought it!'

The lead truck had veered into the left-hand embankment and come to a shuddering halt with its cab ablaze. The trailer had overtaken, snapped its links and gone flying off over the other side of the track on a mission of its own. It tried to climb the opposite slope, failed and fell over on its side, wheels spinning in the air like the legs of some stricken insect.

Luckily there was enough room between the crashed truck and trailer for the convoy to pass through. But not at speed.

Rocky had slowed quickly through the gears and finally braked, tucking in hard to the right. He was on the convoy intercom again. 'Leader to Convoy Gold. Don't stop! Keep rolling! Brum Taylor's down, I'm checking on him.'

One of the lorries was having trouble with its brakes and I watched its driver struggle to slow his beast sufficiently to avoid the wreckage. It was a close thing, but he made it. As the lorry crept slowly through the debris I recognized the white, scared face of Lizard behind the wheel.

I suddenly realized someone was getting out of the far door of his cab. As Lizard's truck squeezed through and accelerated away down the track I did a double-take. Tali van Wyk was standing there, large rucksack on her back and a camera to her eye, snapping away at the burning vehicle.

Rocky had already begun running back to help and I followed. As he neared the flaming cab, one of the doors flew open and Brum's co-driver leapt out, yelling and with his clothes smouldering. He threw himself to the ground in desperation, rolling in the snow. My instant assessment was that he was hurt, but not too badly.

Then the charred and buckled driver's door opened and Brum himself half-jumped, half-fell clear. He landed hard and his scream was pitiful. His clothes were on fire and his face was charred beyond recognition. With a sudden feeling of sick horror, I realized that his right hand had been severed above the wrist.

Tali sprinted between the moving convoy trucks, frantically picked up handfuls of snow and throwing them on the writhing man in an effort to quench the flames.

I turned and ran back to the Discovery, dived into the driver's seat, threw it into reverse gear and backed up fast until I was just a few metres from the crashed truck.

By the time I'd got out again, Rocky had joined Tali and between them they'd put out the flames on Brum's clothes and covered his face in snow in an effort to ameliorate the burning. He was still screaming like a soul in hell. I ripped the morphine syrette from around my neck, rolled up the driver's sleeve to find an area of still-pink flesh and shot in the full load.

I looked up at Rocky. 'Back of the Discovery,' I said. 'We've no time to lose.'

As Rocky pushed his hands under the man's armpits and I held his legs, Tali took off. 'I'll get the rear door open,' she shouted.

We struggled with Brum's generous weight, slipping and sliding in the snow, while all the time the convoy trucks kept flashing by.

Nigel Cuthbert pulled up in his Land Rover and, after a brief exchange with us, picked up the injured co-driver before carrying on to Una Drina.

Meanwhile Rocky and I finally managed to manoeuvre Brum into the back of the Discovery. Tali climbed in with him, holding his unscathed left hand and whispering earnest words of reassurance to him.

At that moment, one of two Warriors appeared further down the track, running alongside the UN trucks going in the opposite direction. Hal Watkins was in the turret of the first vehicle and quickly assessed the scene. As he did so, another rocket-propelled grenade swept over his head, missing it by inches, and exploded in a fireball in the embankment.

Hal snapped an order into his mike and the turret swung, bringing the 30mm cannon to bear on the source of the attack. The gun stammered out half a dozen rounds, chewing up the Muslim position that had attacked Brum's truck.

'That'll teach the fuckers!' Rocky said with grim satisfaction, and proceeded to swing the Discovery into a gap between the convoy trucks. I gave Hal a thumbs-up as we passed and he grinned widely as we resumed our own helter-skelter run back into town.

By the time we reached the outer suburbs it was just daylight and the word of our arrival had spread. Townspeople had gathered in small groups along the street that ran past the school. They weren't people given to great emotion, they had suffered too much for too long, but some actually waved as we passed, and I could see that there were tears in many eyes.

The kids had gathered outside the school with Anita and they were not so reticent, jumping up and down with excitement, laughing and waving handkerchiefs at the drivers.

Rocky pulled over briefly and I wound down my window. 'How's it going, Anita?'

She leaned forward and kissed me on the lips. 'Now it is wonderful. It is not a Christmas that I or the children will ever forget.'

It was only then that I remembered that this was Christmas Eve morning. 'We've got to go,' I said. 'We've an injured man on board. At least the kids should have something on the table for Christmas dinner tomorrow.'

She waved as we drove off again and I wondered if she had noticed Tali in the rear of our vehicle.

There were more people than I remembered in the little squatter camps that had grown up along the main drag. They, too, stood and watched by their burning braziers as the nine remaining trucks and trailers of One Section trundled past on their way to company HQ. In the meantime Two and Three Sections had gone the opposite way and were parked along the high street, ready for their onward journey to Donji Vrbas and Sarajevo.

Rocky headed straight for the clinic where I'd arranged by radio for us to be met by a British Army medical team. They would lend their equipment and expertise to do their best for Brum Taylor.

Then it was back to company HQ to catch up with Gordy Cromwell in the Ops Room. On the way I dropped off Tali at the Splendid. We had hardly spoken since she'd unexpectedly appeared beside the burning truck. We both knew that she'd disobeyed my specific instruction and had smuggled herself onto the convoy – Lizard once again proving himself totally hopeless at resisting any female on the planet. But it was done and I didn't want to exacerbate the situation.

In truth I think it was already too late then. Before she went, she held out her fist and dropped a cassette of film into my palm. 'You might be able to use this, Jeff.' And in case I didn't fully understand what she meant, she added: 'Pictures of the UN convoy being shot up by the Ramoza Brigade. I do hope that poor man will be all right.'

Her voice sounded very flat. It had lost its charming lilt and suddenly I thought those usually laughing pale-blue eyes of hers looked ice cool.

'Thanks,' I said. She turned, shouldered her rucksack and disappeared inside the hotel.

I knew then that it was over. I just couldn't believe I'd been crazy enough to believe that it would go anywhere in the first place. Strangely, I didn't feel as depressed as I would have expected, more a sad acceptance of the inevitable. At least I'd been lucky enough to have known her and to have loved her at all. Besides, I didn't have time to brood. There was too much to do.

I think Rocky sensed that something was wrong, but he had the good sense to say nothing as he drove us back to company HQ. The trucks and trailers of One Section had already dispersed to one of Mayor Jozic's warehouses, where UNHCR staff were waiting to unload the supplies and arrange for their distribution around the town.

When we walked into the Ops Room there were smiles all round. Nigel Cuthbert was already there, regaling everyone with the previous night's adventures on the snake.

Billy Billings was true to form and had two mugs of hot sweet tea thrust into our hands almost the moment we stepped through the door. To these were added a couple of welcome shots of festive whisky.

'Well done,' Gordy Cromwell said. 'I think even Major Tring is secretly impressed. He dived off to sulk in his room as soon as he heard you coming in. Can't bear to congratulate you. Mind you, he's still muttering about rubbing the Ramoza Brigade up the wrong way.'

I sipped at the tea; at that moment it seemed like the best I had ever tasted. 'Well, he has a point. My next job is to sweet talk General Aganovic. We've still got to get the bulk of the convoy through his lines to DV and Sarajevo.'

'And don't forget,' Rocky added, 'Convoy Silver remains stuck out on the road, waiting to be let in.'

I remembered the film cassette that Tali had given me, and fished it out of my smock pocket. 'This might help to swing things. Pictures of the Ramoza Brigade's handiwork on the convoy just now.'

Cuthbert stepped forward and held out his hand. 'I'll get a copy transmitted to London, Jimbo. With any luck it'll be in the newspapers tomorrow morning.'

'No papers on Christmas Day,' I reminded, giving him the film.

He shrugged. 'Well, maybe they'll show the stills on TV news. The Bosnian government will hate it, but it'll put pressure on them to put our choice of Major Herenda in charge of Ramoza—' He realized then he'd said too much, and his mouth clammed instantly shut, leaving an awkward silence hanging in the air.

But no one at company HQ knew about the secret plans being hatched to get rid of Almir Aganovic, and thankfully the duty staff were too preoccupied to pick up what Cuthbert had indiscreetly admitted.

I left Gordy discussing the next piece of convoy strategy with Rocky, and went off to the Den to set up my satellite telephone.

Ten minutes later I was through to the Muslim general himself. His voice was low and terse, finding it difficult to hide his anger. 'I suppose, Captain Hawkins, you and your UN friends are very pleased with yourselves.'

'Not really, General, we were just doing our job,' I replied evenly. 'A job, I hasten to add, you and your men have made ten times more difficult. Not least by badly injuring a civilian driver.'

But Aganovic clearly couldn't care less. 'No doubt he knew the risks of the job when he took it on.'

You blind bastard, I thought, but held my feelings in check. 'I'm calling to advise you that the larger part of the convoy will be moving through your lines on the main road to Donji Vrbas and Sarajevo later this morning. I trust we will have your fullest co-operation.'

The laugh at the other end was as dry as bones. 'The devil you will.'

'Let's leave the devil out of this,' I came back at him. 'Just face
the fact, General, that the siege of Una Drina is broken. The
town now has enough supplies to get it through to the spring.
It's over. It is now pointless to keep the other UN convoy out of
town or to prevent the main one from moving on to DV and the
capital, where your own government is anxious for the aid to
arrive.'

There was a slight hesitation and I knew I had him on the
back foot, for a moment, at least. I added, 'But there is also some
very good news for you if you co-operate fully.'

'Oh yes?' He sounded suddenly wary.

'Mayor Jozic and Colonel Zec have agreed to a withdrawal of
their forces from the town, if you do the same.'

'That again!' The anger was clear in his voice. 'I'm not falling
for that. I have told you before, I will talk only *after* they have
taken unilateral action – not that I believe they would willingly
do so for a moment!'

'Allow me to come and talk to you personally,' I persisted.
Then added the idea I'd been toying with since I'd met the
three Muslim militiamen laying mines the previous night. 'It's
more complicated than you might think.'

'How so?'

'Mayor Jozic is leaving office.'

What I didn't tell General Aganovic was that the mayor didn't
know it yet.

Nevertheless, that announcement really did seem to catch the
Ramoza commander on the hop. After the briefest of pauses he
said in a low voice, 'You are trying to make a fool of me.'

'Not at all,' I came back quickly. 'It is well known that Mayor
Jozic is thoroughly disliked by the Muslim population of this
town. He has agreed to step down in return for you allowing the
convoy to run . . . Then he wants to meet with you to agree –
if possible – to a suitable candidate to succeed him.'

'I am still not sure I believe you.'

'Then let me come and talk to you.'

'When?'

'This afternoon,' I said, and pushed home my advantage, 'but only once the convoy has been allowed to leave town.'

Another pause. 'Very well. It is the season of goodwill. I will allow just that, your convoy to go on to Donji Vrbas and Sarajevo.'

'No,' I insisted, 'and the second convoy stuck out on the main road to enter town.'

'You are pushing your luck, Captain.'

'There is a lot of press on that convoy, General. They will be told of your generosity of spirit.'

'All right, but nothing else until we have met. I will expect you at my camp at three o'clock this afternoon.'

His order given, he hung up abruptly.

I think it was the sweetest sound of silence I'd ever heard. Elated, I left the Den for the Ops Room to announce to delighted Gordy and Rocky what General Aganovic had promised. The convoy was free to leave and Convoy Silver and its UNPROFOR resupply tail was free at last to roll into town.

They wasted no time in getting it organized, before the Muslim leader had a chance to change his mind. Within the hour the main convoy would be running on to relieve DV and then Sarajevo itself, escorted by every available Warrior in the Royal Wessex deployment.

'How in God's name did you get the bastard to agree?' Gordy asked.

I tapped the side of my nose, not a little smug and pleased with myself. 'Need to know, chum, need to know.'

He grinned. 'You've been mixing with Nigel for too long. It's catching.'

'Yeah,' Rocky agreed. 'Secret-squirrel disease.'

Deciding that they were both probably right, I returned to the Den and got through on the satellite phone to Mayor Jozić.

He was in ebullient mood, no doubt because UN provisions were back in town and soon he'd be up to his old tricks with a flourishing black-market business again. 'Of course, Captain, when would you like to see me?'

'No time like the present.'

'Excellent. You may join me in a glass of slivovitz to celebrate Christmas.'

I took my time to gather my thoughts, tracked down Ivana and asked her to join me on my visit to the town hall, where I wanted her to be a witness to events. We ambled out to the compound and my Land Rover. The place was a hive of activity with the Warriors firing up, ready for the final push. We saw Gerald Kemp in the middle of them all with his news crew going into overdrive to get some good pictures back for showing on TV in the UK that night.

The clear weather had given way to low cloud and a persistent icy drizzle and it was a slow drive to the town hall through the main drag packed with UNHCR trucks and trailers. As I turned off into the little square, one truck in particular caught my eye. It was parked under the trees, away from all the others. Unless I was very much mistaken it was the load of 'ladies' toiletries' that had been handed over at the Croat roadblock the afternoon before. Strange that it should have ended up outside Mayor Jozic's office with one of his guards taking care of it – but then again, perhaps not!

Being the day before Christmas it seemed that most of the Croat sentries and headquarters staff had already deserted their posts for the usual round of drinks parties. The place was almost empty and we had to make our own way up to the mayor's parlour, where one guard at least had remained at his post.

He knocked on the doors to announce our arrival and as he did so Nigel Cuthbert emerged with Colonel Zec right behind him. I don't know which of us was the more surprised.

'What are you doing here?' he asked me, and glanced at Ivana with an insipid sideways smile.

'Setting up the meet you want with Almir Aganovic,' I

answered. 'We're seeing him this afternoon and I *think* I can get him to agree to meet with Mayor Jozic.'

'Excellent. But I'm still not happy to be involving Ivana.'

'He trusts her. We've been through all this.'

He smiled at her again. 'If you're sure, but please be careful, won't you?'

She nodded. 'Of course. I am not afraid, Almir loves me.'

Cuthbert said, 'I've just been putting the idea to the mayor and Colonel Zec here.'

The general nodded, a conceited smile on his face at getting one over on his avowed enemies.

I frowned. 'That's why I'm here . . . that's what you asked *me* to do . . .'

Cuthbert looked as guilty as only Cuthbert could, his schoolboy face blushing fiercely. 'Slight change of plan, Jeff, that's all. I was passing and thought I'd save you the trouble. I needed to know where we stood. Anyway, they've both agreed to our little subterfuge. You can sort out the details with the mayor.'

'When will everything be in place?' I asked.

'Boxing Day. See if you can get Aganovic to come for talks then. Come to the school in the early evening. There's some entertainment for the kids, we can use the room next door. It'll be good cover.'

I nodded, it made good sense. There weren't many suitable places to hold talks in Una Drina that Aganovic would consider neutral territory. 'OK,' I said, 'I'll talk it through with Jozic.'

Cuthbert grinned, looking sort of relieved. 'Fine. Colonel Zec and I have a few more things to discuss in private. Looks like we might get this damn siege ended once and for all.'

I watched the two of them descend the stairs. I just didn't trust Cuthbert. Something was definitely up.

But I pushed my concerns to the back of my mind, put my arm round Ivana's waist and guided her through the door which the guard still held open.

Mayor Jozic, dwarfed by his huge desk, looked even more

pleased with himself than had Colonel Zec. He already had the bottle of slivovitz open, standing on a silver platter before him with half a dozen shot glasses.

He rose to his feet. 'My dear Captain Hawkins, what a pleasure it is!'

'Of course, you know Ivana,' I said, by way of introduction.

He took her offered hand. 'My dear, yes, yes.' His hatred of Muslims clearly didn't stretch to their womenfolk, for he proceeded to plant slobbery kisses all over it. 'Such an excellent interpreter for so long a time.'

Ivana finally managed to retrieve her hand, and the mayor began slopping spirit into three glasses. 'But tell me,' he said, beckoning us to be seated. 'You speak excellent Serbo-Croat, Captain, so why the presence of the lovely lady?'

'Because Ivana knows General Aganovic well,' I explained, 'and she will have to persuade him that you are genuine in your intention of withdrawing Croat forces from Una Drina.'

I saw the concern in his eyes. 'Er, well, yes, your Mr Cuthbert has explained it to me. You can tell General Aganovic what the hell you like, anything to get him to attend these talks. They will never actually happen.' He raised his glass. 'Merry Christmas!'

I left my drink untouched. 'That is true. General Aganovic will be safely removed so that Major Herenda can take command under orders from the Bosnian government in Sarajevo. That will mean an end to this siege and the convoys will run again.'

'Quite so.' Jozic had finished his slivovitz already and poured himself another. 'Cuthbert explained all that.'

'I'm afraid there is a little more to it than that. A part that he did not tell you.'

'Why not?'

I was tempted to say because he didn't know, because this was my personal part of the plan. Instead I just shrugged. 'You see, the plan is to demilitarize Una Drina and, hopefully, Donji Vrbas as well. Both the Muslim and Croat militias agreeing withdrawal with an UNPROFOR guarantee of protection for all ethnic parties.'

Jozic nearly choked on his brandy. 'Over my dead body, Captain! Not as long as I am mayor!'

He'd walked neatly into it. 'Ah, that is the other point. You are stepping down as mayor.'

From the corner of my eye I saw Ivana staring at me in disbelief.

'What the hell are you talking about!' Jozic blustered.

I put on a sympathetic expression. 'I hate to be the bringer of bad tidings, Mr Mayor, especially at Christmas time. And please, you understand that I really should not be telling you this . . .'

'Telling me what?'

'I've seen a secret memorandum from the Bosnian government. They have set up a special war-crimes unit within the police service. In the New Year you are to be investigated—'

'I do not believe you!'

'—for inciting racial hatred and organizing the ethnic cleansing and perhaps even murder of Muslims in the town, of abusing your power to perpetrate fraud and obtain UN aid for your own personal gain . . .'

'That is preposterous!' Jozic boomed.

I raised my hands in a gesture of helplessness. 'Of course, I'm sure it is . . . but unfortunately for you there is a lot of circumstantial evidence against you. I and other Royal Wessex officers may even have to testify for the prosecution.'

The Christmas spirit seemed to have left Jozic in rather a hurry. He suddenly looked very deflated. 'There must be a way around this nonsense.'

'I'm afraid not, because that is only the *good* news. The bad news is that the Ramoza Brigade has secretly put a price on your head.' I paused for effect. 'And they may well move faster than the police department in Sarajevo.'

Jozic now looked decidedly unwell.

I added quickly, 'That's why you must step down as mayor and leave for your motherland. In Croatia you will be safe. It's that simple.'

He blinked at me. 'Are you seriously suggesting—?'

'Even if you escape a Ramoza death-squad,' I said, 'these are still very serious crimes, Mr Mayor. You could be facing a long jail sentence and the police may arrive at any time. The big convoy will be returning to Croatia before then. I *insist*, for the safety of you and your family, that you are on it. I will facilitate your escape in any way I can, arrange for your personal posses- sions, valuables and so on to go with you. Keep in touch with me.'

'You mean this, don't you?' There was moisture in his eyes behind the thick pebble lenses.

'Get out while you can. Leave your lawyers to tie up the loose ends of your businesses. Leave the demilitarization nego- tiations to your successor.'

He was flustered, panicking. 'I can't think who else could do the job . . .'

'That's for later. I suggest you write your letter of resignation now. Go home immediately and explain the situation to your wife.'

He drew a blank sheet of crested paper from the wad on his desk. 'What do I put?'

I smiled. 'Just keep it simple.'

His hand shaking, he wrote off his career in local government in three brief sentences with an expensive fountain pen. When he'd blotted the letter I reached across and took it. 'I'll hold on to this for safe-keeping. Nothing will be said until after General Aganovic attends the talks. No one will know about your resig- nation until you are safely in Croatia.'

He looked at me oddly. 'I am touched, Captain, at your con- cern. I always had the feeling that you didn't like me.'

I smiled again. 'That just shows how wrong you can be, Mr Mayor.' Then I turned to Ivana. 'We'd best go now.'

She looked pale and somewhat confused as she stood up and

walked with me to the door. As we stepped outside, she said, 'I cannot believe what I have just witnessed.'

'Now,' I said, 'you have to make General Aganovic believe it. If you do, we just might bring some peace to this town, enough to last until the day this conflict is finally over.'

Her eyes were dark and wide. 'That would be so wonderful.'

When we got outside to the Land Rover, the rain had become heavier and, as we drove back past the stolen UN truck and its trailer of tampons, a small group of bemused Croats had gathered to watch a very bizarre event. The tarpaulin-less loads of sanitarywear had greedily soaked up the moisture and begun inexorably growing out of the top and sides of the vehicles like a gigantic soufflé.

I hoped that I was witnessing the ruin of what would have been Mayor Jozic's very last scam. It really had not been his day.

I dropped into the Splendid with Ivana for a late lunch, during which I quietly briefed her in preparation for our meeting with General Aganovic.

She listened intently, but seemed rather subdued. I said softly, 'Are you really *sure* you're willing to go ahead with this? I know Nigel isn't keen.'

'Yes, Jeff, I'm sure. I know Almir is far more likely to believe me and go to the talks if I can persuade him.' She gave a wan smile. 'It is just so sad that it ends like this. He has changed so much since the blindness struck him. And it is a bitter irony that it is me who will deliver him into the hands of his enemies . . . but that is the only way he will be stopped.'

I placed my hand reassuringly on hers. 'Not his enemies, Ivana. I don't know exactly what the British government has planned, probably some legal ruse to keep him out of circulation for a few months until things settle down.'

'The massacre at Stavac?'

'Maybe. We know it wasn't his forces who did it, but the rumours still persist.'

She shook her head. 'I know . . . just because it suits Mayor

Jozic's purpose to keep repeating the lies against the Muslims. This really is a mad, upside-down place, Jeff.'

'It is,' I agreed with feeling. 'And what about you and Nigel? Forgive me for asking.'

'Since you and he had that row, we have not been seen together in public. He has even been using your interpreter, Senic, rather than me.'

'That's good. Poor Senic has been feeling rather redundant, I'm afraid.'

'When Nigel and I are together, we are very discreet.'

'So you *are* still seeing him?' I'd been hoping my suspicions were unfounded and I was really annoyed that Cuthbert could be so stupid and selfish. 'You know how dangerous that is.'

It was Ivana's turn to look angry. 'We are in love, Jeff, and it is all I have left to cling to now . . . But as I say, we are very careful. We only ever meet at the home of a trusted friend of mine. No one else knows.'

'There are no secrets in a place like this,' I told her, and immediately felt such a hypocrite when I thought of my supposedly discreet liaison with Tali.

Ivana looked a little uncomfortable and shrugged. I let the matter rest there; it was her decision, after all.

We finished our drinks, then I drove us back to company HQ. Given the tenseness of the situation in Una Drina and the obvious anger, at least in the Ramoza Brigade's officer corps, that we'd managed to break their siege, it seemed sensible to exercise a little extra caution.

With all the Warriors now deployed in escorting the bulk of the convoy onward to DV and Sarajevo, Gordy had arranged for two additional Land Rovers of heavily armed Royal Wessex troops to escort us to our meeting with General Aganovic.

Our patrol set off north, through the Croat checkpoint and through several hundred metres of no-man's land to the Muslim lines. To my surprise, the sentries were expecting us. They were so much more efficient and well turned-out than the regular militia they had replaced. We and our escort were in our turn escorted by a couple of small trucks inherited from the former Yugoslav Army. The soldiers in the back watched us suspiciously, keeping their weapons at the ready.

We followed the familiar route over the hill to the farm where the local Muslims, led by Major Herenda, and the Ramoza Brigade both had their headquarters. Their tented city now looked decidedly bleak and uncomfortable sitting in a field of slushy snow.

Stopping outside General Aganovic's tent, our Royal Wessex escorts faced down the Muslim escorts, each side trying to look meaner than the other, while Ivana and I were led inside by a single aide.

General Aganovic was seated behind his desk, wearing an Afghan-style soft cap and swaddled in a military greatcoat and scarf. A blow-heater running off a generator noisily failed to make any impression on the near-freezing temperature.

'Captain Hawkins and Miss Ivana,' the aide announced.

Aganovic turned his head in our direction. 'No Nigel Cuthbert?' he asked.

I thought I detected a hint of sarcasm in his voice. I said, 'No, General, I'm dealing with this.'

'So, explain to me again exactly what is happening.'

'You may have lost the siege, General,' I began. 'But you have won the battle. Mayor Jozic has decided to stand down his forces and withdraw them from the town. Likewise, he will obviously expect you to do the same. In effect, Una Drina will become demilitarized.'

'Almir,' Ivana intervened, 'he wants to discuss with you how best to do this. I promise you this is true.'

Aganovic turned towards Ivana. 'And why should I believe you, a woman who has betrayed me?'

I felt my jaw tense as I heard his words. But Ivana came back swiftly. 'I have not betrayed you, Almir. These are stupid rumours and lies by troublemakers, just because I spend so much time with Mr Cuthbert. But I *have* to spend time with him, I'm his interpreter! It is my job, you know that.'

Aganovic fell silent for a moment and stared sightlessly out into the middle distance as if trying to make a difficult decision. At last he said, 'Right, Ivana, so explain to me precisely what are Mayor Jozic's proposals?'

Slowly and patiently she went through the proposals that, in truth, Nigel Cuthbert and I had concocted. At least we'd done a thorough job so that they sounded utterly convincing and, if actually followed through, would make Una Drina a safer and saner place for its inhabitants to live in and for the convoys to pass through. There was a proposed timetable and full details of unit positions and numbers of both Croat and Muslim forces. The embryonic agreement was well balanced and favoured neither side. It all made good political sense.

Not surprisingly, Aganovic didn't quite see it that way. 'Obviously this is skewed in the Croats' favour,' he announced suddenly. 'I knew that infidel Jozic would try to gain advantage.'

'He is prepared to be flexible,' Ivana assured him. 'That is the reason for the talks. These are just his initial proposals.'

Aganovic looked unhappy. 'And if I withdraw my men, who will protect the Muslims of Una Drina when Jozic goes on another ethnic-cleansing rampage?'

I said, 'There will be no need to protect them, General, because he won't be there. As I told you, he's leaving.'

'I still cannot believe this.'

'Mayor Jozic *is* stepping down.' I confirmed, 'This is top-secret, and there must be no word to anyone. Once the deal is done with you, he is leaving the country.'

'He would never leave Una Drina!'

'We have Mayor Jozic's letter of resignation,' I said, handing it to the general's aide.

The man read it out slowly, the expression on his face showing that he was just as surprised as Aganovic himself.

But even this did not satisfy the general. After a few moments' grudging thought he said, 'And who will replace him? Another Muslim-hating infidel?'

Somehow I knew this would be the clincher. 'No, that's the other reason for the talks. To settle on a new mayor for the town. Someone that both Muslim and Croat citizens will trust and be happy with.'

Another dark silence fell, this time a long one. Suddenly he raised his head and pronounced, 'I shall come. But the siege will stay in force until everything can be agreed. I smell a trick, because I cannot believe all this.'

'Fair enough,' I said. 'It is to be held the day after tomorrow. Three in the afternoon at the schoolhouse. There is also a children's entertainment going on — that'll help mask the activities. I will have a two-Warrior escort sent when your vehicle is ready to cross the Croat lines into town.'

And so the deal was done.

I shook his hand, even though Aganovic was not enthusiastic.

'Time to go,' I said to Ivana.

'No,' the general said sharply. 'She stays.'

The woman looked startled. 'You want to talk to me?'

'Yes, we have much to discuss, but also you will remain here in the camp until after the talks.'

Now I understood. Aganovic was so ruthless that he'd even use his fiancée as a hostage to acquire a deal. I said, 'No way, General. Ivana comes with me. You and she can talk some other time.'

She placed a hand on my arm. 'No, Jeff, it is all right. I shall stay. It will only be for a couple of days.'

'Or a lifetime,' Aganovic said, which I thought sounded ominous. Or maybe he was going to try and persuade her to marry him.

'Please go, Jeff,' Ivana insisted.

Reluctantly I agreed. It was her decision, her life. Maybe she'd even go back to him. 'OK, Ivana, if you're sure. Thanks for your help. I'll see you in two days, on Boxing Day.'

She smiled.

I replaced my blue beret and strode out into the cold twilight to rejoin the escort.

We'd not even cleared the line of tents when I heard a single shot.

I told myself it was most likely someone letting off steam or a negligent discharge, but still my hands began to tremble. I had just gambled with Ivana's life and I prayed that I had not lost. But in my heart I feared the worst.

Seventeen

I drove on, telling myself not to be so damn stupid. Just because I'd been unhappy about leaving Ivana behind didn't mean that any harm had befallen her. Surely Almir Aganovic wouldn't be stupid enough to kill her in cold blood and risk a death sentence himself? On the other hand, sexual jealousy is a very unpredictable emotion . . .

By the time I was back in Una Drina I'd convinced myself that I was just too tired to think straight. I hadn't slept for over thirty-six hours and it was starting to show. But when I returned to company HQ, it was clear that sleep wasn't going to be on the agenda for a few more hours yet.

As if by magic the Ops Room had been transformed into Santa's Grotto. The coloured spokes of a wheel of old-fashioned paper chains were strung out from the central lampshade. Some sad squaddies must have made them during their hours of off-duty boredom. Tinsel glittered around the tactical maps and there was even a fir tree in one corner with a flickering set of fairy lights – you could always rely on REME in a crisis!

Billy Billings was hard at work mixing a hot punch at a table designated as the duty-staff bar, littered with bottles of beer and spirits.

Everything was winding down. Only the duty staff were on station, but there was very little radio traffic. Soldiers were standing around in small groups, laughing and joking and recounting adventures past and present.

Suddenly Gordy Cromwell was at my side, pressing a glass into my hand. 'Have a drink, Jimbo, you deserve it.'

I accepted the whisky. 'I don't know about deserve it, I damn well *need* it.'

'The lads are on a high,' he said, his face already flushed from the alcohol. 'The rest of Convoy Gold got all the way through to Sarajevo. No trouble from Muslims, Croats or Serbs. Now that *is* a bloody Christmas miracle. When the convoy arrived, apparently the people couldn't believe their eyes. There was dancing in the streets.'

'I'm pleased,' I said. After all, it's what we were there for, and it was good to feel – only too rarely – that you'd really made a difference.

'The convoy will take a couple of days to unload,' Gordy said, 'but Rocky's driving back here tonight, leaving Shaun in charge. In fact, Tring's invited Rocky to our Christmas lunch tomorrow as guest of honour. He supplied four huge turkeys and sacks of veg. Billings was having an orgasm just looking at them.'

I was just contemplating the prospect of a decent meal when Nigel Cuthbert made an appearance. He looked to be in good humour as he approached. 'Hi, Jimbo,' he greeted, and took me to one side. 'How'd it go with General Aganovic?'

'Bingo,' I replied. 'He's insisting on maintaining the siege, but he's agreed to come to the talks on Boxing Day.'

'The siege will be over as soon as we've got Aganovic out of it and Major Herenda takes command. I've just come from a meeting with him. He's one very happy bunny. And the government in Sarajevo will be very relieved once Aganovic's gone.' He glanced around the Ops Room. 'Where's Ivana?'

'She stayed on to talk with Aganovic.'

Cuthbert looked horrified. 'You have to be joking!'

I shook my head. 'It was her decision. I think maybe they've got some personal matters that need to be sorted, don't you?'

He didn't look pleased. 'That could have waited. After Boxing Day, he'll be off the scene.'

I shrugged. 'Maybe she'd rather tell him it's over face-to-face. Women are like that.'

At that point Gordy came up behind us and draped an arm round each of our shoulders. 'I'm off duty now,' he declared. 'How's about my two favourite buddies join me for a drink at the Splendid? Wet the head of the baby Jesus?'

It was as if someone had suddenly thrown a switch and – rather late in the day, and despite my desperate need for sleep – I suddenly felt a congenial wave of Christmas spirit wash over me. The bad dreams could keep.

Minutes later the three of us were in my Land Rover, driving out of the base. To the north on the main drag we heard and saw the lights of the chugging column of Warriors returning from their escort duties to Sarajevo. No doubt Rocky would be amongst them in his UN Discovery. It wouldn't be long before he joined us at the hotel bar.

I couldn't find a parking place anywhere within a whole block of the Splendid. There were vehicles all over the place, even double-parked in the road. I think every aid worker, UN official and driver, off-duty UNPROFOR soldier, journalist and Croat militiaman had been drawn by the magnetic pull of the hotel's bar that Christmas Eve.

The place was a pulsing, seething mass of humanity. The tinny crackle of carols from a ghetto-blaster barely made itself heard above the hubbub of excited, drink-fuelled conversation and laughter. Finally, the dangers and tensions of the previous weeks had found a release.

As we fought our way doggedly through the crowd to the bar, I scoured the sea of faces for a glimpse of Tali. There were many people I recognized, including Colonel Zec and ITN's Gerald Kemp, who grinned and waved in my direction, but not her.

We ordered a double round, plus a couple of beers in anticipation of Rocky's arrival, and fought our way back to a table just vacated next to Kemp and his television crew.

As we sat down he yelled, 'We're making the evening news back home tonight, Jeff. Great pictures – including a few stills from Tali. Powerful stuff.'

'Well done,' I called back, but somehow I couldn't share the newsman's professional appreciation for the absorbing footage of vehicles on fire and people dying. Maybe some good would come of it, but to me it all seemed very cynical.

'The editor was over the moon,' Kemp continued.

'Talking of Tali,' I said, 'I suppose she isn't planning to join you?'

He shook his head, then indicated the far side of the bar. 'With her American chum over there.'

Momentarily a gap developed in the forest of bodies and I caught a glimpse of the candle-lit window table. She looked glorious, wearing make-up for once, her hair down and dressed in a simple black number with a slashed front that revealed a little too much. Leaning forward with her elbows on the table, she was looking into Kirk Grundy's eyes and smiling as he stroked her hands with his. Then he said something and they both laughed. He reached for the bottle of wine beside them and refilled her glass.

Then the gap between the other revellers closed again and the cameo scene was cut off. I felt sick.

'C'mon, Jeff,' Gordy said, nudging me. 'Drink up. You look like you've swallowed a wasp. It's Crimbo, Jimbo.'

I took a mouthful of beer. It tasted like dishwater. 'Maybe I'm just not in a festive mood.'

'Yeah, but that's the thing about Christmas. Try to ignore it and it'll still come out and grab you!'

'Dead right,' Cuthbert agreed.

I made a snap decision. 'I'll see you guys in a minute.'

Leaving the table, I worked my way through the crowd until I reached Tali and Grundy.

They were so wrapped up in what they were talking about that they didn't even notice my presence until I spoke. 'Hi, Tali.'

I didn't address Grundy, but gave him a curt nod of acknowledgement. 'Enjoying yourself?'

'Yes thanks, Jeff.' Her voice sounded flat and I wondered if I detected a note of irritation in her voice. 'And you?'

'Over there with some of the lads. Join us later, if you like.'

'Thank you, maybe we will.'

'Have you got a place to stay?'

She nodded. 'My old room's been let, but Kirk's going to let me share his room here.'

'I see.'

Grundy had been silent, but his eyes had been glinting with cynical amusement. 'Don't worry, Jim-bo. She refuses to share my bed. Reckons I snore. So she'll have to curl up in her sleeping-bag on the floor. I'm much too old to do that!'

His words seemed to amuse her and she landed a playful punch on his arm. 'Kirk Grundy, I don't think you're too old for anything!'

I wasn't going to give up that easily. 'I was wondering if you've made any plans for tomorrow, Tali?'

She looked back up at me. 'Kirk's taking me to DV. Apparently there's a big slap-up lunch and a dance after. The hotel's even got electricity on at the moment.'

My heart didn't have room to sink any further. 'Well, I hope you have a good time.'

'Thank you,' she said, then added, 'Enjoy your evening.'

Fat bloody chance, I thought as I turned away and returned to my table.

'Eaten another bloody wasp, Jimbo?'

I forced a smile. 'Sorry, miles away.' I sat down and picked up my bottle of beer. 'Cheers, let's party!'

But the party spirit was to be short lived. Half an hour later, when we'd just finished our first double round, I glanced at my watch. 'Where's Rocky got to?' I wondered aloud.

'Talk of the devil,' Gordy said, looking up.

I turned round to see Rocky Rogers' bulky frame, still dressed in his tartan lumberjacket, squeezing its way through the crowd. It was difficult to tell in the poor light, but I thought he looked decidedly angry.

Cuthbert must have missed that. 'Hallo. Bit late on parade, aren't we?'

Rocky made a beeline for him, reached over the table, grabbed him by the lapels and hauled him to his feet. 'Don't give me that crap, Nigel, you devious fucking wanker!'

Cuthbert looked terrified, his eyes bulging. 'W-what the hell's up with you!'

Rocky released his grip. 'You – you're what's up with me!'

Cuthbert felt his neck and straightened his collar, forcing a smile that just didn't want to come. 'I don't know what you're talking about.'

'Oh, I think you do!' Rocky retorted.

'Then tell me!' Cuthbert pleaded.

'Not here!' Rocky snapped. 'Outside – now!'

Cuthbert raised his hands. 'OK, OK, I'm coming.' By the time he'd picked up his combat smock from the back of his chair, Rocky was already storming back towards the hotel entrance.

I was curious to know what was going on and followed them. Gordy volunteered to keep an eye on our seats; to be honest I think the man was so exhausted after weeks of holding the company together that he wasn't going to let anyone or anything spoil the evening for him.

Outside on the hotel steps, the raw cold of night air caught in my throat. With the drop in temperature the earlier drizzle had turned to fine snowflakes which were beginning to overlay the frozen grey slush on the street and pavement. Rocky and Cuthbert were standing a few metres away in the doorway of a derelict shop. I could hear their raised voices as I approached.

'Those four fuckin' trucks!' Rocky was saying accusingly.

'What trucks, specifically? There are UN trucks all over town.'

Rocky pushed his face close to Cuthbert's. 'But those four trucks aren't UN trucks, are they? That's the fuckin' point!'

I knew Rocky well and I was seriously worried he was in a mood to knock Cuthbert's teeth out. I said, 'Hey, you two, cool it, eh? What's the problem?'

Rocky turned to me. 'Remember those four trucks that arrived late – just before the convoy left?'

I nodded. 'Back from the repair workshops.'

'Bollocks,' Rocky rejoined. 'They're fakes. They were pushed in at the last minute knowing full well there wouldn't be time to check their loads or paperwork properly. They've got switched plates to match four vehicles still sitting in the workshop back on the coast!'

'How d'you know?'

'While I was running with Gold to Sarajevo today, my section leader Sputnik – you know, the big Russian – was looking after things here. Got a bit suspicious when our chum Nigel started interfering, saying he'd had some special request from UNHCR bosses.'

Cuthbert looked a bit sheepish. 'Sputnik misunderstood.'

Rocky shook his head. 'He understood your bullshit perfectly, especially when he found you'd had them parked way up on the school playing field and that the so-called UN drivers were bloody well armed!'

'I can explain . . .' Cuthbert began.

'Don't bother. Sputnik checked the consignment notes and established they were elaborate counterfeits – you've obviously got some excellent UN contacts! Then he got his staff to search the vehicles while the drivers stood around, nearly tearing their hair out and shitting themselves.'

'What did you find?' I asked.

'Three of the loads were full of gas cylinders.'

I shrugged. 'So what?'

'Only the ones by the tailgate – those most likely to be checked – contained gas. Sputnik used to be a smuggler, so he investigated further. The rest were filled with gunpowder.'

'I can explain,' Cuthbert interrupted, his face ashen. 'It's part of a deal with Major Herenda. The Muslim munitions factories are desperately short of gunpowder.'

'No *wonder* none of the militias trust the UN,' I said. 'How often have you compromised their neutrality, Nigel?'

Feeling cornered, Cuthbert rounded on me. 'Don't ask damn fool questions, Jimbo. You know full well I can't answer them.'

Again the image of Kirk Grundy parked in a lay-by beside four UN trucks leapt into my mind.

I said, 'The CIA's mixed up in all this, isn't it?'

Cuthbert smiled uncomfortably. 'The Americans are developing a secret long-term strategy to end the war. And we're sort of co-operating with them as they're not officially involved on the ground.'

'And what sort of strategy might that be?' Rocky jeered.

Cuthbert stared at him. 'I said *secret* strategy. I can hardly tell you, can I?'

Rocky took a deep breath. 'OK, so instead tell me about the fourth truck? A truck in *my* convoy! And I *don't* have secrets in my convoy, got it?'

Cuthbert blinked, but remained defiant. 'Sorry, Rocky, no can do.'

'The one with the secret compartment,' Rocky prompted. 'But not so bloody secret, because Sputnik found it. And if he could find it, any proper checkpoint search could find it too.'

It was my turn to feel guilty. 'That'll be to get General Aganovic out of town.'

'What?' He turned on me, eyes blazing. 'Are you in on this, too, Jimbo? Bloody hell!'

'Not the details,' I told him. 'But HMG is planning to snatch Aganovic on Boxing Day, get him out of the area. They've done a deal with the Bosnian government to install Major Herenda as commander of the Ramoza Brigade. Then the siege will be lifted.'

Rocky stared at me for a few moments as the significance of my words sank in. His expression softened. 'Why the hell didn't someone have the decency to tell me?'

I said, 'I think they were afraid you'd say no.'

'Dead right, too.' He paused and looked thoughtfully back along the street at the guttering fires of the refugees huddled in shop doorways and under makeshift plastic shelters.

Cuthbert was seething at me. 'That's privileged information you've just disclosed. I'll see you're court-martialled for this, Jimbo, so help me.'

I turned on him, exasperated. 'Oh, do shut up, Nigel.'

Rocky ignored our exchange and lit a cigarette. He exhaled and said, 'Then we'd better make *sure* the convoy gets out of town on Boxing Day night – before anyone knows what's happened.'

'The Muslim siege will still be holding,' I reminded him. 'It might be days before Herenda has full command.'

'We can't wait for that,' Rocky said. 'Nothing to do with General Aganovic either. There are people going to die if they don't get out. And that includes one of my own men.'

'What do you reckon?' I asked.

'It'll mean getting out the way we came in. The hard way.' He drew heavily on his cigarette. 'There's a lot of planning to do, a lot of thought.'

Cuthbert couldn't believe his ears. 'You'll co-operate?'

Rocky looked down at him with disdain. 'Without my co-operation you won't succeed. And I don't like being used, Nigel, so never do it again. Ever. But I just happen to reckon – *personally* – that this is in the UN's interests. Even if the politicians at the top don't see it that way. It's worth risking my job for the poor bastards who have to live here and in DV.'

'That's very noble of you,' Cuthbert said.

Rocky groaned. 'Get the fuck out of my sight, Nigel.'

Cuthbert needed no second bidding. He turned and scurried back towards the warmth of the Splendid, skidding and sliding on the newly fallen snow as he ran.

Rocky and I watched with shared amusement. 'I'm sorry,' I said. 'It was out of my hands.'

Rocky slapped me on the back, a little too hard to be truly playful. 'Forget it, you scheming bastard. I'm parched and ready to party. Let's go!'

We began to follow in Cuthbert's footsteps back to the Splendid. Just as we reached the steps, I heard a familiar female voice. 'Hey, Jeff! Rocky! Merry Christmas!'

Anita Furtula hurried across the street, huddled in a dark and heavy winter coat.

I waved, my spirits immediately lifting at the chance encounter. 'Merry Christmas to you, too.'

It was great to see her smiling, her pinched white face almost lost between the fur of her hat and the astrakhan collar of her coat. 'It is *you* two people who have made it such a wonderful Christmas!' she said excitedly. 'I cannot tell you!'

I laughed. 'Well, thanks, but I think a few others might have been involved, too.'

I'd never seen her look so happy. 'You know what I mean,' she scolded, a quicksilver look of disapproval in those expressive sable eyes. 'The children woke when the convoy passed the school. The convoys never come that way.'

'We had to use a back way in,' I said.

'They woke each other up, screaming and shouting with happiness. We wondered what had happened. So many trucks, they seemed to never stop coming! The children may be young, but they know what it means. Food and blankets, and for some an escape when the convoy leaves.'

'All tucked up in bed now?' Rocky asked.

She chuckled. 'Yes, but not asleep for all the excitement. There are some nice UN people looking after them. I have sneaked out to celebrate with my best friends.'

I laughed, catching her mood. 'Then I guess we'd better buy you a drink.'

She tilted her head coquettishly to one side. 'That would be nice, kind sir.'

Back inside the hotel, the party in the bar had already cranked up a couple of notches; the press of laughing, chatting people seemed to have doubled and the volume of voices had totally overwhelmed the carols from the ghetto-blaster.

Anita shed her coat and joined our table along with more subalterns from company HQ. Everyone was in high spirits although Rocky and Cuthbert managed studiously to avoid eye contact with each other. The drinks just kept on coming.

I think it was to everyone's surprise, given her former reputation as the dragon-lady of Una Drina, that Anita produced a large sprig of mistletoe from her shoulder bag and proceeded to do a circuit of our table, kissing every soldier and convoy worker there.

I watched on, grinning at the jokes and innuendos, until she finally came to me. 'I'm surprised you've got any breath left,' I laughed.

'Oh, plenty left for *you*, Jeff, believe me.'

Before I knew it she was sitting on my lap, her arms wrapped round my neck and her lips on mine. For the first couple of seconds I was embarrassed by the jeering onlookers, then I thought, to hell with it!

'Hey, steady on!' someone called. 'You're suffocating him!'

'Take your tongue out of her lungs, Jimbo!' cried another.

'That's not fair! He's had twice as long as I had!'

I no longer cared, I was just lost in her arms, the taste of her mouth, the soft weight of her body, the fragrance of her hair. Eventually, almost reluctantly, we eased apart. By this time the rest of the table had lost interest and were busy ordering more drinks from Jelena.

'I will have to go in a minute,' Anita announced.

I was disappointed. 'Do you have to? I think we should talk.'

She nodded. 'I agree. I think I have been very jealous, very stupid. I apologize.'

I shook my head. 'No, it's me who should apologize. I've behaved like an idiot. I think it's called a mid-life crisis.'

She raised a questioning eyebrow. 'So we are still friends?' Her eyes were close to mine, more beautiful and expressive than I'd ever quite realized before.

'Very much so,' I said hoarsely. 'Very special friends.'

Another smile lit up her face and she kissed me again, quickly on the lips. 'I am so happy about that. But I must go.'

'Why?'

'To visit the clinic. I have two little gifts for Dario and Mara. And cards the children have made for them.'

To my shame, I'd almost forgotten about them in the events and traumas of the past few days. 'How are they?'

'Not well at all. I hope the convoy will not be too late for them. They urgently need to be in a proper hospital. To receive specialist attention.'

I lowered my voice. 'The convoy will be leaving again in the next day or two. The UN will take them.'

She nodded. 'It cannot be soon enough.'

I added, 'And they will take any orphans who do not have relatives, or who want to leave.'

'That will be such a relief. Suddenly the fewer pupils I have the better.'

I wanted to offer her hope. I said, 'Things will improve here soon, I think.'

'How? I don't see it. Not while we have a mayor who hates the Muslims, and Muslims who hate us Croats, how can it?'

'I can't explain,' I said. 'Just trust me.'

The smile returned to her face. 'All right, but my mother told me never to trust men who said "trust me"!' She hesitated, as though coming to a decision. 'What are you doing tomorrow?'

'It'll be busy,' I replied. 'There'll be a lot of convoy planning to do and then the company Christmas dinner. The officers serve the men.'

She giggled. 'Really? That is so funny, I don't think that

happens in Bosnia . . . Does that mean I won't be able to see you?'

'I don't know. I'd really like to.'

She touched my hand lightly. 'Maybe you could come to my place for a drink in the evening. I will have some cold meats and I make the best chutneys in the country.'

I laughed. 'How can I refuse that? I'll see what I can do.'

She fixed me with her eyes, held my gaze. 'Please do. But there is one thing . . .'

'Yes?'

'We will be *good*, yes? It will be platonic. No more misunderstandings.'

I felt surprisingly relieved to hear her say that. I had enough turmoil going on in my head, enough confused emotions and feelings. I liked Anita a lot, a hell of a lot. But I wasn't yet sure exactly how much, or how deep it ran. The last thing I wanted to do was hurt her again. I said, 'Yes, we will be good.'

She stood up, pulled her coat back on and shouldered her bag. 'Merry Christmas, Jeff.'

I climbed to my feet and kissed her quickly on the mouth. 'And may next year bring you everything you want.'

'Peace,' she said, her voice barely audible. Then she smiled and left.

As I watched her go, Rocky's voice intruded into my thoughts. 'Think you've scored there, mate!'

I glanced down at him and his stupid lascivious grin. 'We're just good friends, Rocky, just good friends.'

He smirked. 'Whatever.'

Jelena returned with a tray of drinks and placed it on the table. 'Jeff,' she said, handing me a small pink envelope. 'Tali left this for you.'

My thoughts were elsewhere and it took a moment for me to realize what she'd said. 'Left? Where's she's gone?'

'To Donji Vrbas. She left with Kirk Grundy about an hour ago.'

I remembered he was taking her to lunch there on Christmas Day. 'They're not travelling at night?'

She shrugged. 'It seems so.'

I was angry. 'God, what sort of idiot is that man? Anything could happen. The Muslims, even the Croats.'

Jelena blinked for a moment, then looked at me as a mother might regard a naive child. 'Don't worry, Jeff, they will be safe. Kirk is *everybody's* friend.'

Her words jolted me. Yes, of course, she was right. Kirk Grundy was everybody's friend. It was his job, until it was time to stab them in the back.

I thanked Jelena, stuffed the envelope into the pocket of my smock and sat down for another drink. But I'd really had enough and could tell that even the redoubtable Rocky was beginning to flag. We agreed with Cuthbert and Gordy to have a meeting the next morning at ten to thrash out the details of the convoy departure, then Rocky and I went our separate ways, he to his hotel room while I drove back past the long line of refugees' fires on the main drag to company HQ.

The building was the quietest I'd ever known it, and even the skeleton duty staff in the Ops Room had little to occupy them.

I reached the door of my billet and pushed it open. I could swear it still smelled of Tali, her hair, her body. And in the darkness I could almost hear her voice, her quiet laugh, her sighs. Pushing the images of her from my mind, I lit the lamp and stretched out fully clothed on the camp-bed. For a moment I stared at the ceiling then, suddenly remembering the envelope, I fumbled for it in the pocket of my smock.

I tore it open and held the single sheet up to read with both hands. The writing was very small and neat:

Darling Jeff,

 Our time together has been magical and wonderful, and I will never forget you and the things that we have done together. Thank you for showing me so much.

*But we have different roads to travel, and it is time for us to
part. Maybe if it had all been at a different time and place . . .*
    Enjoy your life
    All my love
    Tali x

That was it. I wanted to cry, but the tears would not come. I
was just too damn exhausted. I shut my eyes and was instantly
asleep.

By more luck than judgement I snapped suddenly awake at
nine on Christmas Day morning, still fully clothed and with the
Tilley lamp still burning. I reckoned I'd slept straight through for
ten hours and even an earthquake wouldn't have woken me. Yet
I still felt groggy and half-dead as I sat up on the bed. It just
served to remind me that soldiering was a young man's game.

But after a shave and wash in a bowl of cold water, I felt a lot
better. By the time I'd pulled on a fresh set of combat fatigues
and ran a comb through my hair, I actually felt ready for breakfast. Before I left the room, I glanced down at the crumpled pink
envelope and the note it had contained still lying on the camp-
bed.

I felt vaguely angry and disappointed. With Tali, with myself,
with the circumstances that had brought us together. Of course,
she was right. I'd always known it, always known it would never
work, yet still I'd gone on fooling myself.

I still wondered what she had really felt about me. Had she
really cared about me, really felt excited and complete in my
presence, as I had in hers? Or had I been just another new
adventure? Now I would never know, and somehow I doubted
that she did herself.

I picked up the letter and envelope from the bed and screwed
them into a tight ball, before putting a match to it in the ash-
tray. It flared momentarily, then curled and shrank into a tiny
foetus of black carbon. I left the room and slammed the door
shut behind me in a final act of closure.

I was glad that I would be having a very busy day. I caught up with Gordy and Cuthbert in the canteen, where I snatched a mug of hot sweet black coffee and a bacon butty before our meeting was due to start. Life was feeling sweeter again already.

I then took advantage of one of the perks of being an LO with a satellite telephone – I called home. Both the kids were back from university and my daughter Lucy answered. We had a quick chat and a laugh, then Joe came on. He was the serious one, so I asked him how his academic work was going. Not too well, I gathered, and he was loath to say too much about it, or anything else either. He went to fetch Marcia.

My wife's first words were, 'I'm in the middle of making the mince pies.'

'A bad time to talk then?'

'Not the best.'

It struck me as odd. 'You usually make them days ahead, don't you?'

'Yes, but I've been busy . . .' She allowed the sentence to hang.

'Oh?'

There was a long pause. Then I heard her take a deep breath. 'There's someone else, Jeff.'

I wasn't sure I'd heard right. 'Pardon?'

'I'm seeing someone else.'

'Seeing someone?' I echoed.

'I've known him some time. It's serious.'

I'd realized for several years that Marcia and I had been drifting slowly apart, but to hear the cold and clinical confirmation that it was now really over still came as quite a shock.

I said the first thing that came into my head. 'Who is he?'

'No one you know. He sold me that new home contents insurance last year. We just . . . got on.'

'Oh,' I replied lamely.

'It's the real thing, Jeff. I'm leaving to be with him after Christmas.'

A million confused thoughts rushed through my brain. 'Do the kids know?'

'Not really, not yet. They think he's just a friend.'

'But he's more than that?'

'A lot more. I want a divorce.'

I hung up in a pensive mood. Merry Christmas! I'd only called Marcia a couple of times since my deployment, and on both occasions she'd seemed distant and uncommunicative. Now I knew why.

But I had no time to brood over our conversation as, again, work came to the rescue.

I hurried along to Major Tring's office, just in time to catch the start of the meeting. Gordy, Cuthbert and Rocky were already there, waiting.

'Good of you to deign to join us, Jeffrey,' the major said, looking up.

Some things never change, I thought, as I muttered my apologies. However, I was wrong on that score. With the company having received so much praise in recent weeks for its more robust actions – and being buoyed by the siege-breaking success of the convoy – Major Tring had found a new self-confidence and can-do attitude.

When Rocky kicked off the meeting by saying how important it was for the convoy to return quickly to the coast with refugees and the wounded and sick from the clinic, Tring did not throw up one of his usual objections. Even when it became clear that the Ramoza Brigade had already reimposed its siege of the town.

Of course, of those present only Rocky, Cuthbert and I were privy to the fact that there existed a plot to abduct General Aganovic the next day. It was difficult not to give away accidentally some of the underlying reasons for our plan of action.

'I intend to roll out on Boxing Day evening,' Rocky concluded. 'Back the way we came, via the snake, avoiding Muslim lines and roadblocks to the south of town.'

Cuthbert added, 'We've got SAS teams in the hills, monitoring Muslim positions. The route back may not be so easy, because the Muslims are now aware that it has been successfully used once – and could be again. Some mortars and artillery have been repositioned to cover it.'

'Nevertheless,' Rocky said, 'I'd like Jimbo to open negotiations with the Muslims for the convoy to leave by the main road on the twenty-seventh of December, the day *after* Boxing Day.'

'Fine,' I agreed.

Tring nodded his understanding. 'The Muslims will think you're negotiating for the twenty-seventh, but you *actually* slip out under cover of darkness the night before.'

Cuthbert added, 'An SAS team will create a diversion to the south of the town to get their attention.'

'I plan to use the school playing field as our marshalling area,' Rocky said. 'And I would be pleased to have an UNPROFOR escort in this instance. I appreciate that attempting to break a siege without prior negotiation is pushing your official remit to the wire—'

'No problem,' Tring cut in, to everyone's astonishment. We all glanced at each other in a stunned silence while the major added, 'Time we showed some of these people what's what.'

While we were all agreeing with everyone, I decided to lob in my little surprise, just to make everyone's day complete. 'By the way, gentlemen, I hope you might be pleased to hear that Mayor Jozic has decided to retire from office.'

Tring's mouth dropped. 'What?'

'He's had enough of the siege, of life here, and wants out,' I said quickly. 'He's requested that he and his family be allowed to travel with the convoy.'

Rocky laughed loudly. 'That sonofabitch! You bet he can come with the convoy. He can even travel with me if he likes. Anything to get rid of him.'

'Who's his successor to be?' Tring asked. 'Could be someone even worse, even more hard-line.'

I said, 'I don't know yet, Reg, haven't been told. I'll let you know when I am.'

And that was that, everything was set and all just in time for the splendid Billy Billings Christmas Special.

As usual the man had come up trumps with magnificently dressed turkeys and a side of ham, plus a mountain of vegetables and a giant plum pudding with a vat of custard. Tring, Gordy and I together with the rest of the officers served the men at the trestle tables, which were clothed with white linen borrowed from the Splendid. The beer cans, mess tins and foldaway army cutlery rather spoiled the effect, but everyone was too busy enjoying themselves to notice. After the food, Santa Claus arrived in a red crêpe-paper suit and cotton-wool beard to distribute gifts from the men's families in the UK.

Then followed a series of ribald seasonal ditties, including 'Christmas Day in the Workhouse' – allegedly a lost work of Charles Dickens – and a pornographic variation of 'The Twelve Days of Christmas'.

Rocky, our guest of honour, treated the gathering to his favourite party-piece: 'He laid her on the table, so white, clean and bare. His forehead wet with beads of sweat, he rubbed her here and there. He touched her neck, then felt her breast, then, drooling, felt her thigh. The slit was wet and all was set, he gave a joyous cry. The hole was wide – he looked inside, all was dark and murky. He rubbed his hands and stretched his arms . . . And then he stuffed the turkey!'

As the troops dissolved into laughter, I slipped away to the Den and put a satellite call through to General Aganovic. Not surprisingly he was unavailable, but I left a message with an aide that at our proposed talks the next day I also wished to discuss the planned departure of the UNHCR convoy for the coast on the twenty-seventh.

That job done, I returned to the officers' mess to enjoy our own dinner, a superb game stew with dumplings. No one complained that there hadn't been enough turkey for us. The port was passed and we settled down for a long and cheerful after-noon. Even Major Tring, having fed the leftovers on everyone's plate to the insatiable Trojan, was pleasant company for once.

In the early evening, I made my excuses and left the com-pound to drive the short distance to Anita Furtula's flat.

She greeted me at the door wearing an attractive blue satin frock and a wide smile.

I handed over a bottle of red wine. 'Best I could manage, I'm afraid.'

'It'll be lovely. Come in.'

It was warm and cosy. Paraffin for the stove had come in on Convoy Gold along with the candles that now lit the small apartment. Their romantic glimmer reflected on the simple tinsel decorations.

We sat and talked. And talked. Our agreement to keep our relationship cool for this tête-à-tête was proving to be a good idea. It diffused the sexual tension between us and allowed us to relax properly and get to know each other as friends should. We began to laugh a lot, too. By the end of the evening, which included a simple meal of cold cuts and her legendary chutney, I think we were both beginning to realize that we wanted to spend a lot more time in each other's company.

I was downing the last of the wine and it was nearly time to leave when I said, 'I've got some news that might make you very happy.'

She frowned. 'Yes?'

'Mayor Jozic is resigning.'

Her face, so expressive as always, was a picture of incredulity. She closed her open mouth and then said, 'Is this *really* true?'

I nodded. 'And I've some more news that I hope will make you even more happy. He's going to name his successor.'

Her eyes clouded. 'Oh, no! Who?'

I looked at her and tried to keep a straight face. 'You.'

Eighteen

'What! Is Jozic crazy?' Anita demanded.

I said, 'I don't think so. You are one of the most respected people in the town. Croats and Muslims like you. The town is going to be demilitarized. When it is, the new mayor must be someone whom both sides trust implicitly.'

'It is incredible, I don't know what to say.'

'Think about it.' I smiled. 'With you as mayor, I think this will be the best-behaved town in Bosnia.'

We both laughed at that; it was infectious, and was the perfect end to one of the best Christmas Days I could ever remember.

There was little for me to do on Boxing Day morning and I was able to catch up on more sleep. By the time I reached the Ops Room in mid-morning, the A Company troops had already been out on the streets, telling all the refugees they could find to be packed and ready to move at a moment's notice. Other soldiers had been dispatched to the clinic to help the doctors and nurses prepare to move any patient who was likely to survive the journey. In the meantime, all UNHCR trucks in town had marshalled on the playing field near the school, where their drivers and mechanics gave their vehicles a final check.

I tracked down Mayor Jozic at his home, a very smart and large chalet-style house on the edge of town. When he opened the door, I could see packing cases stacked in the hallway.

He didn't look especially pleased to see me. 'Mr Mayor, I'd like you to be at the school playing field by 1500 hours this afternoon.'

'That's impossible,' he protested. 'My wife hasn't packed half her wardrobe yet.'

'Be there, or I'll come and fetch you at gunpoint,' I warned. 'You can arrange to collect anything else later when the siege is over.'

He glared at me, but I could read defeat in his eyes. 'Very well.'

'One more thing I want you to do.'

'Yes?' he asked wearily.

'Another letter, on your official notepaper. This time naming your successor as Anita Furtula.'

'What? Her?'

'Yes, her.' It was not a Christmas he was ever going to forget. 'Bring the letter with you to the playing field and give it to me then.'

I didn't wait for his reply but turned and walked back to my Land Rover.

The rest of the day seemed to fly by. At 1400 hours four of the twenty UNHCR trucks and trailers left the playing field and made their way down to the clinic, where the nursing staff were waiting to load their patients.

Meanwhile three of the fake trucks loaded with explosives had mysteriously disappeared. Rocky, I knew, was mightily pleased to see the back of them.

Royal Wessex troops quietly fanned out over town and along the main street, telling all the refugees to start making their way to the playing field, leaving any fires to continue burning.

I arrived in my Land Rover with Cuthbert at the playing field as the first of the refugees began to appear. I found Rocky standing beside a battered brown truck having a heated argument with Mayor Jozic, who wore a fur hat and a bright red puffer jacket that seemed to double his size so that he resembled a huge medicine ball on legs. His wife and two heavies stood to one side, watching the exchange with bored expressions on their faces.

'It's hardly fit for normal roads,' Rocky was saying, 'let alone a snow-bound mountain track!'

'It will be fine,' Jozic insisted.

Rocky turned as I approached. 'Ah, Jimbo, just the man. You didn't tell me the mayor planned to bring his own truck.'

'I didn't know,' I replied. 'Does it matter?'

'It's falling to bits.'

'If it doesn't go,' Jozic said defiantly, 'then I don't go.'

I took Rocky to one side. 'Let him take it, Rocky. If it breaks down, it's his problem. I must get him and his family out of here tonight.'

He hesitated, clearly reluctant. 'OK. I'll let my mechanics have a look at it. See if they can do anything before we leave.'

Jozic looked distinctly smug and self-satisfied when Rocky gave him the news.

Cuthbert was getting agitated. 'Hurry up, Jimbo. General Aganovic could be arriving at any time.'

I turned to Jozic. 'Right, let's go. Have you got that letter?'

He nodded, reached inside his puffer jacket and handed me an envelope. 'Perhaps Mrs Furtula would be a good choice after all,' he conceded.

Cuthbert hurried him into the Land Rover and we drove the short distance to the school. As we parked and climbed out, I noticed a new, white, unmarked van parked at the side door. It was incongruous to see the clown from the Wildchild street-theatre company standing at the entrance with bright ginger hair, a huge red nose and baggy polkadot pantaloons greeting parents who were bringing their children to see the show.

We stepped inside and made our way to the left-hand door that led to a classroom that until today had been used as the orphans' dormitory. A handful of Royal Wessex troops had put away the camp-beds and were just finishing rearranging the furniture so that the place resembled a conference room. The trestle tables A Company had used during Christmas dinner the previous day were being placed together to create a single, large one.

'ads of paper, pencils and water glasses were being set out to
reate an authentic pretence.

Cuthbert began fussing about, clearly irritating the soldiers, so
left him to it and wandered into the main classroom. The little
,roup of orphans who would be leaving with the convoy that
night had been joined by a couple of dozen of the town's children and their parents to watch the show. The theatre group
members were all dressed as clowns, some as juggling clowns,
some as stilt-walking clowns and some as, well, just clowns. The
one holding everyone's attention was a puppeteer with a fantas-
ic range of marionettes, currently working a female violinist to
he strains of Mozart from a portable cassette player. Marionettes
had always fascinated me, and this puppeteer was one of the best.
And the kids were loving it, too.

Anita was standing at the back by the door and turned her
head as I entered. 'Hallo, Jeff. Aren't they good? It is wonderful
o see the children so happy.'

I leaned forward and whispered in her ear. 'Your orphans will
be even happier tomorrow – when they find themselves safe in
Croatia.'

'Yes, I hope you are right. They've suffered so much.'

I added, 'After the performance, just take them up to the
playing field. Everything's waiting. Be as quiet as possible, no
lights.'

'Of course.' Her gaze held mine for a moment. 'How long
before you return?'

'A day or two.'

'Hurry back. And take care.'

I said, 'I will,' and then I turned back to the other classroom.

Cuthbert was still fussing around and had persuaded Jozic to
sit centre stage at the conference table so that he was the first
person you noticed when you entered the room.

Suddenly Cuthbert was on his radio, talking to the Warrior
escort that was bringing General Almir Aganovic into the town.
Yes, OK, yes, we're ready.'

A couple of the Wildchild clowns had come into the conference room, put up a small mirror in a corner and were re-applying their make-up.

Cuthbert moved towards the door, nervous and jittery. 'Aganovic's coming,' he announced.

The Muslim general appeared at the entrance of the school flanked by two tall Afghan bodyguards. They regarded the red-headed clown who greeted them with flamboyant gestures of welcome suspiciously and with total incomprehension. They shifted their sub-machine guns into a ready position.

I stepped forward. 'Sorry, gentlemen, no arms here. These are *peace* talks.'

Aganovic recognized my voice. 'Captain Hawkins? My men keep their weapons.'

'OK,' I conceded, 'but not at the ready.'

Aganovic turned his head and gave the order for them to shoulder their arms. Reluctantly they obeyed.

'What is going on?' Aganovic asked. 'My bodyguards say there are men here in strange costumes. Like from a theatre.'

'Just clowns,' I said. 'They are entertaining the children in the next room. I told you when we met the other day.'

Just then, almost to prove the point, there was a peal of childish laughter through the partition walls. He looked more relaxed then. 'Where is Jozic?'

I turned towards the mayor and nodded. 'Mayor Jozic, please let the general know you are here and ready to talk.'

Jozic looked as though he was chewing broken glass as he spoke. 'General Aganovic, I am here. Here to negotiate with you.'

Two more clowns had wandered into the room, joining the first two. The Afghan guards still looked unsettled by them.

I gave a smile of reassurance that didn't really work. 'We are awaiting the arrival of a few more people. Why don't you relax and I'll arrange some drinks, maybe tea?'

Aganovic was still tense. 'Very well. But who else is coming?'

I rattled off Colonel Zec's name and half a dozen of the town' dignitaries. As I spoke, the four clowns had edged towards the two Afghans and were making exaggerated mime movements, heads tilted in curiosity like aliens examining a strange new life-form. The bodyguards were utterly bemused and shifted uneasily at this benign inspection.

I could barely keep the grin from my face, but I wasn't sure it was a good idea for these Wildchild hippies to be having a joke at the expense of such dangerous men, however well-intentioned.

I turned to Cuthbert. 'These guys shouldn't be in here, Nigel. They could get in the way, witness something they shouldn't.'

Cuthbert didn't seemed bothered, just smiled as he looked on with amusement.

Then, in a split second, I knew why. Two of the clowns had found their way behind the bodyguards, crouched as if to inspect their feet. The other two clowns stood in front of them, peering curiously into their faces. Whether they stepped back or were pushed, I couldn't see, but the two Afghans were suddenly top-pling backwards over the backs of the crouched clowns. It was precisely executed, the bodyguards' guns snatched from them before they hit the floor. And, before they could recover, Plasticuffs like large freezer-ties were produced from nowhere and snapped tight around their wrists. Then rags were stuffed into their mouths before they had a chance to utter a word.

Aganovic heard the scuffle and turned round. 'What is hap-pening?' he demanded, his hand reaching for the handgun holstered on his hip.

Suddenly two more clowns entered the room, moving swiftly up behind the Muslim general. An automatic pistol was jammed against his neck. 'Not a word!' hissed the first of the two new clowns. I recognized the voice of Chas, the SAS trooper I'd met earlier in my tour. He added, 'Co-operate, General, and I assure you that you and your men will not be hurt.'

Aganovic's blind eyes blazed. 'You infidel scum! I knew this was trickery!'

That was all he had the chance to say before he was trussed

and gagged as speedily and expertly as his two Afghan henchmen, who were now being bundled unceremoniously out of the side door to the waiting white van.

Jozic sat watching and blinking in total shock. He, too, had clearly been as fooled by the bogus clowns as I had. He looked at me across the room. 'I am glad now, Captain Hawkins, that I did not argue with you.'

'So am I,' I said. 'Thank you for your co-operation.'

He rose to his feet. 'Can I go now?'

'Of course.'

He pulled on his red puffer jacket and walked to the main entrance hall. There he paused and looked back at me. 'That was one of the most satisfying sights I have ever seen.' That was the nearest thing to a smile on the man's face in days. 'Aganovic, the Antichrist, getting his due desserts.'

I said nothing as he turned and left.

Cuthbert said in a whisper, 'You've seen nothing, Jimbo, right? Aganovic came to some proposed talks, but they never happened. He just disappeared among the refugees. Simple as that.'

I looked at him. 'Still playing with your smoke and mirrors, Nigel?'

He just smiled rather enigmatically, missing the sarcasm in my voice. 'Someone has to, Jimbo.'

I said, 'If I were you, I'd ask him about Ivana. Where's she staying – at the Ramoza camp or somewhere else?'

He looked thoughtful. 'I will, but Ivana can look after herself. When our man Major Herenda is in command, she'll be allowed to leave. If she's there by her own free will, she could even be back in town tomorrow.'

I didn't want to alarm him, but I still had horrible doubts nagging at the back of my mind. 'I hope so,' I said.

He looked around the now deserted classroom, satisfied. 'Job done.'

I nodded. 'And now we've got a convoy to catch.'

Next door the entertainment was over and the real Wildchild

clowns were packing away their props, apparently planning soon to go to DV and Sarajevo to do more work. The youngsters and their parents from Una Drina had left and Anita was organizing the orphans, each clutching a pathetic little bundle of personal possessions, into a crocodile, ready to walk the short distance to the playing field.

When Cuthbert and I arrived there in my Land Rover, the convoy drivers and mechanics were completing their final checks. Although there was a considerable amount of noise, spookily there was not a light to be seen. Queues of refugees were standing in the twilight, being guided by UN staff to their designated wagons.

By nightfall the lorries had returned with the sick and injured from the clinic, including Dario, Mara, Brum Taylor and his injured co-driver. The orphans were finally aboard in the care of UNHCR workers, and the last of the refugees had been allocated their personal floorspace.

Elsewhere in the convoy, General Aganovic and his two Afghan bodyguards were trussed in a secret compartment in the back of a supposedly UN lorry in the custody of their SAS captors.

While his wife had joined the other refugees, ex-Mayor Jozic had insisted on riding in his own battered brown truck. I recognized his driver as one of his regular minders.

Two Warriors were being fired up, the redoubtable Hal Watkins commanding one of them. I walked over and shouted up to him above the roar of its engines. 'Cuthbert and I will be in the lead behind Rocky's Discovery. You come in behind us and have your second Warrior come up the rear.'

He grinned and gave me a thumbs-up 'roger'.

I rejoined my Land Rover in time to hear Rocky's voice over the radio. 'OK, Convoy Green, we leave in five. No lights and radio silence from now on.'

It was the longest five minutes of my life, sitting in the noisy warmth of the Land Rover and peering out at the dark mountainside through the feathery, gentle fall of snowflakes. I just hoped that there was no Muslim up there watching us, realizing that we were about to make a bolt for it.

The sense of anticipation was nerve-chewing as I wound down my window and listened. One minute to go, fifty seconds, forty, thirty, twenty, ten. My lips moved silently as I watched the illuminated digits of my watch. Eight, seven, six, five, four . . .

Then I heard it. A distant sound of high-explosive detonations from the south of the town. The SAS's diversion had begun . . .

Two, one.

'Here we go,' Cuthbert said.

Rocky's Discovery began easing away in front of us. I slipped into first and followed, guided by the chemical convoy-lights fitted to the UN vehicle's rear bumper. Hal Watkins' Warrior lurched noisily forward behind me and we headed for the field gateway and swung right onto the suburban road that led to the back way out of town. I knew that in the darkness each column of parked trucks would be taking its turn to peel off and join the procession.

Subdued Croat militiamen stood by their roadblock, weapons shouldered, and ushered us through. Rocky increased speed, moving as fast as he dared over the soft snow before turning off at the track which eventually led to the snake.

At last we were clear of the outlying farms and running up the long, slow incline towards the first high pass. The snow-covered embankment closed in on both sides. It was nerve-racking here, the area where we had come under fire on the way in. Sure enough, a few hundred metres farther on, we were slowing to negotiate the wreck of Brum Taylor's truck and trailer. My palms were damp with sweat on the steering wheel, anticipating the blast of a mortar round and the deadly, violent fireball of a rocket-propelled grenade at any moment.

But nothing happened as the caterpillar of trucks continued grinding its way up the side of the mountain. I could only imagine that the diversionary fireworks display by the SAS team had successfully caught the attention of the Muslims.

I began to breathe more easily as we finally crested the high pass and began the slow descent of the easier of the two zig-zags. This one dropped to the river valley; the bends were fairly easy but still had to be negotiated with care. One slip and a vehicle could plunge hundreds of feet into the gorge with its fast-flowing, near freezing mountain water.

Rocky slowed the pace and I gently changed down through the gears. I began to feel confident that we'd get negotiate this section without mishap.

But then I hadn't accounted for one thing.

'Convoy leader! Convoy leader!' an excited voice suddenly burst out over the radio. 'We have a runaway!'

Rocky's voice snapped back. 'Convoy Green halt! Slow down and halt!'

I eased on the brakes. 'What the f—' Cuthbert began.

I was about to throw open my door to see what was happening when a huge brown truck flashed past me. I glimpsed the driver's pale and terrified face as he tried to steer between my Land Rover and the precipice. He made it, but only just. Now he found himself hurtling towards the next bend of the zig-zag.

'Christ!' Cuthbert exploded. 'That's Jozic's truck. Must have been a brake failure.'

I watched it, praying that the driver would have the sense to steer the thing into the left-hand bank, where the spindly baby firs would at least slow it down.

Well, he did have the sense, but it was too late. Sparks flew into the night as its front wheel crashed into the undergrowth, gouging out rocks and ripping away the foliage. The truck's descent was slowing, but not by enough. In desperation Jozic's driver swung the wheel hard to the left. The nose of the lorry hit something, a tree or a large boulder, with a horrendous crunch of metal and shattered glass. The rear doors flew open. But the back end of the truck kept going, overtaking the cab and ripping the nose free.

Now, in horribly slow motion, the lorry slid gently backwards

for the final ten metres towards the bend with nothing to stop it
from plummeting into the gorge below.

I watched on in horror as the rear wheels refused to find a
grip in the soft snow and kept on going, slowly, tantalizingly
slowly, until the back end finally jutted out over the abyss. There
was a sudden lurch as the rear wheels went over the void and the
chassis crashed down onto the edge of the drop.

Only then did the vehicle finally stop moving, its rear wheels
free-spinning over the gorge. I breathed again, climbed out and
raced to the scene. Rocky got there moments before I did but
even as I ran to join him I could see that the lorry was balanced
on a fulcrum and that only the counter-weight of ex-Mayor
Jozic and his driver was preventing the whole thing from top-
pling over.

Through the windscreen of the cab, I could see the ashen
faces of the two men. Jozic had his eyes closed and was feverishly
crossing himself, praying for divine intervention.

Something caught my eye at the rear of the truck. Paper was
fluttering out of the open tailgate. 'What the hell's that?' I asked,
pointing.

Rocky squinted. 'Fuck me, Jimbo. They look like banknotes.'

I realized he was right. 'That explains why Jozic insisted on
staying with it.'

'Ill-gotten gains,' Rocky muttered as he weighed up the situation.

Then we heard the lead Warrior behind us, Hal Watkins leaning down from the turret. 'Want a hand, guys?' he shouted.
'We can fix a tow hawser.'

'Excellent,' I replied.

Cuthbert joined me as the Warrior disgorged its Royal
Wessex troops to get the steel hawser rigged between the
armoured vehicle's front end and the stricken lorry. 'Just heard
from Gordy on the radio,' he said. 'Some official's been on to
him from the local agricultural bank. Ranting that he went in to
do some overtime and found the vault's been raided.'

I frowned. 'Isn't that the bank Jozic's involved with?'

Cuthbert scratched his chin. 'Yes, that's one of his business interests. Smart thinking by Gordy.'

Gordon Cromwell had been spot-on in guessing that somehow Jozic might have smuggled the loot onto the convoy.

I turned away to watch the troops securing the hawser to the precariously balanced lorry.

'Ready, Captain?' Hal Watkins called. 'I can start backing up now.'

I shook my head. 'No, just hold it steady while the driver and passenger get out.'

I went to the cab of the lorry, reached up and opened the door. Jozic stared down at me, wide-eyed. He was visibly shaking.

'C'mon down,' I said. 'It's safely secured now.'

'Are you sure?'

I offered my hand. 'Certain. Let me help you.'

While I assisted Jozic down onto the road, the driver needed no such persuasion. He jumped clear and stood to one side, hands trembling as he fumbled feverishly to light a cigarette.

'Put that bloody thing out!' Rocky snapped.

Jozic looked back at his lorry. 'Thank you so much, Captain Hawkins. I am so grateful.' He seemed to be regaining his composure. 'But now can you tow my lorry back onto the track, please? All my worldly wealth is in there.'

'All *your* worldly wealth?' I asked sharply. 'Or the life savings of Una Drina's peasant farmers?'

Cuthbert added, 'Whoever's wealth it is, it's now been blown to the four winds. You can come back and pick it up when the war's over.'

Jozic glared at him, his mouth shrinking into a sullen pout.

'Meanwhile,' Rocky intervened, 'I've got a convoy to run. Sorry, pal, I can't have that thing blocking the track. Go and find yourself a place on one of the UN trucks.'

Jozic looked crestfallen and deflated as he watched the final remaining banknotes fluttering out over the gorge.

I turned to the two soldiers standing next to the lorry. 'Release the hawser, will you?'

'Sir!' the corporal called back and bent to release the heavy-duty retaining clip. With the centre of balance shifted, the lorry began to rock gently of its own volition for a moment or two. Then the cab slowly began to up-end and the bodypan of the truck started a dignified slide like a coffin being buried at sea. Then it was gone, sunk in an ocean of darkness. We all heard the crash of tortured steel as it hit the bottom of the gorge.

Jozic slunk away and we all returned to our vehicles.

We were on the move again, making good, steady progress travelling downhill, negotiating each bend slowly and calmly. I was actually getting complacent, certain that we were over the worst of it. I found my mind wandering, remembering the Christmas evening I'd spent with Anita and the enjoyable time we'd shared. Life had dealt her some lousy cards and she took her responsibilities very seriously, so it had been good to see her happy and relaxed for a change . . .

That was when tragedy struck.

At the end of the zig-zag descent the track levelled out as it reached the timber bridge. There was a sharp dip on the approach that was perpetually in the shade of the roadside pine trees. Polished by the wind, it was pure sheet ice. Even with snow chains it was difficult to establish any real grip and I was aware of Rocky's lead Discovery trying to fishtail ahead of me.

I changed down, gently touched the brakes and immediately felt the sideways shift. But it was nothing much, and I knew it wouldn't cause a problem for the experienced drivers who ben-efited from the heavy weight of their vehicles and trailers.

I never gave the tracked Warriors a thought. In my army career, I'd never had many dealings with armoured vehicles. If I had I might have thought to give Hal Watkins some warning.

His great beast hit the ice slope like a toboggan on the Cresta Run. Metal tracks are good in mud and snow, but pretty useless n hard ice. If their sheer weight didn't crack the crust, they ended to slide straight over the top of it.

I wasn't really aware what was happening until it was too late. 'd just crossed the bridge when I heard the crack of rending mber. I hit the brakes and leapt out. The Warrior had come own the dip in a slide, gathering speed. The driver tried to egotiate a slight turn to the left to line the AFV up for the ridge. The tracks had clearly refused to obey and the huge nass just went straight on, clipping the rail of the bridge and earing it away with the force of the impact. Then the Warrior ad toppled slowly over the embankment.

I ran back to see, with great relief, that it had fallen only ome twenty feet before being arrested by a combination of oulders and trees. Now it sat with its tracks still churning like helpless upturned tortoise.

It didn't look that dramatic but I knew that inside the men vould have been tossed around like rag dolls if they weren't elted in, crashing into any number of hard steel obstructions. he injuries could be horrendous.

Rocky, Cuthbert and I were soon joined by other drivers, all ushing down to help. Miraculously we were able to get clear ccess to the rear hatch. After a few minutes it was opened and he first of the groggy, disorientated Royal Wessex troops stag- ered out. Fortunately, they had all obeyed Hal Watkins' order o belt up and wear helmets during the descent. There were a lot f cuts and bruises and two suspected broken arms, but that was ll.

I breathed a sigh of relief.

It was then that one of the soldiers looked around at his gath- red comrades and frowned. 'Where's the boss? Where's Hal?'

Hal Watkins was the commander. His position was in the urret. Unbelted. We found his body ten metres away, where he ad been thrown clear. His neck was broken.

The sudden realization that Hal was dead stunned everyone. or a few moments we stood around in disbelief. Sometimes it is impossible for disinterested observers to appreciate the constant human cost of so-called peacekeeping work. Now Hal ha become the latest to pay the price.

I broke radio silence and called the Ops Room. Gordy immediately arranged for two more Warriors with half-crews t evacuate their stranded comrades and retrieve the body of thei dead commander.

Meanwhile the Warrior from the rear of the convoy replace Hal's vehicle at the front, behind my Land Rover. We continue on a little more cautiously, and in sombre mood.

At least the driving conditions were more relaxed as the trac meandered along the river's edge. The fine snow had stoppe and the clouds had mostly cleared to reveal a black velvet sky an a fine dusting of stars. We were at the very extremity of know Muslim-held territory and the threat to the convoy was dimin ishing with every kilometre we travelled. Or so we thought.

Suddenly Rocky's Discovery braked hard as he took a fairl tight right-hand bend around the shoulder of a hill.

His voice crackled over the radio. 'Green Leader t convoy . . . hostiles ahead! Close up and stop!'

I slowed as we rounded the bend and pulled up behind th Discovery.

There were two old pickup trucks parked across the trac between the river bank on the left and the hillside on the righ Half a dozen armed men stood around, staring back at us. Fror their demeanour and the almost regular uniforms, they were Ramoza Brigade squad. My first impression was that they wer foreign recruits. In front of them, clearly visible in the snow, wa a neat line of anti-vehicle mines.

Rocky opened his door and climbed out.

'Let's see what's going on,' I said to Cuthbert.

We pulled on our blue berets and walked along to wher Rocky was talking to the militiamen across the line of mines.

Their obvious leader, a skinny man with sunken eyes and a unkempt goatee, was jabbing his finger in the direction of th

Warrior. 'This is an illegal attempt to break the siege of Una Drina,' he declared in heavily accented English. 'You go no further!'

Rocky smiled and held up a packet for cigarettes as a peace offering. The militiaman declined with an angry shake of his head. My friend shrugged and pressed on, 'I am afraid the siege is illegal, not our right to free passage. We operate under the mandate of the United Nations.'

I wondered just how many times Rocky had trotted out all his stuff at various times to indifferent thugs and warlords.

The militiaman was unimpressed. 'You turn around and go back.'

Rocky's smile remained fixed. 'Ever driven a truck, my friend? A truck with a trailer attached? Track four metres wide, a mountain on one side and a river on the other?'

The man frowned suspiciously, looking left and right.

Rocky said, 'Can you explain to me how we turn round?'

The man realized his request was decidedly absurd – not to mention impossible to fulfil. He looked a little sheepish but was in no mood to lose face. 'Then you stay here,' he pronounced suddenly.

'There are refugees, injured people and orphans in this convoy,' Rocky replied. 'They will freeze to death.'

'Then you should not have tried to break our siege.' Adamant.

I thought I'd have a go and stepped forward. 'Captain Hawkins, UNPROFOR. I think you should be aware that earlier this evening, your leader General Aganovic ordered the end of the siege. Call him on your radio, he will confirm it.'

My hope was that, in Aganovic's absence, Major Herenda might be asked to deputize.

'I cannot do that. Our radios are having reception problems.'

I then remembered the CBF's promise of radio-jamming when the convoy was on the move. That bright idea had rather backfired on us now. 'All right, but it's true,' I continued. 'So please remove the mines and let us through.'

The man thought for a moment. Then, ignoring me, he turned to Rocky. 'You stay here tonight. By tomorrow we will make contact and confirm with General Aganovic. Meanwhile we will search your convoy for contraband and illegal shipments. Please bring me all your official paperwork and documentation.'

I saw Rocky clench his fists, but his fixed smile remained. 'Of course.'

The three of us walked back towards our vehicles. It was clear Cuthbert was terrified these Muslims would search the convoy and discover their abducted commander in the secret compartment of his fake UN truck.

He was beside himself. 'Christ, this is all we need! Can't we shoot our way out? We've got a Warrior, for God's sake!'

Rocky was scathing. 'Don't talk like an arsehole, Nigel!'

'We can't do anything unless they shoot at us first,' I reminded him. 'I know the rules are bloody galling, but blame the UN.'

Cuthbert took on the expression of a condemned man. 'If they find Aganovic, we'll be so much sausage meat.'

Rocky was unsympathetic. 'Then let's hope they made a good job of the secret compartment.'

We left Rocky at his Discovery to unearth the paperwork and returned to the Land Rover. Once back in its welcome meagre warmth, Cuthbert was still wringing his hands. 'What a bloody mess! Is there no way out?'

'Thinking of the wounded and the orphans, are you?' I goaded. 'You were quite happy to put them at risk to suit your own game.'

'Oh, Jimbo, for God's sake get real!' he flared. 'And stop being so bloody sentimental.'

Sentimental or not, I *was* thinking about the wounded and the orphaned kids, especially Dario and Mara. And the wretched Brum Taylor with his horrific burns. Several of the injured might die if the convoy was kept overnight and I didn't want to think of the children and many older refugees cooped up like sardines until the following day, or very possibly longer.

I made a sudden decision. 'OK, Nigel,' I said. 'I'll get real. We're prevented from picking a fight with the militias, but someone *else* isn't.'

He frowned. 'What d'you mean?'

I reached under my seat and pulled out the SA80. 'Nothing to say a Croat unit hasn't wandered into the area.'

'You?' he asked in disbelief.

I shrugged. 'Hell, why not? I leave the army this year anyway. I can't believe anyone's going to complain if it works. None of the Royal Wessex is going to grass me up.'

Cuthbert raised an eyebrow. 'There'll always be gossip.'

'As long as that's all it is,' I replied. 'I don't really want to lose my pension.'

'Your decision, old son,' he said, just letting me know where he'd make sure any blame would lie if my plan went wrong. Nevertheless, he clearly liked the idea of me getting him off the hook.

I said, 'Go and tell the Warrior commander what to do. If he gets the opportunity, shoot up those mines and go through, stopping for nothing . . . Just make sure you stop to pick me up.'

Cuthbert grinned. 'As if.'

I looked at him. 'Yeah, as if. Got any spare mags?'

He handed over two spare magazines for the SA80 which I stuffed into the cargo pocket of my smock.

We synchronized our watches. Up ahead Rocky was walking back to the militiamen with all the UN paperwork. I pulled off my blue beret and stepped out of the Land Rover. Confirming that the Muslims' attention was diverted, I sprinted to the right-hand side of the road, just hidden from view by the bend. I quickly threw myself at the wall of rock and began scrambling up as fast as I could, my feet slipping precariously on the ice. It was hard going but it took me only a couple of minutes to get to where the ground levelled out a little and I could stand under the first pines of the treeline. Sweating heavily from the burst of exertion, I ripped the camouflaged scrim scarf from my neck, opened it up and wound it round my head and face, leaving a gap for my nose and eyes.

I unshouldered the SA80 and, crouching low, scrambled along the embankment until I was parallel with the line of mines on the track below. I edged forward, hidden by the crumpled dead undergrowth of winter.

The militiamen were still with Rocky and arguing about something; I could hear their voices clearly across the fifty metres that separated us.

I raised the sight of the SA80 to my eye, tucking the butt into my shoulder. It was now or never. I released the safety and gently squeezed the trigger.

The snow around the Muslim militiamen's feet began erupting as half a magazine emptied into it. Both they and Rocky were totally shocked, starting an involuntary dance. I stopped firing. I hoped against hope that the militiamen would rush to their vehicles and drive off.

Of course, they didn't. Instead the Muslims dived for the cover of the river bank, hurriedly trying to bring their weapons to bear. Rocky raced back to his Discovery like a lunatic.

I put in a few more rounds to keep the Muslims' heads down and prayed that the Warrior commander wouldn't hesitate to seize the moment. He didn't. The AFV's engine roared and the turret swung round, the elevation of its cannon dropping. Then the 30mm Rarden spat out its deadly seed along the line of the mines. One by one they exploded in a geyser of rock and snow.

They were small targets to hit, and it took several minutes and a hell of a lot of rounds, but finally the job was done.

I fired another short SA80 burst at the militiamen's position, as the clanking tracks of the Warrior began to grind forward. The vehicle lumbered across the small craters left by the exploding mines and crashed headlong into the two pickup trucks. With contemptuous ease it pushed them aside, smashing one against the rock wall and sending the other toppling over the river bank. It landed with a loud splash and was immediately sucked away by the swirling current.

The Warrior kept on going and I guessed that Cuthbert was telling Rocky over the radio what had been going on. Suddenly the UNHCR Discovery was moving forward and the rest of the trucks began to follow.

I abandoned my position and ran forward as fast as I could until I was out of range of the militia. Below me, Cuthbert had pulled the Land Rover over to one side of the track. I went down the slope on my backside in a barely controlled slide until I reached the bottom.

Cuthbert threw open the passenger door and I dived inside.

'Bloody hell, Jimbo, that was close!' he said as he hit the accelerator.

He overtook the lead vehicles of the convoy as they gathered speed, then tucked in behind Rocky's Discovery.

That was when all hell broke loose. Small-arms fire began raining down from the hillside and fountains of snow flew skyward all around us as mortar shells landed.

'Convoy leader here!' Rocky's voice came over the radio. 'Let's rock and roll the hell out of here! Sorry, Royal Wessex, we may have to leave you behind for a while!'

He meant, of course, that the trucks would probably overtake the trundling, slower Warrior.

Suddenly our radio was carrying stirring strains from Meat Loaf's 'Bat out of Hell' as Rocky's Discovery eased ahead and we struggled to keep up, the trucks all accelerating behind us. Bullets momentarily rattled across our Land Rover's bonnet and more exploding mortars tried to drive us into the river.

The convoy went for it pell-mell, pushing to the limits of safety and sanity. It was as terrifying as it was exhilarating.

Then, as abruptly as it had begun, it was over. We were out of range. Rocky eased up, Meat Loaf quietened down and the convoy thankfully slowed. Some trucks and trailers had taken incoming rounds, but miraculously no one was reported hurt.

I lit a miniature cigar, savouring its aroma, and looked out over the eerily beautiful landscape of dark pines, white snow and black mirrored water beneath an indigo sky. I began to feel both relaxed and very tired. While we still had the treacherous stone bridge and a perilous uphill zig-zag to negotiate, we could take our time. The Warrior we'd left behind would probably catch up with us again then. Now we were well beyond Ramoza Brigade lines, safe in Croat territory.

So it came as a real surprise to hear Rocky's curt voice over the radio, 'Convoy leader here! Slow down! Roadblock ahead!'

'Oh God,' I groaned. 'What now?'

Cuthbert braked gently. 'No problem, Jimbo. Just some Croats.'

I glanced sideways at him. 'How the hell d'you know?'

There was an inscrutable smile on his face. 'I was expecting them.'

'What's going on?' I demanded.

He tapped the side of his nose. 'Need to know, old son.'

When he opened the door and climbed out, I followed.

Rocky was standing beside his Discovery, looking puzzled.

'It's OK!' Cuthbert called out, running forward. 'I'll take care of this. Nothing for you to worry about.'

I was close behind him and could see the Croat vehicle and a group of men who wore the insignia of the notorious Black Swan commandos. I recognized the man standing at their head: Colonel Zec.

Cuthbert approached him and shook his hand. They looked like old friends.

Rocky wandered over to me. 'What the hell's all this about?'

I shook my head. 'Search me.'

I was then aware of movement behind me. I looked back to see General Almir Aganovic and his two bodyguards, all hand-cuffed, being frog-marched alongside the line of parked UN trucks accompanied by men in British Army uniforms and bal-aclavas. I had no doubt that they were the clowns from the school, members of the SAS or some other clandestine unit no one even knew about.

They walked past Rocky and me until they reached the spot where Nigel Cuthbert waited with Colonel Zec. Without ceremony Aganovic and his henchmen were handed over to the Black Swan commandos. Silently they manhandled the prisoners into the back of their four-wheel-drive vehicle with its smoked-glass windows. A shiver went down my spine as the engine began its soft purr and the Croat contingent slipped away into the night with their prisoners.

Instead of returning to the convoy, the SAS men, or whoever they were, just disappeared into the forest without a word. I could only guess they had their own transport waiting for them somewhere nearby.

Rocky looked concerned but there was nothing he could do. He had a convoy to get to safety.

Back in the Land Rover, I started the engine.

As Cuthbert climbed in, I started to pull away. 'You've just handed over General Aganovic to his sworn enemy,' I accused.

Cuthbert shrugged. 'It was part of the deal the Croats made with Grundy. Otherwise they wouldn't agree to pull their militias out of Una Drina and DV.'

'Grundy?' I queried. 'The bloody CIA again. The Americans aren't even supposed to be involved in all this.'

Cuthbert gave a quiet laugh. 'Don't believe everything you read in the papers, Jimbo. Or rather, believe the things you *don't* read.'

I didn't find it funny. 'They'll murder him.'

'They've promised not.'

'And you believe them?'

'It's not my job to believe or otherwise. General Aganovic was loose cannon, a thorn in everyone's side. Including his own government's. The Croats wanted a guarantee he'd never be in that position again. To them that meant they had to have him in their custody.'

I had nothing left to say to Cuthbert. Wars are always dirty, and civil wars are the dirtiest of all. Bosnia was no exception. And I'd played my part in it and other conflicts. But now I really felt I'd had enough. Enough of using people like pawns, regardless of whether they were innocent or guilty. All that mattered was that *your* side won, it really didn't matter how.

We drove back to the depot at Metkovic in silence. It was a long, slow drive, especially negotiating the ascent of the second zig-zag, but the stone bridge held – just – and everyone made it.

When we arrived at the depot at first light, there was a lump in my throat as I watched our bedraggled passengers disgorging from our battered, white-painted trucks, hundreds of lost souls standing around on the tarmac, wondering what was going to happen next. They waited patiently to be dealt with by UNHCR reception staff.

Meanwhile the ambulances were lined up, ready to receive the injured and the wounded, and ranks of coaches appeared to spirit the refugees to somewhere safer, where they could begin to rebuild their shattered lives.

There was a message waiting for me to meet my old friend Dave McVicar at the Seavu hotel. I didn't tell Cuthbert, but deliberately left him stranded at the depot and headed off in my Land Rover for Split.

It was eleven when I got there. McVicar was waiting and we had a coffee together in the otherwise deserted bar.

'The brigadier's pleased with what you've achieved, Jimbo,' he began. 'Within a couple of days Major Herenda will be promoted and put in command of the Ramoza Brigade. He's expected to rein it back under Bosnian government control. Both Una Drina and DV will become demilitarized. That'll make running the convoys easier and safer. And it's a real surprise bonus that Mayor Jozic has decided to leave town. understand that schoolteacher's going to replace him. Popula choice by all accounts.'

I smiled. 'I think she'll be a real asset.'

'And I think the Royal Wessex have turned themselves around,' McVicar added. 'Not the embarrassment they once were.'

'They're a good bunch,' I agreed. 'I'll be pleased to get back to them.'

McVicar held my gaze. 'Ah, well, I don't think that's on the cards, Jimbo. Now your job's done, the brigadier would just prefer you quietly slip out of theatre. You've been involved in a few – er, let's say controversial and difficult decisions. Best you're not around for anyone to ask you any embarrassing questions. Anyway, the battalion's tour finishes at the end of the month.'

What he meant was I knew too much, had witnessed too much. I suspected my removal was at Nigel Cuthbert's request.

I didn't bother to question the decision. 'When do I leave?'

'There's a Herc flight to Lyneham this afternoon at four. Any kit you've left at Una Drina, we'll get forwarded on to you. Your predecessor, Captain Wells, returns tomorrow.' He looked at his watch. 'Sorry, I can't stay. Lots to do. We'll meet up for a beer some time soon back home.'

We shook hands and he left.

I sat down and ordered another coffee. I felt used and empty. But then I was just a small cog in the army's machine. I should have been accustomed to that by now.

Just then the door opened and Lizard walked in with Jelena on his arm.

'Hi, Jeff!' she greeted, throwing her arms round me. 'It is great to see you here!'

'Were *you* on the convoy, too?' I asked.

Lizard looked suitably abashed as she replied, 'Yes, he smuggled me on.'

Some things never changed. 'And how's your mother?'

A cloud passed behind her eyes. 'I am afraid she has died. It is why Lizard brings me here, for her funeral in a few days' time.'

'I'm sorry,' I said.

But her expression lightened immediately. 'But there is good news, too. Lizard and I are getting married. Then he will take me to England.'

I glanced at Lizard, unsure. But the way he was looking at her, I think he really meant it. Perhaps he had finally found the right girl for him, and would actually settle down.

I had my doubts, but I still said, 'Congratulations to you both.'

'Have a drink with us,' Lizard invited.

I shook my head. 'Sorry, I've a flight to catch.'

'Back to England?' Jelena asked.

'Yes.'

'You must come and visit us when we buy our first home in the UK.'

'It'll be a pleasure.'

I walked out into the grey, slush-covered streets, my mood having lifted a little. Amid all the broken lives two people were building a new one. Or at least trying to. The work of the various armies and the convoys were keeping innocent people alive, and the light of hope burning. And I'd been part of it.

I looked down at the Land Rover. Over the past few months I'd broken or bent every rule in the book. One more wouldn't hurt. I had someone I wanted to see before I left, and no bloody army edict was going to stop me. They could stuff their afternoon flight.

I climbed into the driver's seat and fired the engine.

As I headed back inland, I was hardly aware of the road.

All I could see before my eyes was the laughing face and sultry sable eyes of Anita Furtula, mayor of Una Drina.

EPILOGUE

Just over ten years later I was standing in the crowd of onlookers at the start of the London marathon.

At my side in the spring sunshine was Anita, who had then been my wife for seven of those years. With us at the event were our adopted children, Mara and Dario.

Mara had grown into a striking and cheerful young woman, who refused to let the disability of being an amputee stop her getting the best out of life. Now twenty-one, she was running her first marathon alongside my old friend Rocky Rogers, who'd done it twice before.

The two of them were away at the organization-point getting registered and badged while Anita, Dario and I were watching the wheelchair athletes prepare to start their own race, a curtain raiser to the main event.

Dario, a year younger than Mara, was more self-conscious about his artificial eye. However, his confidence had been hugely boosted recently since finding himself a very pretty 'serious' girlfriend at university.

Meanwhile, life as Anita's husband had been and often still is tempestuous, but always enjoyable. We have many disagreements about many things, but our frequent spats over trivia are always short-lived, our relationship easily healed by her very passionate and forgiving nature. In truth I don't think I have ever been happier.

Making that split-second decision to miss my flight back to the UK and instead returning to Una Drina was the best thing that I ever did. Anita had been overjoyed to see me and we spent the afternoon and night together. I think we knew then that we had both found what we were looking for.

As I had hoped, Anita's appointment as mayor had proved very popular with the townsfolk, even though the circumstances didn't allow a proper election to be held. Her determined presence helped to speed up the process of demilitarization; she took no nonsense from any of the local militia warlords. It was almost amusing to see such macho characters so uneasy and compliant in her commanding presence.

Major Herenda was duly promoted to take over the Ramoza Brigade and, once he'd purged it of its more radical elements, from then on became a staunch ally of British troops in the area.

There were and are, of course, many reminders about my time in Bosnia, but I soon moved on. I left the army and worked with a private security company travelling the world, including on assignment to the UN, and tried hard to concentrate on the future rather than the past. But meeting Rocky before the marathon had brought it all back again.

'Dario and I are going to get an ice cream, Jeff,' Anita said. 'Do you want one?'

I shook my head. 'No, thanks, I'm fine. I think I'll take some pictures.'

'We'll see you back here later.'

As they walked off, I took out my camera. There were wheelchairs everywhere, really sporty affairs, mostly propelled by youngsters determined to get the most out of their lives, despite the hand they had been dealt.

I began clicking away. Me and a camera, an odd combination. It had never been much of a hobby until after I left Bosnia. Then suddenly, almost overnight, it had grown into an obsession. And I knew why.

I'd been fired up and inspired by the work of Tali van Wyk. Her pictures had always been stunning, and the stirring and

ignant images witnessed through her young eyes had been
en around the world. She had become one of the few top
hotographers whose names were always mentioned in the same
reath as the war in Bosnia.

I had not seen her again since that Christmas Eve when she
ent away with Kirk Grundy, but I had thought about her often
ver the intervening years. Our incredible time together still
aunted me, but I tried not to dwell on it.

However, it remained a small thrill whenever I noticed a par-
cularly good picture in a paper or magazine from some
rouble-spot around the world and saw her credit beneath it. Her
hoto-features were especially good; she had quite a way with
ust a few words.

That was until the American and British so-called 'war on
rror' and the invasion of Afghanistan in a fruitless search for
Osama bin Laden and his al-Qaeda cohorts.

I just caught a snatch of a late-night news report one day:
The well-known war photographer Tali van Wyk had been
ounded along with a Reuters reporter in an ambush near
abul.' I had breathed a sigh of relief when I heard that 'neither
as life-threatening injuries'. But her photographs never
peared in the media after that.

It was odd to think that I'd been there at the very start of her
rief career, and had almost stalled it in its tracks.

Of course, Kirk Grundy had cynically manipulated and used
er to fulfil Washington's and the CIA's secret agenda. I didn't
now then that it was to replace UNPROFOR, whose troops
ways had their hands tied behind their backs, with a more
roactive and robust NATO force. That had made all the differ-
nce, along with the second thrust of the American strategy.
part from keeping the Muslim government supplied with
eapons, they were secretly re-arming and re-training the
Croatian Army. When the time came for it to be unleashed, it
rought about a swift defeat of the Serb forces.

While ethnic animosities remained, the long healing process

began and the newly-freed nation-states of Bosnia-Herzegovin and Croatia found themselves at peace and able to start the slo rebuilding of their countries.

The remains of Ivana's body were not identified until man years later and then only by DNA testing. Her corpse had bee found with those of others at the bottom of a well near th Ramoza Brigade camp just outside Una Drina; she had bee killed by a single shot in the mouth which had blown her brair out. I still have nightmares about that.

General Aganovic was never prosecuted, because he himsel was never seen again after being handed over by Nigel Cuthber to Colonel Zec and his Croat henchmen. Rough justice fo Ivana, I suppose, though there's no comfort there.

Zec was also accused of war-crimes but the court found tha there was insufficient evidence to convict him. The last I' heard, on one of my frequent visits to Bosnia with Anita, wa that he was running a swanky hotel complex on the Adriati coast with ex-mayor Jozic.

When I look back at that time, I feel not a little pride in having made just a small contribution to the international peace keeping effort. Although some 200,000 lives were lost in th war, the convoys and humanitarian effort made a real differenc Perversely, according to UNICEF and the World Healt Organization, infant mortality actually went down and the birt rate up during the war. No one actually starved to death and, i fact, the inhabitants of Bosnia became more healthy as the foo aid included less fat and red meat, but more vitamins and othe essential nutrients.

It was an unexpected, curious, but welcome legacy of the wa that made the sacrifices of so many individuals a little mor worthwhile.

Suddenly a marathon official's voice came over the tannoy *'Will all non-contestants clear the starting-area now, please! Thank you.*

I moved back to watch as the wheelchair racers lined up at th start.

And then I saw her. She was just a face in a crowd of dozens, but I knew with shocking familiarity the toss of that blonde pony-tail as she turned her head and began manoeuvring her wheelchair towards the start-line.

Although ten years older, she looked little different from when I'd last seen her, maybe just a little fuller in the face. A tall, good-looking man of similar age was standing by her. He leaned over, kissed her and then started heading in my direction, carrying the belongings she wouldn't need during the race.

As those powder-blue eyes followed him, her gaze suddenly met mine. For a moment she stared, a small frown forming as she arched a quizzical eyebrow. Was she as shocked as I had been, wondering if it could really be me?

An uncertain shy smile played on her lips, just for a second. Then she turned her head away. They were under starter's orders and the klaxon sounded.

The sun came out from behind a cloud at that moment, gold catching on the hundreds of spinning wheels as they powered away to cheers from the onlookers. And for one freakish moment I was back in Bosnia a decade earlier, watching those huge road tyres turn as another convoy began to roll.

'There you are, Jimbo.' Rocky's voice was suddenly behind me. 'Been looking for you everywhere.'

He was standing in his running shorts and vest, with Mara at his side. His eyes followed mine, watching the spectacle of the departing wheelchair racers. 'You gotta hand it to them. That takes a special kind of guts, a special kind of courage.'

I tried to say, 'You never said a truer thing.'

But I don't think the words came out.

POCKET
BOOKS

Also by Terence Strong
COLD MONDAY

Haunted by the brutal killing of his UN interpreter wife in Bosnia, ex-SAS man Ed Coltrane is consumed with the need to avenge her murder. Drinking too much and spending too much time and money on his search, his life is going into meltdown . . .

When an ex-colleague offers him a chance to make some real money working in 'black ops', Coltrane is interested – until he finds that the job on offer is a commissioned assassination. His disgust, however, is tempered by the knowledge that the target is one of the three men responsible for his wife's death. Against his better judgement, Coltrane accepts the commission. Revenge will be his.

This marks the start of a dangerous journey into the dark heart of modern Europe, where Coltrane finds himself in deadly conflict with the new mafias and the security apparatus of an emerging superstate. What Ed Coltrane is about to discover will rock the western world to its foundations.

ISBN 0 7434 2992 3
PRICE £6.99

**POCKET
BOOKS**

This book and other **Pocket Books** titles are available from
your local bookshop or can be ordered direct
from the publisher.

| 0 7434 2993 1 | **Wheels of Fire** | **Terence Strong** | £6.99 |
| 0 7434 2992 3 | **Cold Monday** | **Terence Strong** | £6.99 |

Please send cheque or postal order for the value of the book,
free postage and packing within the UK, to
SIMON & SCHUSTER CASH SALES
PO Box 29, Douglas Isle of Man, IM99 1BQ
Tel: 01624 677237, Fax: 01624 670923
Email: bookshop@enterprise.net
www.bookpost.co.uk

Please allow 14 days for delivery. Prices and availability
subject to change without notice